Praise for the Dark Warrior novels by
DONNA GRANT

MIDNIGHT'S MASTER

"Time travel, ancient legends, and seductive romance are seamlessly interwoven into one captivating package."
—*Publishers Weekly*

"Dark, sexy, magical. When I want to indulge in a sizzling fantasy adventure, I read Donna Grant."
—Allison Brennan, *New York Times* bestseller

5 Stars! TOP PICK! "*Midnight's Master* is a MUST READ!"
—*Night Owl Reviews*

"Brimming with passion, adventure, time travel, complex and engaging characters, danger, mystery, romance and a forever kind of love, this book may be my favorite paranormal romance of the year."
—*Romance Junkies*

MIDNIGHT'S LOVER

"Paranormal elements and scorching romance are cleverly intertwined in this tale of a damaged hero and resilient heroine."
—*Publishers Weekly*

5 Blue Ribbons! "An exciting, adventure-packed tale, *Midnight's Lover* is a story that captivates you from the very first page."
—*Romance Junkies*

5 Stars! "Ms. Grant weaves a sweet love story into a story filled with action, adventure and the exploration of personal pain."
le Reviews

More . . .

4 Stars! "It's good vs. evil Druid in the next installment of Grant's Dark Warrior series. The stakes get higher as discerning one's true loyalties becomes harder. Grant's compelling characters and the continued presence of previous protagonists are key reasons why these books are so gripping. Another exciting and thrilling chapter!"

—*RT Book Reviews*

4.5 Stars Top Pick! "This is one series you'll want to make sure to read from the start . . . they just keep getting better…mmmm! A must read for sure!"

—*Night Owl Reviews*

4.5 Feathers! "If you're looking for an author who brings heat and heart in one tightly written package, then Donna Grant will be a gift that makes your jaw drop. You don't want to miss *Midnight's Lover*."

—*Under the Covers Book Blog*

4 Blue Ribbons! "Ms. Grant wields her pen with a lot of skill. Her consuming stories and relatable characters never fail to grab my attention. Her latest book, *Midnight's Lover*, is a wonderful example of what a good romance should be about, passion, love and plenty of action." —*Romance Junkies Reviews*

"Every book is an escape from the humdrum into a world of magic and fiery romance." —*Fresh Fiction*

MIDNIGHT'S SEDUCTION

"Sizzling love scenes and engaging characters fill the pages of this fast-paced and immersive novel."

—*Publishers Weekly*

4 Stars! "Grant again proves that she is a stellar writer and a force to be reckoned with." —*RT Book Reviews*

5 Blue Ribbons! "A deliciously sexy, adventuresome paranormal romance that will keep you glued to the pages." —*Romance Junkies*

5 Stars! "Ms. Grant mixes adventure, magic and sweet love to create the perfect romance story."

—*Single Title Reviews*

MIDNIGHT'S WARRIOR

4 Stars! "Super storyteller Grant returns . . . A rich variety of previous protagonists adds a wonderful familiarity to the books." —*RT Books Reviews*

5 Stars! "Ms. Grant brings together two people who are afraid to fall in love and then ignites sparks between them." —*Single Title Reviews*

Praise for the Dark Sword series

5! Top Pick! "An absolutely must read! From beginning to end, it's an incredible ride." —*Night Owl Romance*

5 Hearts! "I definitely recommend *Dangerous Highlander*, even to skeptics of paranormal romance—you just may fall in love with the MacLeods."

—*The Romance Reader*

5 Angels! Recommended Read! "*Forbidden Highlander* blew me away." —*Fallen Angel Reviews*

Don't miss these other spellbinding novels by

DONNA GRANT

The Dark Warrior Series

Midnight's Master

Midnight's Lover

Midnight's Seduction

Midnight's Warrior

Midnight's Kiss

Midnight's Captive

Midnight's Temptation

Midnight's Promise

The Dark Sword Series

Dangerous Highlander

Forbidden Highlander

Wicked Highlander

Untamed Highlander

Shadow Highlander

Darkest Highlander

From St. Martin's Paperbacks

DARK HEAT

DONNA GRANT

St. Martin's Paperbacks

This is a work of fiction. All of the characters, organizations, and events portrayed in this novel are either products of the author's imagination or are used fictitiously.

DARK HEAT

For information address St. Martin's Press, 175 Fifth Avenue, New York, NY 10010.

ISBN: 978-1-250-04378-8

Printed in the United States of America

St. Martin's Paperbacks edition / January 2014

St. Martin's Paperbacks are published by St. Martin's Press, 175 Fifth Avenue, New York, NY 10010.

10 9 8 7 6 5 4 3 2 1

For all the dragon lovers out there!

ACKNOWLEDGMENTS

To my marvelous editor, Monique Patterson. A beautiful person and brilliant soul. Thanks for the phone calls to bounce ideas off of as well as always pushing me—and letting me write my dragons! I couldn't ask for a better editor.

To everyone at St. Martin's who helped get this book ready, thank you.

A special note to my assistant, Melissa Bradley, for keeping me sane during release times and, well, the times in between.

To my talented, amazing agent, Louise Fury. There's no one else I'd rather have by my side in this business.

A special thanks to my family for the never-ending support.

Last but not least, my husband, Steve. I hope you don't get tired of hearing it, because I never get tired of saying it – I Love You! With you beside me, I can do anything. Thank you, Sexy!

DARK CRAVING

CHAPTER ONE

Edinburgh Airport
Edinburgh, Scotland

"My luggage is lost?" Cassie Hunter asked for the third time, hoping that maybe the airport staff might miraculously find it.

Her eyes were like sandpaper each time she blinked, and all she wanted to do was curl up somewhere and sleep. For at least a week. Instead, she had this to deal with.

"Aye, miss," a middle-aged balding man repeated for the third time, his patience running thin if his tightened lips were any indication. "I am sorry, but it does happen. With all your connections out of—" He paused to look at her itinerary on the computer screen. "—Arizona, it's no' surprising."

"Everything I have in the world is in those two suitcases." She was still reeling from the cost of having had to pay for each piece of luggage as well.

The last few hundred dollars she had were all too quickly whittling away. And she hadn't even exchanged them for pounds yet. How was her money going to last her for a few months at this rate?

"At least you have your carry-on."

Cassie blinked at the man before issuing a quick thank you and turning away. There was nothing left for her to do but dig out the address for the house where she was staying to the employee, and pray that somehow her luggage found its way to her.

She glanced at her watch and inwardly winced. Dan was going to be furious. Her brother wasn't known for his patience, and she'd already wasted almost two hours dealing with the luggage fiasco.

But he was going to have to wait some more, because she had to pee. With her bladder about to explode, Cassie found the bathroom and struggled to get into the tiny stalls with her carry-on, jacket, and purse.

It wasn't until she was washing her hands that she dared to look into the mirror.

"Dear God," she murmured in horror as she saw her reflection.

She raked her fingers through her stick-straight brown hair, which was poking up all over the place. There wasn't time to brush it, but Cassie did take a second to wipe away the smudges of mascara under her eyes before she hurried out of the restroom and then left the airport to the passenger pickup to look for her brother.

She shivered against the cold as she scanned the vehicles for the small blue car he'd mentioned in his text, but found nothing. Worry ripped through her. It would be just like Dan to leave after having to wait so long. Renting a car wasn't an option either, with what little money she had left.

She doubted she had enough to rent half a bicycle.

"Dammit, Dan," she mumbled.

"Excuse me," a female voice said to Cassie's left.

She turned to find another airport employee standing beside her; the woman's graying hair was pulled back in a severe bun. "Yes?"

"You're American, aye?"

"Yes," Cassie replied with a tired grin. She could only imagine what her voice sounded like to the Scots.

"Is your name Cassie Hunter, by chance?"

This was getting odd, but there had to be a reason the woman knew her name. "It is."

"Then this is for you," the woman said, and pulled out a small manila envelope from her jacket and handed it to Cassie. "A man named Dan gave this to me two days ago and said your flight would be landing this morning."

"Two days ago?" Cassie repeated as she took the envelope and felt the unmistakable heft and shape of keys inside it. What the hell was going on? "Did he say anything else?"

"Nay." The woman smiled and walked away.

Cassie sighed as she looked at the envelope. It was amazing what a person could get another to do when money was involved, and Dan had a lot of money. She opened the envelope and found a letter inside telling her where Dan had parked the car and also the address where she was to pick up Duke, his dog.

"I'm going to kill you, Dan," Cassie ground out with a sniff as she dumped the keys into her icy hand.

She had been nervous about leaving behind everything she knew to live in Scotland, but the prospect of seeing her brother was too good to pass up. Now he couldn't even be here to pick her up?

No explanation other than it was an emergency. Dan could be thoughtless, but even he had seemed excited at her coming to Scotland. She couldn't help but wonder if the emergency had something to do with Dan's wife. They had been having some marital issues.

Cassie squared her shoulders. She could do this. Or so she thought. Finding the car was another obstacle.

Between the cold, her coat—which was hardly enough to brace against the wind—and her carry-on with wheels so old they didn't roll properly on the pavement, she never thought she'd find the car. And when she was finally standing in front of it, all she could do was laugh.

It was either that or cry.

Cassie was bent over laughing so hard, tears threatened as she stared at what her brother thought was a vehicle but surely had to be a Hot Wheels car.

She fumbled with the keys to open the door and started laughing again at what constituted the backseat. "I guess it's a good thing my luggage was lost, because there's no way I'd fit it and myself inside."

Getting in the opposite side and realizing the car was a standard put another black mark in her brother's column. Not that she'd say anything to him about it. He was giving her a place to stay when she had nowhere else to go.

At least the car had a GPS. Cassie hurried as fast as her numb fingers would allow her to input the address to pick up Duke—another surprise, since she'd no idea Dan owned a dog.

It took no time to get out of the airport, but she couldn't say the same for driving. Cassie had never been very good at driving stick shifts, and using her dumb hand was only making things worse. The sound of her grinding the gears could be heard all over Scotland.

Remembering to shift as well as staying on the correct side of the road had her already exhausted brain on overload by the time she reached the kennel.

And then she saw Duke.

"He's not a dog," Cassie told the kennel worker in a strangled voice. "He's a freaking horse."

The teenager leading the black and white harlequin Great Dane out of the back room smiled. "Duke is a big lad, but he's got himself a sweet disposition."

"A good thing too, considering his size."

Cassie had never seen a Great Dane up close. She really hoped their reputation for "gentle giant" personas was true. Another catastrophe she couldn't take today.

"Oh, shit," she said as she remembered the car.

Somehow the teenager got Duke in the front seat with the window down so the dog could poke his head out.

"Dogs get carsick," he told Cassie, as if that explained everything.

"I had no idea," she mumbled, and bent to look how Duke would have put his head had the window not been lowered.

She signed and climbed back into the car to input the address for Dan's house into the GPS. When she saw it would take her nearly four hours to reach the house, Cassie almost let the tears loose.

Instead, she gripped the wheel and looked at Duke, who regarded her with dark, solemn eyes while he panted. Even with the heater set on full blast, the cold still came in through the window.

"I'm not sure if I'm ready for this," she said to Duke. "I haven't slept in thirty-six hours, I'm freezing, and I'm driving a stick. On the wrong side of the road. This is a really shitty day, Duke."

In answer, he nudged his large head against her shoulder. She smiled and scratched him behind the ear.

Her morale fortified—by a dog—Cassie started the car and headed out on the M90 north toward Perth. For several hours the drive was fine, but then they left the road with shoulders for a narrower one that wound into the mountains.

Duke kept his head out the window and wore what Cassie was sure was a smile while she kept the car in the correct lanes. It was difficult not to look at the magnificent scenery, even in the dead of winter.

With the new year just beginning, Cassie viewed this not as a hiccup in her life, but as a new journey. It was a fresh start, and she intended to grasp it with both hands.

Suddenly there was a loud pop, and the car lurched on the road. Cassie sucked in a startled breath and tried to keep the wheel straight so as not to skid off the road and over the side of the mountain.

She slowed the car to a stop, shut it off, and sat with her eyes closed and her heart pounding like a drum. When she opened her eyes again, a glance showed her that even Duke had been wise and pulled his head back inside.

"It's okay, boy," she said, and rubbed his giant head, her hands shaking from the adrenaline dump. "Stay here while I go see what happened."

Cassie reached to open the door only to find it took her two tries before she could grasp the handle. She climbed out of the car and looked over the side of the mountain to the snow hundreds of yards below.

A walk around the car revealed that one of the tires was flat. She rubbed her hands together and blew on them for warmth. She was already trembling from the cold, and she'd been outside for only a few seconds.

But she had faced far more daunting things in her life than a flat tire, and she wasn't about to fall apart now. Cassie lifted the back hatch of the Vauxhall Corsa and managed to find the spare tire.

Thank goodness she knew how to change a tire, or it would have been even longer. As it was, everything was taking twice as long because her fingers were so numb.

Just as she was fitting the spare on the car, it began to snow. Cassie gritted her teeth and kept working. An eternity later, the flat was replaced and she was back in the car.

"Sorry, Duke, but I need to feel my hands again."

Cassie rolled up his window and turned the heater on full blast, with all the vents pointed to her. The car roared to life, and she hesitantly pulled back onto the road.

Dan had warned her about driving in the Highlands during winter. He needn't have bothered. Since Cassie had never driven in snow she was already apprehensive, and with the steep inclines, descents, and one-lane bridges, she was moving at a snail's pace.

And by the line of cars behind her, she was apparently the only one who felt the need to go slow.

As soon as Cassie was able, she pulled into a layby, which was Scots for "passing lane," and allowed the cars to go by. She might not understand the way the British built their roadways, but she was very thankful for the laybys so others could go around her.

Another thing she never counted on was the sun setting so early. It was only four, and the sun was sinking faster than any sunset she'd ever seen. Which meant she was not only driving in snow, in the mountains looking for a place she'd never been, but she would also be doing it in the dark.

"Lost luggage, Dan bailing on me, having to drive this toy car, getting Duke, a flat, and now snow and dark. Please, God, get me to the house in one piece," she prayed as she narrowed her eyes to see through the snow.

Duke whined softly, as if offering her comfort.

The roads became more winding and the curves tighter the farther north and deeper into the Highlands she drove. Her fingers ached from gripping the wheel so tightly.

Cars zoomed by her while she struggled to read the signs as the snow fell faster and faster. Twice she missed her turns only to have to double back and find them again.

The GPS was taking her farther and farther off what the Scots called main roadways to small two-lane roads with no stripes and what anyone in the States would call one-way roads.

"Shit!" she cried as she swerved to miss an oncoming car.

Cassie had to jerk the passenger-side wheels off the road to miss another car. It jostled Duke so badly, his head hit the roof of the car.

"Sorry, Duke," she muttered when the dog gave a bark.

She'd never felt so relieved as when she found the driveway to Dan's house. At least she didn't have to worry about oncoming cars anymore. As she drove down the long winding drive, she expected to see lights on in the house welcoming her.

But there was only darkness and stillness.

"Dan, where are you?" she asked.

She knew Dan and his wife were having some issues in their marriage, and it was just like Dan to be forgetful about things. But he had never forgotten *her* before.

"There's a first time for everything, I suppose."

Duke's whine only confirmed her suspicions.

She put the car in park and turned off the engine. Duke pawed at the door, letting her know he needed out.

"Wait," she said. "Let me unlock the front door first."

Cassie unbuckled her seat belt and rushed for the door to the cottage. Dan had told her the key was in a black box near the door. What he hadn't told her was that she'd need a code.

"I'm so going to hurt you, Dan. Badly. Very, very badly."

By this time, rain was beginning to mix with the snow. Duke's barking grew louder, and her only choice was to head back to the car and look through everything she had received from Dan to see if he'd given her a code that she somehow missed.

As soon as she opened the car door, Duke jumped out and ran into the darkness.

"Duke!" she called, and tried to go after him.

Her foot hit a piece of ice and slipped out from underneath her. Cassie landed hard on her butt. She sat, the snow and rain seeping into her jeans, immobilized by the pain.

She had no idea how long she stayed there before she crawled back to the car, wincing at the agony of each movement. Her gloveless hands were now so frozen, she couldn't move them. It took her five attempts before she was able to unzip her purse and pull out her cell phone.

Getting any kind of Internet service was laughable, so she couldn't look through old e-mails. However, she was able to sift through the texts, but found nothing.

Cassie dialed her brother and listened to the call ring over and over again before finally going to voice mail.

The tears she'd held back all day clogged her throat. She swallowed and laid her head on the steering wheel. She couldn't get the keys to let herself into the house, she'd lost Duke, and she was most likely going to freeze to death in a toy car that offered no more than a sliver of warmth.

"A fitting day for the beginning of my new life," she said as the first tear fell down her cheek.

CHAPTER TWO

Dreagan Distillery

Hal shut and locked the doors to the distillery for the day before he turned and looked out over the land. Snow blanketed everything and the light the crescent moon cast upon the ground made it look almost as if it were glowing.

The need to lose himself in the land in the forest sometimes was overwhelming, as it was this night. Other times he could ignore the call, but not tonight.

Hal didn't bother to tell the others where he was going. He simply walked down the steps and into the night. The weather didn't faze him.

His boots crunched in the thick snow, but he never noticed. His gaze was trained on the forest ahead. Every one of them answered to something, and for Hal it was the forest.

Always had been.

Always would be.

Once he was in the trees, he took a deep breath and lifted his face to the sky. Snow landed on his lashes and rain dripping from the limbs above pelted his face.

It was glorious.

Hal smiled and spread his arms wide. He touched his chest, through his jacket and sweater, to the tattoo beneath.

A person could get lost in the glens of the Highlands, and there were thousands of glens. Which made it a perfect place for Hal and the others like him to stay hidden.

It had been a long time since he'd allowed his other self to show, his dragon self. And for some reason, this night he desperately yearned to spread his wings and fly.

To feel the wind around him as he soared through the sky.

He still remembered flying low over the trees, the leaves brushing against his underside as the sun beat on him. He hadn't needed to hide then. For once upon a time, he had been able to call to his brethren and listened to their roars fill the forest.

So very long ago he had lived a completely different life. Back before the humans betrayed them, before a war that changed everything.

A sound off to Hal's right had him turning his head in that direction. He dropped his arms as his eyes fastened on a large, fast-moving animal loping through the trees.

Hal let his coat drop from his arms as he sprinted toward the animal. As he neared, he realized it was a dog—a very large dog. And the only person near Dreagan land who had such a dog was Dan Hunter.

With more frustration than Hal wanted to concede, he came to a halt. He had been able to take flight, but now he had to chase a dog. For several moments he watched the Great Dane running, his tongue lolling out the side of his mouth.

There had been a few times in Hal's life where he'd felt that free, been that free. Those times were the barest of memories now.

When a person was as old as Hal, time blurred.

It was so easy to get lost in his memories, of what had once been, and what *he* had once been. But to allow himself to get absorbed in such recollections was not wise.

He pulled himself back from the brink and gave a loud, short whistle, which pulled Duke up short. The Great Dane turned his head to Hal and issued a deep, booming bark in greeting.

"Come here, lad," Hal called.

Immediately, the dog ran to him, his tail wagging.

Hal rubbed the dog's massive head. "It's no' like Dan to allow you to run like this. Nor is it like you to run off. What's the problem, lad?"

Duke jerked against the hold Hal had on his collar. Hal narrowed his eyes. He'd learned very early in life to listen carefully when animals tried to speak. They might not be speaking your language, but they were talking. It was obvious Duke was trying to tell him something.

"Show me," Hal said, and released the collar.

Duke took off at a run and Hal was quick to follow. Dreagan land extended far as the eye could see, and Dan's cottage was the closest anyone lived to Dreagan.

It was because Dan rarely rented the property and didn't cause any problems that Hal and the others hadn't made a point of getting rid of him.

Hal easily kept pace with the Great Dane as they traversed over the land. When they crested the last hill that overlooked Dan's cottage, Duke stopped and whined.

Dan's Corsa could be seen by the light of the moon despite the heavy snowfall. Thankfully, the rain had tapered off, but the snow made it difficult to see where Dan was.

Duke butted Hal's hand with his head before he took off down the slope to the cottage. Hal had memorized the lay of the land centuries ago and knew where the boulders lay hidden in the snow.

He leapt down the slope and landed in thick snow.

Duke caught up with him, and they both ran the rest of the way down the side of the mountain.

Hal rushed to the front door, but found it locked and all the lights out. When Hal turned to look for Duke, he found the Great Dane standing beside the car.

That's when Hal noticed there was someone inside. In three strides he was beside the car. He tapped on the window, but the figure didn't move.

Duke barked. Hal opened the door to find the most beautiful face he'd ever seen. Hair as dark as chocolate silk hung over her shoulder and next to her pale skin.

The same dark brows arched over large eyes. Her oval face was streaked with tears. Thick lashes lay against her cheeks. Lips, full and luscious, were slightly parted and tinged a pale blue.

That pulled Hal out of his perusal. He touched her cheek to find it ice cold. Cursing under his breath, he rushed to the lockbox next to the door and punched in the code. With keys in hand, he unlocked the front door before he ran back to the car.

Carefully, he gathered the woman in his arms and walked into the house. He laid her on the couch and stripped her out of boots that were made for walking the streets of Edinburgh, not traipsing through the Highlands.

He found her socks dry, so he left them on her feet and got to work removing her jacket. The hem of her sweater was wet, which led him to inspecting her jeans, only to find them also soaked.

With grim determination, Hal lifted her sweater and unbuttoned the jeans. He was resolute in ignoring the glimpse he got of her flat stomach and the feel of her smooth skin against his hand.

He gritted his teeth and tried to look away from the long, shapely legs revealed as he peeled off her jeans. Tried—and failed.

Hal took in one long glance and felt a stirring of desire before he covered her with the thick tartan blanket from the back of the sofa. The fact she was shivering from the cold prompted him to take action and build a quick fire.

When the flames were dancing before him, Hal looked over his shoulder to find Duke lying in front of the couch as if to guard the woman.

"Doona worry, lad. I'm no' in the habit of taking sleeping women."

Duke laid his great head on his paws, as if he were satisfied with the answer.

Hal rose and retrieved the single small piece of luggage and the woman's purse from the car. His curiosity awoken, he searched her purse to find her wallet and looked at the ID.

Somehow he wasn't surprised to find she was American. He read over the Arizona driver's license until he found her name. "Cassandra Hunter," he read aloud.

He shifted his gaze to Cassandra. So, she was related to Dan, but how? She wasn't Dan's wife—that was for sure. Dan's wife, Shelly, was British and was well known for being outgoing and a socialite.

Hal leaned a hip against the back of the sofa. "So who are you, Cassandra Hunter from Arizona? And why are you here?"

Hal shut his phone off, ending the conversation with Rhys, and put two more logs on the fire. He hadn't felt right leaving Cassandra alone overnight, so he had called Rhys to bring a few groceries.

Once Hal learned who Cassandra was, and if she was supposed to be there since he couldn't reach Dan, then he would leave the American to herself.

Hal reclined in the chair and stretched his legs in front of him. His gaze returned to Cassandra. She hadn't made so much as a sound since he'd brought her inside. Thankfully, the blue tinge to her lips had faded after an hour of him rubbing warmth into her arms, feet, and legs.

Duke had kept his guard duty. If the dog trusted her, then Hal mostly likely would as well. Animals had uncanny abilities in reading people.

Hal must have dozed because he awoke to the sound of a vehicle approaching. He knew before he looked that it was Rhys. Hal rose and walked to the door to open it before his friend could knock.

"Is she still unconscious?" Rhys asked as he walked inside with a bag in each hand.

"Aye. She's no' moved."

"Duke is with her, I see."

Hal took one of the bags and set it on the counter to unload the milk, orange juice, and water into the fridge. "Aye. Which leads me to believe Dan sent her, but then why couldn't she get inside?"

"You still have no' gotten a hold of Dan?" Rhys asked as he set a loaf of bread, cereal, and some bagels on the counter.

"Nay. What did you discover?"

"I found a Cassandra Hunter from Phoenix, Arizona. She boarded a flight from Arizona, had a layover in Missouri, and then another in New York before coming here. Oh, and her luggage was lost."

Hal raised a brow. "How is she related to Dan?"

"She's his sister."

"Ah. So why is she here, I wonder?"

Rhys shrugged his thick shoulders and smiled, his dark blue eyes creasing in the corners. "That I'm curious to know as well. I'll let Con know where you're at when he returns in the morn."

Hal nodded, his gaze still on Cassandra.

Odd that after so many thousands of years, a female would draw his attention as Cassandra did. Their dragon magic had put a stop to that. Or so he thought. He had stared at her through the night, wondering what color her eyes were and why she was in Scotland.

He ran the pad of his thumb over his fingers as he recalled the feel of her soft skin and the wonderful curves he'd seen as he stripped her.

His fingers still tingled from their contact with her. While his body stirred with desires he couldn't harness or begin to understand.

"Hal," Rhys called from the door. "Be careful, my friend. You know we doona mix with humans."

"She was in need of my help," he answered as he tore his eyes from the woman. "That's all there is."

"Hmm. I see how you look at her, no' that I blame you. She's verra comely. We are—"

"I know what we are," Hal interrupted as he turned away from his friend. "I doona need reminding."

"We all need reminding from time to time. Part of our punishment is that we're forever to be alone."

"Punishment for something we didna do. We are no' the ones who should be punished. We take the humans' penance while they thrive."

"And we hide. I'm no' arguing that. We did what we had to do."

"Forever is a verra long time, Rhys."

"Especially when you're as old as time. Just guard yourself."

Hal heard the door close behind Rhys and the motor of the vehicle turn over a moment later.

"Forever is too long," he mumbled.

They were supposed to be free, but how free could someone be if they were meant to guard, meant to spend eternity alone?

Some centuries were easier to live through than others. Over the past few weeks, Hal had found . . . a hunger . . . growing inside him that had nothing to do with food.

He craved something, but he didn't know what.

All he knew was that it was out there, waiting for him. He just had to find it. But how? They were forbidden to leave for more than a few months at a time.

He and the other Kings were careful to leapfrog through time by hiding through a generation or two. It had been easier in the past. There wasn't computers, video cameras, or cell phones.

Nowadays, a face was logged into a database, and that was it. They took great pains to keep themselves from being seen, but the inevitable would happen. It always did.

So many lifetimes, so many names. Hal didn't even remember his original name, he'd taken so many. He kept his present one for several centuries, but then all of them had. It was easier that way.

They had a responsibility as Dragon Kings, a duty that no others could fulfill. An obligation caused by one of their own so very long ago.

As eternity stretched before Hal, he wondered how he would get through it all alone.

CHAPTER THREE

Cassie was torn from the cocoon of warmth and sleep by something very cold and very wet on her hand. She cracked an eye open and found Duke's face in front of hers.

He ducked his head and nudged her hand with his nose for a second time.

"I'm awake," Cassie said with a yawn.

As soon as she stretched, the pain in her lower back and butt made itself known. Cassie grabbed the injured area and winced.

The day before came rushing back to her in an instant. That's when she realized she was inside a house instead of in the sorry excuse for a car Dan had left her.

"Oh, good. You're awake," said a too-cheerful female voice with a Scottish accent.

Cassie rose up on her elbow and looked over the back of the sofa toward the kitchen to see a young pretty blond woman wiping a plate dry before putting it in the cupboard.

"How did I get in here? And who are you?"

The girl chuckled as she tossed aside the towel and walked to Cassie. "I'm Alice. I work at Dreagan, but Hal asked me to do some shopping for you."

"Hal?" Cassie was becoming more confused as time went on. Who was Hal, and why was he stocking her kitchen?

Alice's smile grew. "Follow the chopping, and get ready for an eyeful. I've been watching him all morning."

Cassie didn't have time for another question before Alice was gone. With nothing else to do, she threw back the covers and then stopped as she noticed her bare legs. Had this Hal taken off her jeans?

She gingerly stood and made her way to the flight of stairs where the bedrooms turned out to be. It didn't take her long to find where her one lone piece of luggage had been taken.

After she donned a pair of sweatpants and socks and combed out her hair, Cassie walked back down the stairs and did as Alice suggested—followed the chopping.

She rounded a corner and found herself peering out a dining room that was all glass. It looked more like a sunroom than a dining room, and the views of the mountains were staggering.

Or at least they might be if she could tear her eyes away from Hal.

He stood well over six feet, his long black hair pulled back in a queue at his neck while sweat rolled down his face. Thick black brows slashed over his eyes, eyes she wished she knew the color of.

His face was all angles and rugged handsomeness. A dusty coating of whiskers covered his square jaw and chin, but even the whiskers didn't hide the slight indent in his chin.

He had a wide forehead and a long straight nose. And his lips . . . Cassie had trouble swallowing as she caught sight of his mouth. No man should have lips so wide and thin, so damned seductive.

A jacket and sweater were discarded on the back of a

wooden chair, leaving Hal in nothing but a skintight white tee that showed every wonderful muscle.

With each move, each swing of the axe, she watched the play of muscles in his back and arms. The blade of the axe cut through the wood as easily as a hot knife through butter. Cassie was mesmerized watching him.

It wasn't just his amazing body or his good looks, there was something different about him that Cassie had never seen in a man. Something that would set him apart in a crowd of thousands.

As if he realized he was being watched, Hal halted just as he was about to bring the axe down again and turned his head. Their gazes locked, and Cassie felt all the air rush from her lungs.

For several moments they simply stared at one another before he sent her a grin and went back to chopping. It didn't seem right to continue staring at him, so Cassie turned away and hurried into the kitchen only to discover it was nearly noon.

"Duke, I've slept the entire morning away," she said in alarm.

With everything Hal had done, the least she could do was fix him lunch. Cassie grabbed her coat from a hook near the door and shrugged it on as she stuffed her feet into her boots.

She walked outside and huddled into the jacket as the brisk January wind hit her full in the face. Duke raced past her and bounded around Hal.

He laughed and rubbed Duke before he tossed the blade into a stump as if weighed nothing and turned to her.

Being this close to him did something to Cassie. Maybe it was because she was hungry and still exhausted from the day before, but it was as if she couldn't get her balance, as if the world kept tilting beneath her feet.

"I hear I owe you my thanks," she said.

His mouth twisted in a half smile. "I did what anyone would."

She had never thought the Scottish brogue sounded appealing until that moment. His deep, almost gravelly voice made goose bumps race over her body. He could read from an accounting book and she'd listen to him. Avidly.

"I didn't know there was a code, and I couldn't get a hold of Dan."

"He gave it to us a few years ago in case there was ever an emergency."

Cassie chuckled. "Thank God he did."

"I'm Hal."

"Cassie," she said, amazed at how breathless she sounded.

Just from being this close to him. Was it his brogue, his eye-catching body, or was it something more that caused the world to fade to nothing around him?

Silence stretched between them. Cassie cleared her throat. "I apologize for sleeping away the morning. Yesterday was probably the worst day of my life."

"Ah, you slept all of yesterday, lass. This is your second morning here."

Cassie snorted, wondering if the frozen ground could open up and swallow her. "Of course it is." She tucked a strand of hair behind her ear that the wind kept blowing into her face. "Thank you for having Alice bring the groceries. I can pay you for that."

"No need."

"I think I owe you my life. Let me fix you some lunch at least."

He smiled once more, making her stomach flutter as if a thousand butterflies took flight inside her.

"That sounds good. Let me finish up here. Dan didna leave you with much firewood, and with the weather we'll be having, you're going to need it."

"I'll see you inside then."

It wasn't until Cassie was walking away that she remembered she was an awful cook. The only thing she could manage without burning it was a sandwich.

She hastily looked through the small pantry and fridge and found different deli meats and cheeses that she cut up and laid out along with bread and mayo and mustard. There was a bag of chips, which she also put on the table.

"They're crisps," she said after reading the label. "I need to remember that."

A glance outside showed Duke was still with Hal, so Cassie rushed upstairs and jumped into the shower. The hot water felt wonderful, as did washing her hair and scrubbing her body. Then she quickly blow-dried her hair.

Unable to resist, she put a dab of blush on her cheeks before she put on a fresh pair of jeans and her thickest sweater over a long-sleeve shirt, which wasn't nearly thick enough for the weather.

She walked downstairs rubbing her hands together from the chill of the house only to come up short when she found Hal standing in the kitchen munching on a slice of meat, Duke at his feet.

"If that's the warmest sweater you have, lass, I fear you need to do some shopping."

She pulled her gaze away from his amazing pale, pale blue eyes and glanced down at her soft pink sweater and nodded. "I know. I was hoping to make it through winter with what I had. I have a few more sweaters I was able to get before I came, but my luggage was lost."

"Maybe they'll find your luggage soon. Either way, you need more sweaters and a thicker coat as well as gloves and scarves. A hat would also be wise."

Cassie sighed as the dollar signs continued to add up in her mind. "I'll get on that as soon as I can. Thank you for letting me know."

"Dan should have told you."

Yes, he should have, but Cassie wasn't going to rag on her brother to a complete stranger. Yet, this stranger seemed to know Dan pretty well.

"Dan is . . . well, he's so busy with . . . things," she finished lamely. "Are you hungry? I'm famished."

"Then let's eat."

Cassie hadn't found any coffee, and she was in desperate need of caffeine, so she grabbed a soda from the fridge and told Hal to help himself.

He spoke of the weather and the snow they were expecting to get over the next few days while they fixed their sandwiches and ate. Cassie found herself relaxed around him, even if she was more aware of him as a man.

A very virile, very handsome man.

But she was under no illusions. She'd seen herself in the mirror. She was nothing to write home about, and men like Hal always had the most beautiful women on their arms.

"How much do I owe you for the groceries?" she asked once they were finished eating.

He waved away her words. "Consider it a welcome gift. How long are you staying, anyway?"

"Ah, that is a question, isn't it? Dan said he needed some work done on the cottage and I needed a place to stay. I'll do the work here in exchange for staying. During that time, I need to find a job."

"All the way out here?" Hal asked, his black brows raised as his moonlight blue eyes watched her.

"When I arrived it was dark. I don't remember much. How far is it to the nearest town?"

"Thirty minutes on a good, warm day."

Cassie leaned her head back against the chair and nodded as she realized her situation here wasn't that much better than it had been in Arizona, but at least here she wouldn't get kicked out because she couldn't pay the rent. "I see."

"May I ask what brought you here?"

She found herself drawn to his eyes. The pale blue against his black hair and tanned skin was spellbinding. She wasn't the type to reveal all her secrets, but with Hal, she found she wanted to share her burdens. Even if it was only for a short time.

"I lost my job during layoffs almost a year ago. I had savings, and I'd have been all right, but my roommate got married, leaving me with all the rent. That sapped my savings quicker than I expected. Finding a job was impossible anywhere. So many people out of work. I couldn't even get hired on at McDonald's."

Cassie chuckled, remembering that interview.

"So your brother offered?" Hal asked.

She rolled her eyes. "Not exactly. Dan has always been the lucky one in the family. He's the one who was able to skip college and land the ultimate job in London because of who he knew. That job is where he met Shelly, his wife. As I'm sure you know, her family is loaded with money, but Dan was doing all right by himself."

"And your parents? Are they proud of him?"

"Our parents died in a car crash my junior year of high school. Gosh, that was over twelve years ago," she said, and mentally frowned. How time flew. "Dan became my guardian and took care of me. I was able to get a couple of grants to go to college, and I paid the rest myself while working. Dan sent money at first, but it stopped when I got my degree and found a good job. Not that I blame him. I was able to take care of myself."

"You didna see much of him, I take it?"

Hal's questions were ones anyone would ask, but somehow Cassie felt as if he was steering her toward something. What, though, she didn't know.

"No. His life was in London, and I understood that. When things got too rough, I called him. We worked out this arrangement."

"Why no' just ask him for money? He has enough of it."

"I could have, and he would've sent it."

"But?" Hal urged, his eyes focused intently on her.

Cassie crossed her arms over her chest. "But . . . I needed a new start somewhere."

And she'd thought that being closer to Dan, she might see more of him. She was lonely, so very lonely. He was all that she had left of her family, and she hadn't seen him in over nine years.

She hadn't even been at his wedding, because it happened during her final exams and she wasn't able to get away. It never occurred to Dan that she might have wanted to be there and that he could have scheduled the wedding a week later.

"You miss him," Hal said.

Cassie looked away from Hal's probing gaze. "He has his own life."

"He left you alone. There's no shame in wanting to be near family, Cassie."

"Dan isn't a bad person," she said, and picked at her short nails. How many times had she railed against Dan because he hadn't come to see her or sent for her? He knew she worked hard for what little money she earned.

She looked up to find Hal's pale blue gaze soften.

"I never said he was."

"He just gets caught up in his life and forgets about . . . things."

"You mean he forgets you."

Cassie took a deep breath and began to gather up the items on the table as she stood.

Suddenly one of Hal's large hands covered hers. "No one should forget their family. No one should forget you."

Cassie's entire body heated at Hal's whispered words. His amazing eyes caught and held hers, and she found herself drowning in them. Sinking, falling.

"Who are you?"

He glanced away. "I'm just a man."

"No. You're more than that. You're different."

He removed his hand from hers and scooted back the chair as he stood. He forced a smile and pulled on his sweater and coat. Cassie wished she could take back the words, to rewind the moment and start again.

She didn't want him to leave, and take with him the warmth and ease he had given so easily.

"If you need anything I've written the number to Dreagan on a card and pinned it to the corkboard near the phone."

The man who had been so interested, so kind was gone. In his place was someone who couldn't get away from her fast enough. As usual, she was forever saying and doing the wrong thing at the wrong time.

"Thank you again. I can never repay your kindness."

"There's no need, lass. This is a lonely place out here in the Highlands. Doona be afraid to call if you need something."

She walked him to the door, all too aware that he hadn't offered to come back and see for himself if she needed anything. She thought there had been a spark of interest in his gaze, but she'd obviously been mistaken.

Hal gave Duke another pet on his head, and then with one last wave, he was gone.

Cassie closed and locked the door behind Hal. She turned and leaned against it, wishing she could take back whatever had changed Hal. He might still be there then.

"Who am I kidding? I don't stand a chance with a man like him."

Duke barked as if in agreement.

CHAPTER FOUR

Hal's heart still hammered in his chest as he crested the hill and disappeared from view of the cottage. And of Cassie.

He stopped and braced his hands on his knees as he bent over and gulped in huge amounts of cold air. He'd known when he first saw Cassie that he was attracted to her.

But talking to her, seeing her dark brown eyes focused on him had sent him reeling, careening.

She was hesitant to trust, lonely, and entirely too innocent. She was kind and a little shy, but determined and resourceful. And too damned pretty for her own good. It had taken all that he had not to gawk at her like an idiot.

Touching her. That had been the worst mistake.

He closed his eyes as he recalled her warm, smooth skin and the way her dark hair had hung straight and thick down her back like a cascade of silk.

Hal straightened and took several more deep breaths to calm his yearning body. He'd looked in on Cassie several times the day before, each time hoping he'd be there when she woke.

He'd wondered endlessly about what color her eyes

would be and how her voice would sound. He found he loved her American accent and how easy a smile came to her full lips.

There was a moment when he'd almost offered to come see her the following day, but Rhys was right. Hal needed to be careful. There was something about Cassie that pulled at him, that ate away at his resolve.

She fascinated him, captivated him.

Excited him.

He wanted to take her in his arms, to savor her sweet lips until they were both breathless and needy. He wanted to strip away every layer of clothing until she stood bared before him. And then he would caress and kiss every inch of her.

Sex was something each of the Kings immersed themselves in, but that's all there could ever be. There was nothing more for them, and never would be.

It was part of who they were. Hal had never thought it a penance until that moment. How had he gone so many millennia without caring that he could have no more with a woman than a night of sex? Why did it suddenly matter?

But this craving, this unimaginable hunger he had for Cassie wasn't something he could ignore when he was around her. The best course of action was to keep his distance.

That was easier said than done when every fiber of his being demanded he turn around to go back to her.

In spite of the secret of being a Dragon King, despite the treachery that changed his world, even through the magic that was supposed to make him immune to human affection . . . he wanted Cassie with an unmovable, unyielding tenacity.

No matter how he looked at it, there was no way he could have her. Too many secrets, too much was at risk for him and the other Kings to jeopardize all they had built and their anonymity.

Hal sighed and pushed Cassie from his mind as he resumed his walk to the main house on Dreagan property. It was set well away from the distillery and even the sheep and cattle barns.

The large stone structure came into view after about thirty minutes. The house was next to the mountain, with part of it actually inside the mountain, making it easier for them to continue their duties as Kings protecting all of humanity.

A side door to the house opened and Hal spotted Guy making his way to him. Guy Royston with his light brown hair and even lighter brown eyes shared patrolling duties with Hal for the next few years.

"Hal," Guy said.

Hal stopped and stuffed his hands into the front pocket of his jeans. "What's wrong?"

"Does something have to be wrong?"

"When you clench your jaw the way you do, aye. So tell me."

"Something's happened."

Hal's stomach clenched. Could they know how he felt about Cassie? "With what?"

"The Silvers."

Hal didn't say more as he and Guy turned as one and walked to the entrance of the mountain hidden by a large hedge coming off the conservatory at the back of the house.

The entrance was low enough that all the Kings had to duck their heads to miss the low rock, but once through the arched access, the tunnel ceiling was high enough that they could stand upright.

Torches lined the walls of either side of the cave as they descended deeper into the mountain. Con had never had electricity brought into the cave, and Hal thought it a wise decision.

It was better to keep things as they were when it came to what they guarded beneath the rock.

The path turned from gravel to large rock steps that were treacherous and uneven.

Hal heard voices up ahead where the cave opened up to a huge cavern. There were multiple caverns, and this one was set farther back and off to the side than the rest.

"The Silvers moved," Guy said, his voice barely above a whisper.

Hal jerked his gaze to his friend. "What? It's been . . . shite, I've lost count how many centuries it's been since the Silvers last moved. They are contained. *He* is contained. We made sure of that. We sacrificed everything to ensure that."

"Aye, I know," Guy said with a sigh. "Still. They moved."

Hal said no more until they reached the cavern and he found several of the other Kings standing around the immense cage where four of the largest silver dragons to ever roam the earth were kept.

Banan, his arms crossed over his chest, turned his head as they approached. "Did Guy fill you in?"

Hal gave a single nod. "Where is Ulrik?"

Banan dropped his arms and sighed. "Constantine is watching him now. Ulrik hasna changed his routine of going to his bookstore, home, and to run a few errands. It wasna him, Hal."

"There's no other explanation," Rhys said from the other side of the cage.

Hal rubbed his hands along his jaw. "Rhys is right. Ulrik is the only one who can call to the Silvers."

"It's no' him. It can no' be him," Guy said.

Hal knew how he felt. They had forfeited so much to contain the Silvers and to take away the magic and rights of one of their own. All to protect mankind.

"Ulrik is a King no matter that we took away his sword and his magic," Banan said.

"And stripped his ability to shift into a dragon," Hal said.

He slowly walked around the cage to look at the long, thick bodies of the dragons. Their scales gleaming metallic silver and shading to dark silver toward the back of their necks, the scales getting thicker around their heads.

A row of tendrils ran from the base of their skulls, down their backs, to the tips of their tails. They had long, muscular limbs with four closely-mounted digits on each foot that ended in very long talons. The dragons had huge mouths and large nostrils. Their wings, usually folded against them, were large and widely set.

But it was their eyes, the color of obsidian and cold as death, that always shocked people most.

Not to mention their size. The Silvers were easily as tall as a three-story building. Their sheer bulk made them terrible when waging destruction, though they weren't the only large dragons who'd once roamed the earth.

"He can no' shift into dragon form," Hal said. "That alone prohibits him from gathering any type of magic in order to call to his Silvers. For thousands of years, no' a tremor has gone through them."

Banan's gaze met his.

Hal stared at the dragons, the evidence impossible to miss before him. "The wing has unfurled."

The wing of the Silver nearest Hal hadn't unfolded completely, but enough that it was unmistakable.

Rhys grunted and shook his head. "If no' Ulrik, then who did this? The Druids? The Warriors?"

"Nay," Guy said quickly. "The Druids and Warriors are dealing with their own evil by the name of Declan. And as powerful as the Druids and Warriors are, they can no' touch our magic surrounding the Silvers."

Banan braced his hands on the metal of the cage and put his face next to one of the sleeping Silvers as he peered at it. "Regardless, we need to keep an eye on them. We've become too complacent."

"Aye, because Ulrik can no' do any more harm," Rhys stated harshly. "We've kept an eye on him for what? Nothing? He's harmless as a fly now."

"Doona underestimate Ulrik," Hal reminded Rhys.

They had all seen the destruction Ulrik and his Silvers were capable of, of what they had done when they attacked the other Kings and dragons. To underestimate him was to forfeit your life.

It was Ulrik and his Silvers who had nearly decimated the humans, not that many of the Kings blamed him. It was only after the humans began hunting dragons that Ulrik took such a stand.

He had been the only one to go against Con, the only one who had demanded the humans remember who had ruled for millennia before they ever walked the earth.

Hal didn't know how Con had held the other Kings back from taking a stand with Ulrik, but that strength was what made Constantine a King of Kings.

The only one who could ever have taken Con's place was Ulrik. But that time was long past. It was a dragon's magic that made him powerful, and only the most powerful became the King of Kings. Ulrik had as much magic as Con, but Ulrik didn't fight Con for the right. Ulrik had been content to rule his Silvers.

"Hal's right. But there is something at work here, and we'd all be wise to discover what it is," Guy said.

They threw around more ideas on who or what it could be, but in the end, they came up with nothing. Hal spent the rest of the day at his duties with the sheep and cattle, all the while Cassie was ever present in his mind.

At supper, all any of them could talk about was the Silvers and when Con would return, but Hal listened with only half an ear. Even when he knew it was important to focus on the Silvers, he couldn't concentrate.

There was a hunger in his chest. What he'd felt in the past seemed to grow with each breath he took until he was drowning in it. He knew it was Cassie, knew she was the root to this need within him.

But the why of it he couldn't answer.

Could there be some correlation between Cassie's arrival and the Silver's movements? Surely not. Humans—and Cassie was definitely human—had no connection to dragons.

With his thoughts going round and round, Hal decided to go for a walk after supper. He was feeding an apple to one of the horses when a bright light ignited the sky and then flared. A heartbeat later, a boom sounded, sending a shock wave across the land.

Hal didn't wait on the others as he took off toward where the flare had hit the earth. Whatever it was, there was magic involved.

Dragon magic.

It crackled over his skin, calling to the dragon within him and demanding its release.

The thought of someone other than a King finding whatever it was that had just landed made Hal's legs pump even faster.

He slid in a thick piling of snow as he hit a valley between the mountains, and when he rolled and came to his feet, he heard the unmistakable sound of Duke's bark.

"Nay," he whispered, and started running again.

CHAPTER FIVE

Cassie had been walking Duke when she saw the bright flame of light, and when it landed not far from her, she could only stand and stare at the way the light blazed in the inky night.

Then Duke began barking.

Before she could tug on his leash, he was gone, the leash ripped from her hands.

"Duke!" Cassie shouted as she ran after the dog.

She lost track of the number of times she sank into the thick snow or lost her footing altogether. Her jeans were wet from the snow and she could no longer feel her nose. The farther Duke got from her, the more determined she was to catch him.

When she finally caught up with the Great Dane he was staring intently at something lying on the ground. Cassie crept closer and peered through the darkness to find a man.

A very naked man lying on his stomach in the snow on top of a mountain.

There was nothing normal about finding anyone lying in the snow, but a naked man? Something definitely wasn't right.

She looked around, hoping to see someone—someone like Hal—who might be near. But she was by herself. The unknown man's only hope was her.

Cassie drew in a deep breath, the cold air blasting through her lungs, reminding her all too well how she had felt when she was locked out of Dan's house just a few nights ago. That propelled her into action.

"Hello?" she said, and took a step closer, noting how close to the edge of the cliff the man was.

Duke let out a half growl, half whine. Cassie was about to turn her head to glance at the dog when the man moved.

At least he wasn't dead, but by the look of him, she couldn't exactly help him to the house.

"Hey? Can you hear me?" she tried again, hesitant to get too close to him.

The next thing she knew, the man was on his feet, a sword in his hands and his long hair blowing in the wind as he looked wildly about him.

Her eyes widened as she took in the sword. "What the hell are you doing walking around *naked* with a *sword*?"

Somehow she wasn't surprised when he didn't answer.

He was tall, his body rippling with muscles as he handled the sword as if he were born to it. His wide were pressed tightly together, a muscle in his jaw jumping.

His dark hair was wavy and damp as it hid a portion of his face. But what she did see was more than pleasant to look at.

Hollowed cheeks and a square jaw, in addition to his piercing brown eyes, would make any woman's heart skip a beat. As impressive as his face and muscles were, the sword wasn't the only thing that caught her eye.

It was the tattoo blazoned across his chest. The dragon stood tall and proud, its massive wings spread wide and taking up the entire width of the man's remarkable chest.

Her eyes couldn't help but follow the lines of the

imposing dragon down to its tail which wrapped around the man's left side. If the incredible artwork wasn't enough to get noticed, she could have sworn the tat shimmered amber for just a second.

"Where am I?" the man croaked, as if he hadn't used his voice in a very long time.

"Uh . . ." Cassie hesitated, yanking her gaze up to his face to find him watching her with narrowed eyes.

"Where?" he demanded, seemingly unfazed that there was a sheer drop behind him as the wind howled.

His hand tightened on the sword. Before she could answer, she heard footsteps pounding in the snow as someone raced toward them. In the space of heartbeat, the man had leapt across the distance separating them and grabbed her wrist.

A gasp locked in her throat as he spun her until his arm wrapped around her stomach and he pressed against her back, the blade of his sword to her throat.

Cassie sucked in a breath of cold air as she glanced at the sword. By the way the chilly blade felt against her skin, she knew it was the real thing.

Duke paced around them, his lips lifting to reveal his large teeth. Cassie tried to swallow but couldn't manage to do anything but stand there.

Suddenly Hal burst through the nearby trees and came to an abrupt halt when he saw her. "Cassie, are you hurt?"

He asked it so casually, as if he came upon women being held at sword point by nude men all the time.

"I'm cold," she answered, trying to sound just as nonchalant when she was anything but.

The man holding her growled, the sound low and dangerous. Then he demanded of Hal, "Who are you?"

"Someone who can help. Let the woman go."

No sooner had he finished the sentence than three other men stepped out of the tree line and stood on either side of Hal. Cassie winced as the blade pressed even harder against her throat.

"Please," she said to the man. "I can't hurt you."

"Who are they?" he whispered in her ear.

Cassie's eyes met Hal's. "The first one who came is Hal. He's a good man. Trust him."

"I doona know where I am."

"You're in Scotland. In the Highlands."

She felt him ease his hold somewhat. With her gaze locked on Hal, she watched him take a step toward her and the man, slowly, calmly.

"What's your name?" Hal asked her captor.

"I'm . . ." His voice trailed away.

Hal shrugged, as if it were of no consequence. "You must have hit your head. I doona need a name."

"I doona know who I am." His voice shook with terror and rage as he took three steps back, dragging Cassie with him.

Hal glared on the man, transforming Hal from good-looking to lethal in a heartbeat. "Let her go before I have to hurt you."

"You can no' hurt me," the man said, his voice filled with confidence.

"Why?" one of the men with Hal asked.

The stranger opened his mouth to answer, but once more found he couldn't.

"You must have hit your head," Cassie repeated. "Sometimes that'll muddle memories. No one wishes to harm you."

"Release her," Hal said menacingly, his voice cold and hard. "Now."

Cassie barely had time to blink before it seemed like darkness surrounded her the same time her captor moved his sword as if to block a blow coming at him, but there was no one and nothing there.

Of a sudden Hal and the other three men rushed the stranger. The naked man pushed her aside, her feet tangling with his. Before Cassie fell, she managed to see the men tackle the stranger and heard Hal shout her name.

She landed hard on the ground on her side and then began to roll. There was nothing to hold on to, nothing to stop her from . . . She didn't know what was below her, but by the tone of Hal's shout, she knew it couldn't be good.

A strong hand clamped around her wrist and jerked her to gut-wrenching stop. Cassie screamed as her legs went over the side of the mountain and dangled upon open air.

"I have you."

Hal's reassuring voice, his cool attitude did wonders to boost her confidence that she just might get out of this predicament alive.

And then she was hauled up and over the side and into his arms. Cassie threw her arms around Hal and buried her face in his neck as she shook from both the cold and the fall.

Hal held her close, and she felt as if she could have stayed there all night it felt so right.

"You saved me. Again."

Hal leaned back and took her face in his hands. His gaze searched hers before he asked, "Are you hurt?"

"I can't feel anything because I'm so cold."

"Come on," he said, and took her hand as they began to climb back to the top of the ridge.

The other three men had the stranger pinned to the ground on his back by his arms and legs, and someone had draped a jacket over his nakedness. His sword lay just inches away.

Cassie could see nothing other than the elaborate dragon tattoo on the man's chest. The man was struggling to get free, his lips peeled back as he growled viciously.

A growl? Could this night get any weirder? As soon as

she thought it, she knew she was tempting fate. Cassie shivered, not from the cold, but from the fierce bellow the man gave when he couldn't get up.

Hal's comforting arm was the only thing that kept her in her skin, she was so terrified. Duke moved against her leg, coming between her and the man.

Her hand delved into the dog's fur, and for the first time since finding the naked man, she felt relatively safe with Duke and Hal beside her.

Cassie was just turning away when she saw the dragon on the man's chest move.

"Oh, my God!" Cassie shouted, and covered her mouth with her hand.

Hal shifted partly in front of her as if to protect her. "What is it?"

"His tattoo. The dragon. It moved, Hal," Cassie said, and turned her eyes to him.

Hal jerked his gaze to the other men, and Cassie watched as they all looked at the dragon on the man's chest. It was as if all four men were noticing the tat for the first time.

There was a moment of eerie silence only broken by the moan of the wind before the man lifted his chin and let out another loud bellow.

"We'll take him back to the house," one of the men said.

The naked man fought against them. "Let me go!"

"You are better with us," another said, and looked pointedly at Hal.

Hal gave a nod, thankful Rhys and Banan had used their magic to defuse the situation. Now it was time to get Cassie away. "Come, Cassie. I'll walk you home."

She didn't fight him when he turned her away.

They had walked several moments before Cassie stopped and turned to him. "The tattoo moved. I know it."

"Tattoos doona move."

As Dragon Kings, they could feel their tats move before they shifted, but no one—especially not a human—had ever said they saw a tattoo move.

Whatever Cassie saw, Hal was sure she thought she was speaking the truth. But what was it she had seen? It gnawed at him.

"I know that," she said. "But I also know what I saw."

He sighed heavily. There were so many things he couldn't tell her. The fact that she came upon the man before they did was just bad luck. She'd seen more than any human since the war, and somehow he needed to keep her quiet.

"Cassie," he began.

She put her hand to her head. "I'm not crazy. Maybe I just hit my head. Maybe it's the cold. I don't know right now."

"Let's get you into the house and warm. I thought I told you, you needed mittens and a scarf in addition to a thicker coat."

"This is all I have," she said as they resumed walking.

Hal noticed how Duke stayed close to her. "Until you're able to get warmer things, I'd suggest you not go out in the snow, especially at night."

"You're right."

They said no more, and even though Hal was curious about her thoughts, he couldn't keep the image of her rolling down the side of the mountain out of his mind.

When they reached the cottage, Cassie stopped at the front door and faced him. "You saw the tattoo move, didn't you?"

"Nay, lass." He didn't lie. In fact, he wished he had seen it. He'd been afraid the questions would come before he had a chance to get away.

"Don't lie to me."

"I'm no'. I didna see anything."

Her eyes narrowed. "You don't think it strange to find a man naked in the snow? With a sword?"

"That's beyond bizarre, but here in the Highlands, the darkness and cold can sometimes break people's minds."

"I'll admit that man's mind wasn't exactly all there, but he wasn't insane. You didn't look into his eyes like I did, Hal. When he didn't know his name, there was fear there."

Hal moved closer to her, the light from inside illuminating her face and making the gold and red highlights shine in her dark hair. "Doona fret. We'll take care of him and make sure he gets medical attention. I didna get a chance to see how you are? Are you injured?"

"I'm sure the bruise I got from falling in the ice when I first arrived will have matching ones, but I think I'm okay other than that."

"You had a sword at your throat, and you nearly went over the side of a cliff. No one would be all right after that."

She chuckled and looked down. "No, I'm going to go inside and fix a large glass of wine while I soak in a very hot bath and try not to think about how close I came to death."

Hal brushed his fingers against the cool skin of her cheek. Her dark brown eyes rose to meet his, and it was everything he could do not to lean down and kiss her.

The longing to do just that was irresistible, overwhelming.

Uncontrollable.

He wanted a taste of her full lips, to feel her curves against him once more. When he held her after pulling her from the snow, he'd never felt anything so perfect in all the years of his life.

She had clung to him, and in that moment Hal would have given her anything she wanted if he could make her forget what had occurred.

As it was, he dared to caress her cheek, dared to get too close. It was a risk he was willing to take because not to take it was wrong.

She placed her hand atop his and closed her eyes while she leaned her cheek into his palm. His blood heated as longing and desire pooled within him, burning his veins with the sheer need of her.

Her touch made him ache to caress more of her, to know more of her. Because she made him feel as he'd never felt before. When it came to Cassie Hunter, he wanted all there was.

Not once since he came into being at the beginning of time had he ever encountered such a woman. She was different in so many ways, and he wanted to tell her all that he was.

But her knowing his secret was forbidden.

None of the Dragon Kings took mates, or hadn't since the war and one woman's betrayal. It was just part of the reason they guarded the Silvers, but it was reason enough for them to keep to themselves.

It was the first time Hal had ever thought to disregard the rules placed upon them, rules decided by the ruler of them all—Constantine.

Cassie's eyes opened, and for once Hal didn't try to hide the wanting, the craving he felt for her.

"I . . . feel something between us, Hal. Do you feel it?"

He wanted to lie to her, to walk away as if she didn't matter. But he couldn't. "Aye."

With that one admission, nothing else signified. Not that he was a Dragon King and a dragon, not that he was putting himself and her at an awful risk because of the attraction between them.

All that mattered was her.

Cassie.

Hal shifted his hand so that his fingers threaded with

the silky strands of her long hair. Her hands came up to rest on his chest.

Slowly, he pulled her to him as he lowered his head. He saw her eyelids flutter close a half a heartbeat before his lips touched hers.

A current of something pure, something strong flashed through him when he kissed her. He moaned and pressed his lips to hers again.

When her arms wound around his neck and she moved against him, Hal deepened the kiss. His tongue swept past her lips to duel with hers.

And the desire searing his blood rose to a fever pitch.

He was contemplating how to get her inside without breaking the kiss when his mobile rang.

It was Cassie who ended the kiss. Her eyes were dazed and her mouth swollen, but those amazing lips were tilted up in a small smile.

"Good night, Hal."

He watched, dumbstruck, as she entered the cottage, Duke at her heels.

His phone rang again, but he didn't need to look to know it was Rhys calling. The bastard had a keen sense of when one of them was getting in over his head.

The problem was, Hal had dived headfirst into all that was Cassie. And for him, there was no turning back now.

CHAPTER SIX

Hal made his way through the cave to where he knew the others would be holding the stranger. Hal rounded the corner and found the man, now clothed, sitting upon a boulder with his head in his hands.

It was no surprise to find the man without bonds. After all, he was surrounded by Dragon Kings.

"I've told you I doona know my name!" he shouted.

The man's head lifted when Hal approached, and he was struck by the desolation in the stranger's dark eyes.

"Is the woman all right?"

Hal nodded to the stranger. "Aye. Cassie will be fine."

"He held the sword as if he's used one before," Rhys said.

The stranger snorted. "Of course I've used a sword. What kind of Highlander can no' wield a blade?"

Hal crossed his arms over his chest and studied the man. "So, you're a Highlander. Where are you from?"

"I—" The stranger squeezed his eyes closed and gave a vicious shake of his head. "—I should know. It's just out of reach," he said between clenched teeth, his fury obvious.

After a moment he opened his eyes and lifted his head.

"I've no memories. Of anything. My name, where I've come from, or what I'm doing here."

Hal rubbed his eyes with this thumb and forefinger. What did it mean for this stranger not to have memories? Would it aid them in the coming weeks? Or hinder them?

"Have you always had the tat on your chest?" Guy asked.

The man parted the jacket he wore and glanced at his bare chest. "I doona think so. Nay, I didna."

"Though we should wait for Con, I think you have a right to know," Banan told the stranger.

The man raked his hand through his chin-length brown hair streaked with gold and twisted his lips in a smirk. "I doona believe I'm going to like what you're about to say."

"You may no' know your name or where you came from, but what Banan is about to tell you will at least allow you to know what you are," Hal said.

"*What* I am?" the stranger repeated, his dark eyes narrowing. "What's that supposed to mean? I'm a man."

Rhys rubbed his hand over his chin and chuckled. "No' exactly, my friend. What you are is one of us."

"And I can say with all honesty, it has been hundreds of millennia since once of us was created," Guy stated.

The stranger looked to each of them before his dark gaze, intense and demanding, came to rest on Hal. "What are you?"

"Immortal and extremely powerful. In short, we're Kings, but no' of people. We're the Dragon Kings."

"Immortal," the man repeated, his eyes going distant as if he were remembering something. "I . . . that doesna bother me as it should."

Hal and Rhys exchanged glances while Guy began to walk slowly around their newest Dragon King.

"You say you are Dragon Kings?" the man asked intrigued.

Banan shook his head. "Nay, you are a King now as

well. You'll be better off considering yourself one of us from the start."

"He needs a name," Guy said. "At least until he remembers his own."

The stranger gripped his head and growled. "Why can I no' remember anything?"

Rhys reached for the new King's sword only to have the stranger move with lightning speed to grab it. The man spun around, his sword raised with the point directed at Rhys as he glared.

Rhys lifted his hands with a half grin full of eagerness and anticipation for battle. "Is that all you have?"

Hal along with Guy and Banan began to close in on their newest member. Not once did he flinch as he looked at each of them.

There was no way he would have been made into a King if he was weak, but by the look gleaming in his dark eyes, he welcomed their attack.

After eons together, Hal and the others didn't need words to convey what each of them should do. With barely a glance at one another, they attacked.

Hal made a grab for the sword while Banan dived for the man's legs. Guy rammed a fist into the man's ribs and Rhys leapt into the air to wrap an arm around the throat of the new King.

With a great roar, the man kept on his feet. Hal managed to knock the sword away, and in that instant the newest King changed.

He was ferocious in his attack, even with four men assaulting him. He didn't back down. He took all four of them on with purpose and intent clear in his eyes.

Hal had no idea how long they battled. Somehow the newcomer's jacket was ripped off, the jeans he wore shredded and barely hanging on to his waist.

A few times Hal was thrown off the new King, and

each time he was surprised. Not once did the man ever stop or back down.

It wasn't until Rhys took one of his arms, and Guy the other, that Banan and Hal were able to pin the newcomer to the ground. And still he fought them.

"Easy, friend," Hal said evenly.

The new King turned his angry gaze to him. "Get. Off. Me."

"You're no' used to being beaten," Guy said, a trace of awe in his voice.

Banan was the first to release the man, and Hal quickly followed. As one, Guy and Rhys let him up.

The King instantly sat up and lunged for his sword. He wrapped his hand around the pommel and backed up until he hit a wall. His eyes moved to each one of them, waiting to see who would attack next.

"Rhys wanted to look at your sword to see if it could tell us something of who you were," Guy said.

"Or what dragons you command," Hal added.

The man glanced at his weapon. Indecision warred across his face before he lowered the sword and moved out of his battle stance. "Each of you have swords?"

Banan chuckled as his lips tilted in a smile. "Oh, aye. We doona carry them as we used to. No' in this time."

"What year is it?"

Hal wasn't at all sure if the stranger was from the present or the past. He was leaning toward the past, which was why he wanted to tread carefully. It was bad enough the new King had no memories—which had never happened before.

"Look at our clothes," Hal said, and spread his arms wide. "What style of clothing was the last thing you remember?"

"Kilts," the stranger answered automatically.

"I doona know how far into the future you've come,

but I believe you are no longer in the same time period as before."

"He needs a name," Guy said. "If he can no' remember his own, we give him another."

The man's jaw clenched. "I can no' remember my own, no matter how hard I try."

"Maybe there's a reason for that," Rhys said softly.

No one said anything for several seconds as Rhys's words seemed to resonate with the newcomer.

"Give me a name," the man said. "A name worthy of a Dragon King, if that's what I am."

Hal grinned. "Look at your tat. Look at your sword. You're a King. Whether you want it or no', you are one of us."

"Tristan," Banan said, his voice echoing around the cavern. "It's from Celtic mythology. Our newest King is obviously Scottish. Let's give him a name worthy of his roots."

Tristan gave a nod to Banan. "Tristan it is."

Hal crossed his arms over his chest and regarded him. "Tristan fits. A good, strong name for a resilient, powerful King."

Tristan licked his lips, a frown marring his forehead. "What year is it?"

"2012," Hal answered.

For several moments, no one said anything until Banan stepped forward. "You are no' just immortal, Tristan, or just a King. As a Dragon King, you'll rule whatever dragons you were given."

"How will I know what dragons those are?"

"You have to shift," Rhys said with a wicked grin.

Hal kept his gaze on Tristan as Rhys removed his clothes and shifted into dragon form. Hal didn't have to look to know a huge yellow dragon stood behind him.

Rhys flicked his long, thin tail where it had a bladelike

extension on the end, causing the cave to rumble from the impact.

To give Tristan credit, he didn't cower, simply stared at Rhys with a mixture of curiosity and trepidation.

Hal glanced at Rhys and the series of tendrils that extended from the back of his head. Rhys's orange dragon eyes, wide and gemlike, watched Tristan. In the next instant, both Banan and Guy had stripped and shifted to their dragon forms.

With all three Kings in dragon form, there wasn't much room left in the cavern.

Hal pointed to Banan, the dark blue dragon, and to Guy, a dragon of the deepest red. "This is what we are."

"So you . . . I mean, *we* are really dragons?" Tristan asked.

"Nay. We are both dragon and human, no' fully either one. Just parts of both."

"Why?"

"Dragons ruled this planet long before man ever did. When man was created, so the rulers of the dragons were also given humanity so we could be a part of both worlds. It was meant for us to live in harmony. Which we did. For a time."

"Where are the dragons now?"

Hal took a deep breath, pain lancing through his chest as he thought of his dragons. "We made them leave to go to another, safer realm when the humans began to hunt them. We tried to make the humans understand that to kill the dragons was to kill themselves and their world, but they didna believe us."

"Yet, you Kings remained."

"Aye," Hal said softly. "We stayed behind to guard the portal. But that is a story for another time. Right now, you need to shift to see what dragons you command, but also to understand the dragon part of you."

Tristan leaned his sword against the boulder and looked at the three dragons in the cavern. "How?"

Hal was looking forward to shifting almost as much as kissing Cassie again. "Feel your dragon inside you. The first shift might be painful, but the more you do it, the less it hurts. The dragon is a part of you, so it will take nothing to bring him forth. Watch."

Hal closed his eyes and thought of the dragons he commanded, of how it felt to have the wind beneath his wings as he soared through the sky.

He felt his own dragon tattoo writhe on his chest a second before the shift took him. When Hal next looked at Tristan, it was through his dragon eyes of emerald green.

"Does the color matter?" Tristan asked.

Hal nodded his head, waiting for him to shift so they could communicate through each other's minds as dragons did.

"So whatever color I am will determine what dragons I am King of?"

Again Hal nodded.

Tristan removed his jeans and faced them, his eyes closed. Hal, Rhys, Banan, and Guy all watched Tristan intently.

To have a new King, it was almost too much to comprehend. First the Silvers moving, now this.

So many Kings were lost in the battle with the humans, leaving dragons without a ruler. Hal and the others had stepped in as needed, but it wasn't the same as each dragon having its own King.

It had been eons since they'd had to train a King to shift. Hal just hoped he'd done it correctly.

The thought had barely flitted through his head before he saw Tristan's tattoo move. Tristan gave a shout as his bones popped and he shifted from human to . . . an amber-colored dragon.

"Shite," Rhys's voice said in Hal's head.

Hal couldn't form words. The Ambers hadn't had a King in so long, they had forgotten when he was lost. Their King had been killed before the war, and for them to have one now was . . . miraculous.

"What the hell," Tristan said as he shook his huge head.

Hal looked over their newest Dragon King. He had a stocky body with scales the color of polished amber. His long tail had a stinger on the end. Each of his four limbs had five digits that ended in long claws. Enormous amber-colored wings flapped, stirring the air around them.

Bladelike bony plates sprouted from the dragon's chin, and bony knobs surrounded his nostrils while hooded, apple green eyes watched them.

"Impressive," Banan said.

Hal grinned. "Verra."

"I can hear your voices in my head, but your mouth isna moving," Tristan said.

Rhys chuckled. "Did you no' hear the powerful part, lad? We are dragons. We have magic. And no need to speak with our mouths."

A smile pulled at Tristan's mouth. "I think I'm going to like being a King." Tristan turned his head to look at one wing, and then the other. A moment later he was flapping both. "Can we fly?"

Guy laughed and beat his own wings. "Oh, aye. No' that we're able to do it as we used to, but we most certainly can."

One by one they shifted back to their human forms and dressed.

Hal was fastening his jeans when Tristan asked, "Why the sword?"

"The sword is part of you," Rhys said. "It's the part given to us as humans. It's also the only way a King can kill another King in human form."

Tristan frowned. "I thought you said we were immortal."

"Ah, but all immortals can be killed somehow," Hal said. "For us, nothing a human does can kill us. It might wound us, but we'll heal. The only way we can die is by a King using the sword when we're human—"

"—Or battling each other as dragons," Guy finished.

"So other Kings have been killed?" Tristan asked.

Banan sighed loudly. "Unfortunately. The King of the Ambers was killed long, long ago in a battle."

"Why was I made into a King?"

Rhys's aqua-ringed dark blue eyes swung to Tristan. "A verra good question, one I hope Con might be able to answer."

"Con?"

"Constantine," Hal answered. "He's the King of the Kings and ruler of the Golds."

Tristan rubbed his dragon tattoo—absently or not, Hal wasn't sure. The dragon tats did move. It was a way they distinguished a King from a human.

Hal listened with half an ear as they told Tristan how they leapfrogged through time and always had to stay near Dreagan. Hal followed as they walked Tristan out of one cavern and into another where the Silvers were caged.

"Why?" was all Tristan asked as he looked at the Silvers.

"Ulrik, their King, commanded them to destroy mankind," Banan said.

"That sounds verra neat and tidy. How much more is there to the story?"

Hal was impressed at how Tristan's mind worked. Hal and Ulrik had been close friends, which was why Ulrik's betrayal hurt so badly.

"It was Ulrik's retaliation for humans hunting the dragons," Guy answered. "Ulrik was betrayed by his woman, a human. She helped her people kill dragons, so Ulrik went to war."

"Despite Con telling him no' to," Banan said.

Hal leaned a hand on the metal bars around the Silvers. "Ulrik had no idea he was betrayed. We discovered it."

"And ended it," Guy stated harshly.

Hal glanced at Guy. "Aye. We ended it. We killed Ulrik's woman before he had a chance to know what was happening."

"That only propelled Ulrik," Rhys said. "His woman's death, along with her betrayal set him on a path he wouldna move from. He wanted war, but Con forbade it. So along with killing humans, he came after us."

Hal gave a small grunt as he pushed away from the bars. "War. Admit we all thought of joining Ulrik in his hunt of the humans." Hal's gaze caught Tristan's. "The humans were killing dragons, the dragons we were supposed to protect."

"Just as we were supposed to protect the humans," Guy added softly.

Banan scrubbed a hand down his face. "Ulrik's actions damned him. He went against Con's orders, and even when Con demanded he halt, Ulrik was relentless in his destruction of humans."

"What happened?" Tristan asked.

Hal looked at the ground, memories he wanted to forget rising in his mind. "Con had only one choice. He stripped Ulrik of his sword and his powers as well as his ability to talk to his dragons. We captured the Silvers we could, and used our magic to make them sleep."

"Ulrik is still a King," Banan said. "He'll always be a King. But even if his dragons were to wake, he couldna talk to them as a King does, or shift into dragon form. So he goes through each day, all the while we watch him. We're always watching him."

The events of that day so long ago hadn't been spoken about in ages. Despite the time that had passed, Hal couldn't forget how Ulrik had gone into a rage when he'd discovered what his friends had done to his woman. And her betrayal.

Hal wasn't sure what hurt Ulrik the most. No matter how many times he and the others had tried to speak to him, no one had been able to get through to Ulrik.

It was as if a switch had been thrown in Ulrik, altering him forever from the great King he had been, to a killer.

Hal couldn't help but wonder if he would have done things differently from Ulrik. If it had been his woman who had been killed, his woman who had betrayed him, would he have had the strength to do as Con demanded?

An image of Cassie filled Hal's mind, and he honestly couldn't answer his own question.

Tristan shifted in the silence that followed. "How many more Kings are there?"

Rhys flashed a bright grin, happy to change the subject. "More than you think, but no' as many as there should be."

"That's no' an answer."

"Get used to it," Hal told him. "That's all you'll get from Rhys."

A few moments later, Banan and Guy led Tristan away to the main house to show him his room. Hal's thoughts turned to another. Cassie. He knew better than to let himself think of her, but he couldn't help it.

"I warned you to guard yourself."

Hal swung his gaze to Rhys. "Meaning what?"

"Cassie. You're thinking of her. Why? You've never been so attracted to a human before, no' like this."

"I know." Hal rubbed the back of his neck. "She's all I can think about. She's all I want, all I care about. I can no' explain it. All I know is that something has changed."

"Aye, just as the Silvers moved. But what has changed? More important, what is it affecting?"

Hal frowned as he realized the impact of Rhys's words. "You doona think our dragon magic has been touched, do you?"

"I doona know," Rhys said with a shrug. "We've no' had to fight in either human or dragon form in many centuries. We spar, aye, but it isna the same."

"Nay, no' even close. We are Kings, though, the strongest of the strong. Ulrik's power to shift was taken from him thousands of years ago. We've made sure he's harmless."

Rhys slowly shook his head. "I'm no' as sure of that as I used to be."

Hal watched his friend walk out of the caves, and all Hal could think about was keeping Cassie from any danger that might be coming their way.

CHAPTER SEVEN

Cassie blinked and found herself looking at the pale taupe wall she was in the process of painting.

"Damn, I did it again," she said, and dipped the paintbrush into the paint.

It had been three days since Hal had kissed her. Three days of replaying the kiss over and over in her mind, of remembering the feel of his mouth and how he had crushed her against his hot, hard body.

How could someone kiss her with such passion and need and then not contact her for three days?

Cassie blew out a breath, causing a lock of hair to lift against her face. She had the phone number he'd given her, but call her old-fashioned, she didn't want to do the chasing.

"With a man like Hal, it's worth considering," she said as she glanced at Duke.

The Great Dane shifted his ears toward her, but didn't move from his position on the floor. Not that she blamed him. He'd found a blanket and claimed it as his, dragging it in his mouth wherever he went.

Except when he got in bed with her at night.

That first night had been an experience. She learned early to claim her side of the bed before he had a chance to.

She hadn't wanted to watch the dog, and had really been pissed at Dan for assuming she wouldn't mind. But the more she was around Duke, the more she thought of the dog as hers. She didn't even want to think about when Dan came to collect him.

Cassie bit her lip and finished painting around the taped-off stained trim of the door before she wiped the back of her hand across her forehead.

One of the conditions of her being able to stay in the cottage was repainting it. The only good thing was that the rooms were fairly small. So far in her three days, she'd managed the ceiling and walls of the guest room and now the hallway.

It wasn't that her brother didn't have the money to have the house painted himself. No, the idea had been hers. She didn't want to be a charity case. She would work for being able to stay at the house.

She glanced at the pantry on her way outside to wash the paintbrushes and realized her stock of groceries was running dangerously low. Whether she wanted to or not, she was going to have to brave a drive into town in the morning.

Cassie passed the door where Hal had kissed her and once more found her thoughts turned to the ruggedly handsome Scot whom she couldn't stop thinking about.

She was going to give him one more night, and then call him. If she could hold off that long.

The water from the outside faucet was colder than anything she'd ever experienced. It was difficult to finish cleaning the brushes before she brought them back inside. There were several sets of other brushes drying in the kitchen since it was too cold outside for them to dry.

At almost four, the sun had already sunk behind the

mountains, casting everything in dark shadows. Cassie rushed back into the warm house and stuck her hands in front of the roaring flames of the fire.

Duke suddenly jumped up and trotted to the kitchen. Cassie looked over her shoulder and spotted Hal through the glass door. She swallowed, her stomach lurching at seeing him.

How could he have gotten more handsome since the last time she saw him? Unable to find an answer, Cassie crossed the living room and kitchen to unlock the door and let him inside.

Duke demanded her visitor's attention, and Cassie was content to let them have a moment so she could look Hal over at her leisure. His black hair looked like it had been trimmed. This time, however, those inky strands weren't pulled away from his face.

For a moment Cassie could picture Hal as an ancient Highlander wielding a sword with his long hair hanging around his sculpted face.

Hal straightened from Duke and smiled at her. "Hello."

"Hello," she said, and put the kitchen island between them. How she had missed his amazing accent. "What brings you here?"

"Do you really need to ask?"

She shrugged and glanced down at the counter. "I haven't seen you in a few days."

"Aye," he murmured as his wide, thin lips crooked up in a half smile. "There were things I needed to take care of."

"And the man we found?"

"He's with us and adjusting. His memory hasn't returned. We're calling him Tristan for now."

"Tristan is a good name."

His smile faded as he stared at her with his intense moonlight blue eyes. "I wanted to come sooner."

"You're here now."

His brow furrowed as he looked away from her. "I'm no' sure what it is about you, but I can no' stop thinking of you."

"And that's a bad thing?" she asked with a grin.

Hal's pale blue eyes met hers. "Nay. Just . . . curious."

"You make it sound as if you haven't felt anything for a woman before."

"I have no'. No' in . . . years."

She wanted to laugh off his words, but the truth of them was shining in his beautiful eyes. It was difficult to believe, impossible to comprehend.

"There are things about me I can no' tell you, Cassie, no matter how much I want to. Can you accept that?"

"Are you married?"

He shook his head.

"Are you some kind of criminal?"

This time he gave a slight smile as he shook his head.

She was crazy even to listen to him, foolish to consider allowing him into her life more than he already was. But to refuse him would be like throwing herself into the giant black hole of misery she had nearly fallen in while in Arizona after losing her job and running out of money.

His gaze never wavered as they stared at each other. The attraction, primal and wild, was there, but the glance also held more. If only Cassie dared to reach out and take it.

If only she dared to open herself to Hal.

"Then I can accept it," she whispered.

His smile was slow, but soon spread across his face, crinkling the corners of his eyes. "I know I ask a lot, but I can no' walk away from what is between us. You feel it, do you no'?"

"Yes." Why was her voice so breathy and her breathing so ragged? Hal was across the kitchen, yet it was like invisible strings had wound around them, tying them together.

He came around the island gradually, as if he expected her to bolt at any moment. The way her heart hammered in her chest and her body heated as he neared, there was no way she could move.

A part of her brain advised her to run away, because she instinctively knew that whatever secrets Hal had could be dangerous.

But she couldn't deny the attraction, couldn't deny him. It was as if all her life she had been waiting to find him. And there he was.

Tall, dark, and wickedly handsome.

Everything her mother had warned her about. But everything most women fell for.

Cassie swallowed as he closed the distance between them. She only had to lift her hand and she could lay it on the thick sinew of his chest.

"Who are you?" she asked.

"A man who will do anything for another kiss."

"Just a kiss?"

"Nay. I want it all, but I'll take whatever you give me."

The world faded away as his head bent to her. A dark lock of hair fell forward and tickled her cheek. Hal's pale blue eyes ensnared her, trapped her. Captured her.

And then his lips were on hers.

He released a deep breath, then he pulled her against him, against his rock-hard body, and plundered her mouth.

The kiss was fierce, untamed, and full of the same yearning that was in her heart.

She opened herself to him, to all he was giving her. And Cassie had never felt anything so amazing in her life. With just a kiss.

He touched her heart, her soul. Her very essence.

And she never wanted it to end.

Hal deepened the kiss as she threaded her fingers into his hair. She rose up on tiptoe so that she could be closer to him. Which only caused him to moan low in his throat.

Cassie's stomach fluttered. For the first time since arriving in Scotland, she was warm. Her skin felt on fire, her blood pounding in her ears.

Somehow Hal had steered her out of the kitchen and into the living room before the fire. She was so caught up in the kiss that nothing else mattered.

She moved her hands to his chest and shoved his thick leather coat over his shoulders. He released her to let it drop to the floor.

Cassie was reaching for the hem of his sweater when his hands touched her bare stomach as he lifted her sweatshirt and the tee beneath it. With one tug, he had both over her head and cast aside.

As if they couldn't be kept apart, their mouths found each other again. The kiss was frantic and consuming, desperate and wild.

It took her breath away the same time it filled her soul.

Their limbs became tangled as they struggled to get closer together, and then the next thing Cassie knew, she was lying on the rug with Hal leaning over her.

"Cassie," he murmured before he kissed her again.

He straddled her and straightened as he reached for his sweater. She bit her lip in awe at the specimen before her when his bare chest was revealed.

The tattoo of the dragon was spectacular. It covered his entire chest with the head starting at Hal's right shoulder and the dragon's tail disappearing into the waist of his jeans.

Cassie spread her hands wide and caressed up his abdomen from his waist to his shoulders. Her gaze lifted to find him watching her with passion darkening his eyes.

He groaned deep in his throat as he cupped the back of her head and kissed her once more as he laid her back. She clung to him as he rolled them so he was on his back.

She clutched his chest, loving the feel of his skin

against hers. There was a slight tug, and then the straps of her bra fell off her shoulders.

Never had Cassie been so desperate to get out of her clothes. Hands tangled while they continued to kiss and remove the rest of their clothes.

And then finally they were skin to skin.

Cassie inhaled and closed her eyes, letting her body feel every inch of Hal.

Once more he rolled her onto her back with his weight braced on one arm as his other hand stroked down her body to her hip before leisurely caressing back up until he cupped her breast.

He stroked his thumb over her nipple, causing her to cry out. She strained for more of his touch. And then he was touching her everywhere.

His mouth, his hands, his body.

Every caress, every lick sent her passion higher. She was breathless and shaking for more. She wanted to touch him, to run her hands over his magnificent body from his wide shoulders to his tapered hips where the dragon tail ended.

But Hal had other ideas.

Cassie was powerless to do anything other than lie there and feel the exquisite pleasure.

When his hand slid between them to thread in the curls of her sex, she opened her legs wider. Needing him with a hunger she couldn't deny or explain.

His fingers slid inside her before finding her clitoris and swirling his thumb over the tiny bud. His mouth closed over her nipple and began to tease the tip with his tongue.

It was too much for Cassie. Her skin felt too tight, her nerves taut and ready to break apart. It had been so long since she'd had release, and the passion and pleasure were too great for her to hold off the climax when it took her.

She screamed Hal's name as stars exploded behind her eyelids and she was swept away on a wave of bliss.

Somehow Cassie knew, this night, this amazing, wonderful night was just the beginning.

CHAPTER EIGHT

Hal couldn't stop touching Cassie. She was so responsive, so beautiful. So damned wonderful.

He watched as she peaked, his name on her lips, and he wanted to see it time and time again. He'd been a fool to think he would be strong enough to have her once and keep his distance.

That one kiss had stayed with him for days, waking him with dreams of her beneath him just as she was now. If he couldn't shake her after one kiss, how did he expect to do it after making love to her?

But he didn't want to think that far ahead when he had such an alluring, fascinating woman in his arms.

Hal watched her eyelids flutter open and her dark brown eyes meet his. His cock ached to bury inside her, yet he found himself wanting to prolong the exquisite torture.

And then Cassie took his arousal in her hand.

Hal squeezed his eyes closed and groaned, his hips automatically moving against her. He'd never experienced such need before, and he knew there was only one woman who could satisfy him.

Unable to wait another moment, he moved between her legs. He watched as she guided him to her entrance.

Hal clenched his jaw when he felt how incredibly hot and wet she was.

Her hands went around him while one of her feet rubbed back and forth over his calf. Hal shifted his hips forward and sank inside her.

Nothing had ever felt so wonderful, so absolutely right. She was slick and gripped him like a glove. He pulled out only to thrust deeper. Her soft cry of pleasure urged him onward.

With one more plunge, he seated himself fully.

Hal wanted to give in to his passion and let the orgasm take him, but he was determined to bring Cassie with him. He moved in and out of her with short, slow strokes until her eyes rolled back in her head and her nails dug into his shoulders.

Their harsh breaths filled the cottage as he set up a rhythm that sent them spiraling toward pleasure all too quickly.

When she wrapped her legs around his waist, he leaned up on his hands so he could thrust deeper, harder inside her. Her cries of passion propelled him toward his climax no matter how much he tried to resist.

And when her dark eyes locked with his as her sex clenched around him, he was powerless to hold back the tide.

Hal gave one last thrust that buried him deep and let the orgasm take both him and Cassie. The ecstasy took them, wrapped them, swept them over an abyss of never ending pleasure.

He pulled out of her and rolled to the side before he collapsed atop Cassie, and cradled her on his chest. A smile tugged at his lips as he found true contentment that had eluded him for centuries.

Cassie was warm and more relaxed than she had been in months. As she slowly woke, she realized the reason she felt so good was because Hal was still holding her.

She was surprised to find him asleep, his face turned toward the fire. She couldn't stop herself from running her finger along his jawline.

Cassie leaned up to kiss him when her attention was snagged by his tattoo once again. To say it was incredibly odd that the man she'd found naked on the mountain also had such an elaborate dragon tattoo was stating the obvious. Coincidence?

Maybe, but she didn't think so.

It was probably one of the things Hal had said he couldn't tell her. Cassie didn't like secrets, but she hadn't been able to resist Hal. Even now, if he gave her the same option, she'd take him over knowing his secrets.

She took a closer look at the tattoo. Though she wasn't an expert, she didn't know that ink could be an intricate swirl of red and black. It was a startling contrast to Hal's tanned skin and made the dragon appear almost be alive. Whoever had done his tat was an amazing artist.

Cassie reached out to touch it when the dragon moved. She jerked her hand back, her heart pounding as she stared at the tattoo.

What the hell?

Had she just seen it move?

When she looked to Hal's face, it was to find him opening his eyes. He gave her a heart-stopping smile.

"Who are you?" she asked in a whisper, the words almost too much to get past her lips.

"The man who can no' resist you. The man who doesna want to lose you."

She looked at the tattoo again, wondering if she should tell him it moved.

"I doona want you worrying about pregnancy or disease. I doona have anything, nor can I get you with child."

Cassie blinked. Belatedly she realized she should have worried about that before they'd slept together, but the passion had taken her.

"Um . . . that's good about the pregnancy thing. And I . . . uh . . . it's been a couple of years since I've been with anyone. I'm clean as well."

He put an arm behind his head and regarded her. "What's wrong? You seem like something is bothering you."

"Besides the fact I have a gorgeous naked man in my living room?" she asked with a teasing smile.

He chuckled. "Aye. Besides that."

"Your tat. It's similar to the one I saw on Tristan."

"It was dark. Are you sure you know what you saw?"

She sat up and faced him, though she didn't move away. The need to keep touching him was too strong. Yet there was no doubt she had heard an undercurrent in his voice. "Is this one of those things you can't tell me? Just say so, and I'll stop asking questions."

For long moments he simply stared at her. "What is it about my tattoo?"

"It moved."

Hal's brow furrowed deeply. "That's the second time you've said that. First with Tristan's, and now mine."

"I'm not crazy. I saw both of them move. There's a connection between you and Tristan, isn't there? For each of you to have such intricate dragon tats seems . . . well, odd."

He sighed and gently tucked a strand of her hair behind her ear. "They're just tattoos. Tristan seems to appreciate dragons as much as I do."

Cassie let him lie. She'd known as soon as she asked the question that he might not be able to answer. But his lie told her one thing—the tats were important.

She let the matter drop, however, as Hal jumped up and began to rummage through the kitchen. Still completely naked.

Her gaze raked over his tall body and all the wonderful bulging muscle. He was a feast for her eyes, and she wasn't about to waste a moment.

He returned to the rug a few moments later with an array of food and some wine. She couldn't stop grinning. A picnic in front of a fire. It was as if he had delved into her most sacred fantasies.

She sat up as he handed her a glass of wine. There was no denying the desire in his eyes as he bent and gave her a quick, mind-blowing kiss before handing her a piece of cheese.

They sat before the fire and sampled the food before them. With the flames casting the room in an orange glow and her body sated and warm, Cassie had never been happier.

"My first winter picnic," she said.

"Winter picnic? I've never heard it called that, and lass, you've been missing out."

"Apparently. What else have I missed out on?"

His moonlight blue eyes darkened. "I'd love to show you."

"Is that a promise?"

"Aye."

He said it with a smile, but she saw something flash in his eyes. Regret? Apprehension? But it was gone too quickly for her to be sure.

"I have a feeling the Dreagan Distillery is more than just a job and a home. Are the others your family?"

He offered a piece of bread and shrugged. "In a way, aye. We've been together a verra long time."

"They don't approve of me, do they?"

He paused with cheese midway to his mouth. Slowly he lowered it and shook his head. "It's difficult to explain. I'll deal with them."

"Is there anything I can do?"

"Just be yourself," he said, and covered her hand with his.

Around Hal she found that remarkably easy. She loved

to hear his laugh and watch him smile. And when she would find him watching her, it made her stomach flutter.

It was as she was on her way back to the living room from cleaning up that Hal grabbed her and spun her toward the wall. He pressed her against the wall as he molded himself to her back. She felt his arousal against her, the heat and hardness of it causing liquid to pool between her thighs.

"I need you," Hal whispered.

Cassie turned her head to the side, her mouth open in a moan as Hal reached around her and parted her folds. She closed her eyes as he spread her slickness over her sex.

"So damned wet," he said.

And then the blunt head of his cock replaced his fingers. Cassie gripped the wall as he filled her, stretched her. He wrapped his arms around her middle to hold her as his hips began to pump.

Her desire was only banked, and flared quickly and brightly at his touch. No one had ever touched her body like Hal, and certainly no one had ever made her feel such passion, such lust.

Such hunger.

His face moved beside hers, their rough breaths mixing as he thrust inside her. He was plunging so deep that he was moving her against the wall.

And she loved every moment of it.

The angle from which he entered her allowed him to go deeper than before, touch her in ways she had never thought possible. He commanded her body and demanded she give him everything she was. It never entered her mind to refuse him.

All too soon she felt the tightening in her lower stomach, a signal that she would soon peak. Hal must have felt it as well, because he increased his tempo.

And then her world shattered into a million pieces. She tipped, fell into a chasm of profound pleasure. Her scream was locked in her throat as Hal gripped her hips and pumped desperately until the climax took him as well.

The passion sent her higher, winding tighter and tighter inside her until it burst free in another orgasm, wringing a strangled cry from her lips.

The splendor once more took them, enfolded them and swept through them until they were holding each other up.

Gradually, the afterglow faded.

Cassie wrapped her arms around Hal when he turned her to face him and then lifted her in his arms. She rested her head on his shoulder as he climbed the stairs to her bedroom.

She had no idea how he could still move after such lovemaking. Her body still tingled from the orgasm, but more from his touch.

There was a smile on her face when Hal climbed into bed beside her and covered them with the blanket. Then he pulled her against him so that she rested her head on his chest. Her last thought before she fell asleep was how lucky she was to have found him.

Hal stayed at Cassie's as long as he dared before he made himself crawl out of her bed and her arms to find his clothes. He was loath to leave her, but he had no choice. He had to get back to Dreagan before they realized where he was.

He closed the front door behind him and turned to look out over the early morning land. The sun was hours away from finding the sky, but Hal could tarry no longer.

He'd taken but three steps before a voice stopped him cold.

"You tread on dangerous ground."

He turned to find Rhys leaning against the corner of

the cottage, hidden half in shadows. Hal took a deep breath. He'd expected this, just not so soon. "We've each taken our pleasure with women plenty of times before."

"Aye. But none have ever affected you the way Cassie does. I see the way you look at her."

Hal glanced at the window above them that was to Cassie's room. He didn't want to have this conversation where she could hear, so he walked away.

Just as Hal knew he would, Rhys caught up with him.

"You know I'm right."

Hal gave him a glacial glare. "Enough. I told you. I can no' explain what's happening, but I feel different. I couldna keep away from Cassie if I tried."

"Then we make you."

Hal skidded to a stop and slammed his hands into Rhys's chest, sending his friend flying through the air to land heavily in the snow. "Try it," he ground out.

Rhys leisurely got to his feet and dusted the snow from his clothes. "This is worse than I thought."

"This is none of your business." With one last glower, Hal left Rhys standing on the side of the mountain.

CHAPTER NINE

Cassie wasn't surprised to find Hal gone when she woke the next morning. She kept looking over the snowy landscape as she ate her scrambled eggs and toast, half expecting to see him.

Hoping to see him.

Snow fell in an unhurried coating, but that's not what concerned her. She was preoccupied with how he had assured her he could take care of the others regarding her.

Did the others at Dreagan dislike her that much? Was it because she was American? Or was it something else?

The idea that Hal's friends didn't think she was good enough hurt her far more than she would have liked. They didn't even know her. How could they decide if they liked her?

But apparently they had already made their decisions.

The last thing Cassie wanted was to put Hal in any kind of tough predicament. He'd said the men were like his family. She knew all about having no family. Even now, being in Scotland and that much closer to Dan didn't help the ache in her chest at wanting to be with family.

She set down her plate with a sigh. With her hands resting on either side of the sink, she tried to discern her feelings. There was no doubt that in the time she'd spent with Hal, she was falling for him.

Hard.

The attraction between them was undeniable, and her feelings went deeper. Did his? She could be worrying about him and his family for no reason if she was nothing but a shag.

Cassie turned from the sink in disgust. The way Hal had looked at her, touched her. There was no way she had just been someone to relieve him.

"I could've been," she murmured.

There were men out there skilled enough to make women think they cared, and women out there desperate enough that it happened all the time.

"I'm not that woman," Cassie said. "I'm not that woman!"

She *wouldn't* be that woman. If all she got was one night with Hal, she would treasure it. But, God help her, she wanted so much more.

It had felt right when he'd climbed into bed with her. To have his warm, solid body pressed against hers. To have someone hold her with such care.

There was more between them. There had to be.

Duke rubbed against her, throwing her off balance. She bent over to wrap her arms around his neck and laid her cheek atop his head.

"I'm glad you're here, Duke. I don't think I'm going to let Dan have you back. I'm going to claim you."

Cassie gave the dog a rub before she inhaled and turned to painting. But as she painted the kitchen, her mind wandered to Hal and every conversation they'd had.

He went days without seeing her, but always he would turn up. He had groceries brought in so she didn't have to travel. He worried after her.

She also recalled how he had gotten her away from his friends the night she found Tristan. The others seemed harmless enough even if they did look at her like a panel of judges sentencing a criminal.

As the day wore on, the more she thought of Hal, the more she knew his secrets could very well tear whatever had begun between them apart. Not because she couldn't handle the secrets, but because of his family.

There was no doubt the others at Dreagan were part of Hal's secrets. And though Cassie desperately wanted to know those secrets, she was doing her best to keep from trying to learn them.

If she gave Hal time, if he learned to trust her, maybe he would eventually tell her.

But that was a big maybe.

By noon, Cassie couldn't look at a paintbrush anymore. She cleaned up her mess and fixed a hasty sandwich. After she ate, she took a shower and rummaged through Dan's closet until she found a thicker coat and a beanie for her head.

"Let's go for a walk, Duke," she said as she went down the stairs and out the front door.

Though every fiber of her wanted to walk in the direction she had seen Hal leave, she went the opposite way. The snow had stopped for the moment and she wanted Duke to enjoy some time running around.

And she needed a break from her thoughts. There was no need for her to get worked up until she knew some facts. It wasn't unusual for Hal to go a couple of days without visiting, so she would give it those couple of days.

Then she'd get worked up.

She smiled at herself and stood atop a large hill as she watched Duke. Duke's head snapped up the same time she jerked as she swore she heard a . . . roar.

"Thunder," she told herself and the dog.

The ground shook beneath her feet, but it was just for an instant, leaving her thinking she had imagined it. The roaring, however, sounded again.

Duke's ears were perked as he took two steps in the direction of the sound.

"No, boy," she said. "Stay with me."

Thankfully Duke's attention was diverted by something else, and they continued their walk. When Cassie next checked her watch, they had been walking for about an hour, and she was fast turning into an icicle.

She whistled to Duke so they could start home, but when she turned around, she realized that somehow Duke had made a large circle around the cottage and brought them near Dreagan land.

Cassie cut her eyes to the Great Dane to find him staring at her, his tail wagging.

"No. I promised myself I wouldn't go to him. Besides, they don't like me."

Duke's mouth opened and his tongue lolled to the side, making him appear as if he were smiling.

"I'm so glad you think this is funny." Cassie burrowed into the large coat and rolled her eyes.

Suddenly a roar, loud and deep, sounded again, this time much closer. And Duke was off.

Cassie tried to run after him, but the snow was too thick. She whistled and called to him, but Duke wasn't listening.

"Dammit, Duke. I'm tired of chasing your huge ass."

Cassie cursed as she trudged up the side of the mountain. The snow felt as if it were pulling her down, making her use three times as much energy just to walk. When she reached the top, she caught a glimpse of Duke disappearing into some trees.

"Duke!" she shouted, and started after him.

Cassie kept racing after the Great Dane long after he was out of sight. She heard his barks, which kept her going in the right direction.

When she climbed out of yet another valley to the top of a ridge, she stared awestruck at the sprawling mansion before her. Sheep and cattle were everywhere, and farther afield she could make out more buildings, which had to be the distillery.

"Holy shit," she murmured.

The mansion was at least four stories from her vantage point. She could make out one column, and she imagined there were many more around the front of the house.

"Mansion," she corrected herself.

She hesitantly walked down and to the side so she could get a better look at the structure. She counted six columns that were easily sixty feet tall. The gray stones and architecture of the house were stunning.

"Are you lost?"

The deep voice startled her so that she spun around, her foot getting caught in the snow and sending her tilting to the side. Cassie's arms swung in a circle as she fought to get her balance.

Then a hand grabbed her wrist and righted her.

"Thank you," she said as she turned to find a man with light brown hair that just grazed his shoulders. His pale brown eyes were ringed with black, and gave him a predatory look.

He looked vaguely familiar, as if he might have been one of the men on top of the mountain with Tristan, but she couldn't be sure. It had been so dark that night.

"I'm Guy," he said. "And you're on Dreagan land."

She had to clear her throat twice before she found her voice. "I know. My dog ran this way. I was trying to catch up with him. I'm C—"

"Cassie Hunter," he interrupted her. "I know. We all do."

She calmed her ragged nerves and lifted her chin. So much for being nice. "So, you don't like me."

"I doona know you," he said with a shrug, as if she were as insignificant as a gnat.

"But you know who I am."

"We make it our business to know whoever it is that stays in Dan's cottage."

Cassie considered his words and fisted her cold hands in her pockets. "Protecting your secrets, I suppose."

"Everyone has secrets." Guy's unusual eyes pinned hers. "Everyone."

"Not me." She laughed then, her breath puffing around her. "I'm an open book."

"Then tell me what you've done to Hal."

Her smile faded as alarm took hold. "What's happened to him? My God, is he hurt?" While her mind churned out all possibilities, fear took root and she grabbed Guy's arm. "Please. Tell me if he's all right."

Guy hadn't moved during her outburst other than to narrow his gaze on her. "You care that much?"

She rolled her eyes and said, "Yes! Is that so difficult to believe? Hal is . . . special. I've never met a man like him, and I don't believe I ever will again. Now, please tell me, is he hurt?"

"He's no' hurt, lass," Guy said, his voice softer, kinder.

Cassie took a step back, releasing her hold on him. "Why did you scare me then?"

"You took my meaning wrong. I wanted to know what you had done to make Hal act as he has been. It's no' like him."

"People change."

"No' us."

"What makes you so different?"

He cocked an eyebrow at her question. "More than you could possibly imagine, lass. Let's go find Duke."

"Wait," she called when he began to walk away. "Hal he . . ."

"Will be there. Now, come, Cassie."

She licked her lips and followed Guy down the mountain. Her gaze took in the large barn off to the far right of the mansion, and the paddocks where sheep and cattle were sectioned off.

But what really caught her attention was how the mansion seemed to be a part of the mountain itself. It almost appeared as if the structure was built into the mountain. She'd never seen the like before.

Guy glanced over his shoulder at her, and she promptly closed her mouth, which had been hanging open. She could have sworn she heard Guy chuckle.

Cassie began to shake from being out in the cold for so long. Guy walked in it as if the weather didn't bother him at all.

The mansion and barn were quickly left behind as he took her down a path that had been well traveled even in the snow. Through the thick line of trees, she caught a glimpse of buildings she'd assumed were part of the distillery.

"Do you have a taste for scotch?" Guy asked.

She smiled ruefully. "I admit I'm not much of a scotch drinker."

"You need to give ours a try. I think you'll find something to your liking."

"Is that the distillery we're approaching?"

"Part of it. We own the sixty thousand acres around us, and though people know we live here, we like to keep it as private as we can."

"Which accounts for the trees."

He opened a gate and stepped aside for her to enter. "Aye."

Cassie walked through to await him. She counted four buildings nearest her, and by the shouts of men inside, that was where the scotch was made.

Guy paused beside her. "Hal told you we had secrets?"

"He said the only way he could be with me was if I understand he had secrets that he'd never share."

"And your no' curious about those secrets?" Guy asked, incredulous.

Cassie chuckled, wondering if she'd ever feel the tip of her nose again. "Of course I'm curious. Anyone would be. But, as I said, there's something about Hal. If there's a choice of being with him and not knowing his secrets, or never seeing him again, I'll accept those secrets."

"Cassie."

Her heart stopped as she recognized Hal's voice behind her. She turned and found his moonlight blue eyes watching her with a mixture of happiness and surprise.

CHAPTER TEN

Hal had never expected to see Cassie at Dreagan, but one look at her and he never wanted her to leave. Her nose and cheeks were red, but the smile she gave him loosened the hold upon his chest at seeing Guy with her.

"I found her on the ridge above the house," Guy said. "It seems your Cassie has lost her dog."

Warmth spread through Hal at Guy calling her *your Cassie*. He wanted to claim her more than anything, but as he'd been reminded in the early hours of the morning by Rhys, it wasn't possible.

"Duke heard something and took off," Cassie explained, her eyes bright as she looked at him.

"Aye, I found him wandering a little bit ago. I was just about to bring him home."

There was so much more Hal wanted to tell her, like how much he hated to leave her sleeping. How he'd have given anything to stay with her. How he longed to tell her every secret.

And how he wanted nothing more than to be with her forever.

He knew Cassie felt something for him. It was in the

way she looked at him and in the way she gave herself to him the night before.

She hated the secrets, he knew, but she'd accepted them to be with him. If he asked, she'd continue on that way. But it wasn't what he wanted.

How could they have any kind of relationship if she didn't know who he was, what he was?

Hal never thought to find anyone, especially not after the Kings' magic ensured he would never feel anything deeper than kindness for any human.

The shock left him reeling. Their magic had prevented him and the other Kings from feeling for millennia. Something had changed. But what?

And how?

"I had to see it," Guy said, breaking into Hal's thoughts. "I had to see it with my own eyes."

Cassie frowned and turned her dark brown gaze to Guy. "What are you talking about?"

"What's between you and Hal."

Hal waited for Guy to continue, but his old friend merely gave a slight nod of his head and turned away.

"That's it?" Cassie asked. "One look and you're satisfied?"

Guy paused and turned back to them. He stared at Cassie for a long moment before he looked to Hal. "Con is back. He wants to talk to you."

Hal couldn't take Cassie to see Constantine yet. He knew Con would want to know what was going on, and Hal was willing to fight to have Cassie.

But how could he ask her to be with him when she had no idea what she was getting involved in? After the betrayal by a human so long ago, none of the others were going to like what Hal wanted.

"As Cassie so bluntly told me, things change," Guy said. "Maybe something already has that we have no control over."

"I know something has changed," Hal stated with a glance at Cassie.

"Then you know what you have to do. I'll stay with Cassie while you talk to Con."

Cassie had been looking back and forth between them before she held up a hand and said, "Wait. I have the feeling both of you are talking about me without actually talking about me. If anything involves me, don't you think I have a right to some say in it."

Hal grasped Cassie's arms and smiled down at her as he pulled her to him. "Do you trust me?"

"I do."

"Then trust me in this. Give me a wee bit longer. Go with Guy while he shows you the distillery. I'll find you soon."

"Hal," she whispered, concern marring her forehead.

He silenced her with a kiss. Her taste was just as sweet, just as tempting as the night before. She wrapped her arms around him, and Hal allowed himself to deepen the kiss for a brief moment before he pulled back.

"Trust me," he urged her as Guy steered her away.

Hal waited until they were out of sight before he took a deep breath and made his way to the caves. Con had an office in the mansion, but King business was always done in the mountain.

It was no surprise to find Con standing in front of the cage holding the Silvers, his brow furrowed in thought. Constantine's hair was cut shorter than his, but still left long enough that it curled at the ends.

Con's black gaze swung to him. "Even across the miles, I felt the disturbance of the Silvers' moving. Has there been anything since?"

"Nay." Hal went to stand beside the King of Kings and folded his arms over his chest to wait. There was no need in rushing Con. Whenever his leader wanted to talk about something, he'd broach the subject.

"After so many centuries of nothing. Why now? What could have caused the Silvers to move?" Con walked slowly around the giant cage.

"We were hoping you'd know."

Con shook his head, the heels of his expensive leather shoes tapping against the stone floor. "It isna Ulrik. We've been watching him for too long. We'd have known."

"Would we?" At Con's sharp look, Hal said, "We've become lax. We could have overlooked something."

"Ulrik's power as King was taken from him. I took it. He can no' even shift into dragon form anymore, much less talk to his Silvers. He was left alone and desolate with only his immortality and memories to get him through eternity."

"You know why he attacked the humans. He did it because they were killing dragons. Someone had to take a stand, and that someone was Ulrik."

Con banged his hand against the metal bars of the cage. "He was my friend, too, dammit!"

Hal looked away from Con. "You know I'm right. You know we've become lenient. There is other magic in the world, as we've known by watching the Druids and Warriors. A Druid could have helped Ulrik."

"Nay." Con's voice was soft after his outburst, barely above a whisper. "No Druid has been near Ulrik, nor has he sought one out. There is something else at work here, something we're missing."

"We lived in harmony with the humans for such a short time. It seems like another time when dragons could fly through the skies without anyone becoming frightened. I remember the freedom we had, Con, the joy of being a Dragon King. I long for it once more."

"I as well."

"I agreed with Ulrik that we should have fought against the human hunters killing the dragons. Ulrik was only doing what he thought was right."

Con lifted his black eyes to Hal. "We were made to protect both dragons and humans."

"But we were dragons before we were ever part human."

"Your point?"

Hal rubbed a hand over his chin. "I've been thinking of Ulrik's woman."

"The one who betrayed him? The one who conspired against us?"

"Aye. I know she deserved her fate, but I still remember the look upon Ulrik's face when he discovered we'd killed her."

Con swallowed and ran a hand down his face. "It had to be done."

"Ulrik will never forgive us for that."

"Hal, you are no' telling me anything that doesna haunt my thoughts every single day. What is it you want?"

"Your word you willna harm Cassie!" Hal's breathing was ragged as his chest moved rapidly up and down. He was prepared at that moment to battle Con to the very end if it came to it.

Constantine blew out a harsh breath and pushed away from the cage. "We used our dragon magic. We made sure that we'd never fall victim to a human's betrayal again."

"As you just reminded me, we are part of both worlds. It's been thousands of centuries since dragons roamed the earth. We are part of the human world. I doona know what happened, all I know is that I care—deeply—for Cassie. And I willna let anyone stand in my way of having her."

"I can see that," Con said as his black eyes locked on Hal's. He walked to Hal and crossed his arms over his chest. "She can no' know of us, of what you are."

"She has to. I willna have a relationship with her that I can no' be honest."

"Then you can no' have a relationship. Whatever this

is between you and Cassie Hunter should never have happened, but now that it has, I place conditions on it."

Hal took a step away from Con. Con had given in too easily, which wasn't like him at all. Something was up.

"Hal?" Con asked, his gaze narrowed.

"If you've harmed Cassie in any way, I'll kill you, Con, my King or no'."

Con blinked, surprise flashing across his face. "You care for the human that much?"

"I do. Apparently I've no' made that clear enough."

"It's no' Cassie that I'll be doing anything to, Hal. It's you. The magic that kept us from feeling must be put into place again. You'll see clearly once it's over."

Hal shook his head in disbelief as Rhys and Banan were suddenly on either side of him. Hal glared at Con. "I may see clearly, as you put it, but you know I'll always remember this. This is a betrayal, however you want to color it."

"We can no' allow a human to betray us again, and in this modern age if the world got wind of what we were, we'd never have a moment's peace," Con said. "We'd be hunted, Hal. No' even this mountain would keep the humans out."

"You have no idea what peace is. I found it, and it's being taken from me. It's a betrayal, Con. One I willna ever forgive," Hal said, enunciating each word so his King would understand his rage.

Con's face blazed with anger as he leaned in close to Hal. "Do you honestly think you're in love with this human? You know nothing about her."

"I know more than you," Hal said with a tight smile. "I doona know if what I'm feeling is love or no', but I know its powerful, and I doona want to live without Cassie."

"So you feel something, it's no' love. This is a reaction to feeling after so long with nothing, with the first woman you came across."

Hal didn't want to consider Con's words, but they brought him up short. Was Con right? Was this not really a deep caring as he imagined, but something as simple as the magic wearing off and him falling for the first woman in his path?

"You know I'm right."

Hal snorted. "You're no' right. You could have a point, but that doesna make you right."

"Then let's see. Allow me to use my magic to set things right. If your feelings are as deep as you think, you'll still feel something for your human."

Hal hesitated, unsure of taking the chance of losing what he felt for Cassie.

"Look around you," Con said. "Would you put what we've built, thousands upon thousands of years of time, on the whim that you *might* care about a human? Would you be Ulrik and bring about another war?"

"Cassie wouldna betray me!" Hal bellowed, and stood nose to nose with Con.

"Hal," Rhys said. "Listen to Con."

Banan touched his shoulder. "We lost Ulrik. I wouldna lose you as well. Not over a woman."

Hal squeezed his eyes closed and took a step back from Con. These men were his brethren, his family, the last of his kind. He couldn't ignore their wishes, but how could he cast aside his need for Cassie?

"Let Con do his magic," Rhys urged in a soft voice. "Cassie deserves better than a life of lies and secrets. Let her find a man who can give her children, a man she can grow old with."

Hal fisted his hands at his sides. He knew Rhys was right, but it hurt to even think of giving Cassie up. But he couldn't give her children, and if he couldn't tell her who he was, he couldn't make her his mate, which meant she would die.

While he never aged.

That was no kind of life for her. She was vibrant and alive, full of hope and love. She longed for family. It was one of the reasons she came here, to be near her brother.

"All right," he choked out, hardly able to stand the words.

He was selfish in not wanting to give Cassie up, but he had to think of her and not himself. Con's magic would make right what had gone wrong, he would forget Cassie, and she could continue with her life.

Hal's eyes flew open and he turned to Rhys. "Tell Guy to erase Cassie's memories of me. I doona want her to suffer. Make sure she can no' remember anything, no' one single moment with me."

"I'll see it done," Rhys said.

Hal looked at Con. "Get on with it."

With a nod, Con turned on his heel and started through one cavern after another. They followed, silent. Each step was like a knife to Hal's heart. He couldn't get Cassie's image out of his head, couldn't forget the taste of her sweet kisses.

Couldn't forget how she had made him feel after eons of nothing.

"Our magic has never failed before," Banan said when they reached the small cavern.

Con looked to each of them before his gaze returned to Hal. "Mankind's safety is our concern."

"How can you care about their safety when you blame them for what we've had to become?" Hal asked with a sneer. "You can barely look at them sometimes because of the betrayal. You can no' loath them and want to protect them at the same time."

Con rolled up the sleeves to his pristine white button-down and shrugged. "We were created to keep the peace. When Ulrik decided to start a war, we then had no choice but to protect both dragons and humans. As long as Ulrik is alive, he'll always be a threat."

"We are bound to a world without dragons," Hal said. "I'm King to nothing because of treachery by a human. Eternity stretches endlessly in front of me. We were no' meant to be alone, Con."

"Then the humans shouldna have betrayed Ulrik."

Hal closed his eyes and tuned out Con as his King began to draw in his magic. Hal thought of Cassie and how her smile could melt his heart. How her laughter made his days brighter, and her voice made his balls tighten with need.

He didn't know what love was, but he was sure if he hadn't already fallen for Cassie, he would have very soon. Her touch sent his body blazing with yearning, and her kisses left him hungering for more.

It was as if she had been created just for him. She completed him in every way, and no matter how he fought against it, he'd been moved by her. First by her beauty, and then by Cassie herself.

Love. Was that what swelled his heart when he saw Cassie? Was that what made him want to touch her all the time, to hold her in his arms and feel her softness and her warmth?

Was that what made his chest heavy each time he had to leave her?

Dimly, Hal realized Con's voice had ceased, as had his magic. Hal opened his eyes to find Con, Rhys, and Banan staring at him.

"Why did you stop?" Hal asked Con.

Con cocked his head. "I didna stop."

"Then why do I still have feelings for Cassie?" Hal could hardly believe it. She was there, every touch, every word, every kiss. The desire, the longing hadn't been squelched.

"I doona understand," Con said as he frowned. "My magic should have worked."

It was true. Con was King of Kings because his magic

was the greatest out of all of them. For his magic not to have worked seemed too good to believe.

Hal looked at his hands and then up at Con. "What did you do?"

"Nothing," Con said wryly from beside him. "Apparently."

CHAPTER ELEVEN

Cassie tried to appear interested in all that Guy was telling her, but her mind was on Hal. She had a bad feeling about him going to see Con, whoever the hell that was.

"This is where we add in the . . ."

She looked at Guy when he paused to find him with his hand against the outside of the building and his face etched with an expression that could only be called euphoric.

"Guy?"

He opened his eyes, and the small smile upon his face faded as he caught sight of her.

"What is it?" she asked. "What just happened?"

"I'm so sorry, Cassie," Guy mumbled before he turned his face away.

The lump growing in Cassie's stomach plummeted to her feet. She knew in her heart that she had lost Hal. There was no explanation, just a certainty that made her want to drop, to curl up in a ball, and cry.

"Your magic didna work," Hal said.

A muscle in Con's jaw leapt. "I know."

Elation filled Hal, but he held it in check. He had won

a small skirmish, but the battle was just about to begin. "That means what I feel for her isna just some passing emotion for the first human I came across. It means what I feel is real."

"Oh, shite," Rhys muttered from behind him.

Hal couldn't stop the smile that pulled at his lips. "It means I love her. You know as well as I, Con, that nothing else could stop your magic."

"Love shouldna have stopped it either," his King ground out. Con raked a hand through his blond hair. "It worked before. It should have worked now."

"I love her," Hal said again. "Which means Cassie isna going anywhere. She's going to be a part of my life."

Con's black eyes pinned him with a harsh stare. "You might have proved your feelings for the human, but she has yet to prove them for you."

Hal refused to allow his trepidation to show. Cassie was strong, but was she strong enough to learn he was a Dragon King? "I'll tell her everything, in time. She can prove herself in the meantime."

"Nay," Con said, his voice deep and final.

Hal closed the distance between them and got in Con's face. "She's mine. Nothing—and *no one*—will stand in the way of that."

"We'll see. I'll be telling Cassie everything. Today."

Hal felt the rage build into a frenzy, knowing Con would do everything he could to scare Cassie off. "Hell no."

"I'm your King."

"In this, I doona care," Hal said, refusing to back down as he should have. "If anyone is to tell Cassie, it's me. It's my right."

Con peeled back his lips. "I'm trying to protect you, you fool."

Hal stood his ground, waiting, ready for the battle he knew was coming.

"Stand down, Hal," Con threatened, his eyes beginning to brighten with his power.

"Relent and I will."

"Never."

It was all Hal needed to hear. He tackled Con, his arms wrapped around Con's waist as he propelled him backwards and into the wall.

The sound of Con's breath leaving his lungs in a whoosh brought a grin of satisfaction to Hal's lips. In the next instant, he was flat on his back. He blinked to find Con leaping toward him, a battle cry bellowing from his lips.

Hal rolled away and came to his feet before Con's fist could land upon his chest. In that brief second, Hal kicked out, his foot connecting with Con's chin.

Con went flying backwards, and Hal pressed his advantage. He dove for Con, but missed him by inches when Con rolled away. Just as Hal was trying to gain his feet, Con landed on his back, pressing his face into the rock.

But Hal wasn't done yet. He let out a roar and threw back his head, connecting with Con's chin once more. It was enough so that Con's grip relaxed and Hal was able to get free.

He got to his feet and went to charge Con again, when he saw something out of the corner of his eye.

Cassie was momentarily stunned at the brutality she saw in Hal and the man he fought. There was no quarter, no pulled punches. They meant to kill.

And there was no way she was going to stand by and watch it happen.

She dodged Guy's hands as she raced toward Hal in the cavern set ablaze in light from the many torches along the walls. He and the other man were running toward each other again. She called Hal's name, but she knew she couldn't get through to him in his furious state.

And then she was in front of him, her hand on his chest. "Hal," she said, panting from her frantic run into the cave, and then to him.

He halted instantly, and looked down at her.

Cassie glanced over her shoulder to see the other man had also stopped, but the violence radiating off him was undeniable.

"Stop," she told the other man, and then Hal. "Stop this at once. You'll kill each other."

Hal's forehead furrowed as his hands came around her arms. "Cassie. You need to leave. I must finish this."

"No. If this is about me, then I'm not worth it. These people are your family. Don't fight."

"Cassie," he said, and closed his eyes, his chest heaving.

Cassie blinked back her tears as she turned to Con. "I know you don't like me, and that's all right. I'm an outsider. I get it, but shouldn't his feelings matter? If he's family, shouldn't you accept whoever he choses and be happy for him, whether that person is me or not?"

The silence was deafening. Cassie swallowed past the lump in her throat and dropped her hand from Hal's chest. More than anything, she wanted to throw her arms around him and hold him.

She and Dan never fought. How could they when they rarely spoke and never saw each other? But it killed her to see Hal fighting with his family.

As much as she wanted to stand by his side and tell his family to kiss off, she wouldn't do that to Hal. Because she knew, better than most, what it was like not to have family around.

"This, I didna expect," came a cool, deep voice behind her.

Cassie looked over her shoulder. His golden blond hair remaindered her of a surfer. His eyes were so black and in complete contrast to his hair, and when she looked in his eyes it was as if she were looking through a mirror of thousands of years.

Hal's fingers tightened before he dropped his arms altogether. "Wait outside, Cassie. I'm no' done here yet."

She rolled her eyes and moved so she could look at both men. "Yes, you are," she told Hal. "This fighting will accomplish nothing."

"It'll do more than you know."

His words brought a frown to her face. Cassie's gaze shifted to Con to find him watching her with cool indifference. A quick glance found Guy and two other men watching her intently.

"Guy, care to explain how Cassie got here?" Con asked.

Guy leaned a shoulder casually against the rock of the cavern. "I wasna paying much attention to her."

Cassie cleared her throat at Guy's lie. "I'm going. I just wanted to stop this."

She started to move away, when Hal dragged her against him, his mouth on hers in a scorching kiss. She clung to him, her body engulfed in desire so hot, so needy that she trembled with it.

Hal ended the kiss and rested his forehead against hers, their breathing harsh and erratic. "You shouldna have come here and seen me like this."

She couldn't shake the feeling there was an undercurrent of something dangerous and not exactly dark, something she couldn't understand, going on.

"How much do you care for Hal, Cassie?" Con asked, his voice ringing in the cavern.

"A lot," she answered without looking at him.

Hal's head jerked up as he looked at Con over her head. "Con," he warned.

"Cassie, I've something to tell you."

It was only when Hal tried to talk that she put her fingers over his lips to silence him. Then she turned toward

Con. "So that's what this is about? Let me guess. You want to tell me something to frighten me away? But Hal wants to be the one to tell me."

One of Con's blond brows lifted. "Aye."

"All right."

"Nay," Hal growled. "I'll be the one to tell you."

Cassie smiled at him. "Nothing Con will say will scare me off from you. Let him tell me."

"Cassie." His voice was low and deep, and it tore at her heart because she could see the anguish in his eyes. He feared what Con would tell her.

The only way she could prove to Hal that she wasn't easy to scare away was to come back to him after Con was done. Only then would Hal understand.

She leaned up and gave him a quick kiss before she turned to Con. "Shall we get on with it then?"

Hal kept a hold of her hand as she followed Con. With one last squeeze, Hal released her hand. Every step she took away from him was like a piece of her heart was being torn from her. And left behind.

Cassie didn't look at any of the other men, for fear she might lose control of the tight rein she had on her emotions. She inhaled deeply as she reached the outside and let her eyes look over Dreagan land.

It was beautiful blanketed in a thick layer of white, but she imagined it was stunning in the summer when everything was vibrant and green.

Would she be around to see it, was the question.

Hal watched his King and Cassie walk away, knowing Constantine was going to do his damnedest to scare Cassie away. He'd have won against Con, Hal knew it. But it had been Cassie who stayed his hand and took the decision from him.

It killed him to see her walk away with Con, recognizing she might never return to him.

Banan came up beside Hal and laid a comforting hand on his shoulder. "Cassie feels for you, old friend."

"Aye. But is it enough?"

"We'll soon find out," Rhys said.

Guy pushed away from the wall and stared out the cavern entrance. "I didna want to believe our dragon magic had failed and Hal felt something for a human. But none of you were standing there when Cassie wanted to return to him. She was prepared to fight me to get to Hal."

"Has dragon magic ever failed before?" Banan asked.

"Kellan would know."

Hal looked to Guy. He was right. If anyone knew everything of dragon history, it was Kellan, who did nothing but keep track of it. "So we walk to Kellan."

"Only Con knows where he's at," Rhys pointed out ruefully.

"Then all we can do is wait." Hal slumped down on a boulder and dropped his head in his hands. "I was selfish, wanting to be with Cassie. I knew nothing good could come of it. Even when I knew I needed to stay away, I couldna."

Rhys sat down beside him. "I thought Cassie might have done something to disturb the Silvers and the magic preventing us from feeling, but I doona think that anymore."

"Then it's something else that caused this," Banan said, his lips twisted in a sneer. "I was quite content no' having to battle the treachery of humans."

Guy began a slow circle around the cavern, his forehead furrowed as he thought. "It can no' be Ulrik. The only ones who could break dragon magic would be us, and we all know no' to touch that magic."

"Which leaves what?" Banan asked.

Rhys snorted. "And what does that mean for the rest of us?"

Hal looked to each of his friends. For the first time in

eons, their futures were uncertain once more. They would have to stay on guard, to be vigilant against everyone and everything.

"So many years of peace," Guy said.

Banan rubbed his hand over his chin. "I doona relish battle again, but I long to soar freely in the skies. We dare it at night, but to fly during the day with the sun upon my scales. I long for it."

Hal knew exactly how Banan felt. He, too, longed for days when they hadn't had to hide what they were. When they could take to the skies as often and as long as they wished.

"Maybe our time here is done," Rhys said.

Guy stopped beside them and sighed. "This was our planet long before the humans inhabited it. I doona want to give it up so easily, but maybe Rhys is right. Perhaps it's time we took the Silvers and Ulrik and went with the other dragons."

"We could be the Kings we were meant to be," Banan murmured.

All Hal knew was that he wasn't going anywhere without Cassie. Regardless of what evil or magic or whatever it was that nudged the Silvers and changed dragon magic, Cassie was his.

CHAPTER TWELVE

Cassie watched Con as he stopped beside her and gave a small smile.

"Let me formally introduce myself. I'm Constantine, and I run Dreagan."

"I would say it was nice to meet you, Constantine, but I'd rather you just tell me whatever it is you need to say."

"You get right down to the heart of things. I like that."

"I get the feeling there isn't much you like about anyone." Cassie didn't know what had come over her. She knew agitating Con wasn't going to get her anywhere, but she couldn't seem to help herself.

He smiled then, only half a smile that didn't quite reach his eyes. "You doona like me."

"Not really, no."

"Honesty, good. How about I tell you everything, every secret we hold. But in exchange, you have to answer any question I pose truthfully."

She frowned. It sounded too easy. There had to be a catch somewhere. "Why didn't you want Hal to tell me?"

"Because he would try to soften the blow, and I believe the best way to approach this is by telling . . . and showing . . . you exactly what you'll be getting into."

Cassie didn't see that Con had any maliciousness planned. Only a frank talk that she might or might not like.

"First, I need to know what you feel for Hal."

She was unprepared to answer that question, since she herself hadn't dared to look too deeply into her feelings. "I don't know."

"I asked for honesty, Miss Hunter. If you can no' give it to me, then this discussion is over."

"Wait," she said, and grabbed his arm. When he looked down at her hand, she hastily released him. "I was speaking the truth. I haven't been brave enough to think about what I feel for Hal. I'm afraid of what I'll find."

"That you'll love him? You're afraid to love him?" Con asked, frowning.

"Yes. And no." Cassie rubbed her cold nose. "What I feel for Hal I've never felt for anyone before. I'm afraid that if it is love, I'll grasp it with both hands and give it my all. Only to lose him. I'm not sure I'm strong enough to survive that."

For long moments, Con simply stared at her. "I think you're stronger than you realize. Come with me, Miss Hunter. We'll go to my office, where you can get warm and we can talk privately."

Cassie glanced over her shoulder into the caves before she followed Con. It was a short walk from the entrance to the mansion hidden by a small garden to a side door of the solarium.

Green was everywhere. Large potted trees to small pots of plants. Green and an array of flowers like one could only find in a tropical forest surrounded her.

"It's one of my favorite places," Con said.

"I can see why. It's like another world in here."

For the first time, she saw his eyes soften a fraction. Then he continued onward with Cassie at his heels.

She was so busy looking around the mansion at the

colorful rugs against the stained wood floor, the dark molding, and the same dark wood covering some of the walls that she had no idea how many times they'd turned corners or how many flights of stairs they'd taken.

He took her down a long, narrow hallway where there were massive paintings of dragons over ten feet high and six feet wide. Some simply flying through the air, some in battle.

"These are lovely," she said as she stopped beside one canvas to stare at a green dragon locked in battle with a silver dragon. "I've never seen paintings like these. The artist is amazing."

"Why did you stop beside this one?"

Cassie looked at Con and lifted one shoulder. "I don't know. Something about it drew me. The eyes of the green dragon look like emeralds, and the way its scales fade from the dark emerald green to a lighter green toward the front of its body is . . ." She shrugged and grinned. "Well, it's beautiful."

Con grunted and proceeded down the hall. Cassie wanted to stay and look at the painting some more, but she reluctantly followed Con to where he stood next to an open door.

She walked into the lavish office where floor-to-ceiling windows sat behind the large mahogany desk and looked out over the mountainside where sheep were grazing.

"Please, sit," he said, and motioned to the two leather chairs while he sank into the chair behind his desk.

Cassie lowered herself into the chair and looked around her. Expensive lawyer's paneling covered the walls. A fireplace stood at one end of the office with a burgundy leather couch positioned before it. The paintings were of more dragons, but these pictures were much smaller, and each one showed just one dragon though each were different colors and sizes.

On the right-hand side of Con, where the windows stopped, was a sword that gleamed in the lamplight.

The office appeared to be a private one, not one that Con used to run the businesses. Cassie turned her gaze to him then. He was young and handsome if one could get past the cynical look in his eyes.

"This is your personal office. Why bring me here?"

He shrugged and locked his fingers over his abdomen. "What I have to say is private. No one from the distillery or the farm would dare to bother us here. I have no idea how long this conversation will take, but I refuse to be interrupted during any of it."

"All right. Then get on with it."

Con chuckled. "What has Hal told you about us?"

"Nothing other than he has secrets he can never share."

"Well, Cassie, I'm going to share those secrets. What I'm about to tell you can never be uttered again."

She inclined her head and said, "I understand."

"Nay, you willna until you've heard what I have to say."

Cassie sniffed as feeling came back into her nose from the warmth of the room. "You're going to try to scare me off from Hal. It's going to take a lot to do that. What, are you all part of the mob or something? Drug dealers?"

"Nothing like that," Con said with a laugh.

"Then what?" She was becoming nervous the longer they talked.

Con leaned forward so that his elbows rested on the impeccably neat desk. "We're no' human, Cassie. No' fully."

Of all the things he could have said, that she wasn't prepared for. She could only stare at him, waiting for him to continue.

"We're immortal with powers unlike anything you could imagine. We were created to guard mankind. And dragons."

She glanced at the paintings of dragons. "Dragons? As in . . . *dragons*?"

"Aye. Dragons. We're part dragon. Since the beginning of time, dragons have inhabited this earth. We used to fill the skies. And then man was created. In order for dragon and man to live in harmony, there had to be someone who was a part of both worlds.

"Each of us was leader of his dragons. And then we were created so that we could shift between dragon form and human form. The Dragon Kings."

Cassie hadn't realized she'd gripped the arms of the chair so hard until her hands began to ache. She couldn't tear her gaze away from Con.

"You're saying you're dragons?" she asked slowly.

Con lowered his head before he looked at her, his black eyes pinning her to the chair. "That's exactly what I'm saying. Shall I prove it to you?"

He rose and motioned for her to stand beside him at the window. Cassie wasn't sure her legs could hold her, but she managed to rise and walk stiffly to the window.

They didn't have long to wait. In the valley, sheep began to scatter as a man ran down the mountain. It took a moment, but Cassie recognized that it was Tristan. He fell to his knees and grabbed his head as if he was in great pain.

"I—"

"Watch," Con interrupted her. "Tristan is new to us. The tattoo signals him a King. He's learning how to listen to the dragon within him. Each day at this time he comes out here."

Before her eyes, he shifted into a large amber-colored dragon and roared. Suddenly she realized the sound she had heard earlier hadn't been thunder, but a dragon roar.

Tristan's dragon wings unfurled from his body, and he raised his great head to the sky.

"Shite," Con said, and started to unbutton his shirt when four men ran into the valley.

Cassie watched, transfixed, as Rhys, Guy, Banan, and Hal surrounded the dragon. Tristan charged Hal, and just when she thought Hal would be eaten, a green dragon stood where he had once been.

She stumbled backwards and ran into the desk, her hand on her mouth.

"Now you see," Con said.

Cassie's words were locked in her throat as she realized the green dragon she looked at now was the same one in the picture she'd gazed at so long in the corridor.

That dragon was Hal.

One by one, the other men shifted until there was a yellow, a blue, and a red dragon standing around Tristan. When he tried to jump into the air to fly away, it was Hal who grabbed his legs and threw him back to the ground.

Cassie wanted to turn away, but she couldn't. She was fascinated with what she was seeing. Hal, her amazing, gorgeous Hal, was a magnificent dragon.

Just when she thought it was over, Tristan rose up and opened his large mouth and roared. He slashed his talons at Hal and the others as they closed in around him.

"You said you're immortal. Does that mean you survive everything?" she asked as Hal let out an angry roar as his chest was sliced open.

"The only ones who can kill us are other Dragon Kings."

She glared at Con. "So do something. Get down there and stop this before Hal or someone else is hurt."

"Hurt?" Con asked with a frown. "Cassie, he'll heal. Tristan hasna fully mastered all that he is. Hal and the others are as old as time itself. They can handle themselves."

She wasn't convinced, especially when Tristan landed

several more strikes against Hal and the others. And then it was over as quickly as it had begun.

As Tristan lay in human form, naked in the snow, she let her mind absorb the fact that Hal was as old as time itself. It seemed impossible, yet after seeing men shift into dragons, believable.

When Tristan shifted, Hal and the others shifted as well. Cassie longed to go to Hal, but she knew Con wasn't finished with her.

While Rhys and Guy took Tristan's arms and draped them over their shoulders so they could walk away, Hal remained with his back to her.

Slowly, he turned and looked right at her.

Cassie put her hand to the window, hoping to let him know she might be afraid, but she wasn't running away.

"He can no' see you," Con said.

She dropped her arm and looked at him. "I've yet to run screaming from the room. I assume there's more you want to try and frighten me with."

"There's much more, Miss Hunter."

Cassie resumed her seat and waited.

"We are bound to this place," he said as he took his chair. "We can leave for a few weeks and sometimes a month at a time, but always we must return."

"Why?"

"Verra long ago, some humans began to hunt dragons. Several dragons were killed. Because we were meant to protect both, we Kings stayed our hand."

"Was that wise?"

Con shook his head. "Looking back, probably no'. One of us, Ulrik, thought the same as you. When he came seeking my approval to find the hunters, I refused. Ulrik took it upon himself to avenge the dragons that were killed. His retaliation started the verra war I was trying to avoid."

"Is that why you hate humans so much?"

"I doona hate humans."

Cassie raised a brow in question.

After a moment, Con continued. "It wasna just the war. I could've stopped Ulrik easily enough and punished him for disobeying. But he had fallen in love with a human. She used her influence and kept pushing Ulrik into more and more battles.

"What Ulrik didna know was that somehow she was communicating with his silver dragons and having them attack settlements, killing women and children."

"Oh, God," Cassie said, feeling sick to her stomach as she pictured the events in her mind.

"Every dragon has a King, and every King answers to me. Ulrik was a friend, though he was closer to a few others, such as Hal. I was prepared for those loyal to Ulrik, those who had wanted to fight with him to find the hunters, to balk when I issued the order that we find and kill Ulrik's woman."

"Did they?" she asked.

Con sat silently for a moment. "Nay. We cornered her easily enough when she left Ulrik's stronghold. I didna know she was on her way to meet him. My sword was the first to strike her. Every King then pierced her skin."

Cassie didn't have to hear the rest of the events. She knew. "Ulrik discovered what you'd done."

"Aye." Con rose and walked to the fireplace where he squatted and placed another log on the fire. "His rage was uncontrollable. My plan was to tell him what his woman had been about, but he never gave me time. He used his Silvers to attack the rest of us.

"The battle was immense. Many humans lost their lives because they happened to be in the way. And then more joined the hunters and killed the wounded dragons before they could heal. It was utter chaos. And we had only one option left."

"Which was," she urged when he paused.

Con rose to his feet and turned to her. "I used my dragon magic to take away Ulrik's ability to shift or talk to his Silvers. We caught some Silvers and caged them in the mountain there. And then we sent the other dragons to a different . . . place . . . where they could be safe."

"Why didn't you go with them?"

"Ulrik might be immortal and human for all intents and purposes, but he's still a Dragon King. His rage and need for revenge fester even after all these millennia. He had to be watched, for the sake of mankind. With the bound Silvers in the mountain, the only way to keep them caged is with dragon magic."

"You mean the Kings. It's why you can't leave, right?"

"Aye.

Cassie exhaled sharply and looked out the window where she'd seen Hal shift into the splendid green dragon, and then shift back again to human form.

"Why tell me all of this? I thought you wanted to scare me."

"I did," Con said with a chuckle. "But I observed you watch Hal when he shifted. You were concerned for him, even though I saw a spark of fear in your eyes. I told you I'd tell you our secrets."

"And you did. What do you want me to answer?"

"My question from before. Do you love Hal?"

Cassie thought about her life before Hal, and how he had changed everything. Even with him being not quite human, she couldn't imagine her world without him in it. He made her laugh, he awakened passion inside her she hadn't known was possible.

"Yes. Yes, I love Hal."

"Can you face him in dragon form?" Con asked softly.

Cassie licked her lips and stood. "Yes."

Con walked to his office door and took the handle. "I'll warn you, when a dragon finds his mate, there's no going back. If you have any doubts, now is the time to voice them. If you go out there and confront Hal in his dragon form, he will claim you forever."

"Not forever," she said as she realized he would go on without her. "I'm not immortal."

Con didn't say anything until he opened the door. "Prove to Hal you want to be with him. But I caution you, Cassie, if you run away from him, if you hurt him, I'll make you suffer."

"You mean you'll kill me."

He smile was cold and deadly. "I doona kill humans. You'll have your life, but no one hurts one of my Kings and doesna feel my wrath."

Cassie walked out of the office and to the painting of Hal. She gently touched the green dragon. "Take me to Hal," she told Con.

CHAPTER THIRTEEN

Hal didn't bother to put on any clothes. He'd known Cassie was watching him with the others as they tried to rein in Tristan. He hadn't wanted her to see him like that.

He'd have shown her differently. But as usual, Con had to have his way.

Hal put his head in his hands as he sank onto a boulder and squeezed his eyes shut. Anyone seeing a dragon for the first time would have to be witless not to be scared out of their minds.

And Cassie had seen five of them.

Fighting.

"Fuck," Hal muttered.

He knew he'd lost Cassie. It ate at his soul to realize she was probably halfway back to Arizona by now, with Con helping her board the plane.

For the first time in a very long time, Hal hated Constantine. Why was it so bad for one of them to be happy? What was wrong with feeling?

"You act as if she's gone," Rhys said as he tossed a pair of black jeans at him.

Hal caught the jeans before they could hit him. "To a

human who thinks dragons are no' real, what do you think she did when she saw us shift?"

"Why don't you ask me?" Cassie questioned from behind him.

Hal jumped to his feet and whirled around. There stood Cassie, her hands buried in the pockets of her oversized tan coat with Con behind her.

It took everything Hal had not to go to her and pull her into his arms, to feel her softness against him and just hold her.

"Con told me everything," she said into the silence. "I . . . well, I saw everything."

Hal was afraid to say anything and frighten her off, but he had to know. "And you're still here?"

"Yes."

Con stepped around Cassie and gave her a brief nod. "There's one final thing I need from you and Cassie, Hal."

Hal turned his gaze to Con. "What?" He'd do anything as long as Cassie stayed near him.

"Shift."

Anything but that.

He'd wanted her to know who he was, what he was, but he saw the thread of panic and hesitation in her beautiful dark eyes. She'd seen him from far away, but up close and personal was something completely different.

She looked ready to bolt at any moment, as if she wasn't sure about any of them. Where there had always been trust and acceptance in her gaze, now there was indecision.

How Hal hated that. Maybe keeping the secrets to himself had been the best plan. Then he'd have her. Her acceptance of him as part dragon didn't seem to matter anymore.

"Hal," Con urged.

Cassie licked her lips, her smile shaky as she said, "Go ahead."

He released his hold on the jeans. In less time than it took for the pants to hit the ground, he shifted. He lifted his head and stood as tall as he could in the low ceiling of the cavern.

Through the emerald green dragon eyes with their sharp eyesight, he saw Cassie's eyes widen as she took a step back. As much as Hal wanted to turn away, he didn't.

She wanted to see him as a dragon, so he would show her everything.

He blew a breath out, the force of the wind making her dark locks billow around her. Hal transferred his weight, and the sound of his talons scraping against the rocks was loud in the silence.

And to his amazement, she came toward him.

Cassie hadn't realized the immense size of Hal until he stood before her. The green scales were even more beautiful up close.

The scales grew finer and less thick on his neck and tail, but on his broad body they were dense and hard. On the end of his long tail was an axelike extension that she had no doubt could cleave another dragon in two.

His thick limbs had three splayed digits on each foot with long claws that gave her pause. The semitransparent green crest that ran from his shoulders to the tip of his tail only made him look more intimidating, as if he needed any help.

With his emerald gaze watching her, she could see Hal in them. His mouth was shaped so that it looked like he was smiling, and his fine, sharp teeth were there for all to see.

But she also saw the sadness, the doubt in his eyes.

She took a step toward him and he stretched out his large green wings the same instant he moved back. Cassie sucked in a breath when she saw the wings up close. Just that small movement stirred the air so that she nearly lost her balance.

"You're beautiful," she told him. "Yes, I admit, it's scary to see you like this, but to know dragons are real . . . It's incredible."

She stroked his front arm, feeling the hardness of his green scales. His head gave her a gentle nudge, and she found herself smiling up at him.

Her hands shook as she caressed down his long muzzle to his oval nostrils. Fear mixed with excitement the more she touched him.

She was scared shitless, but she was determined to prove to him—and Con—that she cared enough to weather whatever they threw at her.

"You're a dragon shifter. A Dragon King," she whispered. "Of all your secrets I thought you had, this wasn't one of them."

The scales beneath her hand began almost to shimmer. She watched, mesmerized, as the dragon faded and Hal stood before her once more.

Cassie's hand dropped to her side as her gaze locked with Hal's pale blue eyes.

"You didna run," he murmured.

She shook her head as tears filled her eyes. He'd been afraid she'd leave. Everyone always left her. No one had ever worried about her leaving.

"No. I didn't leave, and I won't. Not until you tell me you don't want me anymore."

"That willna be happening," Hal said as his eyes darkened with desire.

Con cleared his throat where he stood with the other three Kings. Cassie had no idea where Tristan was, and didn't care.

"Before the two of you head off for some private time," Con said with a grin, "There is something else Cassie needs to know, and something Hal needs to be reminded of."

Hal sighed loudly. "What might that be?"

"Dragons mate for life."

Cassie looked from Hal to Con and then back to Hal. "But I'm not immortal. I'll die and leave him to find someone else."

"Nay," Hal and Con said in unison.

"Now I'm confused," Cassie said with a nervous chuckle. "Would someone care to explain?"

Hal stood naked before her and opened his mouth to talk, when Con spoke over him.

"It means, Cassie, that you can be bound to a Dragon King. As long as your King lives, so shall you."

Her head could hardly wrap around what they were telling her. "What is this binding?"

"Think of it like a wedding ceremony," Hal said.

A wedding. They were talking eternity, and he'd yet to tell her he loved her. But then again, she hadn't even admitted to herself how deep her feelings for him went.

She had to be sure, because if she bound herself to him, it was forever. There was no divorce.

"Children?" she asked.

Hal looked away.

"A few Kings were able to get their wives with child, but no' a single babe was carried to term. I doona believe we were meant to have families," Con said softly.

Cassie had always thought she'd have two children. She'd pictured holidays with her kids many times in her mind. Leaving cookies for Santa, picking costumes for Halloween, hunting eggs for Easter, and pretending to be the Tooth Fairy.

When she tucked a strand of hair behind her ear, she found Hal watching her quietly. He had yet to say anything, as if he were waiting on her.

"This happened between us very suddenly. Are you sure?" she asked him.

One side of his mouth lifted in a smile. "I know what I feel, Cassie."

"Then tell me."

His brow furrowed for a moment before he closed the distance between them and covered her mouth with his. He tongue slid between her lips and he kissed her deeply, soundly.

Completely.

Every ounce of his feeling was put into the kiss. Every need, every want she felt as keenly as if it were her own.

When he ended the kiss, she clung to him to keep upright. She forced her eyes open and found herself drowning in his moonlight blue gaze.

"I love you, Cassie. I can no' imagine life without you, nor do I want to try. I know it's a lot to ask, but will you bind yourself to me so we can spend eternity together?"

She swallowed as her mind struggled through all she had learned that day. "I knew the first time I saw you that you were different. Now I know why. I didn't want to think or hope that I might be falling in love with you, and when I knew I was, I couldn't stop it."

"But?" he asked when she paused.

"But . . . I don't want to live without you either. How can I know something with such certainty in so short a time?"

"Because it's right," he murmured before he kissed her again.

There was a loud whoop as someone shouted, "It's about fekking time we have something to celebrate!"

The kiss was cut short as they both began laughing. Cassie looked at the men around her. Rhys, Banan, and Guy were talking amongst themselves as Con stood off to the side, his arms crossed over his chest and a smile on his face.

"He approves of you," Hal whispered in her ear.

Cassie chuckled and rested her head on his chest. "The only one I want to approve is you."

His arms tightened around her, and Cassie found herself smiling for the first time as she thought of her future.

CHAPTER FOURTEEN

A month later . . .

Cassie might not have seen every inch of the caves, but she had seen all there was of the distillery, the mansion, and even the sheep and cattle farms.

Since she'd agreed to bind herself with Hal, she'd spent every waking moment at Dreagan, Duke right beside her. Hal had somehow found her lost luggage and gotten everything moved to the mansion within a day.

She stood in her room in the mansion and looked in the mirror and smoothed her hands down the dark green velvet gown she wore. The dress was simple, but she thought it suited.

The sleeves were long and clung to her arms. The bodice was cut into a low vee and showed off her breasts as the material hugged her to her waist. From there, the heavy material draped to the floor.

She lifted her skirts high enough so she could slip on the black stiletto heels. Her hair was left hanging down her back, with only the sides pulled away from her face.

"Come in," she called when someone knocked on her door.

Con poked his head inside and smiled when he saw her. He closed the door behind him and nodded. "You look verra beautiful. Hal will love the green."

"I hope so. I chose it because it's his color."

"Hal said you had no changes to your suite of rooms?"

She looked at the huge room. There was a giant four-poster bed, a couch and two chairs situated in front of the fireplace. There was a separate, smaller room where their clothes were kept.

Hal had brought in a vanity table for her, even though the mirror and lighting in their connecting bathroom would have been enough. And then there was the other living area with two couches and a large flat-screen TV.

"There is nothing I'd change," she said.

Con cleared his throat. "Cassie, it's been a long time since one of my Kings took a mate. I didna ever expect it to happen again, but I have no' forgotten my duty."

"Duty?" she asked with a frown.

He moved his arms from behind his back to present a small black box that he handed to her. "This is a token of thanks from me for bringing such happiness to Hal. I apologize for being so harsh in the beginning."

"You were protecting Hal. I knew that then, and I know it now. There's nothing to be sorry for."

"Hal is a lucky man." He smiled and glanced at the rug he stood upon. "I'll wait outside to take you to him."

Cassie smiled as Con departed. He was a strange one, and just when she thought she had him figured out, he surprised her again.

She looked at the box and slowly opened the lid. A gasp tore from her throat as she found herself staring at a large emerald that had to be at least four or five carats.

It took some doing with her shaky fingers, but she was able to get the necklace secured around her neck. She touched the large rectangle emerald and instantly thought of Hal in dragon form.

She glanced at the clock and realized it was time. When she opened the bedroom door, Con waited for her just as he'd said. He took her down the long corridor and three flights of stairs to a hidden door in the library bookcase that stood open for them.

There would be two ceremonies. One that was just for the Dragon Kings, and another one outside under a massive tent Con had brought in for the wedding, where hundreds of guests had been invited.

Cassie stepped over the threshold into the cave to glimpse men she'd never seen before lining the passage to where Hal waited for her. She walked past the Kings she had yet to meet, feeling their eyes watching her, measuring her. But she didn't care.

Let them measure her, because the only one she cared about was Hal.

Once she spotted him, she couldn't take her eyes off him. The closer they drew together, the wider their smiles got. She barely noticed when Con handed her over to Hal.

When Hal's warm hand closed over hers, all the nervousness vanished. They followed Con into a cavern, the other Kings falling into step behind them.

"There's still time to change your mind," Hal whispered.

"Not on your life. You stole my heart, so I'm yours."

"For eternity."

"For eternity," she said as they stopped before Con and she looked into Hal's moonlight blue eyes.

Con glanced at them before he said, "It's been a long time since we've had a binding, but it's something to celebrate. We welcome Cassandra Hunter to our family, as mate to Haldor Wilson."

There was a pause as Con looked to Hal. "Do you bind yourself to this human Cassie? Do you swear to love her, protect her, and cherish her above all others?"

"Aye," Hal said with a smile, his gaze never leaving hers.

"And you, Cassie," Con said. "Do you bind yourself to the Dragon King Haldor, lord of all Greens? Do you swear to love him, care for him, and cherish him above all others?"

Cassie smiled as tears of joy filled her eyes. "Yes."

She expected to hear Con announce something like they were now bound, but there was nothing. And then she felt something sear her arm. She gasped in surprise and pain as Hal steadied her.

"It's all right," he said softly, reassuringly. "It's part of the ceremony. What you find will prove we are bound, Cassie. There's no turning back now."

"As if there ever was," she replied with a wink.

She moved the gown off her left shoulder and down her arm where she saw a tattoo now inked on her skin. It was about the size of her fist, but with a design that made her catch her breath it was so beautiful.

"It's a dragon eye," Hal said, and traced the pattern with one finger. "A dragon's eye sees things a mortal eye never will. This mark with the eye and the flames coming out around it signifies you as one of us."

She stared in awe at the design, noting the way the eye seemed to be staring at everyone. It made her feel protected and a part of something. "It's stunning."

"How does it feel to be immortal?" Hal asked.

Cassie rearranged her gown over the tattoo and covered it with her hand. "That's a perk, but one I don't really know how to answer. I've never been immortal before. What's really special is that I have you. I never thought I'd find someone like you, Hal, or that you'd want me to."

"Oh, I want you," he whispered as seductively. "It's too bad we now have to go to the wedding when I'd rather take you to bed."

She wanted nothing more, but thankfully the wedding went almost as quickly as the first ceremony. She briefly noticed Dan and his wife, the only people she knew, as she walked once more down an aisle to Hal.

They had decided on an evening wedding with candles everywhere. Cassie hadn't been sure about having the wedding outside, but Hal promised her she would be warm and it would be beautiful. And he hadn't disappointed.

She found her gaze trapped by his, saying the right things at the right time. And then something was slipped on her finger.

A glance down gave her another surprise in an emerald that matched her necklace with a wide hammered platinum band that had small diamonds on either side all the way around the band.

"Oh, my God," she murmured.

"I like surprising you. I need to do it often," Hal said with a grin.

She had chosen a ring for him as well, but since they hadn't spoken about exchanging wedding rings, she had planned to give it to him later.

Cassie pulled it from her thumb and took his left hand in hers. "You're all mine, Hal."

She slid the wide band on his finger and then ran her thumb over the Celtic design etched into the platinum.

"For eternity," Hal whispered.

"For eternity."

Applause erupted along with barking from Duke as Hal kissed her.

The first day of her life as mate to a Dragon King had begun. And Cassie had never felt so blissful. She had the *happily ever after* she thought wouldn't be hers.

And with a man who was part dragon. Maybe the fairy tales really were true.

NIGHT'S AWAKENING

CHAPTER ONE

The Highlands, June
Deep in a cave . . .

Elena Griffin adjusted her helmet while praying the LED light atop it didn't go out. She wasn't the adventurous, adrenaline junkie kind, but when her new boss told her they were going caving, there wasn't much Elena could do but go along with it.

"This will be fun," Sloan said with a wide grin.

Elena forced a smile and projected confidence she didn't feel. "Of course."

She'd done many things while growing up in Atlanta, Georgia, but caving wasn't one of them. Something about the dark, musty place wasn't somewhere she wanted to be.

Everything in her told her it was a bad idea. No matter Elena's objections, Sloan had shown her the safety equipment, as well as how to use it, and assured her everything was going to be fine.

"I've been caving for years, Elena. I've been wanting to explore these caves for some time now, and it's the perfect opportunity."

"Did you get the go-ahead from the landowners?"

Elena asked as she felt the thick rope and carabineers at her side. Mentally she went through how to use them, trying to become familiar in case something unexpected happened.

Despite Sloan showing her the Italian hitch knot at least three dozen times, Elena hadn't been able to get the hang of it, and all she could pray for was that their lives didn't depend on her tying a knot.

"What the Dreagans don't know won't hurt them," Sloan said in her cheery British accent. She winked at Elena. "Get that American ass moving!"

Elena watched Sloan walk into the cave. This was Elena's last chance to turn back, to tell Sloan to forget it. But this new job was everything she'd spent the last six years of her life working toward.

So what if she had to spend a day in a cave to cement her relationship with Sloan. It was worth it to finally be in London, to finally be climbing that ladder of success that had always seemed out of reach.

She took a deep, fortifying breath and followed Sloan.

The warm fleece hoodie she wore over her long-sleeve shirt didn't stop the damp from settling into her bones almost instantly. It was going to take Elena a while before she got used to the cold, especially the damp cold of Scotland. In summer.

The only thing she could be happy about was knowing that she wouldn't be staying in Scotland for long.

Since Elena knew nothing of caving, she'd done some research in the early hours of the morning when she should have been sleeping. She knew they should have at least four members to their party, but Sloan had assured her they'd be gone only a few hours and would be fine with just the two of them.

Elena didn't exactly want to start off her new job by questioning everything Sloan said. Still, the fact of it was that it was just the two of them. And it worried the hell out of her.

That and they were on private property.

She ducked her head, thankful for the hard hat as she managed to hit a low-hanging rock with enough force that it made her take a step back.

Elena knew of Dreagan. The scotch distillery was famous all across Britain, as well as being one of the nation's oldest distilleries.

Dreagan Industries was known to be highly private. Only the CEO, a man named Constantine, was known to the public. No last name, just Constantine. He was the face of Dreagan, though no actual face of Constantine had ever been photographed. Back through the years, it was only the person running Dreagan who was ever named.

Which was more than odd, Elena thought. Finding photos of past managers/CEOs had been impossible.

"Watch your knee," Sloan called over her shoulder.

Elena looked up the same time she slammed her knee into a boulder. She grabbed the injured leg and bit back a string of curses. Her hatred of the cave was growing with every bump and bruise littering her body.

Sloan laughed. "You won't offend me. Let loose with a *fuck* every now and again. I do," she said and winked.

Elena found herself smiling despite the pain. She really was going to have to pay attention. Her mind needed to be on the cave and where she was putting her hiking-boot-clad feet or she might find herself dead.

"Take heed, Elena," Sloan said, seriousness deepening her voice. "We need to stay focused. This is fun, but it can also be dangerous."

"No kidding," Elena said under her breath.

The light on her helmet was trained on Sloan. There was no way Elena was going to let her out of her sight.

The last thing she wanted was to be stuck in this hellish place alone.

"Tell me again why we're on Dreagan land?"

Sloan chuckled, the sound bouncing off the cave walls. "Because it's one of the best caves in Britain, and because they don't want us here."

Elena could imagine Scotland Yard waiting for them when they came out of the cave. "And you aren't worried about what will happen if they find out?"

"They won't find out. Trust me."

Trust. Elena had no choice but to trust Sloan. "Shouldn't we leave like a trail or something?"

Sloan's laugh was loud and long. "Ah, you Americans. I didn't realize you played it so safe, not after how you worked to get here. I thought this would be right up your alley."

Elena rolled her eyes and sighed. "Nope, definitely not up my alley. Seriously, Sloan. How will we find our way back?"

"I've been looking back every now and again to make sure I know where we're at. I've gotten lost in a cave before, so I make sure I can get out now."

"Wonderful," Elena murmured.

The farther she went into the dark cave, the more she knew the outing was a terrible idea. But she continued to follow Sloan. Crawling, sliding, climbing, and ducking her way deeper and deeper into the mountain.

And farther away from sunlight and fresh air.

It took every ounce of her concentration, on where and how she put her hands and feet, so as not to die that she couldn't carry on the conversation Sloan tried to have with her.

Elena had heard caving was a sport, and she never realized she'd end up using every muscle in her body. She was gasping for breath when Sloan called for a break.

She didn't hesitate to reach into her backpack and pull

out a bottle of water, which she quickly downed. It was damp and chilly in the cave, but Elena was sweating and fast becoming dehydrated.

"Oh, look," Sloan called from her seat on a boulder. Her head was tilted to the side and her light atop her helmet shone into the darkness. "There's a shaft here. I think we should explore it."

"I don't think I can. I'm beyond tired, and we still have to go back. The muscles in my arms are shaking, I've used them so much."

"I thought you said you worked out."

Elena lowered the water bottle and tried not to glare. "Lifting a few weights in the gym along with running and doing kickboxing doesn't equate to what I've put my body through today."

As if Sloan hadn't heard a word Elena said, she looked into the gap again. "It doesn't look far. I think it'll be fun."

"No." Elena had had enough. She couldn't go any farther and feel safe. Her job was important, but not as essential as her life.

Sloan's head swiveled to her. She stared at Elena for a moment before a slow smile spread. "Good for you. You need to learn to stand up to everyone, including me. Now rest here while I do a bit of exploring."

"On your own?" Elena asked, her voice pitched high in disbelief.

"I won't be but a moment. I'm just going to put a bolt into that rock, clip on a carabineer, and tie the rope to my sling, where I'll slowly lower myself down."

Elena was shaking her head before Sloan was finished. "Alone? Not a good idea."

"I've done things like this alone before. It'll be fine. Trust me."

All Elena could do was watch as Sloan rigged everything together. And before she knew it, Sloan had her feet on the side of the crevasse as she leaned back ready to plunge into the darkness.

"I promise to stay close enough that you can hear my voice."

Elena took the boulder Sloan had been sitting on when she first noticed the open space in the ground. With her gloved hands clutched in her lap, Elena watched Sloan begin to lower herself.

"Wow," Sloan said a moment latter. "You should see this."

"Another time perhaps." Elena could see the light from Sloan's hard hat reflecting off the cave walls.

"I'll hold you to that."

Elena peered over the side as Sloan went even deeper. A glance at her watch showed they'd been in the cave for almost three hours, which felt more like three lifetimes.

"We need to be heading back to the surface soon," Elena called out.

Sloan said something, but Elena couldn't make out what it was.

"Sloan! You've gone too far. I can't hear you."

The light from Sloan's helmet shifted upward as she raised her head. "I'll be up in just a moment. I'm just looking around."

"Come up higher."

But Sloan only went lower.

Elena's stomach clenched in dread. She was cold and getting colder, and they had been in the cave far longer than Sloan had promised.

And then Elena heard something give a loud pop. Her head jerked to where Sloan had hammered in the bolt and discovered it coming loose.

"Sloan! The bolt! It's coming loose. Get hold of something!"

Elena prayed Sloan heard her as she jumped up and

looked through her pack for the small hammer. She slammed it against the bolt, banging it back into the rock, but that would only buy Sloan a little more time.

She rushed back to the gap and leaned over to find Sloan looking up at her.

"I hammered it back in, but it won't stay long."

"Put in another bolt!" Sloan shouted.

Elena looked around. "Where?"

"Just find a place, and then tie your rope and throw it down to me."

"Shit," Elena muttered as she rushed around doing exactly what she prayed she wouldn't have to do. "If only Sloan hadn't gone down that damned hole."

But she had, and now Elena had to get her out.

Elena put in the new bolt and reached for the rope. Her fingers weren't doing as she wanted and her hands were shaking, but she was determined to tie the Italian hitch.

"Almost done!"

"I'm coming up!" Sloan shouted.

She looked to Sloan's bolt to see it barely hanging in place. "No! Stop, Sloan!"

Before the words were out of her mouth, the bolt jerked from the rock and down into the darkness. Elena's stomach fell to her feet like lead as she could only stare in bewilderment at the missing bolt.

There was a second of silence and then she heard Sloan scream before that, too, faded to nothing.

"No. No, no, no, no, no," Elena said as she ran to the hole. "Sloan? Can you hear me? Sloan!"

Only silence met her calls.

She refused to panic. Elena crawled to her pack and searched for her cell phone, hoping she could call someone, but just as she feared, there was no signal.

Tears stung her eyes, but she brushed them away. She had three choices. She could lower herself in the hole and look for Sloan. She could leave and try to get help—that was if she could find the way out. Or she could stay where she was.

Elena lay on her stomach and looked over the side of the gap again. There was no sign of Sloan's light, and she had no idea how far the chasm went.

"Oh," she said and reached for a small rock.

She held it up over the hole before dropping it, slowly counting to see how far down the shaft went. When she hit forty and still hadn't heard the rock hit, she knew it was bad.

When she was on her feet again, she looked to where she thought they had traveled so she could retrace their steps only to find she was so disoriented, she wasn't sure which way to go.

"Which means going for help is now out of the question."

But Elena wasn't quite ready to give up. She didn't have the experience to rescue Sloan, and waiting was not an option, since no one knew they were there. So, she slung her pack over her shoulder and picked the direction she was sure they'd come from.

Elena had no idea how long she walked or how far she traveled, but the cave was becoming more treacherous. This couldn't be the same trek they had made earlier, surely.

She turned to look over her shoulder, and her foot slipped on the moist rock, sliding between two others. Elena cried out as she felt something snap in her ankle.

With her jaw clenched and tears flooding her eyes from the pain, she slowly pulled her leg free. The agony was unbearable, made more so because she couldn't put any weight on her leg.

Somehow she managed to hobble to the closest spot she could find to sit down. Her harsh breaths were the only thing she heard in the cave, and they resonated around her ominously, menacingly.

"I knew this damn place was a bad idea," she said as she wiped away her tears. "I'm not going to die in this place. I'm going to get out. I am."

CHAPTER TWO

Dreagan Land
In the mountain . . .

"I tell you, I know what I heard," Banan said.

Guy ran a hand down his face. The world he'd known, the world that hadn't changed in millennia had been rocked to its foundation not too long ago when his friend and fellow Dragon King had fallen in love with a mortal. And he still wasn't sure how he felt about it.

He glanced at Banan. "The only woman who would venture in here is Cassie, and she and Hal are gone for the next week to Paris."

"I know," Banan ground out, not bothering to hold back his irritation.

Rhys, who had stood listening with his arms crossed, released a long breath and met Guy's gaze. "I was in here with Banan. I heard something, but I wasn't sure what it was at the time. Banan was closer to the back of the caves than I was."

"You know as well as we do that the caves go all through the mountain," Banan said.

Guy grunted. He knew all too well about the caves.

Every Dragon King would spend centuries sleeping in the caves within the mountain before awakening for a few decades. It was just one way they kept their existence hidden. "Aye, but most end into nothing."

"There are two that go all the way through," Rhys said. "I've walked both. They're extremely treacherous to humans."

"Which means no human will venture there." Guy wasn't sure why his friends were so adamant that it could be a human. Nothing had happened in the five months since Hal and Cassie's marriage. The spell that kept them from feeling anything deep for humans was still in place.

At least he thought it was. Rather, he prayed it was. Guy wasn't sure he wanted to feel anything as intensely as Hal loved Cassie. Their life as dragon shifters was difficult enough without adding in a female.

But Guy couldn't deny the loneliness that a quick fuck from a woman in a nearby village only made worse. He might ease his body, but the ache of detachment never went away. Thanks to Hal and his happiness, Guy realized all too clearly what was missing from his life.

He was King, a leader. It's what he did best. It was why he had ruled the Reds. But what was a ruler to do when he had nothing to rule?

The years blurred drearily as Guy did his job at Dreagan, whatever that happened to be at any given moment. He, like the others, would take to the skies at night. Only then did he feel remotely like the Dragon King he remembered himself to be.

Would he spend the rest of eternity as discontent as he was now? It was no wonder other Kings like Kellan went into the caves and hadn't come out in . . . eons.

Banan exhaled harshly. "I'll wager a month of pay that a human is in there."

"A female," Rhys said.

Guy looked at his friends and shook his head. There

was no way he was getting out of going to look. As much as he'd rather be roaming the glens, he was going to be stuck for hours searching the many—and various—caves throughout their mountain.

A mountain that was in the middle of several thousand acres of land belonging solely to Dreagan Industries.

The more he thought about it, the angrier he got. He turned and looked at the narrow opening that led deeper into the mountain. They didn't use it, because they had all the space they needed in the caverns at the front of the mountain, where the Dreagan mansion was built into it.

But others who desired to disappear to sleep for several thousands of years were known to venture farther in the mountain.

It wouldn't be long now before it was Guy who had to make that journey and sleep. It was part of their existence, part of who they had become so many eons ago. It also helped to pass the ever slow amount of time he endured. Ever since they had sent the dragons out of the world and into another realm to be kept safe, he'd felt the loss of who he really was.

A dragon. Deadly. Huge.

Unbeatable.

Where once they roamed freely, ruled freely, now they hid who they were because the world couldn't know that dragons truly did exist.

"Constantine needs to be told," Guy said, thinking of their leader.

Rhys held up his iPhone and smiled. "Just texted him."

"Let's get going then," Guy said and led the way into the cave. He wanted this over with quickly.

There might be things that irked him about having to stay in human form, but there were perks to being a Dragon King. Like being immortal. He and the others didn't need to don special gear to go into the cave. There was nothing there that could kill them.

When they came to a junction where the path veered off in three different directions, Banan pointed to the farthest to the left. "That's our best bet. It's the longest, but also one where a human could easily think they could go caving."

Guy seriously hoped Banan and Rhys were wrong. The thought that humans had ventured onto private property and then into their mountain left him cold.

What if they saw something? What if they saw Tristan, who was still learning he was a Dragon King?

Tristan had appeared in January with the dragon tattoo upon his chest, signaling him as one of theirs, with no memories of who he was. It had been ages since one of them was created.

Tristan was mastering shifting between human and dragon, but the fierce, insistent call of his dragon to take to the skies complicated things. Some days were good, and others volatile. He was kept away from humans, but if anyone had trespassed, they could very well see something they shouldn't.

"We need to put up security cameras," Guy said.

Rhys's mouth twisted in agitation. "I'd hoped it wouldna come to that, but it looks as if we doona have an option."

"*If* there is someone in the caves," Guy stated.

Banan pushed past them and growled. "I know what I heard."

Guy shrugged at Rhys, and they continued onward. It was only because of their skill, athleticism, and strength that they were able to climb up the steep cliff.

He was the last to make it to the top. When Guy straightened, it was to see Banan and Rhys staring off to the right.

"What is it?"

Banan looked at him and frowned. "You doona smell it?"

Guy then closed his eyes and inhaled deep. There, just

the barest whiff, but it was a scent that had no business in their mountain.

"A woman," he said as he slowly opened his eyes.

Rhys nodded. "There's no mistaking the smell of scented lotion."

The three forged ahead, their focus now on discovering where the woman was. They searched for almost two hours before Guy saw a flash of light in the darkness.

"There," he whispered, and pointed.

Banan and Rhys were on his heels as they made their way to the light. Guy wasn't sure what he expected to find, but it wasn't the sight of a woman slumped over either unconscious or dead.

She'd taken off her helmet so that her wealth of dark blond hair could be seen. It was held back in a ponytail, but the wavy locks that had come loose to frame her face made him want to see the rest of it down as well.

The woman sighed and turned her face toward him, and the beam from her hard hat crossed her face. Guy was arrested by the fragile beauty.

Her heart-shaped face was smudged with dirt on her forehead and chin. Her nose was small and her forehead wide, but she had incredibly high cheekbones and a mouth made for sin.

Guy looked at those tempting lips and felt his balls tighten. He took a hasty step back, and touched his chest as something peculiar seemed to move within him.

"What is it?" Banan whispered.

He ignored the question because he couldn't explain it. It had begun five months earlier with Hal. The dragon magic they had used to bind their feelings so as never to be betrayed by a human again somehow stopped working with Hal.

Hal not only felt emotions for humans but fell in love with one. Cassie had proved herself to Hal, and to Con and the rest of them. Which had been a good thing, because no amount of dragon magic could reinstate the spell on Hal.

Guy thought something special had occurred with Hal and Cassie, something that might not happen again for hundreds of years.

Yet, there was no mistaking the feeling within him was stronger than the lust he usually felt. It was lust, but . . . there was more.

As if he just now realized what was missing from his life, as if a part of him was missing.

He lifted his gaze to find Rhys and Banan staring at him curiously. Guy gave a nod and squatted behind the woman while the other two knelt before her.

Her eyes suddenly opened, and Guy clamped a hand over her mouth to keep her quiet. "No screaming," he said, his voice deep and gruff.

The smell of her hair and the lotion on her skin made him almost forget she was human, almost made him forget why they had spelled themselves from feeling for humans.

"What's your name?" Banan demanded.

Guy slid his hand from her mouth over her chin and down her throat. He should have released her, but her skin was wonderfully smooth and entirely too tempting. He wanted to touch more of her.

And when she pressed back against him, he kept still, amazed at her warmth and how small and soft she was. Her pulse beat rapidly beneath his hand as she tried to swallow.

"Sloan. She fell. I tried to get help, but I got lost. I think . . . I think . . ."

Rhys lifted his hands palm out and said in a calm voice, "Easy, there. Calm down so we can help. Do you know where you're at?"

She nodded, her gaze darting to her pack. "Dreagan land."

"Private property," Banan said.

She licked her lips and leaned farther away from Banan and against Guy. "I told her it wasn't a good idea."

Guy noticed how she was careful not to put any weight on her left side, and the way she held her hand on her left leg signaled she was injured. He caught Rhys's gaze and motioned to it with his head.

Rhys went to touch the leg, when she reached out a hand and said, "No. Please. I think I sprained my ankle in the rocks over there. Just don't . . . don't touch it."

"We have to in order to get you out of here," he said.

Her head shook, causing her hair to tickle Guy's face. He angled his head away from her so that he could watch her expressions.

She was terrified, but she was holding it together.

"Your name," Banan repeated.

"Elena. Elena Griffin."

Guy liked the sound of her American accent. It was almost Southern, but more cultured. "Well, Elena, what are we to do with you?"

She turned her head and looked at him, her eyes widening a fraction. Her lips parted and she simply stared. He was trapped in her sage green eyes.

He was drowning, sinking. Falling.

And there was no way to stop it. Guy didn't like the emotions swirling around in his chest. He worried over whether she was cold, and if she was hungry.

"Please find Sloan," she said into the silence.

He gave a nod, thankful to have something to focus on. "Where did she fall?"

Elena's green eyes shifted as she pointed to where she had been. "I came from that way. There is a large hole in the ground that Sloan wanted to explore. She didn't anchor the bolt right, and it came out before I could help her."

"It's all right," he said, and wondered if it really was.

It seemed the right thing to say, especially since she stopped talking a mile a minute.

Banan straightened and turned on his heel. "I'll go look."

"I didn't want to come," Elena said. "I told her I had a bad feeling. I heard her scream, and then nothing."

Guy fisted his hands to keep from touching her. The need hammered within him and became so overwhelming that he stood and moved away from her. "Have you been caving before?"

"No."

"Then it is no' your fault," Rhys said.

Guy stood off to the side, staring at Elena while Rhys managed to move her leg a bit to see if it was broken. His small shake of his head told Guy the bones were intact.

That was the only good news.

It took only one look at Banan when he returned to know Sloan hadn't survived the fall.

Elena covered her mouth with her hand and squeezed her eyes closed. "No," she whispered with such anguish that it tore at Guy.

Being so near her caused a riot within him that he couldn't stand there, but he couldn't move farther away either. It baffled him, and set him on edge.

"I want out of this mountain," Elena suddenly said, her voice shaking with her emotion.

Banan caught Guy's gaze. "She willna get back through injured as she is."

"And taking her back with us is no' wise either," Guy said.

Rhys shrugged. "We doona have a choice."

There was movement as Elena used the cave wall to pull herself to her feet. "I'm not going anywhere with any of you. I don't know you."

"We're here to help," Rhys said.

"Really?" she asked, her voice laced with sarcasm. "Then who are you? How did you get here without any kind of equipment?"

One thing at a time, Guy thought. He pointed to Rhys first. "He's Rhys, that's Banan, and I'm Guy. We work and live at Dreagan. We're no' here to harm you, simply to get you safely off our land."

"And the gear?" she asked pointedly.

Guy smiled and lifted a shoulder in a shrug. "We're good at what we do. We've lived near this mountain for—"

"Seems like eternity," Banan interrupted sarcastically.

Guy cut him a look before he turned back to Elena. "In other words, we know these caves. You can no' return the way you came. You need to come with us. We willna force you."

"What?" Rhys asked in disbelief.

Guy held up a hand to stop Rhys. If he had to, he'd knock Elena out and carry her out of the cave himself, but he wasn't leaving her.

"Good or not at caving, only an idiot would go without equipment," she said, eyeing him with distrust. "But I want this nightmare to end."

"Then come with me," Guy said, and offered his hand.

She hesitated a moment, staring at him before she reached for his hand. As soon as she took it, he knew his world was about to turn upside down.

CHAPTER THREE

Elena couldn't stop looking at the three men, but most especially Guy. They were tall, and all incredibly handsome. Even the surly one, Banan.

But Guy was different. Whereas Rhys was quick to talk and was at ease, Guy watched her beneath hooded eyes, his gaze intense and . . . hungry.

It's the only word she could come up with. And it hit her like a freight train. It left her breathless and wanting.

Yet, she knew each time those amazing pale brown eyes of his turned to her—because her stomach would quiver and goose bumps rose all along her skin.

It was as if she was attuned to Guy on a level she hadn't known was possible. She briefly thought about asking him why he watched her so, which was odd behavior for her. She wasn't aggressive with guys. It must be the shock and pain of Sloan's death that was making her see—and feel—things most likely not there.

Elena snapped on her helmet. She was determined to walk on her own as best she could, but before she put her weight on her left leg, she looked at Guy.

His honey brown hair was left long, just grazing his shoulders, and it framed his face so that he looked rugged and lethal at the same time.

He had the square jaw and chin that would make any woman swoon. Combined with his wide, slightly full lips, he was a head turner for sure.

But for Elena, it was his eyes—soft brown and ringed in black—that got her attention.

The same pale brown brows slashed over those powerful wide eyes of his. She was gazing deep into those eyes, captured by their uniqueness, and forgot about her injury. She put all her weight on her injured leg.

Elena cut off a gasp of pain and reached for the wall to support her. Instead, it was an incredibly rock-hard body that slid against her. Guy's arm tightened about her as she leaned against him, and for a moment she pretended it was just the two of them.

"That sprain may be worse than I thought," Rhys said, breaking into Elena's thoughts.

She took in a steadying breath that did nothing to stop the feel of Guy's hot, hard body against hers. His warmth, his strength could be felt from her shoulder down to her thigh.

And that was through several layers of clothes.

What would he feel like skin against skin? Not that she would ever know, but she could fantasize. And she was very good at that.

"I'll be fine," she told them.

Guy's fingers wrapped around her waist as he gave a small tug with his arm to settle her more firmly against him. "Lean on me," he whispered.

His voice sent tremors of awareness through her. She couldn't regulate her breathing, not with him so near. When she wrapped her arm around him for balance, she felt the corded sinew through his thin shirt.

"Let's get moving," Banan said brusquely.

Elena glanced at Guy to find him watching her. She tried to swallow, but her mouth was dry.

"Ready?" he asked.

She nodded her head instead of attempting to use her voice.

Guy took the brunt of her weight, lifting her with his arm to keep her off her left leg. But the slightest touch of her foot against anything had pain slicing through her.

She thought she was doing a good job of keeping her agony to herself when Guy stopped and gently lifted her in his arms. Instinctively, Elena wrapped her arms around his neck and found her face inches from his.

"You were in pain," was all he said before he continued walking.

Out of the corner of her eye, she saw Banan and Rhys stare after Guy. As Guy walked in front of them, Elena looked over his shoulder and caught the other two sharing a look.

Rhys found her observing him, but he said nothing as he quickly moved ahead of Guy while they continued on.

Several times, Guy had to hand her off to Rhys as they reached a narrow passage or where it was difficult to walk. She felt like a bag of potatoes getting passed around, but she wasn't going to complain.

They were careful not to jar her leg, and they were helping her out of the awful cave. That was enough for her.

Words were kept to a minimum. She was too enthralled in Guy's proximity to be able to think clearly enough to carry on a conversation.

Her muscles had begun to ache after the adrenaline rush wore off. She was going to have a tough time moving the next day, but she'd face that later.

Just when she thought they'd have an easy time out of the mountain, Guy stopped beside Rhys, and Banan moved to Guy's other side.

"I'll go down first," Banan said.

She moved her head to follow him and noticed they were atop a sheer cliff that was at least thirty feet tall. Elena could only stare dumbfounded as Banan began to climb down without any type of rope.

"He's going to fall! Without rope. He needs rope."

Her voice must have begun to rise because all three men looked at her, but Elena kept hearing Sloan's scream in her head. She'd fallen, and she'd been harnessed.

Rhys nodded and motioned Banan back up. "Of course."

Guy gently set her down, and all three began taking rope, carabineers, and bolts from her belt. She didn't hinder them, but watched as they expertly hammered in a bolt, tied a quick knot, and tossed the rope over the side.

That's when she realized she was going to have to go down that rope. Elena took a hobbled step back. She couldn't do it. The knot might come undone or the bolt might not be hammered in securely enough.

Guy put his hand to her lower back and moved in front of her to block her view of Banan going over the side. "We willna let you fall, Elena. I give you my word."

How she wanted to believe him. Desperately so. But she had seen—and heard—Sloan fall.

Elena shook her head. "There has to be another way."

"Banan is already over. Safely on the ground. Look if you want."

She had never been afraid of heights before, but she was quickly developing the condition. "It's okay. I'm good."

Guy turned away, but she saw his hint of a smile before he did.

It was Rhys who said, "You willna believe us until you look yourself."

She wasn't sure if her fingers were cold inside her gloves because of the cool air or because she was scared shitless. One look at the men and she knew they would hound her until she saw Banan.

Elena gingerly put the tip of her left boot on the ground and put all her weight on the right side before she jumped. She hadn't even landed before Guy had a hold of her to help her to the edge.

Her cold fingers gripped his arms as she peeked over the side and her light allowed her to see a brief look of Banan's face as he tilted it up to them.

"See?" Guy said when she leaned back.

"Uh-huh. Sure. It's all good."

Rhys chuckled. "I hope that's convincing you, lass, because it's doing nothing for us."

Elena might have laughed had her life not been on the line. As it was, all she could do was swallow past the lump in her throat.

"See you down there," Rhys said with a grin before he, too, went over the side, one hand barely holding the rope.

The image of him sliding down the rope made her think of Sloan, and she turned away. "Tell me he's all right. Tell me he landed."

"Look for yourself," Guy urged.

"I don't think I can. I don't want to be scared, but . . ."

"It's understandable. All you need to do is trust us."

She looked up at him and said, "But I don't know you."

He didn't answer right away, just tugged a strand of her hair behind her ear. "There are two ways we can do this. I can tie your harness to the rope and slowly lower you down. Both Banan and Rhys are below in case anything happens."

"Or?" she asked, praying the second option was better.

"Or . . . you climb on my back, and I take both of us down."

Elena closed her eyes. "I knew I should have stayed in bed this morning."

Guy knew Elena was close to losing it. She had done

remarkably well, having never gone caving before, being injured, and seeing her friend fall to her death. All in all, he was impressed.

But if he allowed her to continue as she was, they'd likely never get out of the mountain.

He put his fingers beneath her chin and lifted her head so she had to look at him. Her sage green eyes slowly opened to look at him. "I'm going to strap you to me, and then I'm going to lower us down."

"I don't think that's a good idea."

"You keep clenching your hands. They're cold, are they no'? Do you think you can hold on to the rope yourself? And what of your injured leg? You'll need both to help you descend."

"Shit," she mumbled, which caused him to grin again.

He set about getting her harnessed and then wrapping the rope around himself and her before he reached to fasten her to him.

"If you drop me, if I die, I'm warning you now that I'm going to make sure I come back to haunt you."

Her words had meant to threaten him, but he found himself smiling. "And if I get you safely down?"

"I'll kiss you," she said as she glanced over the side of the cliff.

Guy paused in tying the knot. He didn't like how anxious he was for that kiss. It wasn't a good sign at all, but now that she'd said it, it was all he could think about.

"Are you two coming?" Rhys called up.

"Aye. Be down in a moment," Guy replied.

He looked to Elena to find her shaking, her face a mask of apprehension and fear. He knelt down and waited for her to move behind him. They were already locked together via her harness and the ropes, but she had to climb on his back.

"Even if you lose your hold on me, you willna go far.

Once you're on my back, I'm tightening the rope so you'll be almost a part of me."

She mumbled something that he swore sounded like, "That doesn't sound so bad," but he wasn't sure.

A moment later and she wrapped her injured leg around him first before hoisting herself onto his back. She weighed next to nothing, not that he expected more from a woman who didn't even come to his shoulders.

Right before he went over the side, she giggled.

"Something amusing?" he asked.

"I was just thinking of *Jurassic Park,* where the little girl was in this same position and she choked Dr. Grant." Elena laughed harder. "She was so scared of falling, and of the *T. rex,* of course, that she didn't know she was choking him."

"Well, let's no' choke me, shall we?"

He'd grabbed the rope and positioned himself so that she was now hanging off the cliff. Her blond head was buried in his neck, and he felt her entire body shaking.

"I don't want to even be in a cave again. Just get me out of this one, Guy. Please."

Gone was the amusement and anger of earlier. Now, her voice held nothing but fear. And he didn't like it.

"Hold on," he told her right before he slid down the rope.

The quicker he got them down, the better. When the air whooshed around them, her hold tightened, but she never uttered a sound.

They slid to a jarring halt when the rope caught on a rock jutting from the cliff and Guy's hands got caught between the rope and the rock.

He felt Elena lift her head to see what had happened, but he knew if she spotted the blood now coating his hands from his hands being crushed and cut by both the rock and rope her control would snap.

Guy pushed away from the cliff, which allowed him to

yank the rope free of the rock. In no time, his feet touched the bottom, and Banan and Rhys each reached to help Elena off him. Guy loosened the rope holding her when the others took her.

Guy turned to face her, and before he could ask how she was, she took the small step separating them and rose up on her good foot to put her lips on his.

A shock of something electric, something charged went through him.

Something primal.

He fisted the rope in his hands to keep from dragging her close and slipping his tongue past her sweet lips. As it was, he held perfectly still until she moved away.

"I owed you a kiss as promised," Elena said, as if she needed to explain her actions.

All Guy could wish was that they were alone and he could kiss her again. Deeply, until he had her taste running all through him. Until he could feel every inch of her body against him.

Luckily she looked away from him, which allowed Guy to remember where they were and who he was with. He began to unsnap the caribineer when he heard Elena's gasp.

"My God. Your hands," she said.

Guy looked down and saw the blood. Before he could answer, she had taken his hands and turned them over. There, before her eyes, the last few wounds healed.

He waited for her to say something. When she did not, he pulled his hands free. "Just a scratch from the rocks."

"Yeah," Elena murmured, looking stunned.

"Shall we go?" Banan asked.

Guy nodded and began to roll up the rope while Rhys got Elena out of the harness. When Guy turned back, Rhys had Elena in his arms while Banan had her backpack.

He missed holding her, but he wasn't going to yank her

from Rhys. That would mean Guy wanted to stake a claim. Which he didn't.

Right?

Elena looked at him over Rhys's shoulder. Their gazes locked, held for a moment before she lowered her eyes and turned away.

CHAPTER FOUR

Guy knew what awaited Elena when they reached the mansion. They should probably warn her, but the easier she went, the better.

All too soon, they reached the main cave they used daily. Guy prayed no dragons were heard as they carried Elena through one of the caverns and then up the long corridor to the outside.

She inhaled the fresh air and removed her helmet when they stepped out of the mountain. "Oh, goodness," she murmured as she looked at the mansion.

"We'll take you to the house to see to your injury," Banan said.

Elena chuckled. "That isn't a house. That's a palace."

"Mansion," Rhys corrected her. "It's no' grand enough for a palace."

"But it's certainly large enough. I had no idea anything like this was here. Do y'all do tours like other places?"

Guy came even with Rhys when they reached the side door of the conservatory. "No visitor is allowed anywhere other than the distillery sections of our land."

He waited for Rhys to walk through, but Guy's eyes were glued to Elena. He'd lived at Dreagan for thousands upon thousands of years. There were things in the house he didn't even notice anymore, and he was curious as to how she saw their home.

The way her eyes widened, and her lips parted in a silent *wow* while her head swiveled one way and another made him look at his surroundings with new eyes.

"Holy cow," she said when they approached the staircase.

It stood in the center of the large foyer and was wide enough for six men to stand side by side. It went up fifteen steps before there was a landing, and then more steps off to the side to the second floor.

But Rhys didn't stop on the second floor. He continued up to the third. Once more the stairs switchbacked, but now Elena's eyes were glued to the weapons hung on the walls.

Weapons of every century, from every continent.

Guy knew the house was absent of everyone but Con, thanks to them alerting him there was someone in the mountain. When they reached the guest room, Guy found Constantine standing against a far window, his back to them. Guy walked to the headboard near where Rhys carried Elena, not yet ready to be away from her.

Elena let out a sigh when she was on the bed. Then she looked down at her muddy, dirt-encrusted clothes and scooted to the edge of the bed before standing.

"You need to lie down," Rhys said.

"Not on that comforter. There's no way I'm getting it any dirtier," she argued as she glanced at the cream colored comforter.

Con turned to them with a smile. "It's just a piece of fabric that can be replaced." He bent and, with a yank, removed the comforter from the bed.

Guy found it curious that Elena leaned back against him as she stared at Con. "Maybe it's just a piece of fabric, but it isn't mine to ruin."

"I'm Constantine," he said. "As I heard Rhys say, you're injured. Let us get you looked at, a change of clothes, and some food, shall we?"

She nodded woodenly before she cleared her throat twice. "I'm Elena Griffin."

"Welcome to Dreagan, Miss Griffin. We'll give you a few moments to yourself, and then I've some questions."

Con walked past Guy, leaving Elena staring after him. Banan and Rhys soon followed. After a long look at Elena, Guy, too, trailed them.

He closed the door and sighed. He didn't like how anxious he was about how she was going to get her boot off, or if her foot would swell because of it.

He didn't want to worry about her getting out of her clothes, but then he pictured what she might look like nude. Slim, but rounded and soft in all the right places.

"Are you going to stand there all day, waiting for her to call for you?" Banan asked sardonically.

Guy jerked his head around to find all three staring at him. He wasn't sure he liked the way Con's gaze narrowed on him, or how Rhys smiled as if he knew exactly what Guy was thinking.

So, he focused on Banan. "Why be such a bastard?"

"Someone has to be. And it's my turn this month."

Guy rolled his eyes and shouldered his way through them.

For long minutes, Elena simply stared at the closed door. There had been something decidedly ominous about Constantine's parting words.

The only thing that kept her from trying to escape out the third-floor window was Guy's look before he left. She couldn't be sure, but she thought he might have been trying to tell her to be strong without saying the words.

In any case, she was too tired to think past getting out of her grimy clothes. Except when she did finally make it into the adjoining bathroom and sat on the toilet to unlace her boots, she couldn't hold back the yelp of pain.

With the boot off and the laces no longer keeping everything tight, her ankle swelled before her eyes. She was glad she was sitting because the room began to spin. It was only by holding on to the sink that she managed to get both her shirts off. Her pants were another matter entirely.

But she wanted out of the soiled clothes.

With her foot and knee hurting ten times more than before, she slowly made her way back into the bedroom, since a shower was now out of the question. If she couldn't stand on her own, then trying to take a shower would be foolish.

She did manage to open a drawer and find a pair of sweatpants. They were so huge, she had to roll down the waist several times as well as roll up the legs so she didn't walk on them.

The long-sleeve flannel button-down was most likely saved for cooler weather, but it looked too comfortable to pass up. Only once she was dressed did she hobble painfully back to the bed.

Where she readily climbed under the covers.

Elena had no idea how long she was left alone before she opened her eyes to find Guy at the foot of the bed, watching her. With Con beside him, and Rhys and Banan on either side of the bed.

"Why do I feel like I need to call a lawyer?" she asked, and turned her head to hide her yawn.

Con smiled, but it didn't quite reach his eyes. "There's no need for a lawyer, Miss Griffin."

"Really? By the way you're looking at me, I'd say otherwise. You aren't happy we were in the mountain."

"Nay." Con said it with finality, and a hardness that brought her fully awake.

Elena sat up, wincing when the movement caused her

left leg to move. "And Sloan? Have you called the authorities to retrieve her body?"

"The authorities have been called," Banan said. "I showed them where Sloan fell."

Elena frowned. "How long did I sleep?"

"Four hours," Guy answered.

She rubbed her hands over her face as her mind struggled to process everything. "Why didn't the police talk to me? Didn't they want to hear my story?"

"They believed us," was all Constantine said.

Elena shook her head. "No. For all I know, you could have told them I pushed her."

"Maybe you did."

She blinked, her anger spiking in an instant. "How dare you thi—"

"How dare I?" Con spoke over her. "You trespassed on private property. I want to know what you were doing in the caves."

"Caving," she said, her exasperation growing. "It was Sloan's idea to come here. She kept saying she'd heard it was a great spot to cave."

Rhys's usual friendly face grew livid as he leaned close. "Who told her that? Who has been here?"

"What did they see?" Banan demanded.

Elena pushed at Rhys's chest. He hadn't been expecting it, so she was able to shove him back far enough that she threw off the covers and jumped out of the bed.

Unfortunately, she forgot about her leg until the moment of impact. She cried out, reaching for her ankle as she crumpled to the floor.

"Enough!" Guy bellowed. "At least until we get her injuries looked at."

She pushed her face into the rug, wishing with all her might that she had stood up to Sloan the night before when told they were going caving.

Guy's hands gently touched her, but she shoved him

away. Tears that filled her eyes threatened to fall. She glared at him. "Don't touch me."

"You might show them some kindness," Con said. "They were the ones, after all, who got you out of the mountain. If no' for them, you'd be dead."

"Bloody hell. Her ankle," Banan murmured.

Guy, who had been in the process of standing, was suddenly beside her again. This time when she tried to move his hands, he ignored her and lifted her in his arms.

He was so gentle that more tears gathered.

"You should've told me," he said.

She turned her face away and gripped the pillow as the four of them unrolled the leg of her pants and pushed it up over her left knee.

"Can you move your knee and ankle?" Rhys asked.

In answer, Elena squeezed her eyes shut and managed to move both enough to show she could.

"I think her knee is fine. It's the ankle I'm concerned with," she heard Con say.

For several excruciating minutes, they felt all along her ankle to see if anything was broken. She was relieved to hear that nothing was.

"The foot needs to be elevated," Banan said.

It was Guy who tenderly lifted her leg and put pillows beneath her foot. A glass of water was given to her, along with two pills she recognized as aspirin.

She was ready to dull some of the pain and didn't hesitate to take them. The room got quiet. Elena looked at the men staring at her as if they expected her to faint or something.

It was on the tip of her tongue to let out a scream just to shock them, but the pain and events of the day came rushing back at her again.

"A woman is dead, and all you can think about is that we were trespassing," she said, her eyes losing their focus.

The faces of the four men began to blur. She closed her eyes and found it impossible to open them again. She'd never been so tired in her life.

"We're sorry about your friend. But it's our lives that are at stake."

Elena tried to open her eyes to be sure if that was Guy who had spoken, but before she could, sleep took her.

CHAPTER FIVE

"We'll have to keep things to a minimum. No more midnight flights. No more training. At least until she's gone."

Elena wasn't sure at first if the voice was from a dream or real. It sounded muffled, but it had to be a dream to talk of midnight flights.

A mental picture of a man flying through the air flashed into her mind, and she knew it was a dream.

"Tristan willna be happy. He's begun to like having the freedom to release his dragon when he wants."

She was positive it was a dream then. Why would the men be talking of dragons? Everyone knew they weren't real.

"We can no' keep her here indefinitely."

Guy. That was Guy's voice. It was deep, smooth, and near, as if he was just in the next room. But what was she doing in bed?

The fog of sleep began to dissipate as she struggled to consciousness. When she opened her eyes, it was to find herself on her side. The events from before came back to her quickly.

Elena rolled onto her back, but found herself alone.

She sat up to see the door pulled shut. Yet there was no denying the voices had come from outside.

Suddenly, the door opened and Guy poked his head inside the room, his amazing pale brown eyes locked on her face.

Her lips tingled as her gaze lowered to his mouth and she remembered the all-too-quick kiss she had dared to give him. It had been so unlike her, but she didn't regret it.

Recalling the feel of his wide lips against hers made her heart beat double. And her body yearn for more.

A kiss. One simple kiss.

In movies and books maybe, but to happen to her? It didn't seem real. Yet the very presence of the man before her, his eyes darkening with unmistakable desire the longer they stared at each other, said otherwise.

The passion was palpable, the desire undeniable.

The need . . . tangible.

"Elena?" someone said.

She blinked and Guy looked away, the spell that had taken them now broken. Elena watched as the door opened wider as first Guy, then Con, Rhys, and Banan walked in the room.

Con stood with his hands braced on the footboard while Banan leaned against the door with his arms crossed over his chest. Rhys stoked the fire, his head down.

Guy sank onto the foot of the bed, the heat of his gaze making her blood burn. She was all too conscious of how close he was, of how easy it would be to lean forward and kiss him again.

She gripped the blanket and forced her gaze away from Guy's handsome face.

"How do you feel?" Con asked.

She licked her lips and sat up, keenly aware of her hardened nipples scraping against the flannel of the shirt. Longing went through her, longing for Guy's hands on her body.

Elena swallowed and pulled the shirt away from her while adjusting her foot atop the pillows. “Better. Did you give me something?”

“Just aspirin,” Banan said.

Guy raked a hand through his shoulder-length honey brown locks, disheveling it. “You were exhausted after the events. Your body shut down to rest.”

It made sense, so she nodded. “I think the swelling has gone down on my ankle.”

“It appears so,” Con said. “I didna mean to frighten you during our last talk, Elena, but you doona understand how important it is that what we have here remains private.”

“Nothing stays private in this world,” she argued. “Everyone has cameras on their phones, and video cameras at every street corner and store. Privacy is a thing of the past.”

“No’ for us,” Rhys said, and set aside the poker as he faced her. “It’s because of the legacy of Dreagan that there are certain . . . concessions made for us.”

“Such as?” she asked.

Banan pushed off the door, his arms dropping to his side. “No planes or helicopters of any kind are allowed to fly over our land. All sixty thousand acres of it.”

“Why?” It was all she could think to ask. People normally had a no-fly zone when they were hiding something. So what was Dreagan hiding?

Con looked as if he was searching for the right words before he said, “We need privacy. We open portions of the distillery and the gift shop for visitors with the one road in and one road out. It was made that way for a reason.”

“And the sheep and cattle? I know you sell them. Who picks them up?” she asked.

Guy leaned his elbows on his knees. “We take them to sell.”

"You make it appear as if you're hiding something."

Rhys cracked his knuckles one finger at a time. "Privacy doesna equal hiding. None of us wish to be in the spotlight, and so we ask for one simple request: that all that we are, and where we are, stay private."

"But it's an illusion. Everyone knows where you live. Everyone knows the mansion is behind the distillery."

Banan chuckled. "Have you seen pictures of our home before?"

Elena thought about that a moment. "No, but then again, I haven't exactly had the need to do a search. There are few things in this world that aren't on the Internet in some shape or form. And you have to know the government knows all about you."

"Hmm," Con said as he straightened. "An illusion, aye?"

"If there is one thing about people is that the more you try to keep from them, the more they're going to want to know about you. They'll do whatever it takes to find whatever you're keeping secret."

"Is that what you and Sloan were doing?" Rhys asked.

Her head turned to him as she frowned. "What?"

"You said yourself, people will do anything to find secrets," Banan replied. "What were you and Sloan doing in our mountain?"

She opened her mouth to speak, when Con talked over her.

"The road Sloan had to take was hidden, Elena. It was hidden and closed off. How did she know about it?"

Elena had the awful feeling she was being interrogated without being in a small windowless, stuffy room with one bright lightbulb shining at her face.

She took a deep breath to try to calm her racing heart. "I didn't lie to you. I told you all that I knew."

"No' all," Con said. "Start at the beginning. I want to know what you're doing in Britain."

Out of the corner of her eye, Elena saw Guy watching

her, his face devoid of expression. He hadn't spoken much, and she wondered why.

The others were quick to point out what she'd done wrong, but no one was defending her.

"I've worked for PureGems in Atlanta for eight years. I started as a file clerk while I went to college, and then worked my way up the company. It was my dream to work at the London branch and then move on to somewhere else in the world."

"Why?" Banan asked.

She shrugged. "I want to see the world, to experience the different cultures. What better way than to work in those cities and work with what I love—gems?"

"Go on," Con urged.

"I got offered the London position last month. I just moved here two weeks ago. Sloan was my boss. I was new to the office, new to London. When she told me we were going caving, I couldn't exactly tell my boss no."

"When did you know where you were caving?" Guy asked.

It was the first thing he'd said since she woke. She looked at him, desperately wanting him to believe her. "Not until we were at the cave. Sloan kept telling me it was a secret, a place she'd been wanting to explore for some time."

"Who told her of it?" Rhys asked.

Elena shrugged. "I didn't ask, and Sloan didn't volunteer the information."

"Did she say what she was looking for?"

Elena fought to roll her eyes as she glared at Con. "As I told you, no. She told me we'd only be gone two hours max, but when two hours came and we hadn't turned around, I knew it had been a lie."

Banan moved beside Con and asked, "How so?"

Elena struggled to find the right words as she remembered how Sloan hadn't broken stride, but kept moving.

"She knew I was a beginner, that I had never explored a cave before, yet she moved quickly through it. Almost as if . . ." Elena trailed off and looked away from Con.

"As if what?" Con demanded.

Elena wasn't sure if she should say. The men already thought the worst of her, if she spoke her thoughts, they would assume she knew more.

"Elena, please," Guy said. "Finish your sentence. We need to know."

She closed her eyes, silent praying that Sloan forgave her if she was wrong. Elena opened her eyes and kept her gaze on her hands folded in her lap.

"It seemed as quick as Sloan was moving that she knew where she was going. We rarely rested, and there was no time for me to see anything of the cave we were to explore. Until we came upon the opening. Only then did Sloan let us rest. And she was adamant about going into the hole."

When silence greeted her, she slowly lifted her eyes to find all four men staring at her with expressions ranging from of disbelief to acceptance.

Without so much as a thank-you, Con turned and walked out of the room. Rhys and Banan immediately followed, but Guy stayed behind.

Elena turned to him and said, "I'm telling the truth. I've nothing to hide. Why won't any of you believe me?"

"I do."

Those two simple words helped her to relax a bit. "I want to go home."

Guy looked away from her then, but in his pale brown gaze she'd seen a flash of regret. "That's no' going to be possible until Con is satisfied that he has his answers."

"He can't hold me here."

"Aye, he can," he said matter-of-factly, as if Con could do whatever he wanted, whenever he wanted.

"No. I'm an American."

"In Scotland," Guy said, his gaze once more returning to her face. "If he wanted, he could press charges for trespassing. For the moment he's no', but doona give him a reason to."

She put her hand to her forehead and looked at the ceiling. "This is a nightmare."

"Just continue to tell him the truth," Guy urged.

Elena lowered her hand and licked her lips. "How long will he keep me here?"

"I doona know."

"What are you hiding in this place?" she whispered. "What are you so afraid of everyone discovering?"

Guy released a long breath and raked a hand through his hair. "We didna become a powerful company for nothing."

"This is more than just the company." It was a guess, but when a flash of intensity filled his eyes, she knew she'd hit the nail on the head.

"Be careful what you say, Elena."

"Why? Will they hurt me?" When Guy looked away, unease snaked down her spine. "Why didn't you just leave me in the mountain, then?"

His brown eyes, ringed in onyx, swung to her as he rested a hand on the bed and leaned toward her. "You think we're capable of leaving a person to die in the mountain?"

"I don't know you," she whispered, hating how her body craved the hard muscular length of him against her when she was fighting so hard to steel herself from him.

"You trusted me to get you down the cliff. You trusted me to get you out of the cave."

"I had no choice."

One side of his lip lifted in a smile. "Liar."

"I'm not a threat to you."

"Oh, but you are." His words, barely whispered, sent

her heart beating double time when his gaze lowered to her lips. "You're definitely a threat, Elena Griffin."

He gently ran the pads of his fingers along her injured ankle sending chills racing along her skin. With barely a touch, he had her tied in knots. Imagine what it would be like if they kissed, really kissed, not just a brief meeting of the lips.

Guy rose and walked to the door, saying, "I'll have food sent up. You slept through the night, so I'm sure you're famished."

Elena didn't get a chance to respond as he was quickly out the door. She looked around her prison. At least it was cozy and warm.

And her visitor handsome, strong, and so very tempting.

Still the thought of being kept against her will left her feeling sick. If-no, *when*!—she left Dreagan, she knew in her soul she'd never see him again.

And she wasn't quite ready to let Guy disappear, not when she yearned for another kiss.

CHAPTER SIX

Guy walked away from Elena, each step like a punch in his gut. He'd wanted to take her in his arms and tell the others to bugger off as they fired their questions at her. He'd wanted to cover her body with his, to feel her softness and her heat.

But more than that, he wanted to taste her lips again.

She'd been afraid, but she had stood her ground. Yet when her eyes had touched his, he knew she sought someone to be on her side.

Guy did believe her, but like the others, he knew there was something more going on with her and Sloan's appearance on Dreagan land. He prayed it didn't involve Elena. He liked her around the house, knowing she was close by if he wanted to see her.

No one needed to know that he stayed in her room as she'd slept through the night. It had taken everything he had not to climb in bed with her and pull her into his arms for another kiss.

When she'd opened her eyes and looked at him with such passion, with such need, all the blood had rushed to his cock. How he'd stayed in his chair, he didn't know.

He could've kissed her then. He could have taken her

in his arms and pulled her soft body against his, and she wouldn't have refused him. He'd seen it in her beautiful sage green eyes.

Her long, wavy dark blond hair had been mussed from sleep, her eyes drowsy, and her lips slightly parted. She had looked as if she'd just been thoroughly loved.

Guy fisted his hands and walked down the corridor to Con's office, where he knew the others waited. He rounded the corner and stopped, preferring to lean against the doorway than take a seat inside the office.

"She likes you," Con said when he spotted Guy.

"I'm the only one no' ramming questions down her throat."

Banan snorted. "Nay, you just rammed your tongue down her."

Con's blond brows rose. "You kissed her."

"Nay," Guy said as casually as he could. "She was scared witless when we found her, and we had to take her down the cliff to return."

"With her injury, she couldna do it herself," Rhys said.

Guy nodded. "So, I took her down on my back. She said she'd haunt me if she died, but if I got her safely down, she'd kiss me."

"And she did," Banan said with a smirk. "Doona deny you didna liked it, Guy."

Guy shifted his gaze to Banan. Ever since Hal and Cassie were bonded, Banan had gotten even crankier. Hal was the first of them to have found his mate since the dragons left earth.

It had been a rarity when the dragons were still here, but once they had left and the spell was put on the Kings, they all knew they would forever be alone.

They had accepted it. Or had they? Hal hadn't fought against the love he felt for Cassie. He had fought *for* Cassie.

Guy hadn't really understood what Hal went through

before, but he was beginning to. It wasn't like Guy to skirt his duties as a Dragon King, yet every time he thought of Elena, the first thought that came to his mind was to protect her.

Against his own. Never before had he felt that. It unsettled him, just as Elena did. Her mere presence in the mansion drove him to distraction.

"Who doesna like the kiss of a pretty girl?" Guy replied when he realized the others were waiting on him to answer.

Banan lost all trace of anger and peered closely at Guy. "You feel something for her, do you no'? Is what happened to Hal happening to you?"

"Nay," Guy said quickly. Maybe a little too quickly, by the way Con narrowed his eyes at him. "It's been five months since the Silvers moved. Five months since the spell preventing Hal from feeling for a human ceased. That's five months as proof that our dragon magic used for the spell still holds. None of us have been drawn to humans since Hal."

Con tapped his fingers on the desk. "Five months is a blink to us. I've worried since Hal fell in love that our dragon magic had cracked somehow. That worry hasna left."

Guy watched his leader, the King of the Kings. Their history as Dragon Kings was long and bloody. The dragons they once commanded were gone, and because of a human betrayal, they had used their magic to never feel anything deeply for humans again.

Too much was at stake for Guy to lie to his friends. They might have won against one of their own and saved mankind that fateful day several millennia ago, and though Ulrik had been stripped of his ability to talk to his Silvers or to shift, he was still out there.

The silver dragons caged in their mountain had moved five months ago, something that had never happened since they were forced to sleep. Not since the Dragon Kings had sent the other dragons away and took up post guarding the Silvers.

Guy locked his gaze with Con's. No, he couldn't lie to his friends, his brethren, or himself, but especially not his King.

"I want her," Guy admitted. "I willna lie about it."

Con's lips flattened. "How badly do you want her? Is it because you have no' had a woman in a while? Or is it more?"

"It hasna been that long since I took a woman," Guy answered.

Rhys sighed loudly. "Maybe you should stay away from Elena."

"Nay!" Guy shouted.

He backed away at his outburst, more stunned than the others. What was wrong with him? He had no reason to snap at Rhys for a suggestion Guy himself probably would have made.

"Fuck me," Banan mumbled.

Con slowly rose to his feet. "I admit, Guy. I'm worried. I prayed it was only Hal our magic had ceased to affect, but I'm beginning to think it was more than just him. He was the first to fall for a human. You may be the second."

"And if it's all of us?" Rhys asked.

Banan's mouth twisted with concern. "Then we'd better stay at Dreagan."

"We used our magic because we didna ever want to be betrayed again," Guy said. "We made that decision thousands of years ago, but nothing has changed. We still hide what we are from the world, now more than ever. We're no closer to returning the dragons here now than we were the day they were sent away."

"I know," Con said wearily.

Could Guy chance being the one who fell for a human who betrayed them? It was only a matter of time. He knew the longer Elena remained, the more he'd be drawn to her.

He'd touched her, felt her body against his. And kissed her. It would be a miracle if he could stay away, and it had been a very long time since he'd seen a miracle.

"The longer you keep Elena, the worse things could get," Guy told Con, as much as it pained him to do it. "You're keeping the rest of the Kings in the mountain. She'll hear something eventually. How are you going to explain the roars?"

Or the dragons flying in the sky, Guy thought to himself. It had been weeks since he released his dragon and took flight, and just thinking about it made him want to feel the wind around him.

"You're right," Con agreed. "We had to trust Cassie because Hal had fallen in love with her before we realized what had happened. If we had known before, we might have prevented all of it. Cassie proved herself, but I'm no' in any hurry to go through that again. Let's see what Sloan was looking at in the cave and then get Elena home."

Guy left Con's office, knowing they had made the right decision, but the thought of her being taken away from Dreagan—from him—left him cold.

He stopped on the stairs, his breathing labored as he fought against going to Elena.

"The more you fight it, the worse it'll be," Rhys said.

Banan snorted. "Hal didna fight it, and he fell in love. Do you really want that emotion?"

"Nay," Guy said. He didn't want to fall in love, didn't want to be bound to a mate.

But he wanted Elena, needed her with a hunger that took his breath away. It shook him, this unwavering longing for her.

"I promised I'd bring her food."

Rhys slapped him on the back and continued down the stairs. "I hope you know what you're doing, my friend."

Guy hoped he did as well. He'd thought Hal a fool until he saw the love shared between him and Cassie. Guy was under no illusions. There was nothing like that between him and Elena.

With them, it was all physical. And that he could deal with.

He changed directions and went to the kitchen to order her some food, and then Guy found himself taking the stairs three at a time to get to her.

When he knocked, she didn't answer, and he feared she might have tried to escape. So he wrenched the door open and stormed into the room.

Only to be drawn up short by the sight of her silhouette through the clear shower curtain as steam billowed out of the bathroom through the open door.

She stood with her back to the water as she smoothed her hands over the long strands of her hair to rinse it. The motion caused her back to arch and her breasts to push outward.

Her slender arms moved slowly, sensuously over her face and hair. Guy let his gaze rake down what he saw of her silhouette. Small waist, flared hips, and beautiful breasts.

His balls tightened as he took a step toward her. He watched her lather her body with soap and then slowly rinse it away.

There was a grunt, and then Elena cried out. Guy's only thought was to help her. It wasn't until he'd shoved aside the curtain and held her very wet, very naked body against him that he realized what he'd done.

Her sage green eyes were wide as she stared at him. For long moments, they simply looked at each other.

"I heard you cry out."

"My . . . my ankle," she said after clearing her throat. "I put too much pressure on it."

"A bath would have been better." He was valiantly trying to keep his gaze on her face, but it was difficult with her pert breasts against him and her bare ass beneath his hand as he held her up.

"Probably," she whispered.

He knew he should let her go. The shower was soaking him as well as getting the floor wet. However, nothing mattered but Elena.

She drew a blunt nail across his cheek. No matter how he fought it, the overwhelming need to taste her eclipsed everything else. His head dipped toward hers.

When she lifted her face, it was his undoing. As soon as their lips touched, Guy released a breath he hadn't known he was holding.

His mouth nibbled hers, licking and tasting all that was Elena. He angled his head and slid his tongue past her lips. A groan tore from him when her hands plunged in his hair as she opened for him.

He deepened the kiss, the need pushing him, urging him to take more. He was blinded by desire, but it had never felt so good, never tasted so special before.

It wasn't until her hands touched his chest that he realized she'd unbuttoned his shirt. He gripped her wrists and held them from him as he looked at her.

"Don't stop," she pleaded with swollen lips. "Please, Guy, don't stop."

The same hunger that ran through him had taken her as well. What kind of man would he be to leave her with such need? Guy kissed her again and released her hands.

She pushed off his shirt and then reached for the waist of his jeans while he kicked off his boots.

He closed his eyes and tilted back his head when she ran her hands down his chest and knelt before him to slowly push his jeans down.

Her soft touch was driving him insane as her fingers touched the head of his dragon tattoo that came over his right shoulder and the fire that it breathed across his chest. He fisted his hand to keep from taking her, but it wasn't enough. He had to touch her.

His fingers slid into the wet strands of her blond hair. He looked down to find her lips inches away from his cock. Guy couldn't move, couldn't breathe as he waited for what she would do.

With the water beating at her back, she leaned forward and kissed the tip of his arousal before wrapping her lips around him.

It was the most exquisite torture Guy had ever endured. Her hot mouth sliding over his cock was pure decadence. He rocked his hips against her, but the pleasure was too much. He would peak too soon at this rate.

He took her shoulders and pulled her up to take her mouth in a kiss full of need, of longing as he stepped into the shower and pulled the curtain shut.

His kiss was rough, but she returned it with all the fervor she had. With her arms wrapped tightly around his neck and her amazing body against him, Guy wished he could stop time.

He ran his hands down her side so that his thumbs caressed the undersides of her breasts before sliding lower to her trim waist and then over her hips.

For an instant, he held her hips still and rocked against her. She moaned, her fingers digging into his shoulders. It was just the beginning of what he had planned for her.

Guy kissed down her neck to the valley between her breasts. With the hot water cascading from behind him over them, it heightened their pleasure.

He shifted his shoulder so that a spray of water would hit her nipple. Elena gasped, her eyes flying open. He held her gaze an instant before he bent his head and took that same turgid peak in his mouth.

With her nails piercing his skin, he teased the nipple

until she was rocking her hips against him. And then he moved to the next.

Her body shook with need, but he wasn't yet ready for her to climax. There was still so much more he wanted to give her.

Guy followed the path of his hands and kissed along her stomach to her hips. He knelt before her and looked up at her as she had done him.

Her lips were parted, and her glorious sage green eyes were filled with passion. He slowly lifted her injured leg and placed it over his shoulder. His hands grabbed her hips to keep her steady.

And then he licked her sex.

She cried out his name, her head thrown back. It was the most beautiful sight he had ever seen. Guy found her clitoris and continued to lave his tongue against the tiny nub.

Her body trembled, her moans filling the small bathroom. But those moans turned to cries as he moved a finger inside her.

She was so damned tight. He couldn't wait to fill her. Guy could taste her pleasure on his tongue and knew she was close to orgasm. He moved his tongue and fingers faster, propelling her onward.

He had only thought he'd seen radiance until he watched the pleasure erupt on Elena's face as the climax hit her. He continued to lick her, dragging out her pleasure as long as he could.

When he leaned back, Elena's eyes were closed, her head back against the shower as the water flowed freely over her. He took her injured leg and held it as he slowly stood.

Her eyes opened, and the smile she gave him made something move in his chest. He wrapped her left leg around him before he grabbed her hips and lifted her.

The smile vanished as desire flared once more. Their lips met, breaths fused as he lowered her, slowly, onto his aching cock. She released a sigh when she was fully seated.

Elena smoothed back the dark strands of Guy's wet hair from his face so she could see him. The longing and need she saw reflected in his gaze made her stomach clench.

He rocked against her, stretching her as he had filled her. She held on to him, her body no longer her own. It belonged to Guy now, and she feared it always would.

His fingers dug into her hips as he slid in and out of her. Each plunge of his thick arousal sent her higher, her body tightening once again. Their lips met again with their tongues colliding in time with his thrust.

The orgasm took her by surprise, flinging her skyward as her body was swathed in the bright glow of pleasure. She clung to Guy, his hips jerking as he quickened his pace.

She watched, spellbound, as he threw back his head and gave a shout as he climaxed. He looked at her before drawing her into his arms, and for long minutes, they stood beneath the spray of the water, locked in each other's arms.

CHAPTER SEVEN

Guy would've been content to stay just as they were, but a knock on the door brought reality with it.

Elena was the first to move. She searched his gaze, but Guy didn't know what she looked for. When they heard the door close behind the servant who had brought the food, Guy pulled out of her and lowered her feet to the tub.

Still, he wasn't ready to leave her.

"I just need to finish up," she said. "And then I'll be out."

"That was food being brought." It sounded lame to him, but he wasn't sure what to say.

He then gave a nod and stepped out of the shower. He dried off and looked at his sodden clothes. With a sigh, he wrung the worst of the water out in the sink before taking the clothes to the fire to lay them out to dry.

The last thing he wanted was be seen walking down the hall in a towel. Everyone would know what had happened, and he wasn't ready for that.

Not that he cared what they thought, but he wasn't prepared for Elena to be interrogated again. Or worse, for her to learn what he was.

It had torn Hal in two when Con had been the one to

tell Cassie what they were. Cassie hadn't run, but would Elena? And why was he even thinking about it?

He'd wanted Elena, and she'd wanted him. It was that simple.

Or so he thought until she stood in the doorway of the bathroom with her hair combed out and a towel wrapped around her.

"They took my clothes. Even my panties."

Guy bit back a moan at the thought of her panties. Did she wear cotton or silk? Plain or lace? He desperately wanted to know.

"They're being cleaned. You should have them shortly. We thought you might want to have your own clothes back instead of running around in ours."

She licked her lips, her eyes traveling down to the towel tied at his waist. "My clothes are gone. Yours are wet."

It was an observation, but one that had his blood heating.

"What is it about you that I can't seem to keep away from?" she asked softly. "It's like you're a magnet. I don't sleep around, Guy, and even though I knew I should tell you no, I couldn't. Not even had my life depended upon it."

He was taken aback by her words, so full of honesty and truth that they stunned him. "I doona have an answer. I wish I did."

"This has something to do with why you want your privacy, doesn't it?"

"Nay." It was the truth, but that's all he could tell her.

Her gaze lowered to the floor for a moment. "I've never been so reckless or careless before with my partners. We didn't even use a condom. I didn't even think about it."

"You willna catch a disease from me."

"Nor me," she hastened to add. "As for the other—"

"Other?" he interrupted her.

She frowned at him as if he were addled. "Pregnancy."

"Ah. Um . . . I doona believe you need to worry about that either."

"You doona believe," she mimicked in a Scottish accent. "Forgive me if that doesn't relieve me. I assumed I'd have kids when I married, but I'm not ready for them now."

"Trust me, Elena, you doona need to worry."

"Can you not have children?"

It was difficult to explain. No Dragon King had a child. Their women might get with child, but the babe never lasted to term.

Guy shook his head in answer.

"I see," she said, and walked slowly to the tray of food on the table near him. She picked up a chip next to the sandwich and nibbled at it.

He could see how her eyes kept going to his tattoo. He waited for her to ask him about it, but she seemed content to just look from the head and flames to the dragon tail that ended at his left hip bone. Would she ask to see the rest that was on his back?

Guy wanted her to see it. And more than that, he wanted her to ask about it.

"Do you like working with gems?" he asked into the silence.

She smiled and reached for a sandwich half. "Oh, yes. I love finding them and discovering what will be their perfect shape for jewelry."

"Do you design jewelry?"

She laughed, the sound like music to him. "No. I'm not that creative. As much as I love the gems, I'm useless in anything other than determining what kind of gem it is and how best to use it."

"That's no' useless."

Her gaze lifted to him. "Many think what I do is boring."

"Tell them to bugger off."

She laughed again, and he found he wanted to keep making her laugh. He loved the sound. It filled him, which was odd because he hadn't thought anything was lacking in his life until recently.

"There are those of us who actually go looking in places all around the world for gems," she continued.

"What kinds of places?"

She shrugged and swallowed her bite. "They'll dig in the earth, shift through rock and water, and even go into caves." Elena's voice faded as her eyes got large. "Oh, my God. Could that be what Sloan was after? Were there gems in the cave?"

Guy frowned, his mind working. There were gems deep in the earth, but none of them had ever tried to work them from the mountain. They had no need of gems.

"It's a possibility," he said, and looked at the door. "They should be returning soon. I need to see what they've found."

He hated to leave her, but if she was right, it could explain what Sloan had been doing in the cave. But it wouldn't clear Elena's name in Con's eyes. Guy feared nothing would ever clear her name.

Elena didn't have long to wait before her clothes were brought to her by an older woman who not only didn't look her in the eyes, but didn't speak either.

She tried not to make more of it than it was and quickly put on her own clothes. Though they were a reminder of Sloan's death.

For the next hour, Elena hobbled around the room. She'd sprained that ankle before, and it had taken several days before she could put any kind of weight on it. The pain that had filled her when she was first brought to the mansion was gone. Just a little twinge every now and again.

It was just odd to have an injury heal so quickly. Then

she remembered Guy's hands after he'd brought her down the cliff. There had been so much blood. For a moment, she thought she might have seen his wound heal, but she must have imagined it. Right?

Elena looked down at her ankle. The conversation she'd heard outside her door about midnight flights came to mind. There was something going on at Dreagan. Whatever it was, they wanted it kept private.

She checked windows to see if she could escape. The windows opened, but it was a sheer drop from the third floor to the ground. A fall in her current condition would only make things worse.

A glance out into the hall showed that someone stood at the stairs. She couldn't tell who it was, but she saw the shadow. Which meant, she couldn't walk out of the mansion as she'd hoped.

"Well, hell," she mumbled.

She wasn't keen on waiting around to discover what Con would do to her. Guy might believe her, but she could see the others weren't so open minded.

The fact that they were hiding something was obvious. But what could it be? Drugs? Money laundering?

She quickly threw out those ideas. There was money at Dreagan, but none of the people she had met were the drug or money-laundering type.

It had to be something different, something she wasn't thinking of.

"Guy said it was life or death for them," she muttered.

After another hour of trying to determine what the mystery was, Elena felt her ankle throbbing from all the walking. She'd been on it too long. With a sigh, she returned to the bed and stared at the ceiling.

She licked her lips, her heart racing as images of her and Guy in the shower played through her mind. The man knew how to touch her, knew how to give her the most wickedly intense pleasure.

Her breasts swelled just thinking of him thrusting inside her. She might have always played it safe, but up until she met Guy, she'd never wanted to throw caution to the wind before.

With him, however, everything had changed.

Everything.

And it scared the shit out of her because she realized what the attraction meant.

It meant she was likely to do something rash and reckless again. Which could be why she wasn't too upset about having to stay locked in such a gorgeous room, hoping Guy returned soon.

Alone.

"Please be alone," she whispered.

CHAPTER EIGHT

Guy walked out on Con and Rhys. It was the first time he had actually walked away from Con before. But he couldn't stand to listen to them think of ways Elena was plotting against them.

At least Banan was gone. He'd been sent to London to see what he could learn of Sloan, Elena, and PureGems.

Guy paused outside Elena's door. Con had asked him why he defended Elena. It wasn't as if Guy could tell them he'd slept with her, that she occupied his thoughts until he saw her everywhere.

How he wished Hal were there so he could talk to him. But he had to go it alone.

"Bloody hell," he murmured.

He put his ear to the door but didn't hear Elena. She'd been left alone nearly all day. Surely someone had gone to check on her. It hadn't been his intention to be stuck in the mountain with the others, but with her information, it was necessary.

Guy opened the door quietly and peeked in to find the fire dead and the lights out. It stayed light out well past midnight, and with the large windows, there wasn't a need to have the lights on.

He stepped into the room, his gaze riveted on Elena, who lay sleeping on the bed. Her blond waves were stretched out on some pillows, and her injured foot once more raised upon others.

"I thought I'd find you here," Con whispered from behind him.

Guy sighed. He should've known Con would come looking for him after he stormed out.

"You believe her?"

Guy nodded.

"Would you stake your honor on it?"

Guy hesitated and turned to look at his King over his shoulder. "I've followed every order you've ever given us, even when it meant turning against one of our own, even when I knew Ulrik was right. I sent my dragons away because you said it was the best thing for them. I gave you my dragon magic to help put a stop to our feelings. When was the last time I asked for anything, Con?"

"Never," Con answered without hesitation.

"I'm asking you to trust me now. You weren't there when we found Elena."

Con sighed. "Nay, I was no', but that doesna mean she's no' a good actress."

"You can no' fake fear like that. Maybe with words, but no' in how she reacted with emotions and actions. She's innocent in this."

"Then you need to prove it. I have to take action. You understand that. No one can know what we are."

Guy looked into Con's black eyes. "I do understand, Con. And if it isna Elena?"

"Then we discover who was behind Sloan getting onto our land and into the mountain, but if it is Elena—"

"What are you going to do?"

Con placed a hand on his shoulder, his mouth tight with weariness. "It's no' what I'll do, Guy. It's what you'll do."

Guy waited until the door shut behind Con before he looked at Elena. He knew what Con wanted. Part of them being dragons was that they had magic. Guy's specialty was erasing memories. There was no way he'd wipe Elena's memories. If he did, what they'd shared would be gone.

But she'd be safe.

He leaned back against the door, but movement on the bed caused his gaze to turn to Elena. Her brow was creased and her sage green eyes worried as she looked at him.

"What would they make you do to me?"

Guy briefly shut his eyes and wished the conversation had taken place somewhere else so she wouldn't have overheard it. "It doesna matter. I'm no' going to do it."

"If it doesn't matter, then tell me."

Guy pushed off the door and walked to the window beside the bed. He looked out over the land he had walked since the beginning of time.

There had been a era when he'd not had to keep what he was a secret. When he'd been able to take to the skies whether the sun was shining or the moon out.

Now, only the moon saw what he was, and then only briefly.

"You wouldna believe me if I told you," he said.

The bed creaked and then he felt her behind him. He prayed she didn't touch him, because if she did, he wouldn't be able to keep from taking her again, wouldn't be able to stop himself from laying her on the bed and ripping her clothes from her body.

"Try me."

Guy inwardly laughed. If only she'd have touched him, then he wouldn't have to think up some lie. He didn't want to lie to her. But he had no choice. No one could know what they were.

"I can no'."

"Because you think I won't believe you?"

"Because of what you'll think of me after."

He hadn't realized that's how he felt until the words left his mouth, but they were the truth. Guy didn't want her looking at him with revulsion or worse . . . fear.

Suddenly she was between him and the window. Her gaze searched his face before she said, "I know something is going on here. Despite being locked away, I've been treated with kindness. If you were so worried about someone discovering whatever it is here, you could have left me to die in the mountain."

"That's no' our way."

She glanced down and then placed her hand over his heart. "What is so different about you that being with you makes me forget about trying to find a way out or contacting anyone? What is it that . . . draws me to you?"

The desperation in her voice tore at him. He threaded his fingers in her hair and cupped the back of her neck. "I wish I knew."

"Please. Tell me I'm not the only one feeling this. Tell me you don't have a hundred women at your beck and call."

At that moment, he'd have told her anything she wanted to know, and what she asked for was too simple. One side of his mouth lifted in a smile. "I've no other women, Elena."

Her shoulders drooped as she turned her head away. "But I am the only one feeling this, right?"

The only way to make her understand was to make her feel. Guy took her mouth in a fierce, all-encompassing kiss. He ravaged her lips, plundered her mouth.

He seized . . . her.

Her arms came around him as she moaned. His already heated blood blazed with need, a need only she could quench. Being so near to her, he couldn't stop touching her, didn't want to stop.

His hand ran down her back to grasp her buttocks and lift her against his swollen cock. He ground against her, desperate to be inside her once more.

With a flick of his fingers, he raised her shirt so he could touch her bare skin. She was warm to the touch, her skin smooth as silk.

All it took was that one touch of her skin and then they were a tangle of limbs as they peeled off each other's clothes. Guy heard a rip of something, but paid no attention.

He drew Elena to him and kissed her while he backed her against the bed. When her knees hit, he leaned forward and carefully laid her down.

Her hands ran down his chest and back up again. Her lips were parted and moist from his kisses. With her blond hair spread around her, she looked like a sacrifice. For him.

"Elena," he whispered, and kissed her deeply.

Elena wrapped her arms around Guy's neck and held on tight. She was being reckless again, but she couldn't seem to help herself when it came to him. And she didn't want to.

It felt good to give in to the hunger, the desire for Guy. His kisses made her forget everything but him, and his touch drove her to such heights of ecstasy, she didn't think she'd ever come down.

Beneath her hands, the muscles of his back and shoulders moved and bunched, his power evident in each shift of his body. She ran her feet along the back of his legs, feeling the sinew and the strength.

When he rose up on his hands, she lifted her head and kissed down his chest and abdomen, which rippled with tight, honed muscle.

There wasn't an ounce of fat anywhere. He exuded authority and vigor with just a stance. But his hands demanded surrender while his mouth exacted pleasure.

Elena knew she was getting in way over her head, but she couldn't seem to stop herself. She went rushing headlong into the pleasure Guy offered without a backward glance.

She gasped when he cupped her breasts and rolled a nipple between his fingers. Her back arched, her hands running along his trim hips to his butt.

Her fingernails dug into his skin when his hips rocked forward, his thick arousal rubbing against her sensitive flesh. Need flared as she was caught in the pleasure of his mouth on her breast and his rod teasing her sex.

Suddenly his fingers were there, soft and insistent as they parted her curls and delved inside her. Her hips rocked against his hand helplessly.

In and out his finger moved in a steady rhythm. A second finger joined the first. He was absolute in giving her pleasure, and he wanted nothing held back.

As if she could. With one look, she surrendered to him. It was as if her body, her soul knew what her mind couldn't comprehend.

What she wasn't yet ready to understand.

His hot mouth left a trail of kisses down her neck. His tongue flicked over her skin every time his fingers plunged within her.

It was driving her mad. Every nerve ending tingled, stretched taut by the need building. She was so close to peaking, but he wouldn't let her.

He pulled back just before she'd go over the edge, and each time it took her higher and higher until she was delirious with need.

Guy stared down at her flushed skin. She was beautiful to behold, stunning to watch as her body came alive beneath his touch.

Her head moved from side to side as she whimpered when he wouldn't allow her climax to take her. He wondered how much more she could take. Already he was ready to spill, and he hadn't even been inside her.

He spread the moisture of her sex over her and felt her legs tremble when he touched her clitoris. Twice more, he teased her with barely a touch, and each time she cried out, her back bowing off the bed.

With her beautiful rose-tipped breasts tempting him, Guy could no longer hold back. He lifted her leg beneath her knee and bent to flick his tongue over a nipple. And then he slid into her tight, wet body.

He groaned, reveling in the exquisite feel of her. When he opened his eyes, it was to find her watching him. He rotated his hips, wringing a moan from deep in her throat.

Once inside her, he couldn't hold back the tide of his own desire. He began to thrust hard and fast. When her legs wrapped around his waist, he sank deeper inside her.

Elena couldn't look away from his pale brown gaze. He leaned above her with his hands on either side of her head. His honey brown locks fell against his cheek as he rocked against her again and again.

Each thrust wound her need tighter. Her body burned with flames of desire that consumed her, devoured her. Just when she didn't think she could take it anymore, the release took her.

Incandescent light surrounded her, blinded her as she was swept on a tide of rapture. Her only anchor to the world was Guy, and she desperately clung to him.

She held him as he gave a final plunge and buried his head in her neck as the climax swept him as well. They rode the pleasure together, locked in each other's arms.

Gradually the glow faded and their breathing evened out. Elena found herself cradled against Guy's chest as he rolled onto his back, his arm holding her tightly.

She felt wanted and beautiful and desired. A smile pulled at her lips as she realized no one had ever made her feel such things before, and probably never would again.

"Would you believe me if I told you I was immortal?"

Guy's words, spoken softly, quietly pulled her from her near state of sleep. She didn't move, because she felt he didn't want her to look at him.

She didn't respond right away, but there had been something in his voice. Hope? Fear?

Once more, the imagine of his wounded hands flashed in her mind. "Are you?" she asked just as softly.

For long minutes, silence followed.

And then, "If I was?"

Everything hinged on how she answered. Elena didn't know how she knew; she just knew. "I'd ask how."

"Would you fear me?"

"Never."

His hand flattened against her back. "Doona ever say never, Elena. It is a verra long time. Trust me."

"There are many things I feel with you, Guy. Lust. Desire. Need. Fear isn't one of them."

"Do you believe me?"

Immortal. It should seem bizarre, but Elena wasn't surprised. She wasn't naïve enough to believe there weren't things in the world that were unexplainable. But immortal?

She lifted her head to look at him then. It was as if his amazing pale brown eyes were trying to tell her something, as if they were silently begging her to trust him.

Her hands cradled one of his. She turned it one way then the other, looking for a scar or even a wound from his injury in the cave. There was nothing, and his other hand didn't show anything either.

Could she believe he had healed himself? She'd dismissed what she saw because she had been exhausted and weary, but maybe she had seen something extraordinary.

It would explain what it was about Guy that was so different. But immortal? If he could heal himself, it wasn't so far-fetched.

"Do you believe I'm immortal?" he asked again.

Elena nodded her head carefully. "Are you?"

"Aye."

CHAPTER NINE

Elena woke on her side with one of Guy's arms draped over her. She caressed his long fingers hanging near her hand.

She couldn't believe he had stayed the night with her. Any minute now, someone was going to come through her door and find them. Not that she cared, but Guy might.

A glance at the clock near the bed proved it was only four. Elena sighed. She was having a difficult time adjusting to the lighting during the summer. It didn't stay dark for long.

Now that she was awake, she couldn't go back to sleep. Especially when she thought of Guy being immortal. She managed to rise from the bed without waking him and wrapped an extra blanket around her. It might be summer to the Scots, but to a Southern girl, it was chilly out.

She turned to find him on his stomach, his face directed away from her. It was then she saw the rest of his tattoo, which covered his entire back. She'd desperately wanted to see the tat earlier, but something had stopped her from asking about it.

Elena wasn't sure what it had been, but she wished she'd had the nerve to ask anyway.

She'd seen the dragon's large head and the flames he breathed, but now she traced the rest of it with her finger. The dragon was vertical with its wings spread out across Guy's shoulders, tip to tip. Elena followed the dragon to where its tail wrapped around Guy's waist.

The ink looked like a peculiar mix of red and black. Many of her friends in Atlanta had gotten inked, but she'd never seen anything like this before. Not just the ink, but the artwork as well. It was beautiful and impressive.

After they'd made love the first time in the shower, she'd sworn the tat looked at her. Elena smiled and started to draw her hand away when she gasped.

The tattoo had moved. She'd stake her life on it.

It was just another thing that made Guy so different from the others. Like his immortality.

Immortal. She thought over that word long and hard as she stared out the window, watching the sky continue to lighten. What did it mean, exactly?

There were hundreds of questions rushing around in her head. She'd wanted to ask them before, but she had a feeling Guy wouldn't have told her the answers. Not yet, at least.

As she looked at the vivid green grass and the sheep dotting the rolling landscape, immortality didn't seem so unbelievable.

Maybe it was Dreagan itself, but the land felt old . . . ancient. Older than anyone knew. Was it the stories she'd heard of the magic of Scotland? Or was it something else?

Strong arms locked around her from behind as Guy kissed her neck. "Couldna sleep?" he asked.

She leaned back against him with a smile. "I was asleep. I can't get used to the sky lightening up so early. For me, when I see light, it's time to get up."

He chuckled and turned her to face him. "There's a switch next to the bed that will lower the blinds to block out the light. Now, is that all?"

"It was. Until I started thinking about what you asked me last night."

His smile slipped. "Elena—"

"Wait," she interrupted him, and put her hand on the flames across his chest. "Let me talk, please. I'm not saying I've changed my mind. I believe you." She shook her head with a laugh. "As impossible as that is for me to imagine, I believe you. Why did you tell me?"

"Most people would think I've gone mad. Instead, you accept what I say. No questions or anything."

"Oh, I've questions. Plenty of them, but I was still wrapping my head around the immortality bit. Plus, I saw your hand heal in the cave."

He ran a thumb down her cheek. "You were no' supposed to see that. And I shouldna have told you about my immortality. If the others learn that I've—"

"I won't tell them," she assured him. "But you still haven't answered me. Why tell me?"

"I doona know. I wanted to." He sighed and looked over her head out the window. "For so long we've kept what we are secret. We knew it wouldna last, but we were hoping to keep it going a little longer."

"Which is why everyone freaked the hell out when Sloan and I were in the mountain?"

He nodded and looked at her. "There is only one other human who knows we're immortal."

Elena blinked and leaned back a ways. "Human? What do you mean *human*? You aren't human?"

Guy was opening his mouth to talk, when there was a single knock on the door and Guy's name was called.

"Bugger," he muttered, and began to gather his clothes.

Elena followed him. "What is it?"

"Con's on his way. Get dressed and hurry."

Elena let the blanket drop and gathered her clothes before kicking her pants ahead of her in the bathroom. She caught Guy's gaze before she closed the door.

There was something about the way he said *human* that she had a feeling had nothing to do with immortality. Would he have told her had they not been interrupted?

"Guess I'll never know," she said.

Elena dressed, brushed her teeth, and combed her hair. When she walked out of the bathroom, Con was standing next to Guy at the fireplace.

Con smiled at her, though much like last time, it didn't quite reach his eyes. "Good morn, Elena. How is your ankle?"

"It's improving. Rather rapidly, actually. I can put a little weight on it now."

"I'm glad to hear it. Sometimes just resting will heal an injury."

She didn't believe him. There was something in his tone, a look in his eyes. She knew in her gut they had done something to help speed the healing of her ankle.

Con chuckled while Guy looked at the rug with no emotion showing. Elena put her hands in her khaki pockets and waited. She assumed the interrogation would begin again, though she wondered where Rhys and Banan were.

"Would you like for me to answer the same questions as before?" Elena asked. She figured she'd be better getting right to the point than beating around the bush.

Con shrugged with a grin. "We could. Or you could actually tell me the truth."

"I'd be happy to take a lie detector test if that'd help. I'm not lying. And regardless of whether you press charges for trespassing or not, you can't keep me here forever."

Her gaze moved to Guy as she finished, and she could have sworn she saw a flash of hurt.

"I want to believe you," Con said as he slowly walked toward her. "Too much is at stake for me to accept what you're saying so easily."

"I don't know what's at stake, but I can see it's important. Is there some way I can help to prove my innocence?"

He studied her for a moment before glancing at Guy. "You said you're a gemologist."

"Yes."

"Do you think there are valuable stones in our mountain?"

She was nodding her head before he finished. "Of course. There are stones everywhere in the world. Below the water, below dirt, beneath rock. You name it, the stones are there. I imagine there are stones that have yet to be discovered."

"Do you want to be the one to discover one?"

Elena thought of the cold, damp cave and shuddered. "No," she said, and took a step back. "No. That's not something I ever wanted to do. I'm not daring enough. At *all*. My idea of running is on a treadmill at the gym, not at a park where some madman might rape or kill me."

"Hmm," Con said, and rocked back on his heels. "You think Sloan might have found something in the cave?"

"As I told Guy, it's a possibility. She was in a hurry, that much was obvious. Once we reached that spot, she was fine for me to sit and rest as long as I needed."

"Did she have a map?" Guy asked.

Elena thought back over the ride to the mountains and while in the cave. "No. She seemed to know where she was going. There were a few times she hesitated when the cave branched off, but I just assumed she was trying to determine the best course to take."

Con and Guy turned to each other.

"She could've been there before," Guy said.

Elena hurried to say, "No. She was adamant about finally getting to cave in such a private place."

Con's face grew grim. "Which means someone else was."

"Ulrik?" Guy offered.

"We'd know."

"Then who, dammit?"

"Let's hope Banan finds out."

Elena looked from one to the other as they spoke rapidly. "Where does that leave me?"

Guy looked up from his musing, his amazing light brown eyes softening as they met hers.

"It means," Con said, breaking into their stare, "that we need your help."

Elena smiled at Con. Eagerness filled her as she realized she could finally help him see she wasn't lying. "I'd love to help. What can I do?"

"We need you to go back into the cave."

"Nope," Elena said, and limped out of her room and into the hallway. "I told Guy I wouldn't go back there, and I'm not."

"No' even if it clears you of suspicion?" Con asked as he followed.

Elena gripped the wall as she put too much weight on her ankle, but she kept going. "I want you to believe me. I really do, but if it means going back into that . . . that . . . cave . . ." She shook her head. "Forget it. I don't care what you think of me. Press charges, do whatever you want, but don't make me go back there."

Guy stood in the doorway of Elena's room and watched her gradually limping down the corridor. She was going so slowly, Con had to actually stop walking to let her get ahead.

If there had been any doubt in Guy's mind about her innocence, it was gone now after hearing that speech. She wanted no part of the mountain.

And if a cave scared her, what would a dragon do?

Guy leaned a hand against the doorframe and sighed. He'd been about to tell her he was a dragon when Rhys had knocked. Maybe Con was right and it was best to keep their secret amongst themselves.

He'd already done enough damage by telling Elena he was immortal. But to tell her the rest of it . . . he couldn't, wouldn't now. He'd lose her for sure.

"You look like someone just shot your puppy," Rhys said as he walked up. "I'd thought you'd be thrilled to have Con asking for Elena's help."

Guy didn't bother to respond. Elena had reached the stairs and was attempting to make her way down. Con wasn't going to stop her, so someone had to.

He started toward them, lengthening his strides when Elena gripped the railing. She was just about to jump on the first stair when Guy scooped her up in his arms.

"You're going to kill yourself," he ground out.

She looked up at him, her eyes wide and mouth open. "I did all right these past twenty-eight years. Humans are fragile, but we heal well enough."

Guy inwardly winced at her words. Would Con and Rhys pick up on the double meaning? Would they guess he'd told her something?

"No' if you break your neck," Guy said, and started down the stairs.

He didn't know where he was going, but it didn't matter. She was in his arms, and he had to get away from Con and Rhys to calm his thoughts and his breathing.

"I shouldn't have said that," she whispered.

"Nay," he murmured.

She rested her head on his shoulder. "I'm sorry."

He gave her a light squeeze and brought her to the entertainment room. Usually it was full of the other Dragon Kings, but they'd been ordered to stay away because of Elena.

"Such a huge house for just the four of you. Why do I believe there are more?" she asked, her eyes twinkling with merriment.

He didn't answer, but she laughed just the same.

"There are. I knew it," she whispered as he set her down on the couch.

Guy moved away from her in time to see Con raise a brow at him. There was no need to try to deny anything. He wasn't keeping what was between him and Elena a secret.

"Verra protective," Rhys murmured as he walked past. "A sign no one can ignore."

Guy glared at him before turning to Elena and sitting on the arm of the couch. "Will you at least consider going back in the mountain?"

"I can't," she said, and picked at her fingernails. "Have none of you ever been so afraid of something that you can't face it?"

"Nay," Rhys said.

Guy had never encountered anything he feared. Until Elena. She scared the hell out of him because of the feelings she evoked.

"It's no' in our nature," Con said as he walked to a chair opposite her.

"What you're asking me to do is like asking someone who's scared of heights to jump off a building," she said.

It was the tremor in her voice that made Guy want to get up and punch Con for pushing her. Instead he gripped his knees. "You willna be alone, Elena."

"No?" she asked, and looked at him. "I wasn't alone with Sloan when she died. She wanted me to go down there with her. Had I gone, I'm the one that would be dead."

The thought left Guy cold. He stood and walked around the back of the couch, raking a hand through his hair. Humans were delicate creatures. That had always been fact. But he'd never had one he wanted so desperately to be safe before.

"What if I can guarantee your safety?" Con asked her.

Guy jerked his head to Con.

Elena laughed shakily. "No one can guarantee anything but death and taxes, Con."

"Then what can I give you that will change your mind?"

Con rarely made that offer, and when he did, he meant it. Elena could ask for anything, and Con would give it to her. Guy waited for what she would request, unsure of how he wanted her to respond.

"There's nothing I want," she finally said.

Con's blond brows rose. "Nothing? I find that hard to believe. Everyone wants something."

Guy's breath caught when Elena looked at him.

She looked away and down at her hands folded in her lap. "If I asked for your secret, would you tell me?"

A muscle in Con's jaw twitched, the only sign that he didn't like where the conversation was headed. "Aye," he said tightly.

She exhaled loudly. "I don't want your secret. I don't want anything from you." She turned on the couch and faced Guy. "But I'll help. For you."

"In the cave?" he asked.

"Yes, though I'm going to regret it. And my threat still holds, Guy. If I die there, I'm haunting you."

While Con and Rhys were talking, Guy let his fingers touch Elena's on the back of the couch.

CHAPTER TEN

Elena asked herself for the hundredth time what she was doing back in the damned mountain. It didn't matter that she was clipped in and connected to Guy, she was scared silly.

They'd been in the mountain for three hours, forty-seven minutes, and eighteen seconds. She knew because she kept looking at her watch.

What Elena discovered was she didn't mind climbing up something as much as she hated climbing down. She'd managed to keep calm the deeper into the cave they went. Guy was always behind her, helping her up an incline or over something.

Rhys and Con were in front of her, but even they looked back often to check on her.

She'd had them tape her ankle securely and taken plenty of aspirin, but the pain was coming back. She dug into her pocket and pulled out two more aspirin and downed them with water.

"You're hurting," Guy said.

It wasn't a question, so she shrugged and swallowed her water. "I'll be all right."

All three had helped to keep the majority of her weight

off her injured leg, but that didn't stop it from aching. As soon as the tape was off her ankle, it would be swollen once more.

"We're here," Con suddenly called.

Elena's heart dropped to her feet like lead. *Here* meant where Sloan had fallen. And died.

"You doona have to do this."

She looked at Guy and adjusted the strap of her helmet beneath her chin. "I do, and you know it."

Elena put her back to the opening in the floor as Con and Rhys got everything ready for their descent. She touched Guy's hand to get his attention.

When he looked at her, she wondered how she'd tell him what she'd found. Or if she should.

"Elena?" he asked, a frown marring his forehead. "What is it? Do you want to return to the house?"

She paused, contemplating if she should tell him. "I saw something, well a couple of somethings, as we were making our way here."

"Rock?" he asked with a teasing grin.

"Smart-ass." She couldn't stop her smile, though. Her hand covered the marking behind her as she leaned back. She thought of the beautiful dragon tattooed on Guy's body and of the markings.

"First, tell me what *Dreagan* means?"

Guy grew instantly still, all traces of teasing gone. "Why?"

"Please. Just tell me what the word means."

"It's Gaelic," he said slowly. "It means 'dragon.' "

Elena took a deep breath, excitement and fear mixing within her. She stepped aside to reveal the carving in the rock. It was about the size of a man's hand, and would have been missed had her light not fallen upon it as she sat down.

"I've seen a couple of these today," she said as Guy squatted beside the picture of a dragon in flight. "All of them are different. Some in flight, some sleeping, some with their wings spread."

Guy still said nothing. He traced the drawing with his finger before he stood and faced her.

"Dragons. The meaning of your distillery. Your tat. The drawings in the mountain. It all comes back to you, doesn't it? What does it mean?"

Indecision warred across his face. He glanced at his friends, and when his gaze returned to her, there was despair. "You're no' going to like my answer."

"What? That you can't tell me?"

"Do you keep an open mind about things?"

His tone was soft, his question serious. She thought of the way he'd loved her and held her. How he'd kissed her with more passion and need than she had ever known was possible.

"If you mean if I believe in ghosts, the answer is yes. Aliens, well, I'm not sure there. I don't think we're the only ones in the entire universe. There's something else out there I'm sure of it."

"And my immortality?"

She shrugged, growing more unsure of things as the conversation continued. "I don't know how it's possible or why. My first thought is to doubt you, but then I look at you. You aren't like other men. There's something . . . more . . . to you, Guy."

"I want to tell you," he whispered, and grasped her elbows as he pulled her closer. "I want you to know. Keep an open mind, Elena. *Keep looking*."

She was about to ask him what he wanted her to look for, when Rhys took her arm.

"It's time, Elena. I need to get you secured to the line."

She was so caught up in her conversation with Guy that she paid no attention to Con lowering himself into the hole. Not even when she found her feet dangling in the air and Rhys holding her did it bother her.

Rhys was talking, but she didn't hear his words. It wasn't until Guy took her hand that she was able to focus again.

"Elena," he said.

She blinked and looked from Guy to Rhys. "I'm sorry."

"You're frightened. No one blames you," Rhys said.

Elena let him believe the lie. She turned to Guy and took his hand.

"I'll be right behind you," he said. "Rhys is staying up here to watch everything. You'll have both Con and me with you. You'll be safe."

"No one is safe if the bolts come out or the rope unties."

Rhys laughed and rapped his knuckles atop her helmet before he began to lower her. "With us, you're safe. You couldna be safer, lass."

She told herself not to look down, but she did it anyway. She had to breathe out of her mouth as she grew nauseated. Her fingers ached inside her gloves, which gripped the rope.

"You're almost here," Con said from below. "You're doing good, Elena."

A compliment? From Con? Her fear must really show. Elena closed her eyes and put her forehead to her hands.

"Keep looking."

Guy's whispered words floated through the fog of her trepidation. She licked her lips and forced her head up and her eyes open.

She turned her head and thought she caught a glimpse of something bounce off her headlamp. Before she could ask Rhys to slow her descent, she gasped when her gaze landed on something shiny in the rock.

"What is it?" Guy asked from above.

A second later, and he was hanging beside her. Elena leaned toward the rock wall that was easily six feet from her, but even from that vantage point, there was no mistaking the small bit reflecting her light.

"It's a gem."

"A gem?" Con asked, unimpressed.

Elena grunted in answer as she squinted to get a better look. "I think it's a yellow sapphire. Matter of fact, I'm almost positive it is."

She was lowered more until she was even with Con. He hung on one side of her and Guy on the other. Elena could only gasp as she spotted even more sapphires in the rock.

"You've got a fortune down here," she whispered in amazement. But it was Con and Guy's lack of response that intrigued her. She looked at Guy. "You knew the gems were here?"

"Aye," Con answered for Guy.

Elena turned her head to him. "Why haven't you done anything?"

"Why? We doona need the money they'll bring."

"Nor do you want people on your land," she said as understanding dawned.

Con inhaled, his nostrils flaring. "Do you think this is what caught Sloan's interest?"

Elena looked around her and then up to where she could see Rhys. She tried to think back to when she was peering down at Sloan. At one point, she'd barely been able to hear Sloan.

"No," Elena said. "She was farther down."

Guy made a motion, and the next instant Elena was moving downward again. While Con and Guy controlled their own ropes, it was Rhys who had hers.

Every few minutes, they would stop so she could look around, but she had yet to find anything that would draw Sloan's notice.

Until she saw the drawings.

"Stop!" she yelled to Rhys.

She lurched as she was instantly halted. Elena pointed to the drawings of multiple dragons on the stones, some in combat, and said, "That's what Sloan was looking at."

Con didn't say anything, simply looked at the drawings. He looked at each one as if learning it in detail, and then he started the climb back up.

Elena looked at Guy. "This isn't good, is it?"

"Nay," Guy said.

"All the dragon . . . stuff. It involves you, all of you." Everything kept pointing back to Guy, which had led her to this conclusion. But *how* was still a mystery.

"You're no' supposed to know."

"I do. So tell me the rest."

He shook his head slowly.

"Just tell me if the dragons somehow involve you," she begged.

His pale brown eyes met hers. "And if I said aye?"

"I'd ask how."

"And if I said I couldna tell you."

"I'd ask if that was why all of you are so desperate for your privacy."

He gave a single nod and glanced at Con, who was about to reach the opening. "Con willna be happy that you're piecing it together."

"Con doesn't seem happy about much."

"Come," Guy said as they left the drawings behind.

Once Elena had her feet back on the ground, she let out a laugh as she sank onto a boulder. The men turned to look at her with expressions of worry, amusement, and unease.

The more she looked at them, the harder she laughed. Every time she'd try to stop, she'd look at them and start laughing again. Now Guy and Con stood together with arms crossed, sharing an expression of exasperation while Rhys was smiling.

Finally Elena was able to pull it together. She wiped

the tears from the corners of her eyes and looked through the hole. "I feared that so very much. Now that it's over, I can't believe I was so scared."

"Your boss died," Con reminded her. "You were alone in a situation you didna know how to manage. From all Rhys and Guy told me, you handled yourself as well as could be expected."

"Careful, you might actually start to like me," she teased.

Guy's frown grew, and he took a step that put him between her and Con. Rhys was instantly on alert. He dropped the rope he'd been rolling and waited.

"It was a joke, Guy," she said.

But he didn't respond.

Elena couldn't see their faces, not even when she leaned to the side, but it was obvious something was going on.

"There's entirely too much damned testosterone around here. Knock it off, you three," she demanded.

Guy turned to face her. The fury she saw etched on his face instantly turned to desire. She had that second of warning before he hauled her up against his body and kissed her.

Deeply. Fully.

Completely.

They were both breathing heavy when he ended the kiss and rested his forehead against hers. Elena clung to him, her body shaking with need as he held her off the floor so as not to hurt her ankle.

"Guy," Con said menacingly.

Elena moved her gaze to Con. "Leave him alone."

Guy squeezed her as Rhys said something beneath his breath and turned away.

Con's gaze narrowed on her. "You'd defend him?"

"To you. To anyone. Yes."

"Interesting," Con said, and turned on his heel to fade into the darkness.

Guy slowly set her on her feet. "I'm afraid you're going to learn all the secrets you want to know."

"Is that so bad?" she asked as a shiver of dread raced down her spine.

"For me, it is."

CHAPTER ELEVEN

"I already know you're immortal."

Elena's words stopped Guy cold. He didn't bother to look at Rhys, who had frozen in place as well. Guy clipped the length of rope onto Elena's belt.

"You'd be wise no' to inform Con of that bit," Rhys said.

Elena frowned, her large, sage green eyes filled with concern. "I'm a big girl, Guy. I can handle whatever it is you don't want me to know."

He knew she could. *If* she cared for him more. *If* their feelings went deeper than just physical.

Rhys began down the path they had come, but Guy didn't follow. He looked at Elena and drank in the sight of her. If he returned with her to the mansion, Con would want to talk to her as he had Cassie. Which couldn't happen.

Then Con would demand to know if Elena loved Guy, which he knew she didn't. She cared. That, he knew with certainty. By the way she touched him, kissed him. Defended him.

But what Guy truly feared was when Con would ask

him how he felt about Elena. It wasn't a question Guy could answer, because he didn't know.

What he did know was that he couldn't get enough of her. If she stayed any longer, he wasn't sure he could let her go. Ever.

"Guy?" Rhys called.

Guy took one of Elena's gloved hands in his. "I can take you back to the mansion, where Con might want you to stay even longer. Or I can take you out the way Sloan brought you in."

"You don't want me to go back with you?"

Her voice was soft, too soft.

"You know too much, Elena. To know more is to be confined to Dreagan as we are. You have a life out there, a career you've worked hard at."

"Does my mortality have something to do with it?"

He snorted. "Never. I'm thinking of you."

"I knew what was between us couldn't last. It felt too good, too right." She pulled her hand out of his. "If you don't want me to go back with you, then I won't."

"She has to," Rhys said from beside them. "We all need to get moving. Now!"

That's when Guy felt the tremor in the mountain. He grabbed Elena's hand. "Forget the pain of your foot. We need to cover a lot of ground."

He heard her wince a couple of times, but she kept up with them as well as she could. Both he and Rhys shortened their strides to aid her.

What took them over three hours to trek going in took just over an hour returning. The cliff held them up only so long as it took Elena to climb on Guy's back before he could descend down the rope.

Once they were back in the main cavern, he pointed to the corridor that would lead to the outside and the mansion. "Go, Elena. Run as fast as you can, and get inside the house. Doona look back, no matter what you hear or think you'll see."

She nodded and was off.

He watched her for a moment before he turned to Rhys. "Was it the Silvers?"

But one look at the massive silver dragons they had bound in the cage showed they were sleeping as soundly and still as they had for millennia.

"Then what?" Rhys asked.

Guy looked around, wondering where the other Dragon Kings were. That's when realization struck.

"Sod it," he said as he took off running after Elena.

He exited the cave in time to see the amber dragon land in front of her and tilt back his head with a deafening roar.

"Tristan, dammit," Rhys said.

Their newest King was still learning what he was, but regardless, the need to protect Elena was welling up inside Guy.

He felt his dragon tattoo move and knew there was only one way to protect Elena, though in the end, he'd lose her forever.

Elena's foot throbbed so she could barely put any weight on it, but the apprehension she heard and felt in Guy's voice and touch was enough to get her running out of the cave.

She wanted to know what could have gotten them moving so fast, but all she could think about was how happy she was to be back at the mansion.

It meant more time with Guy. Despite the sense she had that he might not want her around anymore.

Elena had stopped running and was limping—slowly—to the house when she heard something behind her. A gust of wind slammed into her back, and a second later hit her in the front so that it knocked her off her feet and onto her butt.

She winced when the heel of her hand landed on a rock. But every ache and pain faded to nothing as the enormous amber-colored dragon landed in front of her.

There was no time to scream as it lifted its huge head back and let out a roar that made her ears ring. Elena took in the large, stocky body and the scales the color of polished amber.

The dragon's tail had a stinger on the end that it slammed into the ground. And then its apple green eyes riveted on her.

It took a step toward her. Its front foot had five digits, each with enormous talons that could sever her in half with just a flick.

The dragon flapped its wings and jerked its head up as something flew over Elena.

She looked up to see another muscular dragon latch on to the amber dragon's back and pull it away from her. Elena couldn't take her eyes off the new dragon. It was a deep crimson, its scales looking metallic in the sun.

The red scales shaded to a lighter hue on the underside of its neck. The short, powerful limbs of the red dragon were easily besting the amber one.

A mane of spines sprouted from the back of the red's neck and his wide head. He and the amber dragon seemed to be evenly matched. At least at first, but the red quickly took an advantage.

Someone grasped her arms and helped her to her feet. Elena glanced over to find Rhys staring at the dragons.

"Well, I guess the dragon's out of the bag," Rhys said.

Elena made a sound in the back of her throat. "Where is Guy?"

Rhys's smile was a little sad as he nodded his head toward the dragons. "You were in danger. Guy reacted as anyone would, protecting what's his."

"Protect . . ." Her voice faded away as she looked at the red dragon. "Are you telling me that magnificent red dragon is—?"

"Aye, it's Guy."

Elena knew she should be completely freaking out at the moment, but all she could think about was how cool it was to have her lover be able to change into a dragon.

"Guy isn't going to kill the other one, is he?" Elena asked.

"Nay. The Amber is our newest member. He's just learning everything. With your arrival, everyone was told to keep out of sight and to make sure no one shifted. I guess it was too much for Tristan."

"Who is Tristan? How did he become a dragon?" That's when she remembered Guy telling her something about a Tristan.

"Questions we'd all like answered," Con said as he came up on her other side. "Tristan is no' his real name. He can no' remember anything, so Guy named him. I'm sorry Tristan charged you. I doona believe he meant you harm."

Rhys gave a loud snort of disbelief. "Obviously Guy thought differently. I'll go break this little fun up."

Elena took a step back when Rhys took off running and then suddenly changed into a yellow dragon. And true to his word, he broke up the fight between Guy and Tristan quickly.

She turned to Con. "You aren't angry that I know?"

"I should be," he said wearily. "The truth is, I've seen it coming since Guy brought you into the house. There was something between the two of you even then."

"It's physical. That's what's between us."

"Hmm. I wonder if it was just the physical that had you defending him, or why he would attack Tristan to keep you safe."

Elena turned to look for the crimson dragon that

seemed to draw her gaze only to see Guy standing naked in the open field alone.

She took a step toward him, and then another. Another and another. For each one she took, Guy took two until they were standing face-to-face.

"Now you know."

She nodded and began to reach out to touch him, but drew back, wondering if he'd even want her touch. "In dragon form, you look like the dragon tattooed on your back."

"That's because I'm King of the Reds."

She looked away, an ache beginning in her chest at the dead tone of his voice. "You wanted me to leave. Was it because you didn't want me to know your secrets? Or was it because you'd grown tired of me?"

Elena kept her gaze on the grass because she couldn't bear to look into his eyes and learn that he was tired of her, not after she'd begun to realize her feelings for him.

His finger touched her chin and lifted her face until she was looking at him. He unbuckled her helmet and let it fall to the ground. Then he cupped her face in his hands and lowered his mouth to hers.

Elation swept through Elena at his kiss. She wanted to delve into the kiss, but he pulled back too suddenly.

"I doona want you to ever leave," he said. "There is much you doona know about me and about the Kings."

"And there is much you don't know about me. I have awful habits, Guy, like switching radio stations constantly until I find a song I like. I can't stand commercials."

"I'm as old as time itself," he said. "I was once a dragon, but was changed when mankind began to roam the earth. I'm, apparently, quite protective of you."

"Tell me your story. I want to know all of it."

He nodded and lifted her in his arms as he walked back to the mountain. She didn't say a word as he took her down several hallway like caves that opened up to a cavern. Inside the cavern was a gigantic cage with silver dragons inside.

Guy set her down and retrieved a pair of jeans for himself before he sat beside her. "Are you sure you want to know?"

"Yes. I want to know everything," she said, and took his hand.

"Each dragon who ruled their clan was changed. We were able to shift from dragon to human and back again as many times and as often as needed. We were created so that mankind and dragon could exist together."

Elena looked at the silver dragons and wondered what kind of world that had been. "Did it last long?"

"No' as long as we'd hoped. Many Kings took humans as their mates."

"How did that work with the humans being mortal?"

"When love is shared, when the King finds the woman meant for him, they can bind themselves together. The human will stay immortal as long as her King lives."

Elena's eyes grew round. "Wow. Children?"

"None were carried to term."

"How sad. Why do I have a feeling this human-and-King relationship didn't go well?"

Guy sighed, his lips pressing into a desolate line. "There was one of us, Ulrik, who was about to be bound to a female. Discord had begun throughout the land amongst dragons and humans alike. We couldna find the source. And then the unthinkable happened. Humans began to hunt dragons."

"Did the dragons retaliate?"

"They wanted to. They begged us, but Con refused. Though we are Kings, it is Constantine who is King over all of us. He said we were meant to keep mankind safe, and that didn't mean slaughtering them in war. Ulrik, however, didn't agree. There were many of us who didn't agree with Con, but only Ulrik disobeyed."

"He went after the humans?"

Guy was silent for a moment. "No' just any human. He and his Silvers were hunting the dragon hunters. They were succeeding, too."

"But?" Elena said, a sick feeling in her stomach.

"We discovered Ulrik's woman was betraying him. She was the one turning humans against the dragons, and dragons against humans."

"Why? I thought she loved Ulrik?"

Guy shrugged and looked into the distance. "She loved him as a man, but no' as a dragon. At least that's what Con believes."

Elena squeezed his hand and put her head on his shoulder. "What happened?"

"We found the female as she was about to betray Ulrik. We killed her, Elena. I think Ulrik would have cast her aside had we gone to him with the truth, but we killed his woman. Whatever chance we had of reaching him was gone in that instant. Ulrik was mad with rage and the need for revenge. He instigated the war between dragons and humans."

Elena winced, but didn't speak. She didn't want to interrupt the story.

"Dragons heal, but not instantly. When a dragon was wounded and fell, the humans killed it. Dragons were killing humans. Something had to be done, and our options were few. We did the only thing we could. We sent the dragons to safety, away from the humans who could hurt them."

"And Ulrik? Did you kill him?"

"Nay, though it might have been kinder had we."

"I don't understand."

"It's a part of who we are to shift, Elena, and to speak to the dragons we rule. We took away Ulrik's power as King. He can no' shift, nor can he talk to his Silvers."

She threaded her fingers with his. "I think you all ended up punishing yourselves as well, then."

"Aye, but we had no choice. We were able to catch a few of the Silvers before they left this world. We keep them asleep with our dragon magic, because the only way they can wake is by Ulrik. If that happens, the war will begin again. And mankind will be wiped out."

CHAPTER TWELVE

Guy looked at the Silvers and wondered if Ulrik's need for revenge had faded over the millennia, or if it had grown.

"So Ulrik is still around?" Elena asked.

Guy nodded. "Oh, aye. We keep an eye on him. It's part of his punishment for attacking the humans to be immortal, but no' to be able to be a King."

"That seems . . . cruel. It was the humans who hunted the dragons. I wasn't there, so this may sound like I'm pitying Ulrik, but I think I would've sided with him. The humans had no right to hunt the dragons if everyone was living peacefully."

He smiled at her and smoothed the furrow of her brow with his finger. "It's easy to look back now and know what we could've and should've done. At the time, emotions were running high and war was imminent."

"So you say you're immortal. Can nothing kill you? You're safe from everything?"

Guy rose and pulled her up with him. He led her to the Silvers and placed his hand atop one of the immense dragons heads. "We can be killed, Elena."

"How?"

"Touch the dragon. He's asleep and can no' feel anything."

She delayed a moment before she laid her hand beside his. "The scales are warm. I wasn't expecting that."

"There is magic in dragons. You should've seen it when we reigned, before there was man. Dragons of every color and size ruled the skies, the water, and the land."

He pulled himself back from the memory he had held on to through the passage of time. "In dragon form, another dragon can kill us. It isna easy because we're Kings, but it can be done. It has been done. We lost many Kings during the war before we contained it."

"What happened to the dragons who lost their King?" she asked as she slowly stroked the Silver.

"Other Kings stepped in to rule them. We didna think any more Kings would ever be made, until Tristan showed up five months ago."

She frowned and bit her lip. "Is that a good sign?"

"No, especially when it coincided with two other events."

"Which where?"

Guy knelt beside the Silver closest to him and put his hand in front of the dragon's nose as a rush of wind blasted his hand from the dragon's breath.

"The Silvers moved."

Elena yanked her hand away and took a step back. "They moved?"

"Aye. We doona know how. It was just an instant, but they moved. It shouldna have happened."

"And the second event?"

Guy rubbed the Silver's snout and straightened. "With the betrayal of Ulrik's woman, it did something to Con. He didna want us to ever be in that position again. So, we all joined our dragon magic and bound our emotions."

"Excuse me?" she said in half surprise, half outrage.

"We feel things like hunger, laughter, anger, happiness, and such. What we did was prevent ourselves from becoming entangled with a human."

"You have no human friends or lovers?"

He shook his head slowly. "None. Until five months ago when Hal, another King, fell in love with a human. Hal wouldna give Cassie up, and she wouldna give him up. Con tested her to see if she could love the man and the dragon."

"Did she pass?"

"Aye," Guy said with a smile. "They are bonded. I can no' remember the last time I saw a King bonded to a human."

"Is the magic used to sever your emotions gone?"

This was what Guy had dreaded answering, the question he knew she would ask. "For five months, my answer would have been the magic is still in place. And then I met you. I feel things I'm no' supposed to. Things that I doona know what to make of."

She looked away before walking around the great cage. For several minutes, he watched her, waiting and hoping for her to say something.

When she didn't, he asked, "Do you no' have anything to say?"

"I don't know what to say. These past couple of days have turned my world upside down again and again. I hate Con for keeping me here against my will, but when you wanted me to leave, I've never felt so crushed in my life."

She stopped as she made her way back to him. "I thought what was between us was just physical. All I can think about is you. When you're near, I want to be beside you, I want you touching me, even if it's just holding my hand."

"Is that all you want from me?"

"No," she said, her eyes wide with torment. She lifted

her face to the ceiling of the cavern. "Oh, God. This is happening too fast. I can't wrap my head around it."

Guy pulled her into his arms and simply held her. He closed his eyes when her arms wrapped around him. "I've never told a human I was immortal before. You believed me. Even when you saw Tristan and then me change into a dragon, you didna run away in fear. Why?"

"I was scared, which is why I couldn't move. I just knew Tristan was going to eat me. And then I saw you, before I knew it was you. You protected me, fought for me. No man has ever done that."

"I'm no' just a man."

"No," she said, and leaned back to look at him. "You're dragon. Maybe that's what's different about you. Maybe that's why I'm drawn to you so."

He tucked a wavy blond lock behind her ear. "Doona leave me yet, Elena. Give me time to win you."

"That's the problem," she said with a small laugh as her eyes filled with tears. "You already have, Guy."

He could hardly breathe with her revelation. "If you stay, you need to understand things are changing, and I fear the danger could only get worse."

"From Tristan?"

"Nay. The Silvers. And whoever sent Sloan here. If our secret is discovered, war will come again."

She sighed harshly. "And you'll be killed. You know the weapons humans have developed now. Nuclear bombs, rockets fired from thousands of miles away, and poisonous gases."

"We'd survive every one," he said with a smile. "I told you how we could be killed in dragon form. In human form, the only way to kill us is if another King uses his sword."

Elena rolled her eyes. "Oh, please, Guy. Everything immortal has to be killed somehow. I mean, you can't survive if they cut off your head."

"Want to give it a try?"

Her eyes widened again and she hit his arm. "Uh, thanks but no thanks. Can you be serious?"

"I am. When I say nothing can kill us besides a King wielding his sword, I mean it, Elena."

"How?"

"Magic. Dragon magic."

She lowered her gaze to his chest, her nervousness palpable. "Do you want me to stay?"

"More than anything," he said gently as he lifted her face to his. "You've made me feel again, and I doona want to ever lose that."

"How long?"

His brow furrowed at her question. "What?"

"How long do you want me to stay?"

He gazed into her sage green eyes and wanted to speak from his heart, but he paused. It would be asking too much of her too soon. He realized his feelings for her went deep, deeper than he ever thought to feel for anyone, but she had yet to tell him of her love.

"I want you to stay as long as I can have you."

"I get to choose?"

"Aye," he said with a nod. "Understand, Elena, if you stay, you can never bring anyone here. No one can know where you're at or who you're with."

"I know."

"And your job?" He hated asking the question, but she needed to be reminded of why she was in Britain at all.

The fact she looked away caused his worry to grow.

"You mean I'd have to give up the job I've sacrificed everything for?"

"Aye."

Silence stretched, and it nearly killed Guy. He buried his frustration and forced a smile as he took her hands in his. "This is a big decision, one you shouldna make hastily. Besides, you've a lot to take in after today. Let's get back to the house and get you something to eat."

She didn't pull her hand away as they walked from the cave. That the only thing that kept Guy from throwing all caution to the wind and shifting so he could take to the skies.

At the door to the house, he paused before following her in. When she looked at him and tucked a strand of her blond hair behind her ear, he said, "I need to check on Tristan. Maybe my clobbering jarred his memory, and he can tell us his name."

Guy let the door close before she could respond. He walked away, knowing he had lost Elena. He hadn't wanted the feelings she evoked within him, but now that he'd experienced them, he couldn't imagine life without her.

But it was going to be a life without her. Her career was too important. And he . . . wasn't enough.

Guy wasn't paying attention to where he walked until he found himself blocked in the mountain by Rhys and Tristan.

"I doona like the name Tristan," Tristan said.

Guy shrugged. "Then remember your own name."

"I wouldna have harmed her."

Guy looped his thumbs in his front pockets of his jeans. "You frightened her. I couldna allow that."

Rhys crossed his arms over his chest and stepped in front of Guy when he tried to leave. "What happened?" he demanded.

Guy laughed as he looked away. He wanted to be alone with his thoughts, but it seemed his friends wouldn't let him. "It doesna matter."

"Is it as Con fears? Does Elena fear you as a dragon?"

"Nay," Guy answered softly. "I told her everything, and she accepted it all. She even touched the Silvers."

Tristan shifted his feet. “Then I doona understand.”

“She wanted to stay. Until I told her it meant giving up her career,” Guy explained.

“Shit,” Rhys said.

Guy nodded. “Exactly.”

CHAPTER THIRTEEN

Elena sat in her room, her legs drawn up to her chest as she gazed out the window. The sky had darkened, and rain splattered against the windows.

It was as if her own emotions had brought the rain. The storm was able to shed the tears she couldn't.

"You're still here."

She jumped at the sound of Con's voice behind her, but she didn't bother to turn around. "I am."

"Even though you've chosen your career over Guy?"

The anger in his voice made her want to turn around and shout at him, but she didn't have the heart for it. Because Con had every right to be furious at her.

"I've sacrificed everything to get to London."

He snorted. A few moments later, he stood between her and the window. As usual he was perfectly dressed in slacks and a button-down with his long blond hair pulled back in a queue and his black eyes zeroed in on her. "Now you know why I doona want our secret revealed."

"I won't tell anyone," she promised.

"It doesna matter anymore. You've made your choice. In a bit, every memory you have of Guy, the dragons, and everything you learned here will be erased."

That got her to her feet. Her chest heaved with indignation. "You can't do that."

"Aye, I can. I do it to protect what we've kept secret for thousands of years. I do it to protect Guy. After what happened to Ulrik, after what I was forced to do to his woman, I vowed I'd never have another of my Kings hurt again."

"You're going to take away my memories of him, memories that would sustain me in the years to come?"

"It's your choice," he said with finality.

Elena slumped down into the chair. "When I was sixteen, I fell hard for this guy at school. He was a jock and one of the cutest guys, and he started talking to me."

She looked up at Con and laughed. "I thought it was the best time of my life. Up until I allowed my enjoyment of his kisses to cloud my judgment to make a wrong call in my life."

"What was the wrong decision?"

"I chose the football guy over an interview for a scholarship to the University of Georgia. I lost the chance at the scholarship, and it turns out the guy only wanted sex."

Con leaned a shoulder against the windowsill and sighed, his dark eyes taking a far away look. "We've lived in this world as men, but always we pine for what once was. I see my men looking to the sky, the yearning to spread their wings there for all to see. It was my decision that destined us to this life. Was it the right decision? Even now I know that it was."

"But," she urged when he hesitated.

He chuckled and turned his head to her. "But if I had taken just a few moments and thought about what would happen with Ulrik, about what I'd be forced to do, I doona know what I would've done."

"What are you trying to say?"

"That sometimes the decision we think we should

make isna always the right one. You say you want to keep your memories of Guy. Why?"

She looked away from Con's black eyes that saw too much. "Because no one has ever made me feel as he does. And I know no one ever will again."

"Are you frightened of what he is?"

"Meaning a dragon shifter?" she asked, and then shook her head. "No. I think it's amazing that he exists at all. I'll admit the sight does evoke fear at first, but seeing him as a dragon was mesmerizing."

Con rubbed his chin. "You care for him as a man, and you care for him as a dragon?"

"Yes. As odd as that might sound, yes." She laughed then. "If I hadn't known Guy, before I might have died of fright on the spot, but knowing the man he is helped me quickly get past the fear. That and the fact he stopped Tristan from eating me."

Con chuckled at her words. "I doona know what's coming for me and my men in the next months or years, Elena, but I know Guy is going to need you. I could have Guy erase your thoughts of your career to keep you here, but I know he wouldna do that to you."

She stared at him as he came over and placed his hand on her injured ankle. Elena felt something warm rush through her, and instantly the pain of her ankle vanished as if it had never been. She knew without asking that Con had healed her.

He straightened. "All I ask is that you think long and hard about why you care for him so much. And then tell me if your career staring at gems will keep you warm in the years ahead of you."

His words reverberated in her head long after he'd left her alone. Elena knew Con was right, but she'd made a hasty decision once before that had cost her so much. She was afraid of doing the same thing again.

And then she thought of her life in London, a life without Guy. She'd thought she hated it in Scotland, but she was really coming to love the land.

The quiet, the beauty. The enchantment of it all.

London was crowded, noisy, and filthy.

She groaned as she thought of how lonely her life would be in London. Once more, she'd be working long hours late into the night. There would be no social life for her, because she'd continue to try to climb the career ladder.

It's all she'd ever wanted. Or all she'd ever used to want. Now she wanted something else.

She wanted Guy.

Movement through the rain caught her attention. Elena jumped up when she saw Guy walking away from the mansion and into the woods on the far slope.

Without another thought, Elena was running out of her room, down the stairs, and then into the rain. The rain instantly plastered her clothes to her, and the chill had her teeth chattering.

She kept running, even when she slipped on the wet grass again and again. Elena paused only once she was atop the hill and in the trees.

Her side had a stitch in it and her lungs burned, but she wasn't going to give up on finding Guy. She didn't allow herself to think of what she would say when she found him, though.

Elena started running again, searching through the thick forest and the rain for some glimpse of Guy. She cursed inwardly when she saw him heading over the next peak.

It took everything Elena had not to fall on her way down the valley. Her pace slowed, however, and it took her twice as long to climb the next rise.

The rain was coming harder and the wind had picked up, slinging the rain in her face so that it felt like shards of ice hitting her.

Elena raised an arm to help shield her face as she finished the last of her climb. She prayed Guy was there because she didn't think she had the strength to go on much longer in this weather.

And then there he was.

She stopped and watched him as he stood on the edge of a sheer drop-off, his arms spread wide as his face lifted to the clouds and the long locks of his dark hair flying about in the wind. Elena hadn't realized how steep the mountains were until that moment.

The bright green grass mixed with the dark rock face. It was beautiful to behold, but nothing compared to the sight of Guy shirtless, his tattoo and plentiful muscles there for her to see.

The rain and mist surrounding the mountains prevented her from seeing how far up the mountain went, but that didn't matter. Nothing mattered now that she'd found Guy.

She took a step toward him, and promptly slipped. Her hands caught her before she completely lost her balance. When she stood, a scream locked in her throat as Guy jumped.

Elena ran to the edge, sliding to a halt, just in time to see Guy shift into a dragon. His wide crimson wings caught a current and swept him high into the sky.

He flew up, then dived straight down, his wings tucked against his body. As he neared the ground, his wings spread and took him once more into the sky.

With his long tail streaming behind him, Elena watched as Guy rolled and dipped, turned and dived. For the first time, she saw who he really was—man and dragon.

He'd asked for nothing of her, even when he knew she had chosen her career over him. He hadn't yelled, hadn't given her an ultimatum.

He'd let her go.

Guy had protected her, fought for her, and loved her. She had rewarded him by walking away. What kind of woman did that? What kind of woman had the man of her dreams hold her at night and chose cold gemstones over him?

"Not me," she whispered.

Elena didn't know how long she watched Guy before he noticed her. He flew into the valley behind her. She turned and started down the mountain as he shifted back into human form.

"What are you doing here?" he shouted over the rain as he stood naked and glaring at her.

She shrugged as she approached and said, "I saw you from the house."

"You could have fallen. I wouldna have known, Elena. You could have died!"

"I love you," she said, surprising herself and him. She laughed then. "Oh, God. I do. I love you, Guy."

He stood there with his mouth parted simply staring at her for the longest time, and then he jerked her against his body, his mouth sealing over hers.

Elena clung to him and his heat. The kiss was hard and fierce, but she welcomed it, welcomed him.

He ended the kiss and looked down at her. "I thought . . ."

"I know," she said. "I did, too. But then I realized I have no life without you. You are what I've been looking for my entire life, not the gems. I know I hurt you earlier, and I'm sorry. I'll spend the rest of my life making it up to you and proving that I love you."

"Elena—"

"Please," she said over him. "Please let me stay with you, Guy."

He held her face in his hands and smiled. "Are you sure?"

"That I want to stay? Yes."

"No," he said with a laugh. "Are you sure you love me?"

She nodded. "Yes. Oh, yes. I love you."

His eyes closed for a moment before he swept her up in his arms with a wide grin. "I love you, Elena Griffin. I love you!"

Guy would have made love to Elena right then, but he felt her shivering against him. So he gathered her in his arms and ran back to the mansion.

They were laughing and dripping water all through the house as they ran up to her room. They burst through the door and came to a halt when they found Con sitting in a chair with his back to them.

"Con?" Guy asked. "What is it?"

"I just got a call from Banan. Someone knows about us."

Guy gripped Elena's hand as Con's words sank into his mind. All the laughter and happiness faded. "Who?"

"Banan is trying to find out." Con rose and faced them. "I'm glad to see the two of you together. It looks like you made the right decision, Elena."

She smiled as she looked at Guy. "Yes, I did."

"I'm afraid I'm going to have to ask you both to hold off the binding ceremony."

Guy kissed the back of Elena's hand. "I thought we'd wait anyway to give Elena some time, since everything has happened so fast."

"I'm ready right now," she said with grin.

"We have time," Guy insisted.

Con walked to the door and stopped. "I have a favor, Elena."

"Nay," Guy said as he comprehended what Con was going to ask.

Elena looked from Guy to Con and back to Guy. "What is it?"

"Con wants to use you as bait," Guy ground out.

Con sighed. "Nay, I doona wish that. The truth, Elena,

is that I think the only way we'll discover who sent Sloan here is through you."

"I see," she said slowly. She looked at Guy. "It makes sense. No one will suspect that I've fallen in love with someone here. They'll buy whatever story I give them. I'll tell them that I stayed here because of my ankle."

"I doona like it," Guy said. "I willna be able to protect you."

"No one knows you. You can be there, just not with me."

Guy squeezed her hand. "I can no' lose you, Elena."

"I willna let that happen," Con promised.

Elena smiled as she faced Guy. "Think of it as an adventure. I've gotten to see your world. You'll get to see mine until we uncover who is threatening Dreagan and all of you."

"Or until you're in danger." Guy forced her to look at him. "At the first sign of a threat to you, I'm bringing you home."

"Home," she said with a smile. "Yes, this is home now."

Guy was able to return her smile.

"I'm sorry I ask this of both of you," Con said. "I'd ask someone else if I could. Hal and Cassie are on their way back, and I've sent Laith to rendezvous with Banan in London. You'll have those two along with Guy for protection, Elena."

"It'll be enough. I'm glad you asked me. I feel a part of this family now. I'll find what you need to know."

Guy gave Con a nod. "Elena, you've been a part of us since the moment you kissed me."

"You leave in the morning. Get some rest," Con said.

But rest wasn't what Guy had in mind as they ran to her room. He was in such a haste to pull off Elena's long-sleeve shirt that he tore it. They laughed as they fell together on the bed.

EPILOGUE

Elena gave Guy one final kiss before she walked out of the mansion and into the waiting helicopter that would return her to London.

She hated to leave, but it had been worse for Guy. He'd come up with all sorts of arguments as to why she shouldn't go without him. It had taken her and Con both to make him realize they couldn't be seen together lest anyone realize who he was. Still, Elena hated it.

She kept her eyes closed the entire ride back to London. It was her first helicopter ride, but all she could think about was crimson dragons and Guy's kisses.

When she arrived in London, it was to find PureGems had a car waiting for her. She got out of the helicopter and the door to the black Mercedes opened and Richard Arnold, Sloan's boss, greeted her.

"Elena, I'm so glad you've gotten out of this ordeal with nothing more than a sprained ankle. I hope those at Dreagan treated you well."

She shook Richard's hand, but couldn't stop being suspicious of him. "I'm just glad to be home. I still can't believe Sloan is gone."

"A few days off are in order. I insist," he said when she

started to decline. "We can catch up on everything when you get back. And I want to know everything there is to know about those at Dreagan, Elena."

"Of course."

Richard smiled and turned as another car pulled up. "I have a meeting, but you'll be driven home. It's the least we can do."

Elena climbed into the car, a feeling of dread descending upon her. Everyone at Dreagan was counting on her. She wouldn't let them down.

Something caught her attention out of the corner of her eye. That's when she saw Guy. He stood in the shadows, but he was there. Watching her.

Together they would find out who was putting the Dragon Kings at risk. And they would stop it.

"Your address, Miss Griffin?"

She gasped as she looked to the driver to find Banan's gray gaze staring at her through the rearview mirror. A slow smile spread as she realized that no one stood a chance against the Dragon Kings.

No one.

DAWN'S DESIRE

CHAPTER ONE

London, June 2012

Banan glanced at Elena Griffin in the rearview mirror as he merged into traffic from the helicopter pad. They didn't speak, because as far as the world knew, they didn't know each other.

It was a dangerous game they played with Elena's life, but she was their only link to discovering what was going on at PureGems.

Banan tightened his grip on the steering wheel. The realization that someone at PureGems knew the secret so carefully guarded at Dreagan left him furious. He couldn't wait to discover who it was, and when he did, he was going to make sure their secret stayed hidden.

He and the others who called Dreagan home kept what they were a secret for a reason. The world couldn't know about them. It was bad enough that two human females now knew. After several millennia of it being just the men, having females about seemed . . . odd.

And human ones, at that.

But Elena and Cassie weren't just any humans. They had the love of a Dragon King—a rare event for sure.

Because of that, Banan would risk his own life to keep the women safe.

Fortunately for him, he only had to worry about Elena right now. He wasn't alone though. Banan inwardly smiled because he knew Guy was near, watching Elena. There was no way Guy would allow his woman out of his sight for long. Guy had wanted to be the one driving her, but both Elena and Banan knew in order for their careful planning to work, Guy had to keep his distance.

So Guy relented. Sort of.

"I hope we're doing the right thing," Elena said in her American accent as she lifted her mobile phone to her ear and pretended to use it so they could talk.

Banan slowed the car to a stop in front of a traffic light and watched a mob of people walk across the street in front of the vehicle. "There's no other way. We've been over this."

"I know. It's just . . ." She paused and sighed. "I worked hard to get promoted to this position in London. PureGems is supposed to be one of the top five companies in the world to work for. How would they have learned about you and the others? More importantly, why do they want to know?"

They were good questions, and ones Banan desperately wanted answered. The fact he and the others were dragon shifters had been a vigilantly shielded secret since they had sent all the dragons to another realm eons ago.

Banan clenched his jaw as thoughts of the dragons and the life he'd once had began to fill him. Instantly, he shut off those memories. He couldn't allow them.

Ever.

He'd racked his brain, trying to determine how anyone would know what they were. Their company, and their home, Dreagan Industries, was situated deep in the Highlands—very nearly impossible to reach.

He and the others who owned and ran Dreagan had gone out of their way to keep what they were hidden, which was difficult considering they made one of the finest scotches in all the world. But concealing their true identities had been something they'd done since the war with the humans had nearly ended both species.

It wasn't always easy in this time of video cameras on every street corner, satellites, and mobile phones to keep the truth that they could shift into dragons from everyone. People were more aware of others, and if someone tried to hide, they would search even harder to discover just what that person was withholding and why.

Which was why they were careful not to appear as if they were hiding. They were walking on a knife's edge, and one stumble could end it all.

That stumble nearly happened when Elena and her boss, Sloan, had gone caving on Dreagan land. Sloan had died, and the Dragon Kings saved Elena in the nick of time.

Banan glanced up at the sky through the buildings cluttering London as he pressed the accelerator and proceeded through the intersection.

Anger simmered at the freedom he was denied. It had been decades since he dared to spread his wings and take to the sky. There had been a time dragons outnumbered people, but that time was so long ago it almost seemed a dream now.

Banan pressed his lips together. He was a Dragon King, but he no longer had any dragons to rule. They were gone. But at least they were safe.

"All you have to do is discover what they know," Banan said to Elena in order to turn his mind off the past. "Guy will make sure you are no' harmed."

"And you?" she whispered, her gaze meeting his in the rearview mirror.

Banan grinned confidently. "I'm here to ensure that

whoever it is who dared to send people onto our land and see us in dragon form can no' talk anymore."

Elena shivered, but lowered her phone and dropped it into her purse. There was no more need for words. It had been said over and over again. And the plan was flawless.

PureGems contacted Elena after learning Sloan had died while they were caving on Dreagan land. It hadn't taken Elena and Guy long to give in to their attraction, or for Elena to tell him all she knew.

Which, fortunately for Guy, hadn't been very much. Yet Elena wanted to get to the bottom of it just as much as the Dragon Kings did.

So when PureGems offered to fly Elena back to London via helicopter, their plan was set into motion. With all Dreagan's connections, it was easy enough for Banan to take the place of a driver at PureGems.

He, Guy, and Rhys made the trip to London ahead of Elena, and it had taken everything he had to keep Guy from going to his woman and ruining their carefully thought-out plan.

As Banan pulled to the curb in front of PureGems, he spotted Rhys hiding in an alley across the street. Banan would hazard a guess that Guy was up on a rooftop somewhere, observing.

"Remember, Elena, as soon as you have information, get out," Banan said. "Guy willna wait long for you."

She leaned forward and grasped the handle of the door. "Just make sure Guy doesn't get hurt."

Banan turned his head and smiled as he rested his arm across the back of the seat. "You keep forgetting we're immortal."

"I don't forget," she said with a roll of her eyes. "I just can't quite believe nothing will harm any of you. I'm doing this to keep Guy and all the Dragon Kings at Dreagan secret."

"And we appreciate it more than you know."

She put her hand atop his. "I hope I can get the information. I've not been here that long. They don't trust me fully yet."

"And Guy willna allow you to risk your life too long. See what you can get. If it's no' enough, then we'll figure out another way. The main thing is that you come out of this unharmed. Guy would never survive something happening to you."

She gave a nod and slid out of the Mercedes. Banan watched until she was inside PureGems before he turned his head to where Rhys hid.

For eons, the magic they used to block romantic feelings and prevent close bonds with humans had never failed. Why had that suddenly changed? Banan had seen how Hal and Guy reacted upon falling for their women.

He didn't want to do the same.

Too much was at stake for him to allow emotions to get in the way. They would only complicate his duty, which was why—no matter what—he wasn't going to allow some woman to jeopardize that.

Jane Holden twisted her ankle as she stepped onto the elevator. "Damn," she muttered, and leaned a shoulder against the wall so she could take her weight off the injury.

"Beautiful shoes."

For the first time, Jane realized she wasn't alone. She looked over at the blond beauty and realized who she was. "You're Elena Griffin. I'm glad you're back, and so very sorry about Sloan. It was such a tragic event."

Elena's smile was forced, but Jane didn't hold it against her. She'd been through a traumatic experience in that awful mountain in the Highlands of Scotland.

"You're from the States as well?" Elena asked, her sage green eyes kind.

Jane looked at the floor to hide her embarrassment

over her clumsiness and tenderly put some weight on her ankle. She wasn't surprised Elena hadn't noticed her before. No one ever noticed her unless she was being her usual klutzy self.

Whereas Elena was stunning, and literally stopped men in their tracks with her wavy blond hair and green eyes, Jane was plain. She'd prayed as a little girl that she would grow out of the nickname Plain Jane, but she'd not been so fortunate.

Her features were too stark, her eyes too large, and her lips too full. Her hair was an awful shade of auburn that couldn't decide whether to be brown or red.

Jane cleared her throat when she realized she hadn't answered. "Yes. Seattle, actually."

"What brings you to London?"

She was wondering how to answer Elena when the elevator stopped and the doors opened. Jane stayed in the back corner as Elena stepped onto the top floor of PureGems and was immediately surrounded by people.

Jane watched her for a moment. She envied how easily Elena carried herself around people. It wasn't until the doors began to close that Jane leaped forward to stop them and dropped her armful of papers in the process.

Her body prevented the doors from closing as she hastily gathered the spilled papers and straightened. She swallowed and smiled when she realized everyone was staring at her with a mixture of laughter and horror.

Jane was forever doing stupid things. Apparently, being a klutz had been programmed into her DNA. Her mother had often joked that it took skill to fall on a flat surface, which Jane did often.

All Jane knew was that it was mortifying.

She straightened her pencil skirt with her free hand and walked to her desk, praying she made it without incident. After plopping the mound of papers on her desk, she sat down with a sigh.

"Jane!"

She jumped when Richard Arnold's voice bellowed through the speaker on her desk phone. His voice was full of distaste, and he always looked down on her Americanisms, as if his being British made him a better person.

Jane leaped to her feet and hurried to open the door to his office. She poked her head in and asked, "Yes, sir?"

"Did I hear right? Is Ms. Griffin finally back?"

"Yes, sir. I just rode up the elevator with Elena."

"Lift. It's a lift, Jane. How long is it going to take for you to get it right? Now, why isn't Elena in my office?" Richard asked as he leaned back in his large leather chair and steepled his fingers.

Jane glanced out the windows lining his office wall at the stunning view of London. "People are very fond of her, sir. Elena didn't get two steps off the elevator—"

"Lift," he interrupted.

Jane paused. She hated when he interjected terms they used in Britain. Sometimes she used an American term just to annoy him.

"The lift, then. She got off the lift and was instantly surrounded. I'm sure she'll be along shortly."

Richard sat up and braced his arms on his desk, his dark eyes cold. "Go find her. Now."

"Yes, sir." She closed the door and looked at the stack of papers she'd dropped and needed to get to work on. It was going to be another late night.

Jane walked down the hall to Elena's office and found her standing in the middle of the room, staring blankly at her desk.

"Are you all right?" Jane asked softly so as not to startle her.

Elena whirled around in surprise. A sad smile pulled at her lips when she saw it was Jane. "I'm fine. I was just remembering the last time I was here, Sloan was telling me we were going caving."

"I know this must be difficult. I wish you had more time to adjust—"

Elena laughed and set down her purse. "Let me guess. Richard wants to see me?"

"I think it has to do with the necklace the earl wants made for his daughter's eighteenth birthday."

Elena ran her fingers through her wealth of blond hair before gathering the locks into one hand and securing them into a ponytail. "Well, we mustn't keep Richard waiting."

Jane followed Elena as they made their way to Richard's office. Jane resumed her position behind her desk and began to sort through the pile of papers and manila folders.

She lost track of time, but when she finished sorting the papers, she looked up to find Elena standing beside her desk.

"Do you need me to get you anything?" Jane asked.

Elena frowned. "What? Oh, no. I'm just thinking. Jane, did anyone work in my office while I was gone?"

"I know Mr. Arnold went in there a couple of times looking for things while he handled some of your clients. Is something missing?"

"No," Elena said, a small frown marring her forehead. "No, I don't believe there is. How long have you worked here?"

"Since last summer. Just about a year." Jane was beginning to suspect there was more to Elena's questions than met the eye. She glanced at Richard's closed door and lowered her voice before she asked, "Should I be looking for another job? I know Mr. Arnold isn't exactly thrilled with my work."

Elena smiled and leaned down next to Jane. "He's British," she replied in a whisper. "He thinks he's perfect."

Jane couldn't help but return her smile. Elena always put everyone at ease, which was why she'd climbed the

She should be flirting, but Jane didn't know how to flirt. She wasn't coy or beguiling. She hated the games people played, and just wanted to find a man she could be herself around.

Every fall, ditzy moment, and disaster she had.

His half smile grew, crinkling the corners of his unusual gray eyes. "That would be me. I'm Banan."

"Banan," she repeated, letting the name roll through her mind. She liked the name.

He gently guided her to where he had parked the Mercedes. "You must be Jane Holden."

"Yes."

He opened the car door, and she easily slid into the backseat. "I'll get you to the airport in plenty of time."

Jane smiled as she rested her head back against the seat. With a grin like Banan's directed at her, for the first time in her life she didn't feel like a Plain Jane.

And she had managed to walk to the car and get in it without incident. Maybe the day was looking up.

latter of success at PureGems so quickly. Her clients loved her. Coworkers loved her.

Everyone loved her.

"Jane!" Richard's voice shouted again through the desk phone.

She hurriedly rose to her feet, only to be stopped by Elena's hand on her arm.

"He treats you poorly," Elena said, her sage green eyes holding a wealth of sadness and a measure of anger.

Jane shrugged. "Yes, but it's a good job, and I really like my flat. In order to keep it, I need the money he's paying me."

"Jane!" This time his voice bellowed through the door.

Elena's brows snapped together. "I don't care. No one should be treated like that. Don't let him do it to you, Jane."

Jane wanted to acknowledge that Elena was right, but she needed every penny earned—a beggar couldn't be choosy.

"Thank you," she said before she rushed to see what he needed, only to find herself running errands more suited to a mailroom clerk.

Richard kept her dashing about the rest of the day. She even missed lunch. When she finally looked up from the letter she was drafting to grab a drink of water, she noticed it was after six.

Then she saw a sticky note on her computer. She was supposed to go with a company driver and pick up a client at the airport a half hour ago.

Jane grabbed her purse, nearly falling on her face as she jumped up from her chair, and ran to the elevator. Fortunately, she didn't have to wait long for it to arrive, but every second felt like an eternity. She could just imagine how Mr. Arnold would react when he learned she'd been late to pick up his client. It could very well be the end of her employment at PureGems.

By the time she reached the bottom floor, she had all kinds of excuses lined up to present the client, as well as ways to make it up to them.

Jane pushed open the door, and her foot came out of her shoe when she took a step. She tried to turn around to get it—only to find people behind her, stomping on her shoe. Jane dodged several shoulders only to have a briefcase slam into her back as she grabbed her wayward shoe and put it back on.

A rumble of thunder greeted her on the sidewalk as she straightened. A quick look around showed her there was no car waiting. Had they left? Had Richard sent someone else and not told her?

A sick feeling began in her stomach. She parted her lips and took in several slow breaths to stop the queasiness and moved to the side of the building so she could lean against it. The day hadn't started off well, and it was ending even worse.

"You look like you could use a drink."

The smooth, deep voice sent goose bumps over her skin as it wrapped around her seductively. Sensuously.

Wantonly.

Her emotions were so strong, so astonishing that she closed her eyes and savored the feel of each incredible moment.

Then she opened her eyes and slowly turned her head to stare into the most amazing gray eyes. They were stormy, like the sky above her, and she could imagine they would be as cold as steel when he was angry.

His dark brown hair was a rich mahogany, tempting her to delve her fingers into the short strands. The trim cut accentuated his chiseled jaw and square chin to utter perfection. Brows, thick and as richly colored as his hair, slashed over his startling eyes. He had wide, full lips that were lifted in a mischievous, all-too-enticing grin.

"I do. More than you know. Too bad I can't righ
she finally said when she could form words again.

"Ah. An American," he said, and pushed away
the building.

He didn't say it with the usual scorn Jane was use
from Richard Arnold. Rather, this impossibly hands
specimen said it as if American accents were a comn
occurrence.

She swept her gaze over his tall form. He moved wi
fluid grace that seemed at odds with his height and th
bulge of muscle his black suit couldn't hide.

The suit and white shirt were impeccable and fit him as if they were custom made. She let her gaze linger on the breadth of his shoulders and the hint of thickly muscled chest when his jacket shifted.

He looked damned good in the suit, yet it seemed as if he were meant for more than such stiff clothing. She licked her lips as she wondered what he would look like in a pair of jeans and a T-shirt.

Her heart hammered in her chest as her blood heated just looking at the man. She dragged her eyes back up to his face to find him watching her.

Jane had to make her feet stay in place despite the invisible pull she felt toward this complete stranger. I
wasn't just his amazing looks and mouthwatering bod
that attracted her, but also the way he looked at her, th
way he spoke to her.

As if he were really seeing *her.*

That in itself was a heady sensation that made
reach out toward the building with her hand. She le
brick grate against her palm in the hopes it would
her body, which was raging out of control, tilting,
ning. Listing.

"I'm waiting for my driver," she said to fill the s
Then inwardly cringed.

She was always saying the wrong things arour

CHAPTER TWO

"Where is Stan, the regular driver?"

Banan had expected that question, but he hadn't anticipated the husky, sensual voice that passed through such inviting, luscious lips. Jane Holden was anything but typical.

And he hated to admit the lust that flared, when he'd first spotted her.

"He's with Mr. Arnold tonight." Banan said the lie easily. Almost too easily. Some might begin to question his integrity when lying became as effortless as breathing.

Then again, few were as old as time itself.

Banan glanced in the rearview mirror. Jane was looking out the window, her large, guileless coffee brown eyes seemingly staring at nothing. Though she might appear innocent, her relationship with Richard Arnold made her suspect. Like everyone at PureGems.

No matter how appealing she might be, he couldn't let down his guard.

She didn't speak, and he didn't push her. It would have been prime opportunity to gather information. But one look at the dark circles under her eyes and the way she could barely keep them open, and Banan decided not to press her.

For the moment.

He stole another glance in the mirror. Her dark auburn hair was parted on the side, and it hung straight and sleek to her shoulders except for the hair that tapered around her face.

Banan tried not to notice the high cheekbones in her oval face. He tried not to notice the way her tongue licked at her plump lips. He tried not to notice how she ran her finger over her arched eyebrow as she looked into a mirror she pulled out of her purse.

But if he thought that was difficult, it was nothing compared to doing his damnedest to forget the glimpse of her long, lean legs as she'd gotten into the car. Or the straight skirt that fit her arse to perfection.

It was so easy to imagine those long legs wrapped around him while he . . .

Banan shifted in his seat, half-aroused. He had to get his mind off her. "Do you normally pick clients up at the airport?"

"No," she said and tucked a glossy strand of auburn hair behind her ear, revealing a small jade earring dangling from her lobe. "Mr. Arnold prefers to do it himself, but he had a prior engagement. Which is really odd, now that I think of it." She paused, her forehead wrinkled in a frown. "This is a high-profile client. He never would've allowed anyone but himself to pick them up."

"It must've been something important indeed to take him away, then."

She didn't say anything, but he'd gotten her thinking. Just what Banan wanted to do. He had no idea how loyal she was to Arnold, so he had to tread carefully.

Banan said nothing more as they pulled into the airport. He stopped the car by a curb, but before he'd put the car in park, she was out the door.

He watched as she hurried into the airport looking one way then the other. His gaze raked down her frame, from her button-down shirt that fit against her curves to the snug-fitting skirt and tall heels that only elongated her legs even more.

"Damn," he muttered, hating the lust that wouldn't dissipate.

Banan's phone rang then, and he wasn't surprised to see it was Guy.

"Can you talk?" Guy asked.

"Aye. What do you need?"

"I wanted to know if you'd found out anything. I assumed you would've discovered something being alone in the car with the woman."

Banan grinned as he kept watch on the airport doors for Jane. "I found out Arnold is the one who usually picks up clients, but he had Jane do it this evening. She doesna know what kept him away."

"Could she be lying?"

"She could be, but I doona think so. She seems . . . transparent. Unless she's a verra good actress, I think she's telling the truth."

Guy blew out a long breath. "Arnold is the top man in the London office. This has to involve him."

"And if it doesna? It could be someone else in PureGems."

"Doubtful, my friend. He's the only one with the money and connections that could've gotten him our secret."

Banan leaned his elbow on the door. "How is Elena?"

"She willna let me in her flat," Guy said with a growl. "I even tried to sneak in, but she says she could be watched and doesna want anyone to know what she's doing."

"She's right."

"Aye," Guy said angrily. "I know she's right, but I doona have to like it."

Banan chuckled at Guy's frustration. "Where is Rhys?"

"He's trailing Arnold. Hopefully he'll come back with something useful. How much longer are you going to be?"

"No' sure. Jane is looking for whoever it is she's picking up."

"Keep your eyes open."

"I'll be fine. Worry about your woman."

"Doona remind me," Guy replied testily.

Banan ended the call, but Jane had gone farther into the airport and he could no longer stare at her. Which was probably for the best.

He reached into the back and snagged her large purse. With ease, he rifled through the bag. He found her mobile and hurried to check incoming and outgoing calls. He was surprised to see there weren't many at all.

Satisfied there was nothing in her purse that could aid them, Banan replaced everything and set her purse exactly as it had been. Fifteen minutes later, Jane returned. Alone.

She got into the back of the car and closed the door, a worried expression pulling at her features. "I don't understand."

"What is it?"

"The client isn't here. His flight doesn't come in until tomorrow. Did I get the day wrong? God, that would be just like me." She put her head in her hand and let out a long, exasperated sigh.

Banan started the car and pulled away from the airport. "Are you sure the client didna arrive?"

"Yes. I have a friend who works for Virgin Atlantic. I had her check if he was on today's flight. He wasn't. I just don't understand."

"Everyone makes mistakes. Doona worry about it."

She looked out the window. "Yeah. You're right."

But he had the feeling she didn't believe him. The way she held herself and the worry lines bracketing her lips told a different story than her words.

"How about I drop you off at your flat instead of the

office?" he offered. This way he wouldn't have to tail her later.

Their gazes met in the rearview mirror and she smiled slowly, true happiness in her eyes. "That would be great. Thank you."

He followed her quietly spoken directions. There was obviously something bothering her. She was so distracted. He began to wonder if the snafu that night was an accident, or something done to Jane deliberately.

Whatever the cause, Banan intended to discover what it was. Jane seemed like the innocent sort, but sometimes those could be the ones at the heart of all the trouble.

He stopped the car in front of her flat. While he waited for another car to pass so he could get out, Jane had already opened her door.

Banan came around the back of the car and stopped cold at the sight of her long leg poking outside the car as she gathered her purse. Her skirt had slipped up, giving him an ample view of her thigh all the way down to the high-heeled shoes she wore.

He swallowed. It was a shapely leg, but just a leg. Yet there was no denying the need, the hunger surging through him.

Somehow he shook himself and held the door as she looked through her purse. Banan bit his lip to keep from smiling as he watched her.

"They're in this damn purse somewhere," she mumbled.

"Are you sure that's a purse?" he asked as he nodded at its large size.

She stopped and looked at him, then at her purse. And to his amazement, busted out laughing. Then she went back to digging. "It is rather huge. And the bigger the purse, the more crap I put in it. I know I need a smaller one, but I love this purse. Ah-ha!" she cried a moment later, and pulled out her keys.

He helped her out of the car, covertly watching the way she slung the purse over her shoulder and adjusted her skirt before she turned to him.

"Thank you for waiting on me this evening. I apologize for running behind."

"There's no need to fash yourself over it. The client wasna at the airport."

"Fash?" she repeated and frowned. "You're Scottish, right?"

"I am." He was more than that, but it was easier just to agree.

She glanced down the street and fiddled with her key ring. "I traveled there last fall."

"For a holiday?"

"In a manner," she answered evasively. "It's beautiful."

He found himself more intrigued by her with every passing moment. "Where did you go?"

"I spent some time in Oban and Loch Ness."

"Did you go looking for Nessie?"

She smiled and ducked her head. "I did take a boat ride on Loch Ness, but I'm sorry to say, I didn't look for Nessie."

Silence stretched between them as Banan found he simply enjoyed looking at her. She kept glancing away from him, and he knew his staring made her nervous.

She acted almost as if she didn't know what to do with a man's attention. Which was surely wrong. All a man had to do was look at her to see her appeal.

"Um . . . thank you," she said, and took a step back.

Banan saw the heel of her stiletto fall into the crack in the concrete an instant before she shifted her weight onto it. He took the two steps separating them, catching her just as her ankle gave way.

"Oh!" she gasped as he pulled her against him.

He stared down into the large pools of her coffee brown eyes. Her hands gripped his shoulders tightly. He'd brought her against him to help balance their weight so they both wouldn't topple over, but with the feel of her breasts and amazing curves against him, he knew it hadn't been a wise decision.

The lust he'd keep abated raged like an inferno, demanding he close the distance and sample her lips with his own. Slowly, leisurely he'd kiss her until she clung to him with longing.

Despite knowing he needed to separate from her, he couldn't. His blood burned from the desire that licked at his body. He liked the feel of her in his arms, loved the way her lips parted as if she waited for his mouth on hers.

The urge, the pure, primal need to take her was unwavering. Overwhelming. He couldn't remember the last time he'd felt such . . . yearning for a woman.

"Are you all right?"

"Y-yes," she murmured softly.

Her lips were so close to his. They were tempting, enticing.

Inviting.

He wanted to cover her mouth with his, to kiss her deeply and intensely. The impulse was so great, he barely stopped himself in time.

And then wished he hadn't.

Banan stared into her eyes and saw lighter flecks in her irises. "Gold," he said.

"What?"

Slowly, he stood them upright and reluctantly released her. "Your eyes. They have flecks of gold in them."

"You must be mistaken. My eyes are just plain brown."

"I'm no' mistaken."

Their gazes locked and held again. How easy it would be to pull her back into his arms, to lean his head down and place his mouth over hers. How simple it would be to give in to the growing need inside him.

"Thank you," she said nervously, and turned her head

away. "I know that hole is there. I've had my heels caught in it numerous times."

He waited as she walked up the steps, unlocked her door, and stepped inside. She turned back to look at him.

Only then did he say, "Good night, Jane Holden."

"Good night," she replied.

Banan refused to think of his reaction as he drove back to PureGems to drop off the Mercedes. Whatever he'd felt would surely pass before the next time he saw her.

CHAPTER THREE

The next morning, Jane found herself staring at her computer screen without actually seeing it. Instead, she was back in Banan's arms the night before. Sure, she'd gotten there by making a fool out of herself by tripping. Again.

But never once had she found herself in the arms of a man like him as a result. So virile, so gorgeous.

So completely out of her reach.

Her hands clenched atop her desk. She could still feel the solid, hard sinew of his muscles beneath her palms, still sense the steel of his body as she was hauled—firmly and protectively—against him.

He'd been quick and agile and superbly strong, but not once had he hurt her. His hands had held her tightly but gently, securely but tenderly.

Which was so at odds with the fire she'd seen smoldering in his gray eyes. They had darkened to the color of smoke, and for the briefest moment, she thought he might kiss her.

"Jane," someone whispered.

Jane nearly fell out of her chair, she moved so quickly. When she righted herself, she looked up to find Elena leaning her hands on the desk next to hers.

"Are you all right?" Elena asked, her lips quivering as she suppressed a laugh.

Jane nodded, mortified at her continued gracelessness. "Um, hm. Just fine."

But she wasn't. Would probably never be again. Not after Banan's touch, his voice, his eyes.

Every time Jane had closed her eyes during the night, she saw Banan's face. All she could dream about was his body against hers, holding her. Caressing her.

It had taken hours for her to sleep, and then she slept through her alarm, making her late getting to work and missing breakfast altogether.

She'd managed to eat half a granola bar during the morning meeting before Mr. Arnold had her getting his coffee. Even when she tried to leave for lunch, he'd had errands for her.

Jane's head ached from the lack of food, and she was having a difficult time concentrating, though the blame for that could be placed squarely on Banan's very wide, very muscular shoulders.

"Jane," Elena said again, a smile in her voice.

She looked up at Elena. "I'm sorry. I didn't sleep well. Did you need something?"

"Nothing that can't wait. Why didn't you come to lunch with the rest of us? We need to stick together, since we're the only Americans here."

Jane smiled. Her best friend still lived in Seattle, and even though she and Lisa Skyped often, it wasn't the same as having her friend in London with her.

Elena's offer sounded wonderful, and Jane hated that she missed the lunch. Next time, she'd be sure to go.

"Mr. Arnold had some errands for me."

"Did you eat at all?" Elena asked, a frown marring her forehead.

Jane shrugged. "No, but I have a protein shake in my purse that I'll get to in a moment."

After Elena walked off, Jane reluctantly went back to work. Her thoughts, however, didn't stray far from Banan, no matter how she tried to focus.

When she saw Richard Arnold making his way back into the office after his two-hour lunch, Jane stopped him. "Sir, I wanted to ask what happened with Mr. Eto? I had it marked on my calendar to pick him up last night at the airport, but he wasn't there."

One of Richard's eyebrows lifted as he stared at her. "Are you telling me I gave you wrong information?"

Jane ran her thumb across the chipped nail of her index finger. "No, sir. I'm simply asking if I made the mistake and wrote it on the wrong day?"

"I give you the information. I then pay you to keep up with it," he said, and looked down his nose at her, not one strand of his light brown hair out of place. "If you keep making these mistakes, you'll find yourself looking for a new job. Now, get in here. I need you to take notes on a letter you'll write before you leave for the day."

Jane wanted to bang her head on the desk. Instead, she grabbed a pen and paper and followed him into the office.

How she despised Richard Arnold. If he wasn't correcting her American words to British terms, he was telling her how inferior she was.

But she'd never say anything to him. Not only was it just not something she did, but she needed her job as well. Instead, she sat and patiently waited as he rambled for fifteen minutes from one topic to another. She jotted everything down, though most of it wouldn't go in the letter.

Several times both his office and mobile phones rang, and he'd pause to answer them, getting back to her a few moments later. But when he answered his mobile this last time, he'd turned his chair around so he faced the windows and spoke in a hushed tone.

Jane paid no attention to him until she heard something about Dreagan Industries and Sloan. She kept her eyes on the pad on her lap, but her attention was solely on Richard Arnold.

"It's not my fault she died in that godforsaken mountain!" Richard whispered loudly.

A short pause later, he turned around, his hand over the phone. "Jane, we'll continue this tomorrow."

"Of course," she said.

He waited until she stood before he turned back around. Jane wanted to linger, to learn what it was that involved Sloan and Dreagan Industries.

Jane wasn't brave enough to try to remain. She was walking slowly toward the door, her gaze glued to Richard, when she ran into a chair. The impact doubled her over, and when she tried to keep herself upright, she lost the pad and pen in her grasp.

"Bloody hell," Richard said, too caught up in his conversation to know what had happened. "I know you gave me the information, but you didn't bother to tell me how dangerous it was."

Jane's mind was running rampant with scenarios as she stayed bent over. There would be a huge bruise on her thigh tomorrow, but that didn't concern her. The conversation did. Just who was Richard talking to, and what mountain? Surely not the same mountain Sloan and Elena had gone caving in?

That would mean Richard had sent them there. But why?

Suddenly, his chair swung around, and she could feel his black eyes boring into her. Jane made a great show—and lots of noise—as she tried to reach for her pad and pencil. She straightened and looked at him.

I'm sorry, she mouthed, and started limping to the door.

"Jane."

She ignored him and the threat in his voice, her heart pounding so hard she could feel it hitting her ribs, she was nervous and scared. Ice now flowed in her veins, and it took everything she had not to run from the office. And never look back.

"Jane," he barked.

With great effort she stopped and looked at him. "I'm sorry, sir. You know how clumsy I am."

"What did you hear?"

"Hear?" she asked, and shrugged. "You know I would never listen to your calls, sir."

His nostrils flared as he glared at her. "Do you want your job, Jane?"

"Yes," she whispered, growing more terrified with each passing second.

"What. Did. You. Hear?"

She swallowed past the growing lump of dread in her throat. "I heard Sloan's name. Are we going to do a memorial now that Elena has returned?"

It sounded so stupid, but it was the only thing Jane could think to say.

"Get out. We'll talk about your eavesdropping when I'm done here."

Jane stood on legs shaking so terribly she was afraid they'd give out on her. Somehow she made it out of the office, and hastily closed his door before she leaned against it.

"Oh, dear God," she whispered, her chest heaving from her fear.

She looked at the clock and saw it was the end of the day. She didn't care that she was supposed to wait for him to finish his call. All she wanted to do was get out of the office before she suffocated.

There was too much muddled in her mind, too much she didn't understand. And so much she was afraid to even try. But she had to get her thoughts in order.

Jane tossed the pencil and pad on the desk and grabbed her purse. She kept trying to make herself slow down as she headed to the elevator, but it was as if something were pushing her from behind, silently urging her to get away as fast as she could.

She tripped twice and had to grab hold of the wall the second time so as not to fall to her knees, but nothing was going to slow her down.

As usual, everyone crammed into the elevator. This time, however, Jane didn't politely wait her turn. She shouldered her way onto the lift, apologizing the entire time. And just before the doors closed, she saw Richard come out of his office, looking for her.

Jane's heart didn't slow until she was out of the building, but even that didn't help. She looked over her shoulder once, and hurried to hail a cab. There would be no walking home for her today.

Banan caught sight of Jane as soon as she exited the building. It was easy to pick her out of a crowd with her dark auburn hair. But what got his attention was the fear etched on her face and the way she practically ran out of the building while looking over her shoulder.

Then she hailed a cab. As the cab drove away, she looked back at the building once more.

"What happened, Jane?" he whispered.

Rhys came to stand beside him. "Good question."

A moment later, Richard Arnold ran out of the building, looking up and down the sidewalk. Banan narrowed his gaze on the tall, thin man with graying hair at his temples and cold, dark eyes.

"I suspect that's why Jane was rushing away," Rhys said.

Banan had tried to get Jane out of his head, yet somehow she was firmly inside his mind. Her fresh, sweet scent. Her long legs.

Her irresistible lips.

"There was nothing I could find at Arnold's home,"

Rhys said. "I searched everything. He did have a safe, but there was nothing linking him to Dreagan in the papers."

Banan grunted. "There has to be something. We're missing it, is all."

"I'm thinking what we need is in his office."

Banan looked at the top floor. "We need to get him out so we can search."

"You follow Jane and make sure she's no' meeting someone. It would be a good time to search her flat as well. I'll rummage through Arnold's office."

With a nod Banan walked out of the alley and waved down a cab. After he gave Jane's address, he sat back and considered whether Jane was the person they were after.

She had seemed innocent enough, but that initial impression really didn't mean anything. The terror on her face, however, had brought him up short.

Jane must have seen—or heard—something. Could it be the lead they were looking for? Banan knew Guy was fast losing patience at having Elena continually in the office where someone was trying not only to discover their secrets, but also expose them.

And he and the other Dragon Kings had plenty of secrets. They hadn't kept themselves concealed for so many thousands of years by sheer luck, though.

Banan paid the cab when they reached Jane's address. He got out of the car and looked around. Jane was nowhere to be seen. Most likely she was inside her flat.

He was just setting up to get comfortable for a few hours to keep watch when he heard someone shout Jane's name. He looked to his right to find her coming out of a store, carrying a bottle of wine.

The way Jane smiled, so easily and so accepting, made Banan contemplate the last time he'd been happy like that. He searched through the eons of his memories, but found only a couple of occasions where he'd been blissful.

It wasn't difficult to remember the last time he was truly happy, back when he was still a dragon. The time before man had come to the land. A time when the skies, land, and water had been filled with dragons.

Banan turned away from such dark thoughts as Jane walked his way. He wasn't sure what prompted him, but Banan suddenly stepped out in front of her.

There was a flare of distress in her brown eyes before it quickly faded as recognition took hold. She smiled shyly, and he felt another jolt of untamed lust burn through him.

"Banan. What are you doing here?"

He said the first thing he thought of. "How about dinner?"

She eyed him skeptically. "With me? You want to have dinner with me?"

"Is that so odd?" he asked with a chuckle.

"Yes. Yes, it is." She looked around her then.

Banan inwardly cursed himself. He should've known she would be on edge from whatever had sent her rushing out of PureGems.

"Look," he said, and caught her gaze. "I . . . well, I've been waiting for you to get home."

She took a step back. "Why?"

Banan was going to have to convince her he was on her side, and quickly, or risk losing valuable time getting to know more about Jane and PureGems. "I wanted to ask you to dinner. I'm usually more suave," he said with a grin. "I had it all planned out, you see. It didna exactly go as planned."

For several long minutes, Jane simply stared at him. Finally she shrugged and held up the wine. "I've not had a good day at work. I'm not sure if I'm fit company."

"Let me be the judge," Banan said and took the wine from her. "Why no' put away your things and we'll go eat. I know you're hungry. I can hear your stomach growling."

His grin spread when her eyes widened in embarrassment.

"I am hungry." She paused and bit the left side of her lip with straight, white teeth. "As much as your offer appeals to me, I need to cook."

"You need to cook?" he repeated, unsure what she meant.

She nodded and wrinkled her nose with a grin. "I know it sounds silly. Some people exercise, some people garden, but I cook to de-stress. And I really need it today."

His invitation had been a surprise even to him, but he found he wanted to take her out to dinner. He didn't like the disappointment that welled inside him.

"I always make too much when I cook," she said hesitantly. "If you're in the mood for Italian, why don't you come up. I'm a pretty decent cook."

Banan's smile was slow as it pulled at his lips. "I'd like that verra much."

And he was shocked at just how true that statement was.

CHAPTER FOUR

Jane winced when she saw the state of her flat. She wished she'd spared a few minutes that morning and picked up. As it was, there was a small pile of laundry—with her panties—on the couch.

Her empty milk glass from the night before was on the end table, and she hastily snatched it up and threw a pillow over her laundry as she walked past. Jane put the glass down by the sink, grateful that at least her kitchen was clean.

"Why don't you open the wine while I get out of these heels?" she asked.

Banan gave a nod, and once Jane showed him where the opener was, she grabbed the laundry and headed into her small bedroom.

Only after tossing the clean clothes on a chair did she sink onto the bed, wondering what had gotten into her, offering to cook for him. It was so unlike her to be so forward, and though she knew she'd inevitably do something klutzy or say something inane, she still wanted to get to know Banan.

Which, again, was so at odds with her life normally.

She wasn't without her share of boyfriends, but she'd

never felt truly comfortable around any of them. Not that Banan made her feel comfortable, exactly. Quite the opposite, really.

Her body was in a constant state of jumbled nerves, her blood always pounding in her ears, but it was the heat, the unbelievable attraction that pulled her to him yet again.

Even more odd, it seemed being around him appeared to . . . change her. Not that she could explain how. She was nervous, but a different nervous.

Jane inwardly laughed. Those weren't the right words, but it was true. She was a changed person around Banan. Someone who wasn't quite sure how to respond to the way her body reacted to his.

With a sigh, she rose and stripped out of her camel-colored shirtdress and heels, and then stopped in front of her closet. Did she go comfortable in yoga pants and her oversized sweatshirt that hung off her shoulder?

Or did she go for the jeans and a black tee that had been a favorite of hers since she bought it?

Jane opted for the jeans and tee. She ran her hands down the formfitting tee as she looked herself over in the mirror. A quick run of her fingers through her hair, and she walked from the room to discover Banan looking at the shelf of her family photos.

He turned with a smile and handed her the glass of red wine he held. "Is this your mum?"

"Yes," she said after taking a drink. "That was taken during a trip to the coast one summer. It was a girls' week."

Banan's dark brows rose. "A girls' week?"

Jane padded into the kitchen and pulled out a large pot she filled with water. "Me, my mom, and three of my female cousins would try to take a trip like that as often as we could. It was girl bonding, as my mom called it."

"Interesting," Banan said as he slid onto the stool at the bar and watched her. "Can I help?"

"Nope. You talk while I cook."

Jane set the water to boil before she pulled out garlic, onion, and basil to cut up. She placed the cutting board on the counter as she faced Banan and began to chop.

"How is it you love to cook?"

She smiled as she thought of her family. "My uncle owned a restaurant in Seattle. He was the chef, and all the kids in the family worked there. It wasn't always easy working for family, but I developed my love of cooking from him."

"What did you do there?"

"I started as a waitress, but as you've seen, I have a habit of falling and running into things. For the sake of the glasses and dishes I kept breaking, my uncle moved me into the kitchen."

"And there were no more broken plates?"

She chuckled. "Oh, there were a few. At first everyone was hesitant to put a knife in my hands, but it's like I'm a regular person when I'm in the kitchen. I have very few falls or cuts. Something my parents have never understood. Everyone thought I might go to culinary school, and I almost did."

Banan took a drink of his wine and set it down. "What stopped you?"

Jane shrugged, unwilling to delve into that part of her life. No one in London knew why she was there, and for the time being, that's how she wanted it.

"Ah. A secret," he said.

Her heart skipped a beat at his lopsided grin. She was caught in his gaze, trapped. Ensnared.

But she wasn't afraid. It felt almost natural to have Banan in her flat as she cooked for him.

"Everyone has secrets."

His smile faded as he gave a single nod. "Nothing is more true than that, Jane."

She looked away and finished chopping the onions and garlic before she put them into a pan to sauté.

"What are you making us?"

She straightened after grabbing a can of crushed tomatoes and a box linguine from a bottom cabinet. "One of my uncle's recipes, as well as one of my favorite dishes."

Banan couldn't take his eyes off Jane. It wasn't just because she looked good in her worn, faded jeans and black shirt, but he was transfixed with how she moved so fluidly in the kitchen. As if she'd been born to it.

She sidestepped to the stove to cook, but angled herself so she didn't have her back to him. Her wineglass was near, but she only sipped on it.

"What happened today to make you need the wine?" he asked, pushed by a need to know the reason.

There was a slight jerk of her hand, which was the only sign he'd hit upon a touchy subject.

"It was just a bad day."

"Was it because of last night and the client?"

She glanced at him, her smile easy as she said, "No. Apparently I wrote it down wrong. Mr. Arnold wasn't at all happy, but then again, he never is with me."

"Is that what Richard Arnold said you did, wrote it down wrong?"

Her response was a shrug of one shoulder.

"Why do you stay at PureGems?"

She dumped the pasta into the boiling water. "Most people don't care for their bosses. I'm no different from thousands of other people."

"I suppose."

"What about you? Do you like your boss?"

He swirled his wine in the glass, watching the dark liquid. He knew she spoke of his supposed boss at PureGems, but Banan referred to Con when he said, "Actually, I do."

"Interesting," Jane said with a grin.

He'd come to Jane for a reason, and the sooner he did what he was supposed to do, the sooner he and his brethren could get on with their mission. "There have been rumors around the company about Arnold. They say he isna a nice man."

"He can be rude," she admitted, and then frowned.

She didn't like talking about people, that was obvious. But why would she stay loyal to someone like Arnold? Banan couldn't piece it together. He tried another tactic.

"The rumors I'm hearing is that he's mixed up with something that could bring the company down."

Jane's head lifted to look at him. "Do all drivers gossip about Arnold?"

"There's always talk. I'm just asking."

"Yes, but that's a very particular question."

Damn. Banan was going to have to be careful around Jane. She was careful. But why? Was it because she was loyal or had something to hide? "Just something I heard that I thought was odd. It got me curious."

"And you think because I'm his secretary that I would know? Is that why you asked me to dinner?"

"Nay. I asked you to dinner because I wanted to get to know you. I'm just making conversation. We work for the same company."

She pressed her lips together, and kept her gaze on the vegetables sautéing. "I'm sorry. I do this, Banan. I . . . I never say the right things."

"You did nothing wrong," he assured her.

He saw how tense she'd become since his question. She had just begun to relax in the kitchen, and he'd ruined it. But then the image of her frightened face as she left PureGems earlier flashed in his mind.

She didn't trust him enough to talk about Arnold, maybe not because she was loyal. But maybe because she was scared. His time getting to know Jane was going to take longer than he realized.

And somehow that pleased him.

That should have sent him out the door to have Rhys replace him, but he didn't want to share Jane with anyone. Especially not another Dragon King, and not when their magic to prevent them from falling for humans was disappearing.

"Why do you drive for PureGems?"

He met her inquiring gaze and realized she was asking more than what her words said. She wanted to know what had gone wrong in his life to that made him just a driver for a company.

Banan came up with another lie quickly, one that would put him in a good light. And better earn her trust.

"I'm no' just a driver. I'm a bodyguard of sorts hired to look after things."

She stopped stirring the food and said, "Does Mr. Arnold need a bodyguard?"

Banan shrugged and took a drink of wine. "I doona know. All I know is that I was hired by corporate to keep an eye on Arnold. I go where they tell me."

"Interesting," she murmured, and looked back at the food. "Tell me what you did before coming to London."

Banan suddenly hated the lies, so he decided to add a healthy measure of truth to his answers. "I'm part of a large family."

Jane grinned as she got out two baguettes of bread and put them on a baking sheet to heat in the oven. "How large?"

"Large," he said. "So large that sometimes you need to get away for a bit."

"But you always go home?" she asked, and looked his way.

"Always." Partly because he wanted to, but also because he had to.

It was part of who they were. They could venture away Dreagan for a month at a time, but they had to return or the magic holding the deadly silver dragons would no longer keep them sleeping, which would result in a war no one wanted. But Banan couldn't tell her that.

"How long will you stay in London?" she asked.

"That depends on a number of things. I doona care for the city, so I doubt I'll be staying too long."

She turned from putting the bread in the oven and placed her hands on the counter. "That's too bad."

"Is it? Why?"

She glanced at her hands. "I don't have many friends, and no one I can cook for."

"Ah. So I'm just someone you want to feed?" he asked with a grin he couldn't keep off his face.

Jane nodded, her eyes sparkling with laughter. "It gives me the excuse to cook that I need."

"Is it a friend you need?" he asked, his smile gone as he realized the seriousness of his question.

She turned to drain the pasta. "Everyone needs friends."

"Someone you can cook for?"

She laughed, the sound sweet and erotic. "Definitely."

"Someone you can talk to about your bastard of a boss?"

"Oh, yes."

"Someone you can share secrets with?"

Her gaze snapped to his. "Would you share your secrets?"

Banan rose from the barstool and walked around the counter to grab two plates from the cabinet. "I've never wanted to share my secrets."

It was the truth, but he didn't tell her how he found himself wanting to share them with her.

"Me either," she said, and spooned the noodles into the plates before pouring the sauce over them.

She handed him both plates, and then checked the bread. Banan got the forks and their wineglasses to place on the table. Then he watched as she took out the bread, cut it, and put it in a basket.

Once she was seated beside him, he took her hand and looked deep into her rich brown eyes. "Thank you, Jane."

"For what?"

"For this. The food, the conversation. All of it."

"You act as if you've never done this before."

He'd had women cook for him before, but he'd never yearned for one of them as he did Jane.

And that was just the first of many differences he recognized.

One of many that sent warning bells off in his mind that he continued to ignore.

CHAPTER FIVE

Banan and Jane finished their meal and moved to the couch. Soon after, Jane turned off all the lights save the small lamp on the end table. Not that he minded. He kept her talking of her family and her childhood. He was enraptured by her descriptions of Seattle and her life there.

There hadn't been a time in his very long existence where he'd thought to ever care about anything so mundane as her Thanksgiving dinners or the party she and a friend had thrown for their high school graduation.

Yet Banan wanted to know every detail. When it seemed as if she might stop talking, he asked her another question to keep her going.

He found himself laughing at the exploits of her and her best friend sneaking out of her house. A few minutes later, as he listened to her story about the prom, he actually thought about flying to Washington and finding the bastard who had ruined her special night.

She'd been enthusiastic to describe the dances they had in America, and though she chuckled as she spoke of her date, Banan could see the hurt she couldn't quite hide in her eyes.

Her eyes were her most expressive feature. Every emotion she felt could be seen in them.

Even when she couldn't stop yawning, and her lids grew drowsy, he kept her talking. Banan glanced at his watch to find it was well after one in the morning. He'd purposely kept Jane up until she fell asleep so he could search her house.

He'd always been able to keep an open mind about people, but the more he learned of Jane, the more he hoped she wasn't part of what was going on at PureGems.

There had been a few times he tried to turn the conversation to Richard Arnold, but Jane had deftly turned it away with such ease, it always took a moment before Banan realized what had happened.

He rose from his end of the couch and squatted beside her. Slowly, he extracted the wineglass from her fingers before any spilled and set it on the end table, and then switched off the lamp.

Every instinct told him to hurry and begin to search her flat, but he couldn't resist running the back of a finger down her cheek.

For long minutes he simply stared at her, wondering how she might be involved with Arnold, if she was involved at all. Mostly he didn't want her to be a part of it, which clouded his judgment.

Banan rose and, as silent as a ghost, began to search her small flat. He started in her room, moved into the tiny bathroom, and then was back in the kitchen. With every area that he searched and found nothing, the more relief he felt.

He softly closed a drawer and looked at the couch to find it empty. Banan's gaze swiftly scanned the flat and found Jane at the window staring down at the street.

"Jane?" he murmured.

She didn't turn around as she said, "I think something happened at work today."

"What do you mean?" He kept his voice low, like hers, as he slowly made his way to her.

One of Jane's shoulders lifted in a shrug. "I think I overheard something. It was Richard's tone. When he spoke to me it . . . frightened me."

Banan wanted to find Richard Arnold and rip his heart out for making Jane feel afraid. Banan stepped around the couch and over Jane's purse, but stopped short of going to her.

"Tell me," he urged. "What did you hear?"

"I don't know."

"Then how do you know it was something bad?"

She jerked her chin toward the window. "Him."

In an instant, Banan was standing behind her, looking over her shoulder. He spotted the man on the street as he gazed up at Jane's window.

Banan warred with himself about whether to confront the man or get Jane to safety first.

"Why is he watching me?" she asked, and turned her face to Banan.

He pulled her away from the window and turned her so that her back was against the wall. Her fresh, sweet scent filled his senses, making him struggle to keep his lust in control.

"Tell me what happened." When she didn't respond, Banan tried another tactic. "I'm a bodyguard, remember? I can protect you."

Jane's large, coffee brown eyes glanced at the window. "While you're here. You won't always be around, Banan."

"Let me help. Please. Tell me what happened yesterday."

She squeezed the bridge of her nose between two fingers and closed her eyes. "I was in Richard's office, taking notes for a letter he wanted me to draft. His cell, I mean, mobile phone kept ringing, and he kept answering it."

Her hand dropped and she opened her eyes to look at him. "For each call, he spoke as if I wasn't in the room. Normally, if it's important, he tells me to leave. Otherwise, I must stay. It wasn't until the last call that things changed."

"How so?"

"He turned his chair around so that his back was to me before he ever even answered it."

Banan nodded. "So it was a private call. Why no' ask you to leave?"

"I don't know," she said with a shrug, and looked away. "He was acting very odd. Then he asked me to leave. He thought I was gone when he went back to his conversation. But I heard something, and as I was paying attention to his side of the conversation, I ran into a chair. I stayed there listening until he noticed me."

He frowned as her voice faded away. Banan smoothed a lock of hair away from her face. "Jane?"

When her gaze turned back to him, he saw the trepidation in her dark depths.

"His voice was low, almost a whisper," Jane said, her own voice shaking. "But I know what I heard."

"Which was?" Banan pressed.

"Dreagan and Sloan." She leaned her head back against the wall. "I knew then that Richard was somehow involved with sending Sloan and Elena to that mountain. But why?"

Fury welled inside Banan because he'd known Richard Arnold was involved. Having Jane say the words made him itch to find Arnold right then and pound the truth out of him.

"Banan?"

He blinked, and realized he was squeezing her shoulders. Immediately he loosened his hold, but didn't drop his hands from her. "Did Arnold say he sent Sloan and Elena to Dreagan?"

"No," she answered with a small shake of her head. "Whoever he was talking to gave him some information. I know Richard was upset because he hadn't known how dangerous it was, or at least that's what he said."

"At least you got out of there before Arnold knew you overheard anything."

When Jane simply looked at him, a feeling of dread filled Banan.

"Bloody hell." Banan spun from Jane and raked a hand down his face. He still had no idea if Jane was in on it or not. Everything she was saying could be a ruse.

Yet he knew her fear was real.

So was the man watching her flat.

"I like Elena," Jane said.

Banan turned his head to find Jane with her arms wrapped around herself as she stared out the window. "And Sloan?"

"Sloan was . . . well, she could be like Richard. Richard and Sloan were always together. Several times they invited Elena to go to lunch with them, but she usually declined because she was busy with work."

"You think they wanted her to be a part of whatever they were doing?"

Jane blew out a long breath. "I don't know anymore. I had this weird feeling Richard might do something to me for overhearing his conversation. I had work to do. I never leave it."

"Then why did you?"

Her large eyes shifted to him. "Something told me to run. It was like something was behind me urging me out of the building as quick as I could. I even took a taxi home because I didn't want Richard to come down and find me."

Banan simply stared at her, wondering how much of what she said was the truth.

"That's silly isn't it?" Jane said with a forced laugh. "I mean, why would he come after me? I'm just his secretary."

Banan glanced out the window to see the man still staring their way. Banan sighed and made a decision he prayed didn't backfire on them. "Jane, Arnold did chase after you."

"What?" she asked breathlessly, her voice full of shock.

"I saw him. You'd just gotten into the cab when he came out." Banan paused and looked her way. "I think the man at the street was sent by Arnold."

"Oh, God," Jane said, and slid to the floor so that her knees were against her chest. Suddenly she frowned at him. "You saw me leave work?"

"Aye, I—"

"And then you came here asking me to dinner," she said over him. "You continued to bring up work. Why? Why are you following me? Why do you care what happened to me?"

He clenched his jaw when he heard the hysterical rise in her voice. "Jane, I'm no' following you. I'm a driver for PureGems, remember? I was there."

"No," she said angrily. "There's more. I know it. I thought . . . It doesn't matter what I thought."

He inwardly cringed as he realized she was going to say she'd thought he was interested in her. And the kink in the whole situation was that he *was* interested.

"Who are you, really?" she demanded, her eyes shining brightly.

Banan had opened his mouth to reply, when his phone vibrated in his pocket. He held up a finger to her and quickly answered it.

"Well?" Rhys asked on the other end of the phone.

Banan looked out the window. "How close are you?"

"Close. Why?"

"There's an unwanted visitor waiting for Jane. He needs to be taken care of."

"Where?"

Banan saw a form move out of the shadows just a few doors down from the man. "He's the one staring up at Jane's window. I've a feeling he's going to try to force his way in once I leave."

"Why tell me? Why no' take care of him yourself?"

Banan found Jane staring at him with a mixture of trepidation and fury. "Rhys, when you get done, come up to Jane's."

His answer was a click that ended the conversation.

Banan nodded his head to the window. "My friend is going to take care of your watcher."

He'd expected Jane to get up and watch, but she stayed where she was. Banan didn't need to see if Rhys did his job. Rhys was a Dragon King. And Dragon Kings always succeeded.

"Who. Are. You?" Jane asked again, her voice growing angrier with every word.

"Rhys is a friend. He willna harm you."

"Right," she said as she jumped to her feet. "Which is why you asked him to come up here."

"Nay. I asked him up so we could both talk to you."

She leaned to the side and grabbed her purse. Banan knew she was searching for either the can of Mace or the knife he'd found while searching her purse the day before.

Neither would do much damage to him.

There was a soft knock on the door, and then it opened. Banan glanced behind him to see Rhys fill the doorway.

"Whoever that was willna be bothering you again," Rhys said to Jane.

There was a pause as Jane pulled both the knife and

the pepper spray from her purse. She released the purse and flipped the knife open so that she held a weapon in each hand.

"Ah . . . Banan, what's going on?" Rhys asked as he softly closed the door behind him.

Jane lifted the Mace toward Rhys. "Stop right where you are. I didn't invite you, and I don't want you up here."

"I've made a muck of things," Banan answered Rhys.

Rhys grunted and folded his arms over his chest. "Obviously. I gather Jane isna in on whatever Arnold is up to?"

Banan said, "Nay" the same time Jane shouted "What?"

Rhys laughed softly and walked into the kitchen. He leaned over the leftover bowl of pasta and inhaled. "Smells good," he said as he found a fork and began to eat.

Banan ignored Rhys as he focused on Jane. "We work for Dreagan, Jane. We knew there was some kind of plot to learn more about our—" He stopped because he searched for what to tell her.

"Your whisky?" she offered. "I know it's good, but is it that good?"

"It's a moneymaking industry," Rhys said around a mouthful of food. "People have killed for less."

Banan watched her digest the information and wondered if she believed them.

"This has to do with Sloan and Elena caving on your land, doesn't it?" she asked.

Banan leaned against the back of the couch and nodded. "The area of Dreagan land they were on is private. The road going to that part of the mountain is hidden and known only by few. We need to know how Sloan discovered it."

"Why didn't you just ask me?" Jane asked wearily. She dropped the weapons and walked around the couch to sit down. “No lies, no snooping around. I’d have told you all that you wanted to know.”

“True.”

She gave a snort. “Oh. I see. I was a suspect. Why? Because I work directly with Richard?”

“Aye,” Rhys said.

Banan always trusted his instinct, and it had been telling him Jane wasn’t a part of the plot. Or was that just his cock leading him around?

Never had he been more unsure, and never had he prayed more to be right.

Because Jane Holden was quickly becoming someone he wanted to be around.

CHAPTER SIX

Jane couldn't believe what she was hearing. Her. A suspect. She turned to glare at Banan. "How could any of you think I was part of it?"

"We knew nothing about you. We had a strong hunch Arnold was involved, but we didna know how deep it went in PureGems."

"Have you questioned Elena? I mean, I don't know where she was after Sloan died, but it was a few days before she returned to London."

The silence that followed her statement made a shiver race down her spine.

"You've already spoken with Elena," Jane said with a nod as it all clicked into place. "And you believe her?"

Rhys picked up the large pasta bowl in his hand and continued to twirl his fork in it as he walked to the edge of the kitchen. "Aye, we believe Elena. She nearly died in that mountain, for one. And another, she and Guy fell in love."

Jane blinked. Then looked first at Rhys, and then Banan. "She fell in love?"

"Aye," Banan answered softly.

Jane knew Elena had looked different, but she thought it was the near-death experience that had caused the change.

"So, Elena wasn't part of Sloan's plan," Jane said as her mind tried to sort it all out. "I gather you know Sloan's plan."

Banan and Rhys exchanged a look before Banan said, "Aye."

"That's why Richard wanted Elena back so urgently," Jane said as recalled him desperately trying to get a hold of Elena. "He wanted to know if she and Sloan had found anything."

Banan moved to sit on the couch. "That's why Elena is back."

"Do you trust that I'm not involved, or are you seeing if I run back to Richard with any of this?"

Rhys said, "A good question. Banan, I'd like to know the answer as well."

Jane wanted Banan to believe her, needed him to believe her. She wasn't sure why it was important, only that it was. It seemed impossible that she had spent so much time with him and been completely at ease. They had talked and laughed and shared stories.

She frowned then because she had been the only one sharing stories. Banan hadn't said much about his own life.

"I believe you," Banan finally said.

She nodded and ran her thumbnail down her jeans. "Richard knows I heard something. If he chased me yesterday, and then sent someone to watch me, what will he do next?"

"We'll be there whenever he makes his next move," Banan said.

But Jane was already shaking her head. "You can't be in the office with me. What are you going to do? Hide under my desk?"

"If I have to." His voice had dipped low, a hard edge to it.

Rhys set aside the now empty bowl. "If you can get into Arnold's office and snoop around, that would help us out."

"I can do that," she said. "He's always gone for lunch, and I'm in and out of his office all the time. No one will notice. There's just one thing."

Banan met her gaze. "What's that?"

"This is about more than stealing a recipe for scotch, isn't it? I need to know, because I've this feeling that this isn't just my job on the line."

"You're no' wrong," Banan said.

"Damn. Have you gathered any information on who could be in it with Richard?"

Banan leaned forward so that his forearms rested on his thighs. "Nay. Elena is making her way through those closest to Arnold. So far, she's found nothing."

"If I'm going to do this, how do I contact you if I find anything?"

"I'll give you my, Rhys's, and Elena's mobile numbers. And wherever you are, I'll be close by. I can reach you quickly if you're in danger."

Jane grabbed for her wine and drained it in three swallows. It burned as it slid down her throat, but she needed something to steady her after all she'd learned.

"The fact you just said that, Banan, tells me how dangerous this is going to be. Richard is connected to influential families. Money, politics, and God only knows what else. He's not a man to be messed with."

"Let us worry about that," Banan said with a smile that promised Richard would suffer.

Jane just wished she knew what was so important that Banan, Rhys, and Elena would risk their lives to protect Dreagan for it.

Rhys touched her shoulder, and she turned, startled, because she hadn't heard him move.

"You are doing a brave thing, Jane," Rhys said.

Jane swallowed, wishing she had more wine in her glass. "Stop talking now or I might chicken out of this whole thing."

Just as she was about to get up, Banan leaned over and placed his hand atop her. "Thank you."

Her heart skipped a beat at his husky timbre. It hurt that he wasn't attracted to her, but the letdown wasn't anything she wasn't accustomed to. She was Plain Jane after all.

Jane managed a small smile. "Don't thank me yet. I'm not exactly brave, Banan, and Richard has a way of making me feel an inch tall when he talks to me."

"So doona allow him to speak to you that way," Rhys said matter-of-factly.

Jane looked down at Banan's large hand, his warmth sinking into her. She liked his hands, liked how it felt to have him touch her. "Easier said than done."

Banan settled into the shadows as he watched Jane walk into PureGems the next morning. He had followed her from her flat, and it was pure hell. All he'd wanted to do was walk beside her and listen to her amazing voice. Instead, he had to keep his distance.

"Arnold hasna arrived," Rhys said from beside him.

Banan nodded. Rhys kept watch on PureGems while Guy stayed with Elena, and Banan did his best to ignore the growing need to kiss Jane.

The disappointment in her eyes when she thought he'd only wanted information about Arnold had been like a kick in the balls. He hadn't liked the feeling, but nothing could make it go away.

Banan had given Jane everyone's number except Guy's.

He had purposely left out Guy's name. Just in case. Not because he thought Jane might be working with Arnold, but if she was put in a position where she had to give information in exchange for her life, she wouldn't know everyone from Dreagan who was in London.

"She'll be all right," Rhys said.

Banan leaned a shoulder against the brick of the building. "I hope so. I also hope we uncover who it is that's giving Arnold intelligence about us. The sooner we can find that wanker, the better."

"Aye. No' to mention being around all these humans makes my ass twitch. I long to return to Dreagan."

Banan did as well. The only thing that helped to calm him was Jane. Beautiful, intelligent, amazing Jane.

Jane couldn't stop shaking as she walked into PureGems and rode the elevator up to her desk. When she discovered Richard hadn't yet made it into the office, Jane was able to breath a little easier.

She didn't waver from her normal routine and hastily got to work, rarely looking up. It wasn't until she was coming back from the copy machine that she found Richard's office door open. Her knee gave out, and she nearly dropped her papers as she tripped.

"I got you," Elena said as she steadied her.

Jane looked at Elena and smiled. "Thank you."

"I'm here, just two offices down, Jane. If he does anything, give me a shout, and I'll come running. So will Banan and Rhys."

Elena squeezed her arm, and then she was gone. Leaving Jane to face Richard alone.

She returned to her desk, waiting to hear him scream her name, but as soon as he saw her, he stared at her for several minutes before he shut his office door. Which was just fine by her.

Jane didn't see, or hear, from Richard until it was time for lunch. Once more, she was buried in work and saw him leave out of the corner of her eye.

When he was in the elevator, she rose and walked into his office. She'd already sorted out how she would search it. She'd do it a bit at a time so no one noticed how long she was in there.

She checked his desk first, and found nothing. A trip back to her desk, and fifteen minutes later, she returned to his office. This time she went through the credenza behind his desk.

Again and again she repeated her process, but found nothing that didn't pertain to anyone who wasn't a client. She shut the last drawer in his filing cabinet and was turning to leave when she spotted the cell phone he'd been on the day before.

With shaking hands, Jane picked up the phone and quickly scrolled through to the Incoming Calls. She matched the times from the day before and his calls and found the call she was looking for.

Jane wrote down the number and had just replaced the phone when Richard walked in.

"What are you doing in here?" he demanded.

Jane jumped, and then forced a laugh. Thankfully, her tripping over her own feet wasn't out of the ordinary. "Oh, Mr. Arnold, you frightened me. I was finishing up some research on the new mine we were looking to buy in Belgium. I was coming to leave the file on your desk, but since you're here," she said, and handed him the manila folder.

His gaze narrowed as he took the file as if he wasn't sure whether to believe her or not. "That'll be all."

"Yes, sir," Jane said, and hurried out of the office, cautious to keep the paper with the phone number carefully hidden in her hand.

The rest of the day passed as slow as an eternity. When

it was time to leave, Jane didn't check with Richard as she usually did. She grabbed her stuff and left.

Just as she stepped onto the elevator, Elena moved beside her. They stayed together until they walked out of the building.

"Until later," Elena whispered with a smile.

Jane paused and scanned the area, hoping for a glimpse of Banan. As if he knew she was looking for him, he stepped out of the shadows.

She couldn't stop the smile from pulling at her lips, or the relief in knowing he was there. His answering grin made her stomach flutter with awareness.

Her gaze was locked with his, and she was about to cross the street to go to him when someone bumped into her shoulder, spinning her as it knocked her to the ground.

Jane landed hard, scraping her knee and palm. She looked up to the cold, blue eyes of a man just before he pushed through the door of PureGems.

"Jane," Banan said as he gripped her arms and lifted her to her feet.

"Did you see him?" she asked. "Did you see that creepy guy?"

Banan's body stiffened. "What man?"

"The one that ran into me."

"There was a group of people who walked between us. I didna see who knocked you down. Come. Let's get you home. I've got to keep my distance, even though I'd rather take you to your flat myself."

"It's okay," she said as she climbed into the taxi he'd hailed for her.

Banan leaned in. "I'll be right behind you."

He was true to his word. Jane had just gotten out of the cab when Banan came into view down the street. She walked up the stairs to her flat but left her door unlocked.

It wasn't but a few minutes later that his large frame filled her tiny flat. She wasn't sure what to say to him, so she looked through her medicine cabinet for some peroxide and antibiotic cream.

"You're hurt," he said from behind her.

Her eyes closed at his nearness, at the pure maleness of him. "Just a little."

"Let me."

He took the bottle of peroxide and gently held her hand over the sink as he poured the liquid over the scrapes. Jane didn't feel her cuts any longer. Not with Banan touching her.

She couldn't take her eyes off him while he dabbed a towel at the scratches. When his thumb stroked the sensitive skin of her wrist, she shivered with need.

Breathing became impossible with him so near. She wanted to run her hands over his chest, wanted to comb her fingers into his hair. And she wanted to kiss him with a desperation that bordered on madness.

And then his fingers caressed her jaw before sliding around her neck and into her hair. Her gaze lifted to his, and the gray of his eyes had turned molten.

He still held her injured hand between them, which was the only thing separating their bodies. His heat enveloped her, encircled her.

Surrounded her.

His scent, his body, his very essence was sinking in her, through her. All the while, he continued to slowly pull her toward him.

"Jane," he whispered as his gaze dropped to her lips.

A sigh escaped her when his head lowered to hers. He brushed her lips with his once, twice before he took her mouth in a soul-stealing kiss.

He kissed with a skill that sent her senses reeling. His lips were soft yet insistent. She was enthralled from the first touch of his mouth.

His tongue swept into her mouth, each touch a seduction. She was sinking under the weight of his desire. Falling. Tumbling.

And she never wanted it to end.

CHAPTER SEVEN

Banan moaned, the taste of Jane sweeter than he could ever have imagined. He released her wrist so his arm could wrap around her waist to her back. Which allowed him to press her tighter against him.

He loved the feel of her soft curves. As good as she felt, having her hands wrap around his neck while she met his kiss was even better.

A low groan rumbled from his chest as her nails gently scraped his scalp. He tried to keep the kiss slow and casual, but his hunger for her, his yearning was too much. There was no holding back with Jane.

He deepened the kiss, inwardly grinning with masculine pride when she moaned and pressed against him.

His need goaded him into putting her onto the counter and taking her right there, right then. It was so tempting. He could picture the scene in his head, which only made his cock swell even more.

Banan gripped her hips, ready to lift her onto the counter, when his mobile phone vibrated in his pocket.

It was harder to end the kiss than he could have imagined. And when he opened his eyes, it was to find hers closed, her lips swollen from his kiss.

Slowly her lids lifted, and her dark gaze met his. The desire he saw made his balls tighten with a rush of pure, unadulterated need.

He might have ended the kiss, but he wasn't ready to let her out of his arms. Banan reached into his back pocket and pulled out his mobile.

"Aye?" he barked into the phone.

There was a slight pause on the other end of the line before Elena said, "Ah . . . is everything all right?"

He sighed, and then wanted to curse when Jane stepped out of his arms and backed away from him. "Aye," he answered Elena.

"Jane seemed . . . well, anxious when we left work. I wanted to know if you'd spoken with her?"

Spoken? No, Banan didn't remember words. He recalled the kiss very well, however. He could still taste her on his tongue, could still smell the clean scent that was Jane's alone.

"Banan?" Elena said.

He couldn't look away from Jane as he answered, "We just reached her flat. We've no' had a chance to talk."

"Call me after you do," Elena said, and ended the call.

Banan set aside his phone, and wasn't sure what to say to Jane. He hadn't planned the kiss. Nor had he planned the longing he felt for her.

It was baffling, bewildering. And absolutely amazing.

He was painfully hard, and all he could think about was taking off her red dress, exposing more of her satiny skin to see and caress. And kiss.

By all that was holy, he wanted to kiss every inch of her at least a thousand times.

Jane licked his lips, and he swallowed back the moan as he imagined those unbelievably plump lips wrapping around his cock.

"I didn't find anything in Richard's office that was out

of the ordinary, or that had anything to do with Dreagan," she said, her gaze frequently looking away from him.

This would never do. Her shyness was making him want to tug her back into his arms. He'd bend her backwards and run his hand over her breast, testing the weight of it before teasing her nipple.

Would she moan or cry out with pleasure?

Banan wanted to know, he had to know.

He gripped the counter to keep himself from reaching out to her. "Rhys found nothing in Arnold's home either. This isna looking good."

"He left his cell phone behind. The one he was on the day before? Well, I found the number of the person who called him."

To his surprise, she handed him a piece of paper folded into a small square that fit perfectly in her palm. Banan unfolded it to discover the number she spoke of.

"Good work," he said with a smile. "We can find out who this number belongs to."

Jane ran her finger along the edge of the sink. "So, does that mean you no longer need to worry about Richard?"

"He's still part of it. There's no doubt of that now. How deep, is the question. Is he an integral part, or is this much bigger than him?"

"How are you going to find that out?"

Before he could answer her, there was a knock at her door. Banan stayed where he was as she kicked off her heels on the way to the door. He expected it to be Rhys, but one look at Jane's face frozen in surprise, and Banan was at her side in a moment.

He narrowed his gaze at Richard Arnold. Just what was he doing at Jane's flat?

"Mr. Arnold," Jane said nervously. "What are you doing here?"

"That's two days now you've left work on your desk,"

Arnold said, barely masking his effort to peer inside Jane's flat. "That's not like you. I wanted to be sure everything was all right."

"You could've called," Banan said.

Arnold's dark gaze rested on Banan. "I could have."

"Do you make visiting your employees a habit?"

"Not usually."

Jane cleared her throat. "I'm fine, Mr. Arnold. I had an appointment yesterday."

"And today?" Arnold asked.

Banan was finding it increasingly difficult not to reach out and wrap his hand around Arnold's throat and squeeze. "I came into town," he said before Jane could.

After a stare-down, Arnold dropped his gaze to Jane. "If you can't finish the work I give you, I might have to find a new personal assistant."

With those words, he turned on his heel and walked off. Banan stepped into the hallway and made sure Arnold left the building.

"Shut and lock the door," he told Jane before running after Arnold.

He stepped out onto the sidewalk just as Arnold's car drove off. Banan debated on whether to follow him, but he couldn't bring himself to leave Jane.

"What the bloody hell was he doing here?" Rhys said as he walked up.

Banan released a long breath and turned to Elena and Rhys. "He wanted to know why Jane hadna stayed late these last two days."

"That's not disturbing or anything," Elena said sarcastically as she started up the steps.

Banan grabbed the door Elena opened and glanced behind him. "Where is Guy?"

"Doona ask," Rhys said with a loud sigh. "He wasna happy at no' being here."

Elena lightly elbowed Rhys in the ribs. "Guy understands your reasoning for keeping his existence from Jane, but he wants you to know it should've been Rhys she didn't know about."

They walked up to Jane's flat, and Banan couldn't help but smile. "Well, Rhys was near to take care of Jane's watcher, Guy wasna."

Elena grinned. "No, Guy was otherwise . . . occupied."

And Banan could well imagine how his friend had been occupied. It's what he'd like to be doing with Jane. Slowly, leisurely he wanted to discover Jane's body and bring them both pleasure in the process.

It baffled Banan that he'd never thought twice about relieving his body on a human before, but with Jane everything was different.

If the craving, the unimaginable hunger to have her weren't so strong, he might find his growing . . . emotions . . . something to worry over. But he couldn't even think about them, with his need so strong.

Never once in all the long eons of his life had he ever found a human so appealing. He'd seen beauty before, but nothing compared to Jane.

"Banan?"

He started and discovered they were standing in front of Jane's door. Both Elena and Rhys were staring at him. "What?"

"You seem a wee different," Rhys said, his aqua gaze narrowed.

Elena watched him carefully, almost as if she searched for something.

"I'm still wishing I'd wrapped my hands around Arnold's neck," Banan said before he rapped his knuckles on Jane's door. "Jane. I'm back."

He heard her unlock the door, and then it opened and she peeked her head around. Her thick, silky auburn strands of hair had fallen to the side as she leaned her head over. There was relief in her dark gaze when she saw him.

"I wasn't sure you were coming back," she said as she stepped aside and opened the door wider.

Banan let Elena inside the flat first. "I thought about it, but we can no' allow Arnold to know we know what he's done."

"Right," Rhys said. "We need to know all the players in this game first. And then we strike."

Banan grinned at Rhys's comment. Their strike would be quick, silent, and quite effective. Their very lives depended on it.

Not that they could be killed by anything a human could wield. The only way to kill a Dragon King was by another Dragon King, and even then it wasn't easy to do.

Banan tossed the piece of paper Jane had given him to Rhys. "Jane found the number that called Arnold yesterday when she heard mention of Dreagan."

"What a great find, Jane," Elena said.

Rhys shot Jane a smile. "Verra well done, lass."

"I don't know how any of you will determine who the number belongs to," Jane said. "I mean, you'd have to know someone in the government to get you that information unless you're a hacker."

"We're no' hackers," Banan said as he pulled out his phone and searched for a name under his contacts. He clicked the number and put the phone up to his ear, his gaze never leaving Jane's. He wanted to see her face when next he spoke.

There was an answer on the third ring. "I need to speak with Henri North, MI5."

Just as he expected, Jane's eyes grew large, but her slow smile warmed him. The desire that had filled her flat a short time ago hadn't vanished.

It was there, simmering just beneath the surface. From the way she looked at him, to the way his hands still felt her. To the way she touched her lips when she didn't think he was looking.

If only they were alone. He wanted to kiss her again, to feel her melt against him and hear her sighs of pleasure. He yearned to strip her bare and commit everything to memory.

Banan pulled his gaze away from her to catch Rhys staring at him. He saw Rhys's worry reflected in his gaze, but Banan wasn't concerned. It was just a case of lust that he had.

That's all.

That's all it could be.

And he prayed that's all it would be.

CHAPTER EIGHT

Jane couldn't stop looking at Banan. Her lips were still sensitive after his kiss, her body still reeling from his heat and the hard sinew of his chest.

If she hadn't been drowning in desire, she might have reacted differently to seeing Richard. As it was, she was thankful that Banan had been there, because she wasn't sure what Richard would have done otherwise.

No matter where Banan was, she was painfully, utterly aware of him. His every move, his every breath. She couldn't explain it nor did she want to.

She shouldn't have been surprised to learn he knew someone in MI5, because Banan seemed adept at everything he did. As if he were prepared for every eventuality.

What she feared, however, was that they didn't need her anymore. Because that would mean Banan would disappear from her life. That thought made her ill. What would become of her life after Banan? Not only would she return to Plain Jane, but no longer would she experience the wonderful desire just a look from him could give her.

She listened to him give Henri North the phone number to trace. It was as simple as ordering takeout, or at least Banan made it appear so.

How did he know this Henri North, who hadn't questioned why Banan wanted the number traced? Had Banan worked for MI5? Which didn't seem so far-fetched.

He was leaning against the counter, seemingly relaxed. Yet she'd felt the tightly coiled muscles behind her when Richard came to her door. She'd noticed the way Banan's body seemed poised for action, and he hadn't hesitated in following Richard either.

Traits of a spy? Or just someone who knew a thing or two about life?

"Thanks, Henri. I owe you one," Banan said before he ended the call.

Rhys crossed his arms over his chest. "Tell me you have good news."

But it was her that Banan looked at. "The number is untraceable."

"How?" she asked.

"It takes someone with vast amounts of money and skill to pull something off like that."

"Ulrik," Rhys said, his voice dripping with anger, as if it was distasteful even to say the name.

Banan set his phone carefully on the counter as he weighed Rhys's words. "Nay. Con has him watched. Besides, Con ruled him out as a suspect while Elena was still at Dreagan."

Suddenly Elena stood. "I need to go tell . . . well, I need to go."

Her slip didn't go unnoticed by Jane, but Jane wasn't about to say anything. She walked Rhys and Elena to the door, and could hardly contain her excitement when Banan remained.

Elena and Rhys hadn't asked him to leave with them, and he hadn't moved to follow them. But that left Jane feeling a bit uneasy with how to talk to Banan after their fiery, heart-stopping kiss.

"Jane," he called softly after she closed the door.

She turned, her heart pounding erratically. Heat flooded her body when she saw the scorching intensity of his gaze. The desire in his stormy gray depths made her stomach flutter with anticipation and need unlike anything she had ever experienced.

He pushed away from the counter and started toward her. It was like an invisible cord wrapped around her and tugged her to him. She took that first, hesitant step, her chest heaving as if she'd run a marathon.

In seconds he'd crossed the small room. And then she was in his arms. His low moan as his lips touched hers sent chills racing over her entire body.

He held her tightly, crushing her against his muscles. She wrapped her arms around his neck and clung to him. This kiss wasn't gentle. It was full of need, of longing.

Of unquenchable hunger.

He roughly backed her against the door, which only propelled her desire to burn hotter, brighter. His hands were touching her everywhere. And then he cupped her breast.

Jane tore her mouth from his as she groaned from the sensations rushing through her. Even with the material of the dress and bra, her breasts grew heavy, her nipples hard.

His gaze caught and held hers. No matter how she might have wanted to look away, she was trapped in his molten gaze. She quivered as his thumb moved slowly over her nipple. Heat speared through her to her center.

As if knowing her need, Banan rocked his hips against hers. The feel of his thick, hard arousal made her gasp, and then moan.

His thumb continued to tease her nipple, circling the tiny bud several times before thumbing it. He was going to drive her crazy with need, and she was going to enjoy every incredible minute of it.

"Jane," he whispered.

She wanted to answer him, but she couldn't string two words together. So she didn't even try.

Instead, she grabbed at his dark gray shirt and slid her hand under it. Beneath her hand his stomach muscles clenched and shifted. She could feel each cord of sinew under her fingers, and it made her shiver in expectation.

She wanted his shirt off. That wasn't right. She wanted every stitch of clothing he had on gone so she could look her fill at him.

"You doona know what you're doing," Banan rasped before he took the lobe of her ear in his mouth.

"I do," she answered breathlessly.

He leaned back to look at her. "I want you, Jane. I need you."

"Then what are you waiting for?"

His triumphant smile made her stomach flutter in anticipation. And then she was lifted in his arms as he strode to her bedroom.

CHAPTER NINE

Banan couldn't remember a time when he had craved a woman so desperately. His body had needs, aye, but this longing went beyond that.

If he hadn't already tasted her heady kisses, he might think twice about succumbing to the incredible, mind-boggling desire running rampant through him.

He dropped his arm beneath her knees so that she stood before him once more. Every lush curve against him fit to perfection, but he wanted to see that shapely form himself, to feast his eyes on her all-too-tempting body.

Her coffee brown eyes had turned almost golden with her desire. Her pulse was beating as erratically as her breathing. And all of it only aroused him more.

He wanted to kiss her in every way imaginable. To have her so close to him, he all but absorbed her into his body. He wanted to devour her, claim her.

Seize her.

As his. All his.

And only his.

His need burned so hot, he thought he might very well

go up in flames. Her lips parted, and it was all the invitation he needed.

He covered her mouth with his, sinking deep in the kiss as he reached behind her and slowly unzipped her dress. The first bared inch of skin was too difficult to resist.

Banan ended the kiss and smoothed his thumb over her exposed shoulder before placing his lips against her skin. He inwardly smiled as her breath hitched.

He repeated the movement on her other shoulder, and then extracted both arms from the dress. It fell to her hips, where it waited for him to finish unzipping it.

But he wanted to take his time and savor every marvelous, astounding moment of her in his arms. He'd think about the emotions raging within him later. For now, the yearning inside him was too much to ignore.

He hooked a thumb beneath the apricot-colored bra strap. His lips trailed up her neck, Jane's head lulling to the side to give him access.

His balls tightened when she sucked in a gasp as his tongue touched a sensitive spot. Banan reluctantly loosened his hold on her when her hands once more delved beneath his shirt and up his chest.

Her touch was warm and teasing. His eyes slid shut as she continued to caress him, learning him. He was rocked when she lifted his shirt and bent to kiss his chest.

Always he'd been the one to pleasure women. He hadn't cared if they touched him. He got what he wanted and left.

But he couldn't stop Jane. Her touch felt too good. The more she touched him, the more he wanted her to. So when she lifted his shirt, he was all too happy to jerk it over his head and discard it.

"My God," she murmured softly.

He could only watch as her gaze raked over his chest while her hands continued to explore him.

"You're beautiful."

"Nay," he said. "It's you who is beautiful."

Her fingers traced over the two dragons intertwined on his chest. The tattoo covered the entire width of his chest, and her reverent touch moved something within him.

She couldn't know how important the tat was, or why he had it. She had no inkling that he was a Dragon King, nor did she know of his power or immortality.

Yet she touched him as if he were special, as if she understood that the tattoo had a deep meaning.

Her gaze lifted to him. "This is amazing artwork."

"Aye." But he found he wanted to tell her how each Dragon King had such a tat, and that each one was special to the King and to the dragons he ruled.

She gave a faint laugh. "I could look at you all day. And that voice of yours. It makes me shiver."

Her words pleased him to a degree that should have sent off warning bells. But all he could think about was the need to hear her scream his name as she peaked.

He wanted her, craved her—yearned for her on a level he had never thought possible. And had greatly feared.

Yet now, with her in his arms, there was no fear. Just a longing so intense and soul-deep, he had no choice but to follow it. To follow her.

Jane.

Her golden brown gaze lifted to his. "What are you doing here? With me?"

"Is it so odd that I want you?"

"Yes," she whispered.

Banan finished unzipping her dress. With the barest tug, it puddled on the floor. "Then let me show you just how much I desire you, Jane Holden."

He angled his head and ruthlessly, fiercely kissed her. She pressed against him, a low moan filling the room. He was relentless as he deepened the kiss, showing her his yearning, his longing. The insatiable need.

"Banan," she murmured as her fingers grasped the waist of his jeans.

He recognized—and felt—the desperate need within her. With each garment that was discarded, the passion escalated and drove them harder.

Between kisses and fumbling fingers, they were finally skin to skin. Heat to heat.

Banan was perfectly sculpted, and Jane couldn't stop touching him. His heavy shoulders, the muscled expanse of his chest, and his ripped stomach.

The sinew didn't stop there. She felt it shift under her hands as she grasped his neck and back. His legs were just as corded as the rest of him.

His heat surrounded her, just as his arms did. Her breasts ached as they rubbed against his chest. She squeezed her legs together when his gray eyes darkened even more.

One minute they were standing, and the next she was lying on the bed. She loved the weight of him atop her. His arousal pressed against her stomach, causing her to rub against him.

He groaned, and it made her blood burn hotter in her veins. She was about to roll him onto his back so she could explore his magnificent body at her leisure, but he bent and wrapped his lips around a nipple.

Jane cried out as she arched off the bed, her hands sinking into his dark hair. She could only hold on to him as he teased and drew her nipple into a throbbing bud until she was whimpering from the onslaught of pleasure.

And then he moved to her other breast. His expert tongue soon had her head thrashing from side to side, her body shaking with the need for release.

If Jane thought he'd give her that release then, she quickly discovered how wrong she was when his lips left a hot trail of kisses down her body.

He shouldered his way between her legs. Jane was so

focused on his mouth and the desire that threatened to overtake her, that she gave a startled cry when his hot tongue gently licked her.

She grasped her comforter in her hands, another cry locked in her throat when he found her clitoris and began to lick, lave, probe.

He kept her thighs wide, introducing her to an even more intimate onslaught. The assault left her senses reeling. Every nerve was stretched tight, her body drifting on the tide of his carnal prowess.

And he was a master. He knew just where to touch, just how to touch to bring her nearly to the point of no return, only to pull back and leave her wanting and aching.

Banan rose above her and let his gaze rake over the exquisite creature beneath him. Her luscious body was naked and racked with passion. Her nipples were tightly beaded, and his hands craved to take her firm, full breasts again. Her thighs were spread to show him the auburn curls and her sex still glistening from her desire and his mouth.

But it was her eyes, full of blatant, palpable longing that made his balls tighten. No longer could he hold back. He had to be inside her.

Her hands gripped his sides, urging him over her, in her. Banan smiled as he set his aching cock against her slick folds, and with one powerful thrust joined them.

Her gasp, and the feel of her nails sinking into his skin, only urged him onward. He withdrew, and plunged in again, sinking even deeper.

Jane whispered his name, her breaths coming in heaving gasps. She was tender, passionate. Warm, sultry.

Yielding, wanton.

He'd never known such urgency, such a driving, burning compulsion for a woman.

Despite every last lucid, sensible qualm.

He pinned her beneath him, a small smile playing

about her lips before she released a cry of pleasure. Her glorious curves cushioned him as she wrapped her legs around him. He sank deeper still, enveloped in her wet, clinging heat.

She rocked beneath him, silently pleading for release. A dance as old as time took them. He couldn't hold back the tide of passion—and didn't want to.

It was sweeter than he'd ever known, more evocative than he'd ever thought possible. And all because of an auburn-haired, coffee-eyed beauty who had somehow sunk into his soul.

Her cries of pleasure filled the room. He thrust harder, deeper, wanting—nay, *needing*—to see her peak, to watch her face as ecstasy took her.

She suddenly arched, his name falling from her lips. Her strangled cry, combined with the feel of her tight sheath clamping around him, was his defeat.

Banan let the release take him, allowed himself—for the first time ever—to climax simultaneously with another. With every convulsion of her walls, she took him higher, higher than he'd ever been.

To his surprise, her arms wrapped around him, urging him down on top of her. Banan complied, uncertain if he should stay, but knowing he couldn't leave.

Not now. Not after tasting all Jane was.

He'd think about the consequences later.

CHAPTER TEN

Jane had never been so content lying in the arms of another man. But then again, Banan wasn't an ordinary man. She wasn't sure how she knew that, only that she did.

She'd been drifting in that wonderful realm between sleep and wake while Banan's fingers caressed up and down her back.

Jane opened her eyes and saw him staring at the ceiling with his other arm behind his head. He looked lost in thought, the space between his brows wrinkled as if he were contemplating something.

"What is it?" she asked.

Instantly his frown was gone, his face carefully blank. A thread of insecurity she couldn't dispel threatened to ruin the cozy cocoon they had formed after their lovemaking.

And it had been lovemaking. There had been times Jane wanted to think a boyfriend had made love to her, but after just one touch from Banan, she'd known the difference instantly.

"Nothing," Banan answered.

Jane smiled despite the growing disquiet within her. "You're a very bad liar."

His head tilted so that he looked down at her. "What?"

"Are you telling me no one has ever called you a liar before?" she asked with a laugh.

"Nay."

That one word, combined with the intensity of his stormy gaze, unsettled her. "It was a joke, Banan."

"Nay, Jane. You knew I didna tell you the truth. How?"

She shrugged and wished she'd kept her mouth shut. "I don't know. Look, it doesn't matter. Okay? Let's just pretend I didn't say anything."

But Banan couldn't pretend. Just as he couldn't ignore the emotions swirling like a cyclone within him. He hadn't been able to deny or withstand the attraction he had for Jane. Finally having her, claiming her had only intensified everything.

Yet he knew very little about her.

How had she been able to detect his lie? It had been a little one, but that didn't matter. No one had ever been able to tell when he lied.

Ever.

"Why did you leave Seattle?" he asked.

He felt her stiffen, and knew whatever secret she held would be one he'd be lucky to obtain. Banan, however, loved a good challenge.

"Why does it matter?"

One corner of his mouth lifted in a smile. "Because I'm curious about you. I want to know what makes you, you."

"There's nothing more to tell you than what I already have. You know my life growing up in Seattle. You've seen how klutzy I am, and I'm afraid that will never change."

The sigh in her voice, and the resignation he heard, had him rolling over until he was on top of her. "I think there is much more to you than you'll allow anyone to know. We just shared our bodies in the most intimate of ways. I touched you, kissed you, licked you—"

"I know," she interrupted, a light blush staining her cheeks. "Believe me, Banan, I *know.* I experienced every wonderful minute of it."

He grew hard hearing her low, husky voice. How could such a mortal have that ability over him? If he were in his right mind, he'd get dressed and get the hell away from Jane. And never look back.

The thought of doing that left him sick to his stomach, however. Which only made him more confused.

"Jane. Please," he urged.

She turned her gaze away from him and took a deep breath. "My mother thinks I'm in London because I want to see Europe."

"And the truth?"

"I learned I have a half sister."

She uttered it so softly, it took Banan a moment to realize what she'd said. "How did you find out?"

Jane gave a light touch to his shoulder, and to her surprise, he moved off her. She sat up, holding the sheet to her chest. Which was silly, really. He'd seen all of her already.

But what she was about to say still caused her anguish, and she needed all the protection she could get. Even if it was just a sheet.

"Three years ago, my parents decided to sell the home I grew up in and build their dream house. They moved closer to the coast where they'd first met. It was such a sweet story, and one I'd heard for as long as I can remember."

Jane paused and looked at Banan. He was leaning on one elbow, silently watching her.

"They didn't want such a big house, so they had to get rid of furniture. I took some pieces because I couldn't imagine allowing it to go to someone else. One item was a desk my father had kept with him since he was sixteen."

This was where the story took a turn she still, after three years, couldn't wrap her head around sometimes. Jane picked at the sheet.

"The desk was so used and scratched, I thought I'd refinish it. I was sanding it down when I found the hidden compartment in the bottom of one of the drawers. There, secured with string, was a stack of letters. I thought they were from my mother."

"But they were no'," Banan said.

Jane shook her head. "They were from another woman, a Scotswoman, who had come over to visit relatives. She met my father and they began dating. Dad was seeing her and my mother at the same time. He ended up calling it off with the other woman, and asking Mom to marry him. But the other woman was already pregnant."

"I'm sorry, Jane."

His words, spoken so honestly and tenderly, brought tears to her eyes. "It's all right. I learned through the letters that the woman didn't hold any type of grudge. She knew my father was in love with my mom. I also learned that, apparently, my mom knew all about it."

"So why did you lie to them? Why no' tell them why you came to Britain?"

"Good question," Jane said with a wry smile. She turned to Banan then and drank in his dark good looks. "They kept this from me. I was at first angry, then hurt. I have a half sister out there, and I want to know her. I spent most of my savings hiring a private investigator who tracked Samantha—Sammi, as she likes to be called—to Oban, Scotland. Her mother died almost five years ago. She owns her own pub."

Banan's gray eyes narrowed slightly. "You said you went to Oban."

"Yes. I went there to talk to her. I'd seen pictures of her, so I knew what she looked like. But when I stood twenty feet from her, I couldn't do it. I'd been over and over in my mind what I'd say. Then, chickened out."

Banan reached for her arm and tugged her back against him. "Are you ever going to approach her?"

"It's my goal. It's the entire reason I have the damn job at PureGems to support me so I can get to her."

"Why no' move to Scotland? You'd have been closer?"

"I didn't know she was in Scotland until I got here. The last report I had was that she was in London. I already had a job and my flat when the PI found her in Oban."

Banan rested his chin atop her head. "When are you going to tell your parents?"

"I'm not sure I am. I want to meet Sammi first."

"Then you plan to return to Seattle?"

His question wasn't one she could immediately answer. It had been her plan when she first came to London, but she had come to love being in Britain. "I do miss my family, but . . ."

"But," he pressed.

"I like it here."

"Doona go into PureGems tomorrow, Jane."

It was her turn to rise up on her elbow and look at him. "Why?"

"I've a bad feeling about Arnold. No' to mention the fact he came here, threatened you, and had the other man watching your flat."

"We don't know if that was Richard or not."

"Trust me," Banan said with confidence. "It was."

"I need that job."

Banan was trying to figure out how much he could tell Jane to convince her how dangerous things were. "Do you trust me?"

For long moments she stared into his eyes, and then said, "Yes."

"Then, I beg of you, doona go back to PureGems.

Elena willna be there much longer either. G . . . her man," he amended quickly, "never wanted her to return, and he'll do what he must to keep her safe. I doona know how deep Arnold is in what we're investigating, but he already suspects you know something. You're a liability. Do you know what men like him do to liabilities?"

"I've seen enough movies and read enough books to know."

He hated to frighten her, but he would do whatever it took to keep her away from Richard Arnold.

"I've got a little saved," she said more to herself than him. "I can be all right for a few months before things get tight."

Banan pulled her on top of his chest. "Nay. I doona want you worrying about money. I'll take care of you."

And oddly enough, that appealed to him. He wanted to be the one who ensured she was safe, fed, and well loved.

"I can take care of myself."

"Really?" he asked, and kissed her neck. "Is that so, lass?"

"Hmm," she said in answer.

Suddenly, she put her hands on his chest and straddled him. The sight of her auburn hair falling around her face as she leaned over him made him grow instantly, achingly hard.

His gaze lowered to her breasts, and to his delight, her nipples pebbled before his eyes.

"You want to take care of me?" she asked, and leaned far enough down so that her nipple grazed his chest.

He moaned, his fingers digging into her hips. "Aye."

"Then make love to me."

Banan took her mouth in a searing kiss. He thought he was in control, until she wrapped a hand around his cock. He hissed in a breath as she stroked him from base to tip before lightly squeezing.

He groaned, unable to stop his hips from rising to meet

her hand. He was already so far gone, he wasn't sure how much longer he could last. But the feel of her touching him was the most exquisite torture he'd ever endured.

Jane had never been so bold with a man before. She smiled at the deep moan her touch brought forth from Banan. It was empowering.

As much as she wanted to spend time touching him, it took just one brush from the head of his rod against her sensitive sex, and she had to have him inside her.

Jane guided him to her entrance. The feel of the blunt head of his arousal stretching her felt too good. She rotated her hips once, twice. She was about to do it again when Banan growled and jerked her hips down as he lifted his.

He slid in deep and hard. Jane gasped, her eyes closing with pleasure. He was impossibly hard, like steel encased in velvet.

He stretched her, filled her until she didn't know where she ended and he began. Slowly, she rocked back and forth, loving the feel of him inside her.

She sat up, biting her lip when he went deeper. Through her lashes she watched his lips lift in a satisfied male smile that sent a thrill through her.

His hands grasped her breasts, leisurely caressing them. Her breasts swelled and her body burned. Her tempo increased when he drew her nipples into taut, aching buds.

Jane thought she was in control until Banan sat up and fastened his mouth on a nipple. She sank her hands into his hair and dropped her head back.

He scooted them to the edge of the bed, where he carefully shifted her legs until they wrapped around him. And then he began to move.

Jane's breath locked in her lungs. She was overwhelmed with the incredible sensations as their bodies rocked together. His grip on her hips tightened as he slowly raised her and then pulled her down.

He repeated the movement again and again. Ruthlessly, relentlessly he pushed her higher, urged her to give everything.

Jane opened her heart, opened her soul—and never looked back.

Her body was tightening, muscles locking. And then the climax took her, pitched her. Swept her.

She was falling into an abyss, a chasm, and she'd never felt so safe, so protected. So . . . wanted. It was a primal, primitive feeling.

One look into Banan's molten eyes, and she was lost. Forever, endlessly lost to all that was Banan. She didn't panic at the love blooming in her heart. Nothing so beautiful should be feared.

Contentment flowed through her as Banan began to move his hips faster. Their gazes locked, held. There was no looking away, no denying something profound was transpiring between them.

She felt his muscles tighten, heard his breathing hitch, and with a low moan, his release took him.

Jane embraced him as he buried his face in her neck and spilled his seed inside her. She held him, confused and exciting by what had occurred.

Whatever the days ahead held for her, she knew her life would be forever altered.

Because she had fallen heedlessly, helplessly in love with him.

CHAPTER ELEVEN

Banan held the mug of coffee in his hands and stared at Jane as he stood by the counter. He'd rested better last night than he had since it was his turn to take a century or so to sleep in Dreagan's mountain, as each Dragon King did.

Greeting a new day with Jane in his arms had been amazing. And baffling. He'd always made sure never to stay with a woman like that. Somehow, without him knowing it, something had changed.

He'd considered leaving before Jane woke, but he hadn't been able to. One look at her sleeping so innocently, and he'd been unable to look away.

Banan couldn't ever remember watching anyone sleep. Yet it had held his attention for almost half an hour.

"You aren't going to answer me, are you?" Jane asked from her seat at the table. Her voice held a note of sadness, but her gaze was direct, as if she'd known how he'd react.

But what was he supposed to do? She'd asked for his secret, since she had shared her. Yet Banan couldn't tell her. Even though he wanted to.

Another surprise.

He began to wonder if Jane was somehow affecting

him. He should be worried, concerned—anything. Yet it all seemed so natural, being with her.

"I can no'," he finally answered.

"I figured as much."

"I've kept this secret willingly, Jane, and never once regretted no' being able to tell it. Until you."

She set down her mug and put both elbows on the table. "What happens now? Between us? Are you going to leave, and I'll never see you again?"

The thought brought a pain to his chest. "Nay. I've got to see the MI5 friend of mine this morning, and I want you to stay here. Pack a bag or two. I'm going to take you to Scotland with me."

"What?" she asked, a smile lifting her lips.

"Aye. We're going to find your half sister." It would give him time to figure out how to tell the others about Jane, and try to prepare her for what he was. If that was possible.

She rose from the chair and came to stand in front of him. "You keep surprising me, Banan."

"Is that a good thing?"

"Yeah," she said, and rose up on her tiptoes to kiss him. "It is."

"Good. Now, I'll be back in two hours. Be here," he warned sternly.

She gave a salute. "Yes, sir."

Banan didn't want to leave. Something kept telling him to stay, but the sooner he left, the sooner he could get back. Plus, he needed to answer the dozen or so texts and calls from Con and Guy.

He drew Jane into his arms for one last, lingering kiss. "Lock the door behind me."

"I will. Besides, who would want to come after me?" she asked with a laugh.

Banan stepped into the corridor as Jane shut the door. He waited a moment to hear her set the locks. Only then did he pull his mobile out of his pocket to call Con.

Constantine was the leader of the Dragon Kings, the King of Kings. Con was the face of Dreagan, but no one ever actually saw his face. He also ensured that their land, and the fact they were dragons, remained a secret.

Banan exited Jane's building and walked down the steps to his meeting with Henri North, his mobile already dialing Constantine.

"Con," Banan said when his friend answered. "I willna be returning to Dreagan immediately as planned. I've got a stop I need to make."

Jane had packed three bags, showered, and readied for the day, and still it was a half hour before Banan returned. She hadn't quite decided how to quit her job. A phone call would be the best, and probably the safest.

She ran to her cell phone when she heard the chime that she had a text. To her disappointment, Banan was going to be longer than expected.

Jane pulled out her laptop and began to draft an email to Richard with her resignation. She was half done when she realized she had to go to PureGems after all.

"Damn," Jane said, and tried to call Elena.

If Elena was still at the office, she could get the file Jane needed, and she wouldn't have to break her promise to Banan and leave.

But Elena didn't answer.

There was only one thing Jane could do, and that was to go herself. There was no way she was going to leave the file on Sammi there for Richard to find. It was too important. And private.

Jane glanced at the clock. It was nearly lunch. If she left now, she'd time it perfectly so that Richard was gone and she could get in and out of PureGems without him ever knowing. And leave her resignation in the process.

Her decision made, Jane put on her shoes, grabbed her purse, and rushed out of her flat.

She took a taxi to the office and tried to ignore the way her stomach trembled with nervousness. Even as she rode the elevator up, she knew everything would be all right. Richard always left at eleven for lunch, and it was noon.

He wouldn't be there, and she would be safe.

The doors to the elevator opened, and Jane stepped out. She waited for someone to say something, anything, but as usual no one noticed her.

And for the first time, she was exceedingly glad.

Jane hurried to her desk and pulled open her bottom right drawer. She found the file and tucked it in her purse. Then she drafted a quick resignation letter, printed and signed it.

There was a smile on her face as she walked into Richard's office and placed it on his desk.

In a matter of seconds, she had her purse and was on the elevator down. All her nerves were for nothing. She was going to make it back to her flat before Banan arrived, and all would be fine.

There was still a smile on her face as she walked out of the PureGems building and stepped to the curb to hail a cab.

The next thing she knew, she was being grabbed from behind and tossed into a black SUV.

"Fuck," Guy cursed as he watched the black Range Rover drive off with Jane inside it.

Guy knew whoever had taken Jane wasn't going to be nice, but he couldn't leave Elena. He took out his phone, ready to send Elena a text with what had happened, when she walked out of the building next to Richard Arnold.

By the way Elena held her shoulders, Guy knew she wasn't going willingly.

"Bloody hell." Could nothing go right?

With Banan meeting Henri, and Rhys searching Arnold's home computer for hidden documents, it was up to

Guy to do it all. But he couldn't. His first choice was go to after Elena. If he did, he almost ensured Jane's death.

Based on what Elena had told him of how Banan had been acting around Jane, Banan would never forgive him. But he couldn't lose Elena.

Guy got into a cab and said, "Follow that Mercedes."

He then sent Banan and Rhys a text letting them know what had happened.

Banan was about to ignore the text for the third time, when he realized there was only one reason someone would continue to text him.

"A moment," he said to Henri North.

He had to read Guy's text twice. It took him a second to comprehend what the emotions were raging within him— desperation. And fury.

He was going to kill whoever had dared to take Jane.

Banan refused to think about what would happen if he didn't get to her in time. He lifted his gaze to Henri and said, "They have Jane."

"Who does?" Henri asked, his hazel eyes narrowed in confusion.

Banan squeezed his eyes closed, hating the anxiety he felt. "I doona know. What was she doing at PureGems? I told her to stay at the flat until I returned."

"What direction were they headed?" Henri asked.

Banan shook his head to clear it. He opened his eyes. "South."

"I bet they're headed to a warehouse near the waterfront. Come on. We can track her mobile."

Banan followed Henri to his car and got in. Then watched as Henri pulled out an iPad and typed in some numbers. Banan knew Guy had to make a choice, but Banan hated that he hadn't been there to watch Jane.

Each second that ticked by felt like years. He couldn't allow himself to think about what was being done to

Jane. If he did, he'd likely lose what little control he had on his emotions. And he couldn't permit himself to shift into dragon form in the middle of London.

"What's her number?" Henri asked urgently.

Banan hastily rattled off the numbers. Within a matter of seconds, a map of London pulled up and a small red dot blinked, locating Jane.

"I was right," Henri said with a wry smile. "They're taking her to a warehouse."

"Get moving, then," Banan said between clenched teeth.

Henri smiled and started his BMW. "Why is it anytime I get a call from you, I always find myself in the middle of some bloody mess that takes me months to get myself out of?"

"You enjoy it." Usually Banan enjoyed Henri's banter, but he was too concerned about Jane to be able to contribute.

"You care for this chit?"

Banan looked out the side window as Henri sped off. "Aye."

"Love catches us all, doesn't it, mate?"

He couldn't answer Henri. Banan kept seeing Jane's beautiful coffee brown eyes filled with passion and pleasure. He'd had the most wonderful night of his very long existence, and it left him uneasy.

Banan focused on the blinking red dot while Henri maneuvered them through the crowded London streets. They were gaining ground, but not enough. Jane and her abductors were still too far ahead, and with the traffic, they would never reach her in time.

"Nay!" Banan bellowed when the red light suddenly stopped blinking.

"Bloody hell," Henri ground out, and pulled over.

Once more he was punching in all sorts of codes, but nothing he did had the red light back.

"It's gone, mate. I'm sorry. They must've realized she had the GPS turned on her mobile."

Banan looked to the sky. Millions of years ago, he'd have shifted into dragon form and taken to the skies to find Jane. Now, he could do nothing but wait. It was that waiting that would likely get Jane killed.

"Why did they take her, Banan?"

It took a moment for his brain to register that Henri was speaking. "The number I gave you last night, she found it. She also overheard some information."

"You should've bloody well gotten her out of the city." Henri slammed his hand against his steering wheel. "I can do no more here. I need to get back to the office. There I can use satellites to see inside the warehouses."

"And likely lose your job."

"I'm MI5, Banan. My job is the safety of Britain and her people."

Banan turned his head to look at Henri. He was the kind of man a person forgot. Light, sandy brown hair, hazel eyes, plain face, and average height. He was forgettable, the kind of person everyone overlooked. Which was why he was one of Britain's top MI5 agents.

"You need to know this is about Dreagan," Banan said.

Henri gave a slight nod. "I assumed as much when you called. One of these days, you're going to tell me what's so important about a scotch distillery."

"Doona hold your breath, my friend. That day willna likely come."

Henri grinned slyly. "We all have our secrets."

Banan opened the car door as thunder rumbled over him. "If you find anything, call me. I need to find Jane, and when we do, I suspect the people we're searching for are going to be there."

"And does that include Richard Arnold?"

He shouldn't have been surprised Henri knew that much. "Aye."

"We've a large file on him. Taking him down won't be a problem."

"It's no' just him we need."

Jane opened her eyes to the blackness of a hood over her. Her head ached so badly, she was nauseated. She parted her lips to breathe through her mouth, and wished her hands weren't tied so tightly behind her, because she had an itch on her nose.

Banan.

God, how she wished he were there. Or that she hadn't gone into PureGems, as he'd asked. She thought she had gotten in and out without being seen. How wrong she'd been.

"I see you're awake."

The voice was male, and held a slight mocking quality to it. It wasn't exactly British, because she heard traces of a Scots brogue, so faint that it was hard to detect.

Jane knew she could cower beneath the hood, or she could face whatever was before her. She wasn't naturally aggressive or courageous. But what else could she do?

"Who are you?" she asked.

The man chuckled softly. "I wouldn't suggest you try to outwit me, Jane Holden. You wouldn't last long."

"Because I asked who you were, you think I'm trying to outwit you? Talk about an ego," she said with a snort.

She wasn't sure what had come over her, but his attitude, so like Richard Arnold's, grated on her nerves.

Suddenly, his voice was whispering in her ear. "I have your life in my hands. I wouldn't suggest pissing me off."

She was grateful for the hood, because it hid the tear that fell down her cheek. Jane blinked back the rest, but she couldn't dispel the terror that knotted in her stomach.

"What do you want from me?"

She flinched when a finger caressed down her arm to her tied wrists.

"I can make life easier for you. At least until I kill you."

Her heart pounded so hard, she thought it might burst from her chest. Never had she been so terrified.

"If you're going to kill me, why not just do it now?"

"You Americans, always thinking you control things," he said with a snarl. "I knew the moment I saw you that you'd be trouble."

"Because I'm a good secretary who works late?" she quipped.

"Because you meddle. And you had the unfortunate mistake of making the acquaintance of a Dragon King."

Jane frowned. She had no idea what a Dragon King was, but she was positive she hadn't met one. But the image of Banan's intertwined double dragon tattoo flashed in her mind. "I've never met any king, so I can assure you, you're dead wrong."

"Oh, sod off," he said, the heels of his shoes hitting the concrete. "You've met two."

"Who?"

"Banan and Rhys."

Jane shook her head. "I admit, Banan is far from ordinary, but he isn't a king."

"So. He hasn't told you."

The words were spoken so softly, and with a hint of amusement that sent a chill down her spine.

"After all this time, they're still keeping their secret," the man continued. "How . . . archaic. What would you say, Jane, if I told you the Dragon Kings had the ability to rule the world?"

"I don't know."

"What if I told you they once ruled the world? What would you say then?"

She shrugged, wishing with all her might that Banan found her. And soon. "I'd say you're a half bubble off plumb."

Instead of getting irritated, the man laughed a full-bodied laugh. "Oh, dear Jane. You have so much to learn. I wonder if you'd be so willing to take Banan to your bed once you know his deep, dark secret."

"What has Banan done to make you hate him so? That's what this is all about, isn't it? You want to hurt him?"

The man pulled off her hood, and she blinked at the bright light coming through the rows of windows before her. She was momentarily blinded, but quickly forgot about it as her hair was grabbed from behind and her head yanked backwards.

"Banan is one of many," the man growled angrily. "My plan was flawless, but the idiot Sloan had to bring a friend. They both should've died in that mountain. Instead, the other bitch is protected by Guy. But no' for long."

Jane winced as he tightened his hold on her hair. But with his anger, she heard the Scottish brogue come out even more. Now she knew he was masking his accent for some reason. But why?

"Then you had to overhear Richard's conversation with me," the man continued.

"I didn't hear anything."

Strong fingers locked on to her jaw and squeezed. She bit back a cry of pain as tears stung her eyes.

"I know you heard. He knew better than to take my call with someone else around. But doona worry, sweet Jane. Richard will pay for his mistake."

The way the man's voice had grown soft and cold sent Jane's blood pounding in her ears. Whatever awaited her wasn't going to be good.

And Banan had no idea where she was. She was as good as dead.

CHAPTER TWELVE

Banan stared out the window in Jane's flat, watching the water run down the glass as the rain continued to pour. He hadn't known where else to go. He had seen her packed bags waiting on her bed, and a sharp, unrelenting pain went through his chest.

He rubbed the spot on his left side. The ache hadn't abated. If anything, it had gotten worse.

"Henri still has nothing," Rhys said as he ended the call and put his phone on the table. "I'm sorry, Banan."

In all the centuries Banan had lived, he had seen it all. He'd watched wars, famine, and drought. He had been content, if not happy.

Many times he'd held in his anger at not being able to take to the skies as he had as a Dragon King. He had even experienced loss with the death of dragons and Dragon Kings.

Of all the feelings he had dealt with, not once had he felt helpless. Until now.

He was a Dragon King. Immortal and powerful. Yet he could do nothing to save one human female who had touched his heart and soul as no other.

The door to Jane's flat flew open, and Guy and Elena

rushed in. For just a heartbeat, Banan had thought it might be Jane. The disappointment was like a knife to his gut.

He solemnly turned to stare out the window. Everywhere he looked in the flat, he felt Jane, smelled her clean scent.

"Anything?" Guy asked.

Banan didn't bother to reply. He wasn't angry at Guy for doing what was necessary to ensure Elena's safety. Banan himself would have done the same for his woman.

He squeezed his eyes closed. *His woman.* Never had he thought even to think those words, but after last night, that's exactly what Jane was.

His.

"No," Rhys answered. "Henri couldna help us."

"There is one who can."

Banan turned at Guy's words, a thread of hope breaking through. "Who?"

"The Warriors. Broc MacLaughlin has the ability to find anyone, anywhere."

Elena looked from Guy to Banan. "What are you waiting for? Call this Broc. We must find Jane."

"It's been hours since they took her. Besides, Con would never allow us to approach the Warriors of MacLeod Castle," Rhys said.

Nevertheless, the idea appealed to Banan. If he went alone, maybe he could convince the Warriors to help him without ever disclosing what he was.

When Con found out—and he *would* find out—there would be hell to pay.

Banan would take whatever came his way as long as Jane was free. The only way he could contact Broc, however, was to go alone. Something Rhys and Guy wouldn't allow if they knew his plans.

He didn't have time to go all the way to MacLeod Castle, but then again, he didn't have to. He had Henri North as a friend.

"I'm going to go to the warehouse district. Maybe I'll get lucky and find her," Banan said as he headed to the door.

He glanced at his watch to see it was after six in the evening. The rainstorm had turned the sky a nasty shade of gray, and the rumbling thunder announced that the storm was only going to get worse.

"Banan, wait," Guy said.

But he was past waiting. He'd been waiting for hours, hoping whoever had Jane would call, since all his other leads at finding her were gone.

"Dammit, wait!" Guy yelled.

Banan took his hand off the doorknob and turned to his friend. "What? I can no' stay here another minute. Jane could already be dead. And I've done nothing."

"Not nothing," Elena said. "Guy is trying to tell you what I told him. He wants to explain why he didn't follow Jane."

"I know why," Banan said before Elena could say more. "And I understand. I doona blame Guy."

Elena set down her purse and threaded her fingers with Guy's. "Richard ordered me to lunch, Banan. Actually ordered me. He's never spoken to me that way before. He was . . . scared. That's the only way I can explain it."

Banan crossed his arms over his chest and waited for the rest.

"He was in my office when Jane came to PureGems. I never saw her, and I don't believe Richard knew anything about her being taken."

"So," Banan stated.

Elena licked her lips and glanced at Guy. "What I'm trying to tell you is that when we went to the restaurant, Richard didn't eat. He drank. Heavily. But he never ate. He didn't talk much either, just kept looking around him as if he expected to see someone show up at any moment."

Banan dropped his arms as he realized what had happened. "Arnold might no' know they wanted to take Jane, but I'm guessing that somehow he knew Jane found the number of the person who called Arnold the other day."

"Aye," Rhys said. "Arnold must know they're coming for him."

Guy rubbed his chin thoughtfully. "It must be the others, because Arnold has no way of knowing we're closing in on him. Besides, he's no' the big fish we want. We want the man controlling him."

"True, but we didn't know about the bigger fish," Elena pointed out. "Not until we began to look into Richard."

"None of this is helping Jane, or helping me find her," Banan said, and ran a hand down his face. "All this tells me is that whoever this bastard is, he's two steps ahead of us at all times. And he knows what we are."

Rhys scooted back his chair and stood. "Which shouldna be possible. But how do we find this arsehole?"

"Good question." Banan reached for the doorknob again, only to have Guy's voice stop him.

"There's no need to go to Henri for Broc's mobile number."

Banan slowly turned to his friends. "I doona know what you're talking about. I already said it wouldna be a good idea to contact the Warriors."

"Aye, so you did," Rhys said with a cocky grin. "That doesna mean we shouldna do it."

Banan looked at them and found his lips tilting up in a smile. "I've wasted enough time. Call him now. I need to find Jane. And Rhys, see if Henri can put a tracker on Arnold's mobile so we can see where he's at."

Guy already had his mobile out when Banan's phone rang. He pulled it from his back pocket to see PRIVATE CALLER show up on his screen.

"Aye?" Banan answered the call.

"Tell me, Banan, how does it feel to have something taken from you that you care about?"

Banan knew instantly the man was referring to Jane. He squeezed the phone until he heard it crack. Rage burned within him, urging him to find whoever the man was and crush him with one stomp of his massive dragon paw.

"Are you there, Banan? Don't tell me you're too angry to speak. I thought you were the one Dragon King who didn't allow emotion into his life."

Banan took a deep breath and swung his gaze to Rhys and Guy, who had moved closer to him. He lowered the phone and put it on speaker so everyone could hear.

"Who are you?" Banan demanded of the caller.

The man laughed softly. "Oh, you'll never figure that out. Trust me. But, that's not why I'm calling. I'm calling because I have a sweet morsel in my possession."

"Leave Jane alone," Banan stated angrily.

It was too long since he'd felt the need for battle. How Banan longed for it now. He wanted to shift, to spread his wings and take to the sky. He yearned to use his dragon sight to hunt down the scum who dared to touch Jane.

And then Banan would rip him apart with his teeth.

"Jane got herself in this situation," the man said. "Or should I say *you* got her in this. It was you, after all, who sent her searching in Richard's desk. It was you who got to know her. If only you'd left her alone, then we would've left her alone. She is quite the beauty, I must say."

"If you've laid one hand on her!" Banan bellowed.

"*He's been following Jane,*" Guy mouthed. "*It's the only explanation.*"

Banan hated that his friend was probably right.

The man's laughter cut through Banan's thoughts. "What are you going to do? Not even your MI5 friend could help you. With all your power, with all your magic . . . with all your immortality, you're powerless, Banan. I'm going to make sure each of the Kings feels such helplessness. And I'm starting with you."

"Why?"

In answer, Banan heard a scream, a scream he recognized as Jane's. His gut twisted, and anguish snaked through him.

"Jane has given us all the information we need. Her time is up," the man said.

"Nay!" Banan yelled, but it was too late. The call had ended.

The mobile fell from his numb fingers to bounce on the carpet. Jane was still alive, but not for very long. He had precious few moments to find her.

There was no longer time to call the Warrior Broc. There was only one way Banan could find Jane.

He lifted his gaze to find Rhys and Guy watching him. There was no need for words. They all knew what had to happen.

"The storm is getting worse," Rhys said.

Guy nodded. "It'll be to your advantage, Banan."

"They'll never expect you."

"Nay, they willna," Banan said, and removed his boots and socks.

"Uh . . . not to interrupt," Elena said as she moved to stand beside Guy. "But what the hell are you three talking about?"

Banan smiled weakly. "I'm going to risk everything we are as Dragon Kings."

"Oh, God," Elena said, and covered her mouth with her hand.

Rhys took off his shoes as well and rubbed his hands together. "I'm coming with you. No way I'm going to miss this."

"Nay," Banan said. "I'm risking too much. I might be able to get away with it, but there's no way people will miss two dragons in the sky."

"You're no' going alone." The smile was gone from Rhys's face, and the hard edge of a Dragon King took its place.

Guy opened the door for them. "Go. I'll contact Con."

Rhys was the first out the door, but Banan hung back. He looked at Guy and Elena. "Get Elena to safety. Doona risk her life any more."

"I doona plan on it."

With a nod to Elena, Banan hurried out of Jane's building and into the rain. He lifted his face to the sky. It had been a Dragon King's place to protect the humans, but this night Banan was going to break his oath.

He was going to kill a human. And rejoice in it.

"Come on!" Rhys shouted over the rain.

Banan lowered his head and took off at a run to catch up with Rhys. Together they weaved their way to the outskirts of London. They were too large, as dragons, to shift where they were. It was going to take privacy.

Fortunately for them, the sky had grown even darker, and people were in such a hurry to get out of the rain, they never looked up.

By the time they reached a safe spot, the urgency pushing Banan was too much. He barely spared Rhys a glance before he closed his eyes and shifted.

The change happened in an instant. He turned his great head first one way, then the other. Another second was spent stretching out his wings.

It felt so good to be in dragon form that for just an instant he forgot his mission. All too soon, the memory of Jane's scream echoed through his mind.

"Ready?" Rhys's voice sounded in his head.

Banan gave a nod and jumped into the air. The rush of wind as his wings caught a current sent excitement through him. It had been too long since he was in his true form. Too long to deny what he truly was.

It wasn't right he was getting such a thrill of being in

dragon form in order to save the woman who he had fallen in love with.

Banan climbed higher and higher in the sky, soaring in between the clouds as his vision locked on the warehouse area of London. He could see heat signatures through the buildings.

They appeared like bright orange figures, but picking out which one might be Jane wasn't so easy.

The many passes he made over the warehouses were blurred as he got closer and closer, hoping to see or hear Jane. He'd do anything if he could detect where she was.

His heart clenched when he heard her terrified scream. With a roar, he rolled and turned to fly back the way he had come. She screamed again, and it helped him home in on the warehouse. He gave a roar that was drowned out by thunder.

And then dived toward the warehouse.

CHAPTER THIRTEEN

Jane screamed and stumbled backward, tripping over her feet and nearly falling as her eyes locked on Richard Arnold, who pleaded for his life to the thug with the gun. The goon wasn't the same man who had threatened her earlier, but that made little difference.

Villains were villains, and the one holding the gun—along with his malicious smile—stated just how much he enjoyed killing.

For the briefest of moments, when Richard had walked into the warehouse, Jane had thought he was in charge. It had taken less than a heartbeat to realize he was being dragged to the warehouse kicking and screaming.

Richard was merely a pawn. A gamepiece whoever ran this criminal enterprise was all too happy to be rid of.

"Richard, Richard, Richard," said a familiar voice from the shadows. "I warned you what would happen if anyone discovered what you were up to."

Jane searched the darkness for a face. Whoever the man was, he went to great lengths to keep his face from being seen. But why? If they were going to kill her, what did it matter if she saw him?

Richard glanced at her before he looked at the shadowy figure. "Please. You know how valuable I can be to you. My connections—"

"I didna contact you for your connections!" the voice bellowed angrily.

Once more, the brogue was all too clear. Jane took another step back as she tried to distance herself from Richard and the man with the gun.

"She didn't hear anything!" Richard yelled.

He opened his mouth to say more, but the gun exploded. Jane screamed and watched as red blossomed over Richard's heart, staining his white shirt.

Richard turned toward her as his legs gave out. He landed hard on his knees, and then fell to the side. His arm was stretched out to her, and his eyes wide.

Jane couldn't tear her gaze away from him. She'd seen violent movies, but that was nothing compared to seeing someone killed in real life. It was shocking, appalling. Horrifying.

And it was something she would never forget.

Movement from the thug made her look at him. Only to find the gun now pointed at her. She hadn't understood when they untied her wrists after hours of interrogation in which she had lied beautifully, but now she did. They wanted her to run, wanted to chase her. Like some kind of quarry.

Every instinct yelled for her to move, but fear rooted her.

"Banan," she whispered, hating that she would never see him again.

She drew in a deep, shaky breath and readied for the sound of the gun going off. Instead, something crashed through the top of the warehouse.

Jane turned away, raising her arms to block her face from the shower of debris that fell on her. She stumbled against the back wall and quickly covered her ears against the roar that nearly busted her eardrums.

She chanced a look to see what had happened, and stood in stunned disbelief at the massive midnight blue dragon who now stood in the warehouse. Jane blinked through the torrent of water that drenched her to find the dragon's gemlike sapphire scales glistening from the rain.

The dragon had a thick body with a long neck and a tail with what looked like a spiked ball at the end of it. The dragon used that tail, whipping it to the side to take out more men Jane had never even known were there.

One of the dragon's large feet with four digits slammed into the floor as it roared again. It was then she noticed the wings tucked against the dragon's body along with the rows of tendrils that ran from the base of its skull down its back to the tip of its tail.

She couldn't quite believe what she was looking at. And then the dragon's colossal head swung toward her. She let her gaze look from the four horns extending backwards from its forehead to the rows of teeth she glimpsed. Jane knew the instant the dragon's amber eyes trained on her.

Her heart leaped in her throat. Was this how she would die? Not by a bullet, but by a creature that surely couldn't exist?

There was movement near her. Jane watched the thug shoving away debris as he gained his feet. He took one look at her and raised his gun.

The dragon let out another deafening roar before it clamped down on the brute with its sharp teeth and tossed him in the air.

Jane followed the thug's soar, both elated that he was gone and frightened of what would now happen to her. She was about to look away, when she spotted something yellow dip from the sky.

A shriek lodged in her throat when she saw the second dragon, which quickly ate the gunman.

Jane waited until the blue dragon was busy swatting more men with its tail before she began looking for a way out. She fled behind a wall where the roof still covered the warehouse and anxiously looked for some kind of door.

When she found nothing, she turned to retrace her footsteps and found a man standing in her way. His face, along with most of his body, was shrouded in the shadows, but she knew who it was. Despite all the yells from the dying men and the roars of the dragons, this man didn't seem fazed.

"You aren't afraid," she commented.

He shrugged. "It's not the first time I've seen dragons. What do you think of them? Are you frightened, Jane?"

She was terrified, but she wouldn't tell him that. "Move."

"So you can leave? Oh, I think not. You're going to stay to see the end of this. I think you'll be surprised. Matter of fact, I know it. And I want to see the look on your face when you realize what's going on. Better than that, I want to see Banan's face."

Banan. Jane didn't know what he had to do with this, but she couldn't wait to get to him. In his arms she was safe—she knew that with a certainty she couldn't explain.

It was then she realized the screams of the men had stopped. The only sound was that of a dragon's deep, heavy breathing, the rain, and the thunder and lightning.

A large drop of rain landed in front of her. Jane slowly lifted her face to find the dragon looking at her from over the top of the wall, which in her haste, she hadn't noticed didn't go all the way to the roof.

Her heartbeat grew rapid and harsh as terror took hold. The dragon shifted its gaze, searching the shadows. Jane glanced to where the man had been, only to discover him gone. When her gaze returned to the dragon, she watched his head disappear back over the wall.

Why hadn't he killed her? It would take just a swipe from his paw to knock down the wall separating them.

Jane took the opportunity to search where she was for a door out, but found nothing. She had no choice but to go back where the dragon waited. Maybe then she could escape without his notice.

She hesitantly walked around the wall and found not just the blue dragon, but also the yellow dragon. They were standing side by side, and their opened wings blocked the majority of the rain.

Jane looked from one to the other. The yellow dragon's wide, orange eyes looked back at her, and she could have sworn the beast smiled, causing the series of tendril-like sprouts from his chin to move.

There seemed to be no malice coming from either of the dragons, and though the yellow one seemed to have smiled, it was the midnight blue one that drew her attention.

She couldn't stop shaking from the cool air or the fear that gripped her. She was facing dragons!

Suddenly she recalled the man's words from earlier. Dragon Kings.

Jane looked at the blue dragon. "Are you a Dragon King?"

To her surprise, he nodded his great head.

She took a step back, her hand over her heart. "How? How are you here? How do you exist?"

The blue looked away, his amber eyes troubled by her questions.

"They are questions I can answer," said a male voice behind her.

Jane whirled around to see a new form move out of the shadows and into the light. He wore dark slacks and a charcoal gray and deep purple striped button-down. He shoved his hands casually in his front pockets and smiled.

"You must be Jane Holden."

She looked over her shoulder to see the dragons watching her. When she looked back at the man, she took in his tall form, the muscles not quite hidden by his shirt, and the golden color of his hair. It was his nearly black eyes that penetrated her, which told her this man would not be trifled with.

"Yes," she answered. "And you are?"

"Constantine. But you can call me Con. I've a feeling, Jane, you and I will come to know each other quite well. Banan has spoken highly of you, as have Elena, Rhys, and Guy."

Jane put her hand to the side of her head. "Stop. Just . . . stop. There are two dragons behind me, and you aren't even daunted by them. The other man seems to have just disappeared as well. What the hell is going on?"

Con took another step toward her. "First, the other man you refer to is gone. Unfortunately. But I'll take care of that later. Second, those dragons are my friends. You know them, actually."

"The other man said something like that as well. What do you mean?"

Con's relaxed demeanor changed instantly. "Did you get a look at this man? Did you see his face?"

"No, to both questions. He made sure to keep to the shadows so I never saw him. He said he wanted to be here to see my face when I realized what the dragons were. He said he wanted to see Banan's face as well. I don't understand any of it."

"Nay," Con said with a sigh. "I'm no' sure you're ready for the answers, Jane."

Con let out a short whistle, and both dragons shook their heads. Jane grew more confused the longer the conversation went on.

"Look. I'm wet and cold. I've been kidnapped, roughened up, threatened, and had the fear of God put in me. I just want to find Banan and get home."

Con glanced at the ground. "A verra long time ago I swore to protect my men at all costs. We gave up everything, but I feared that wouldna be enough. So, I made sure we never developed feelings for mortals. I thought that would solve things."

"Mortals?" Jane whispered, her brain having trouble deciphering his meaning.

"Jane, look at the dragons."

She took a hesitant step back, but Con walked to her, placed his hands on her shoulders, and gently turned her to the dragons.

"Look at them. What do you see?"

"I saw them kill." But she couldn't leave it at that. There had been more, and she needed to admit it. "They didn't touch me. It was almost as if . . ." She trailed off, not sure if she could say it.

"What? It was almost as if what?"

"They were protecting me," she answered in a whisper.

Con leaned close and replied in the same hushed tone, "Because they were."

"I know them?"

"Aye."

She stepped away from Con and toward the dragons. Jane hesitantly smiled when the blue dragon shifted his wing to keep her dry. Her gaze swung to the yellow, but it didn't stay.

The blue was the one who called to her. She continued toward the massive beast until she stood next to its large front foot.

Tentatively, she put her hand on it. The scales were surprisingly warm. And it was then she noticed the dark blue scales on its back slowly faded to a lighter blue on his belly.

"Are you afraid?" Con asked, his voice echoing in the warehouse.

"Yes. And no," she answered.

She looked up at the blue watching her with its amber gaze, and it was something about those eyes that looked familiar.

It wasn't the color, but something in the gaze that told her she should know who the dragon was.

But . . . surely that couldn't be possible.

CHAPTER FOURTEEN

Banan couldn't look away from Jane's sweet brown eyes. He had seen her fear while he'd been killing to keep her safe, but there hadn't been time to calm her.

Now, he wasn't sure what to do.

He'd seen Hal and Guy show their women their dragon forms, but none had done it while fighting. Jane had seen the worst. His gentle, kind Jane.

All Banan had to do was return to his human form. But did he dare? Could he take the chance of showing her everything he was and not have her run away?

It was because of him that she was involved in such danger. He had promised to keep her safe, when he'd only made things worse.

He turned away, unable to bear looking at her another moment. Yet he had a choice to make. He could return to his human form and hope for the best.

Or he could fly away and never see Jane again.

Banan hadn't understood Guy and Hal's feelings for their women, but he did now. He wanted Jane with him always, to be by his side. He wanted to climb in bed with her each night, and face the dawn with her each morning.

He might have thought himself immune to whatever

was affecting the Dragon Kings, but there was no denying his love for Jane.

"Banan," Rhys's voice sounded in his head. *"Show Jane who you are. She went to you because she senses something about you."*

"She could run."

"Aye," Rhys said sadly. *"She could. But she might no'. I see how much she means to you. Doona let her go. You'll regret it always."*

Banan's gaze shifted to Con, who stood silently watching. Con was leaving everything up to Banan. Regardless of what Banan decided, Con would abide by it.

If Banan flew away, Jane would have no reason to know their secret and could very well live out her life in safety.

But whoever had been on the other side of that wall with her, who Banan suspected was the same bastard who'd kidnapped her, knew how important she was to him. They wouldn't ever stop hurting Jane now that she was connected to him.

Banan took a deep breath and made his decision. He shifted with barely a thought. He kept his eyes closed as he knelt with one knee and both hands on the floor, the rain pounding his flesh.

It was Jane's soft gasp that tore at his heart.

"Banan?" she murmured in confusion.

He lifted his head until he was caught in her gaze. Then he slowly stood as Rhys moved to cover Jane with his wing. "Aye. It's me."

Her hands shook, and the shock etched on her face couldn't be dismissed. All Banan could pray for was that she didn't run. If he had the time to tell her everything, to explain who he was, it might win her over.

But he knew it wasn't going to be easy.

"You were a dragon," she said, her voice wavering

from fear or anger—he wasn't sure which—as her gaze looked over his naked form.

"It was the only way I could find you. The only way I could make sure you were safe."

"Why didn't you tell me?" she asked.

Banan wished they were alone for this discussion. There was no denying the anger rising in her tone. He hated that Con was there, but at the same time knew the King of the Dragon Kings had come to help.

"I couldna," Banan said.

"This," Jane said as she waved her hand at Rhys, "is what you protect at Dreagan?"

Banan nodded his head. "You're the third human to know. Only Cassie, Elena, and you know what we've kept secret for millennia."

Her eyes bulged. "Millennia? This just keeps getting weirder and weirder." Jane turned away from him, one hand on her forehead as she paced back and forth. "I feel like my brain is going to explode any minute."

Rhys slammed his foot on the concrete, his long talons scraping the floor. Banan winced when Jane jumped. He glanced at Rhys and knew his friend was urging him to tell Jane everything.

"Once, a verra long time ago, dragons ruled this world," Banan said. "We filled the skies, the land, and the water. Every size and color dragon imaginable existed. With each species of dragon, there was one with more power and magic than the others. We were made into Dragon Kings. We ruled our dragons as kings, and answered to only one—Con."

To Banan's delight, Jane stopped pacing and turned to him. At his mention of Con, she glanced at Constantine to find him leaning a shoulder against one of the walls, uncaring of the rain that soaked him.

"We lived such a life for eons. Until one day there was

man. In order for both man and dragon to coexist, each Dragon King was given the ability to shift from dragon to human form and back again at will."

"Why?"

Banan fisted his hands at his sides instead of pulling her into his arms as he wanted. "The only way for dragons and humans to communicate was through us."

"Did it work?" she asked, her curiosity bringing her a step closer to him.

"For a time. Then a human betrayed us."

Jane looked away and wrapped her arms around her. "It's the reason you keep yourselves secret, isn't it? Because you fear another human will betray you?"

"It's more complicated than that. The human, a woman, was to be bound to a Dragon King, Ulrik. Discord abounded throughout the land between dragons and humans, and there didna seem to be a reason we could find for it. Nor could we determine the source. To make matters worse, humans began to hunt dragons."

Jane shook her head, her stricken gaze lifting to his. "Why?"

"It was Ulrik's woman causing the discord. It all happened so fast. Many of the dragons wanted to retaliate against the humans for the killing of the dragons. Con refused. We were supposed to keep the peace and protect both humans and dragons. We might no' all have agreed with Con, but we obeyed him. All except Ulrik. He and his silver dragons began to pursue the dragon hunters."

"If this human woman was to be bound to Ulrik, why did she begin such a war?"

Banan glanced at Con to see his face turned away. Banan let out a deep breath. "She cared for Ulrik as a man, but no' as a dragon. There was only one way to stop the war, and that was to stop the female."

"You killed her," Jane stated flatly.

"Aye," Banan said. "It's easy to look back now and

think we should've found Ulrik and told him what we'd discovered. Then he could have decided what to do with his woman. In the heat of battle, in a war that was dividing the land, there isna a lot of time for decisions. We found her, and we killed her."

Banan paused as he recalled Ulrik's devastation. In all the centuries since, Banan had never comprehended why Ulrik reacted so to the death of one human. Now, Banan understood entirely.

He cleared his throat and continued. "Ulrik wouldna listen to reason after what had happened to his woman. He pushed dragons to kill humans, solidifying a war we were desperately trying to halt."

"Did you kill Ulrik as well?" she asked.

"Nay," Con finally spoke. "I had inflicted enough harm with the slaying of his woman. The only way to stop Ulrik was to take his power as King. He can no' shift to dragon form, nor can he speak to his Silvers."

Jane's dark gaze turned to Banan. "So there are still dragons here? Besides the Kings?"

"We captured a few of Ulrik's Silvers. They are under our magic and sleeping at Dreagan. Only Ulrik can wake them, and if that happens, the war will begin again."

Jane's forehead creased with a frown. "Where are all the other dragons?"

"We sent them away," Con said. "I couldna chance them being killed off. They are gone from this world and safe."

"Maybe," Jane said as she looked at Rhys as a dragon. "But they don't have their kings, and you don't have them."

Banan didn't allow himself to think of the dragons he had once ruled. If he did, the ache inside from missing them would eat him alive.

But it was too late not to think of them. Jane had put the thought in his mind, and he couldn't dismiss his yearning to have the Blues around him as they rode the wind currents. He couldn't stop the longing to hear their roars in answer to his.

Suddenly, soft hands cupped either side of his face. He found his gaze staring into coffee brown eyes.

"I'm so sorry, Banan."

He pulled her against him and buried his head in her neck. Just being able to hold her helped to push the gnawing ache to a small corner of his heart.

Her arms were full of strength and tenderness as she held him, and he never wanted it to end. She belonged next to him. But did she know it yet?

"There's more to the story, isn't there?" she asked.

Banan nodded.

She pulled out of his arms and urged, "Tell me."

"I'm immortal, Jane. The Dragon Kings have been around since the beginning of time. After we sent the dragons away, the Kings set up residence at Dreagan in Scotland. We use the distillery as a cover for what we are."

"Don't people tend to recognize you've been alive for hundreds of years?"

Banan rubbed her arms with his hands as he felt her shivering. "We take turns sleeping in the mountain. Con is the only one who doesna sleep. But we are tied to Dreagan because of the Silvers we have caged there. It's our magic that keeps them sleeping. We can leave, but only for short periods of time. Then we must go back or our magic begins to loosen its hold."

"I see," she said, and shoved a wet strand of auburn hair behind her ears. "So you're immortal. Does that mean you can't be killed?"

"No human can kill us. No' even a dragon can kill us. Only a Dragon King." At her frown, he elaborated. "In dragon form, Kings can battle one another and kill. As Dragon Kings, we each have a sword that belongs only to us. Only we can use our swords. In human form, Dragon Kings can battle using these swords and we can kill each other."

"Wow," she whispered. "No wonder you want to keep yourselves hidden. Is that all you can do?"

"Nay. Each of us is given a certain kind of magic as a Dragon King."

She raised a brow. "Interesting. What is yours?"

"I can give hallucinations."

"I wasn't expecting that," she said with a small smile. "Was it Ulrik who kidnapped me and sent Sloan to Dreagan?"

Banan shook his head and met Con's gaze over her shoulder. "Nay. Con has him watched constantly. Ulrik had nothing to do with this."

"Then who was it?"

"A verra good question, and one I had hoped we'd discover tonight."

"He knows you," Jane said. "He told me there were Dragon Kings. He said he wanted to be here to see my face when I learned what you are, and that he wanted to see your face as well."

Banan felt the rage rise in him again. "He thought you'd run from me."

"You are a fearsome sight."

Banan's chest constricted at the note of anxiety he heard in her voice. "You're afraid of me."

"No. No," she said again, and gave him a quick, hard kiss. "I admit, at first, yes. I wouldn't have come to you or touched you if I had been that afraid. I always knew there was something different about you." She ran her hand over his tat. "The dragon tattoo makes sense now. I just wish you'd told me."

Banan rejoiced at her words, but he couldn't hold back anymore. He covered her mouth in a kiss. Her sweet taste enflamed him, the desire licking at his blood.

He wanted to lay her down on the floor and claim her body again, not just as a man, but also as a Dragon King. She hadn't run from him, hadn't left him.

His hands skimmed down her back to cup her round bottom in his hands and bring her against his aching cock. Her soft moan was music to his ears. And just when he was about to start stripping her clothes off, rain pelted them.

Jane tore her lips from him as she laughed. Banan looked for Con and Rhys only to discover them gone, and he hurried to get Jane out of the rain.

She was running toward the door left open by Rhys or Con, but Banan pulled her to a stop.

"I need to know something."

She wiped the water from her face and smoothed back her hair, a smile dancing in her eyes. "What is that?"

"You've seen and heard a lot this night. Is it too much for you to be with me?"

She grew very still. "Be with you?"

Banan swallowed. He'd never been nervous before. He'd never been a lot of things before Jane, but he wanted to experience them all with her.

"Because of the human female's betrayal, Con used his magic so that none of the Dragon Kings would ever fall in love with humans."

"Oh," Jane said, her gaze lowering to the floor.

"All that changed over five months ago. Hal fell in love with Cassie. Then Guy fell in love with Elena. Something has changed, Jane. I used to no' fully believe it. Then I held you in my arms."

Her eyes snapped to his. "What are you saying?"

"I'm say—" He paused because he didn't want to mess it up. "—I'm saying I'm in love with you, Jane Holden. I want you as mine. Always. Will you come back with me to Dreagan? Will you stand by me in all that my now-uncertain future holds?"

For long minutes she didn't reply, and Banan was trying to think of what else to say to convince her, when a lone tear fell down her face.

He stopped the tear with his thumb before it reached her chin. "Jane," he whispered.

"I've waited for you all my life," she said. "I'd go anywhere with you, Banan."

A laugh exploded from him as he crushed her against him. "I love you."

"And I love you," she said between the kisses she placed on his neck.

EPILOGUE

Jane got out of the Jaguar and closed the door, her gaze locked on the same tavern she'd visited months before.

"You can do this," Banan said as he came up beside her.

She smiled as he took her hand. "Yes, as long as you're with me."

"I'll always be with you."

"You didn't answer me yesterday, by the way."

He looked away from her as he asked, "What are you talking about?"

Jane shook her head. "You're lying. Why are you afraid to tell me how this will work? Is it because I'm right, and you just don't want to admit that I'll grow old and die while you live on?"

"Jane," he said, and suddenly had her pinned to the car. "I doona have any answers. I wish I did, but all this is new. For the little time when humans and dragons coexisted together, there were humans who mated with Kings. None of their offspring survived. Hell, half of the women never carried the babies to term. And all the women eventually did die."

She cupped his face and looked deep into his gray eyes. "I'm not really keen on you seeing me all wrinkled and hunched over, but I want whatever time we have, Banan. I understand that you'll grow tired of me one day."

"Nay," he said, and gave her a gentle shake. "You doona understand. I've never, no' once in all my life as a dragon or a Dragon King, felt for anyone what I do for you. You, Jane, are different. I was going to wait until we reached Dreagan to tell you, but you willna relent."

She laughed and raised an auburn brow as she waited.

"A human can be bound to a King. You'll live, staying as you are now, for as long as I live. Only if I die will you die."

"Oh."

"Is it too much?" he asked, knowing she'd taken in a lot over the past few days.

Jane rose up on her tiptoes and kissed him. "No. Is it something you want to do?"

"Aye. Most definitely, but I was going to give you some time."

She rolled her coffee brown eyes. "Apparently, I haven't let you know just how much I don't want to be without you."

"We'll start making plans for the ceremony once we reach Dreagan." He stared at her a moment before he chuckled. "Now, have you wasted enough time? Are you ready to meet Sammi?"

"No, and I don't know. I'm scared, Banan," she admitted.

He pulled her into his arms. "It'll be all right."

Jane took a steadying breath, and then they walked into the tavern. Sammi was behind the counter, drying some glasses and laughing at something a customer said to her.

Her sandy brown hair was pulled away from her face

in a high ponytail as bangs covered her forehead. And then her eyes swung to Jane.

Banan smiled down at Jane as she gave his hand a squeeze and went to her half sister. He stood back and watched while she hesitantly began to tell Sammi everything.

It wasn't until she pulled out the letters she'd found that Banan slid into a bench and relaxed. Everything was good. For now.

How long it would last, he didn't know. Rhys and several other Dragon Kings, with the help of Henri North, were still scouring London for any sign of the man who had kidnapped Jane and killed Richard Arnold.

But so far, they had come up empty-handed.

The unease Banan had felt ever since he'd been unable to detect the man in dragon form had only grown. They hadn't seen the last of the bastard, that was for sure.

"Banan," Jane called.

He lifted his face to her. "Aye?"

"Come meet Sammi."

Banan greeted Jane's smile with one of his own. Today was theirs. Tomorrow, the Dragon Kings would begin to look for their enemy.

He stared at the little tavern in Oban from his car window. It had taken all he had not to get out of his car and kill Jane while Banan had been holding her.

His plan should have worked. It *would* have worked.

But he hadn't factored in Banan and Rhys turning into dragons and attacking as they had. It had broken the rules Con put into place.

Still, though his plan might not have played out as he wanted, it hadn't been a total waste. It had gotten Con to London.

He hadn't been able to stay and listen to the conversation between Jane and the other three since he had to run for his life. Yet in the end, the retreat had worked to his advantage.

The Dragon Kings knew they had an enemy, but they didn't know who. And they had shown a weakness—one he would exploit until they were all dead.

PASSION'S CLAIM

PART 1

CHAPTER ONE

Dreagan Manor
October

Jane surreptitiously glanced at Banan through the mirror of her vanity as he changed his shirt for the third time. He was unusually edgy as they readied for their night out.

"Do you like this one?" he asked as he finished buttoning the black shirt.

"Very much."

He looked at her with a droll expression. "You've said that about all three shirts."

"Because I like all three shirts. I helped you pick them out at the store, remember?"

"Aye," he mumbled and quickly unbuttoned the shirt before he jerked his arms out of the sleeves and wadded it up to toss on the floor with the other two.

Jane dusted the blush on her cheeks, wondering if Banan was growing tired of their relationship. She knew she could be bound to Banan and live as long as he did. He'd offered her that option, and she had gladly accepted it.

Upon their return from London—with a short stop to

introduce herself to her half-sister, Sammi—they had begun to make preparations. But those arrangements had been put on the back burner as the Dragon Kings looked for their enemy and helped the Warriors from MacLeod Castle.

Jane didn't mind. She loved Banan, so it was enough to be with him. Was it still enough for him though? Had he changed his mind about the binding and just didn't want to tell her?

Her stomach began to sour the more she thought about it. Jane didn't want anything to ruin their first night out alone in weeks. She was determined to enjoy it, and if Banan wished to keep their relationship as it was, she wouldn't argue. She had once told him being with him for as long as he wanted her would be enough.

She hadn't lied. She loved him with her entire being, but he was a Dragon King. He had been alive since the beginning of time. He had commanded dragons, flown high in the clouds. When the endless passing of days grew too much, he—like so many of the Kings—would sleep away centuries in the mountains.

How could she compare to everything he was? He was immortal and powerful. He could shift from human to dragon form and back again with nary a thought. The only thing that could kill him was another Dragon King.

And what was she? Mortal—with a life span that passed in a blink to someone like Banan. Many women had shared his bed, and though she understood this, it didn't stop the spread of insecurity that she might be just one of thousands.

"Jane?"

She jerked and found his reflection near hers in the mirror. He had walked up behind her as she had been lost in thought and she hadn't heard him. His brow puckered in concern as he searched her eyes in the mirror.

"Are you all right? You looked to be a million miles away."

"I'm fine," she said and put away her blush as she moved around her makeup in the drawer to search for the eye shadow she wanted.

Banan's large hands came to rest on her shoulders as he straightened. "You would tell me if something was wrong, aye?"

"I would," she lied, briefly meeting his gray gaze in the mirror.

His hands fell away as he turned back to his closet. Jane once more watched him through her mirror. The muscles in his back shifted and bunched as he reached for another shirt, this time a vivid blue with widely spaced thin black lines running vertically. He rolled up the sleeves to his elbows and finished buttoning it before he tucked the front of it into his black jeans.

"Perfect," she said when he looked at her.

He gave her a wink before turning to find his watch. Jane finished her makeup and put on the navy sweater dress that hugged her frame and stopped a few inches shy of her knee. Once she'd zipped her black boots with the four-inch heels and added jewelry, she found Banan waiting at their bedroom door with her coat draped over his arm.

"You look beautiful."

She gazed into his eyes and returned his smile. "And you look very handsome."

"Keep looking at me like that and that dress of yours will be puddled on the floor by the bed."

She loved when his eyes darkened and desire deepened his voice. It sent chills racing over her skin every time. Banan had a way of making her forget everything with just a look, that same look he was giving her now.

"Ah, how you tempt me, Jane," he said as he dragged

her to him and gave her a brief, hard kiss. "It's all I'll permit myself lest I have you on the bed. I know how you've been looking forward to a night out."

"We can stay in," she said and backed into the room.

He gave a firm shake of his head. "No' tonight. Let's go."

Jane walked with him down the hallway to the stairs as they descended to the main floor. Most of the Dragon Kings kept to themselves—the ones who had awoken, at least.

There were only two other couples at Dreagan. Cassie and Hal, who had already been bound together for over a year. Then there was Elena and Guy. Both seemed content in their relationship, neither speaking of making it formal or of binding themselves.

Jane wondered if she was being paranoid. Guy wanted Elena to get used to who he was and the kind of life she would lead if she chose to be his bride. Maybe that's what Banan was doing as well. But wouldn't he have told her?

"You seem distracted," Banan said as they passed the media room where Guy and Elena were wrestling for the remote, their laughter ringing through the manor.

"Just noticing how quiet the house is. Where are Cassie and Hal?"

"Hal took Cassie to Edinburgh for a few days."

They walked out of the house and to Banan's sapphire blue Porsche 911 Carrera. Once she was seated, Banan shut her door and walked around the car to the driver's side.

They had almost an hour's drive before they reached the restaurant. Normally Jane would be talking about her day doing one of the various jobs she, Elena, and Cassie did around Dreagan, but all she could think about was how oddly nervous Banan was.

She glanced at him, noting that he had both hands on the steering wheel, something he rarely did unless the weather was bad and she was in the car with him. It wasn't that he was reckless with his life, he just knew that he couldn't be killed.

Instead of coming out and asking Banan if something was wrong, Jane stared out the passenger window. She was such a chicken. Banan had opened up her world when he came into her life in London. She had been afraid and mesmerized when she saw him in his dragon form that first time.

Now, she eagerly watched for him to take to the skies at night. Under the cover of darkness was the only time the Kings would readily fly. There had been few instances where they had chanced being seen.

One such time was in London where Banan, along with Rhys, had shifted to dragon form to look for her after she had been kidnapped. Most recently, however, was when the Kings, en masse, had fought alongside the Warriors to kill a *drough*, or evil Druid.

Suddenly the car slowed, pulling Jane from her thoughts. She looked around to find they weren't in the city but near a loch. She peered through the windshield and spied lights coming from the water.

When Banan stopped the car and put it in park, he wouldn't look at her. With her heart pounding a slow, sad beat, Jane prepared herself for the end. It was obvious Banan was ending their relationship.

She hastily blinked back the tears and accepted his hand when he opened her door. Jane stepped out of the car and shivered. She might be from Seattle where it was always raining, but there was a dampness coming off the water that settled into her bones.

Or maybe it was her heart breaking into tiny bits that made her so cold.

"Here," Banan said and helped her into her wool coat.

Jane buttoned and tied the coat, grateful that he had remembered to bring it. "Where are we? I thought we were going into Inverness."

"I hope you doona mind, but I changed things."

"Mind?" she said as she looked over the loch. Darkness had fallen over Scotland, leaving the half moon to shed a beacon of light that danced upon the gently moving water. "It's beautiful here."

He put his hand on her lower back and guided her to a set of narrow steps leading to a small dock. "I thought you might like this."

Jane was speechless when the sailboat came into view. All along the rigging small lights had been hung, casting the entire deck in a soft hue.

Banan hurried ahead of her and jumped aboard the sailboat, then held out his hand to her once more as she crossed the small gangplank.

"When did you set this up?" she asked.

He shrugged, beaming as he looked around him. "You didna have any clue, did you?"

"Not at all. You kept this a very tight secret," she said and cut her eyes to him.

His gaze softened as the boat rocked. "Elena packed a small bag for you, which I brought a couple of days ago."

"So that's where my favorite jeans disappeared to," she said with a shake of her head. Jane leaned her head back and looked at the lights reaching high up on the rigging. "You did all this?"

"Aye. You mentioned wanting to sail. I'll take you sailing anywhere you want to go."

Jane looked at the mountains in the distance. "That might be a tad difficult since we're in a loch."

"Och. I meant later," he said and took her hand. "We'll

be spending the next few days getting acquainted with the sailboat."

Was this why he had been so nervous? Jane inwardly berated herself for being so stupid as to think Banan was distancing himself from her. He had gone to a lot of trouble to rent a sailboat for a few days just because she had mentioned wanting to sail.

"I've never sailed any type of boat," she told Banan as she followed him around to the back of the sailboat. "Just because I like boats doesn't mean I know anything about them."

"Good thing I do," he said over his shoulder.

Jane stopped and turned around in a circle. They were the only two on the sailboat, and from what she could see, there wasn't another boat on the loch. It was almost as if they were the only two people in the world.

"What are you doing out here?" Banan said as he came up behind her and wrapped his arms around her.

She snuggled against him as he perched his chin on her shoulder. "I'm just looking at everything. I want to remember every last detail."

"Wait until you see the sunrise."

"Will you wake me for it?"

"Wake you?" he said and leaned to the side so she could see his seductive grin. "There willna be any sleeping tonight."

Jane laughed as he took her hand and dragged her behind him as he went below. Once more she found herself standing with her mouth agape.

In the small space was a table where her favorite dish—salmon—was waiting. A bottle of wine, two glasses, and candles set the mood.

"Banan . . ." She paused, unable to find the words to convey how absolutely perfect everything was.

As if understanding, he unbelted and unbuttoned her

coat before he removed it so she could sit. Only then did he take the wine from the ice bucket and pour.

He sat across from her and lifted his glass. "To us."

"To us," she repeated as they clinked glasses, her love for Banan growing deeper every day she was with him.

CHAPTER TWO

Banan had never been so nervous in his life. Two days ago he'd picked up the ring, which now sat in his pocket. At one time he knew for certain Jane wanted to be his forever. Now, he wasn't so sure.

It wasn't that he doubted her love. He wasn't sure she fully understood what it would mean to be immortal. And once a dragon and his bride were bonded, there was no turning back.

The wind kept the loch rippling enough that the water slapped lazily against the hull. That, added to the sound of Jane's laughter, and Banan was in heaven.

There was a sparkle to Jane's amber gaze that made his blood burn. There had been nights he would pull her against him just so he could hold her.

But he knew he couldn't hold too tight. Jane was human, a mortal. If she was meant to be his, he had to give her the room to make that decision. It's what he had been doing for months, but she hadn't brought up their binding again.

Banan didn't know what to think anymore. It was a chance he was taking bringing her to the loch on the sailboat, but he couldn't go another day without knowing where they stood.

He didn't know what he would do if she said no. Actually, he knew exactly what he would do. He would woo her and seduce her until he won her over completely.

Jane was his everything. She was his reason to face each day, his motivation to do things to please her. He knew in his soul there would never be another to replace her.

And if she didn't want to bind herself to him, he would spend every second of her life with her. As much as it pained him, he would sit by her side until she breathed her last. Then, he would spend the rest of eternity mourning her.

With dinner eaten and the wine bottle now empty, Banan sat back and gazed at Jane.

"What?" she asked and demurely tucked her auburn hair behind her ear.

She had blossomed since coming to Dreagan, but there wasn't a conceited bone in her body.

"That," he answered.

"Me shoving my hair aside?" she asked askance.

He swirled the last bit of white wine in his glass. "Nay, lass. The way you blush when I stare at you."

"Because I know what you're thinking."

"What am I thinking?" he asked, intentionally lowering his voice in the way that made her shiver in excitement.

She visibly swallowed, her fingers idly turning her wineglass on the table. "You're thinking of stripping off my clothes."

"Oh, aye. I'm thinking of much more than that."

"I know," she murmured. "It's written all over your face when you look at me like that."

"I thought you liked it."

"I don't like it, Banan. I love it."

He leaned forward and lifted her hand in his. Banan smoothed his thumb over her knuckles before bringing her hand to his lips. He lifted his eyes and their gazes locked. The desire he saw reflected in her depths made his balls tighten.

Without a word he scooted from his seat and stood beside the table. She looked up at him, her lips parted and waiting for his kiss.

Banan drew her up and into his arms. He ran his fingers through the cool locks of her auburn hair that brushed the tops of her shoulders.

"What are you thinking?" she asked.

He gave a gentle tug on her hair. "I'm wondering how I survived millennia after millennia without you."

"How do you always know what to say?" she asked with a ghost of a smile before she placed her lips on his.

Desire erupted, swift and intense. The sultry woman in his arms dragged him deeper into the all-consuming, never-ending hunger for her. Her kiss, her touch scorched him, seared him.

And still he wasn't close enough.

The passion was indescribable, indefinable. It consumed him, drove him. Compelled him.

He was powerless to deny the pressing, relentless need for Jane. Nor did he want to. She was simply . . . everything to him. She was the light, the air, the spark that kept him looking forward to each new day with her.

They tore at each other's clothes, eager to remove anything that came between them. When they were flesh to flesh, Banan splayed his hands on either side of her head and looked into her amber eyes.

Her lips were swollen from his kisses, her pulse beating rapidly at her throat. Her skin was already flushed. A wicked gleam came into her eyes as she ran her hands over his chest.

"By all that's holy, you are the most beautiful thing I've ever seen."

Her forehead creased as her gaze softened and some

unnamed emotion flitted across her face. Then there were no more words as Banan turned and pushed Jane back onto the bed. With his hand beneath her back, he dragged her up until her head rested on the pillow while he continued to kiss her.

His hand ran up her long legs and over smooth skin to her hip and then up to cup her breasts. A low moan sounded from Jane as he tweaked her nipple.

With a shove against his shoulder, Jane rolled him onto his back. Then, she crawled over him until she straddled him. Banan slid both hands up her thighs and around her waist as he sat up and rained kisses on her neck.

Her nails scraped against his scalp as she tugged against his short hair. All day he had thought of making love to her on the sailboat. No longer could he wait. He had to be inside her, to feel her body clamping around him.

Jane sucked in a breath when Banan lifted her until she was poised over his arousal. She met his eyes, gazed into his gray depths and melted.

He was magnificent, and she still couldn't believe he wanted her. A Dragon King, an immortal who could have anyone had chosen Plain Jane.

But she didn't feel plain in his arms. She came alive, her body awakening. With Banan she was wanton.

Uninhibited.

And utterly shameless.

She became the sensual, lustful woman that she had always known waited for the right man to find her.

Jane sighed as she slowly slid down the hard length of his rod, her body expanding to take all of him in. She wrapped her arms around his neck and held him as she began to rock her hips.

His large hands spread over her back as they kissed, their bodies riding the waves of desire. Already Jane was close to peaking.

As if Banan knew, he cupped her butt and urged her to quicken her pace. The familiar tightening low in her belly began twisting, turning, and sending her closer and closer to orgasm.

Banan nipped at her earlobe, his warm breath fanning over her already heated body. He kissed her behind her ear, a tender spot that always made her come apart.

With just one lick of his tongue on her skin, Jane screamed his name as the first waves of the climax slammed into her. She sank her nails in Banan's shoulders as he continued to move her hips, sending her higher. And then he whispered her name as he too succumbed to his orgasm.

Still entwined, they fell sideways. Jane ran a hand through his short, dark hair. The worries from earlier were far behind her, as if they had never been. A warm glow infused the entire sailboat to cocoon them in their own world.

Banan propped himself up on his elbow and rested his head against his hand as he stared down at Jane. They had talked for hours and made love often through the night until Jane had finally fallen into an exhausted sleep an hour before.

He had intentionally kept their conversation away from any talk of binding, but they had spoken of the future. And, in Jane's eyes, he was still a part of her future.

Banan held up the wide, white gold band. It had taken him months to design the ring with a jeweler in London, but in the end, it had turned out stunning.

He gave Jane a kiss on her forehead as he opened up the curtains. She turned onto her side and snuggled her back against him.

"Wake up, sleeping beauty," he whispered in her ear. "The sun is just about to crest the mountains."

"Tell it to wait," she mumbled.

Banan grinned. If there was one thing Jane liked, it was her sleep. She had the brightest disposition of anyone he had ever known, but if she didn't get enough sleep it took at least two cups of coffee before she was herself again.

The coffee was already made and waiting. Now, he just had to get her to wake up.

"The sun waits for no one. Trust me, you'll be glad I woke you once you see it."

With a dramatic sigh, Jane cracked open one eye, then the second one. "I feel like I slept for only five minutes."

"It was a little over an hour."

The grumpiness seemed to vanish as she suddenly smiled. "Ah, but what a night it was, right?"

It was one he would never forget, that was for sure. "Aye, lass, it was."

He reached over his head where her cup of coffee waited and handed it to her. She rose up on her elbow and took a big whiff of the coffee before taking several sips.

"Ah. Just what I needed."

Banan rested his chin on her shoulder as they both stared out the window, watching the sky turn from a pale gray to being streaked with vivid pinks, rich oranges, and deep reds.

The higher the sun rose, the more vibrant the colors became until the first glimpse of the yellow ball broke above the mountains.

He heard Jane's indrawn breath, and knew she was seeing the beauty that he had glimpsed so many times. Every sunrise was as different as every sunset, and he never tired of watching either of them.

The cry of a golden eagle broke the quiet of the dawn, and it was like a signal to nature. With the sun now chasing away the shadows of night, nature came awake.

For long minutes they continued to stare at the rising

sun until it became too bright. Jane lifted a hand to shield her eyes, squinting them closed in the process, and that's when Banan moved his hand that held the ring into her line of sight.

"That is blinding," she said and sightlessly searched for the curtains. She managed to grab one side and yank it closed. It shut out some of the light, but not all of it.

Banan's heart pounded in his chest as he waited for Jane to see the ring. He'd never experienced nervousness before, and he had to admit he quite hated the emotion. He didn't know if he was coming or going, if he was up or down. He was a wreck, an absolute mess.

All because he had to know if one woman with a propensity to trip on a flat surface would be bound to him.

Jane blinked open her eyes and then stilled. Banan's heart sank. He had moved too soon, asked too much.

"Oh, my God," she whispered, awe lowering her voice. When she lifted her eyes to him, they were awash in tears.

Banan frowned, unsure of what to make of her reaction. "Jane?"

"I thought you didn't want me anymore."

"What?" He was so shocked that he couldn't believe her words. "Why would you think that?"

"You've been acting weird."

"Because I've been planning this for weeks. I wanted everything to be perfect, but I also wasna sure you were ready."

She looked back at the ring he still held. "I'm more than ready."

Relief poured through Banan, quickly mixing with elation. He had seriously doubted whether Jane was ready to give him the commitment that would essentially make her immortal.

Banan sat up with Jane and took her hand. He looked

deep into her amber eyes and asked, “Jane, will you be mine? Will you bind yourself to me?”

“A thousand times yes,” she said with a bright smile.

With a satisfied grin of his own, Banan slid the band onto her left ring finger.

CHAPTER THREE

Jane couldn't stop gazing at the band upon her finger. The design, diamonds in a knotwork pattern set in white gold, was exactly her style. The fact Banan had designed the ring told her that he really knew her, something she'd never thought to claim with another.

She finished dressing by pulling on the cream-colored wool sweater and ran her fingers through her hair. Then she ran up on the deck to find Banan had already cast off from the dock.

"Um . . . do you know how to sail?" she asked, once more looking at the dock growing smaller.

Banan let out chuckle. "Aye. Of course."

"Oh, of course," she said with a roll of her eyes. "I forget you know how to do everything."

"No' everything, lass. I'm still working on perfecting my time with you."

"As if you even need to work on that," she said as she came up behind him. When he made room for her, she slid between him and the wheel. "I can't believe I'm sailing!"

"Do you like the boat?"

"I think she's gorgeous."

"Hm."

Jane looked at him over her shoulder. Banan was staring ahead as if he hadn't just made the most peculiar sound after her answer.

"Hm?" she repeated.

"Hm," he said again. "Can you get me a mug of coffee?"

She nodded, wondering at his acting so odd once again. Though Jane no longer thought he wanted to end their relationship. What she'd learned was that when Banan had a surprise, he grew evasive and quiet.

After giving her the ring, and his commitment to the binding ceremony, she wasn't sure what else there was to give her.

She hurried down the narrow steps below and opened the cabinet for a mug. In the process of pouring the coffee she saw a life preserver hanging on the wall. The ring was white with four blue stripes going at angles. The top of the preserver said Lady, and the bottom portion said Jane.

Jane carefully set down the coffee and felt her heart pounding in her chest. With Banan there were no coincidences. His odd behavior once more and the boat named after her meant . . .

She forgot this coffee as she rushed up the stairs, tripping twice and slamming her shin against a step before she reached the deck.

Banan was at her side in an instant, concern marring his face. "Are you hurt?"

She waved away his words. "The boat's name is Lady Jane?"

His worry eased into a lopsided smile. "Aye. My gift to you."

Jane threw her arms around him and buried her face in his neck. "You are enough," she said. "You're all I ever wanted."

"And you, lass, are all I ever wanted," he said as he held her tightly.

She leaned back and asked as innocently as she could, "You want to give the biggest klutz who ever walked the earth a sailboat? I might run over someone."

"Just make sure they deserve it," he answered without missing a beat.

Jane threw back her head and laughed. Life with Banan was going to be anything but dull.

The day was spent with Jane learning how to sail. It was just after three o'clock when Banan docked them once more. After tying them off, Jane sat back and found him watching her.

"Did I do it wrong?"

He shook his head.

"Then what is it?"

He came to sit beside her at the front. "You have a choice to make."

"You mean I get to decide how we're going to cook the fish?" she teased.

Banan tugged a strand of hair free that was caught against her cheek. "Nay. You get to decide if we remain on your sailboat another night or no'."

She knew what he was asking. They could return to Dreagan and do the binding ceremony that night, but he wasn't rushing her. He was giving her—and would give her—as much time as she wanted.

For Jane there was no decision to make. She leaned forward and gave Banan a quick kiss. "It'll take me just a minute to gather my things."

The smile he sent her made her legs weak. And that smile is what she could look forward to for the rest of her days. She still couldn't wrap her mind around it all as they drove back to Dreagan.

Back at the manor, she and Banan walked hand in

hand through the door. Con was exiting the kitchen when he spotted them. After a glance at her left hand, Con gave them a nod and a smile.

"When?" he asked.

Banan glanced at her before he said, "Tonight."

"How about midnight?" Con suggested.

Jane quite liked the idea. She didn't know anyone who had gotten married at midnight. "Yes."

Banan followed her up the stairs to their rooms. Jane tossed her bag on the bed and sank into one of the overstuffed chairs near the fireplace.

"Cassie had a traditional wedding as well as the binding," Banan said.

Jane hid her smile. She knew exactly what Banan was trying to ask without actually coming out and asking. "I know."

He sat in the chair opposite her and raised a brow. "Well?"

"Well what?" she asked, patiently waiting for him to get it out.

"Do you want a traditional wedding as well? It'll take more time to prepare, but it can be done."

Jane rose and walked to Banan so she could climb into his lap. "No, I don't want a traditional wedding. In my heart I've been bound to you from our first kiss, but most certainly since I came to Dreagan with you. A piece of paper is meaningless next to the ceremony that will officially bind us together as nothing else could."

"Whatever makes you happy." Banan rubbed a hand up and down her back.

"Being with you makes me happy."

His gray eyes darkened just before he tugged her down for a kiss. Their lips had just met when there was a pounding on the door.

"Jane?" came Elena's muffled voice through the door.

Banan smiled and set Jane on her feet as he stood. "That's my cue to leave. I know there is female stuff to see to. I'll see you later," he said and kissed the tip of her nose.

He opened the door and Elena came rushing in. With a wink, Banan shut the door behind him as he left.

"Is it true?" Elena asked.

Jane held up her hand, unable to hold back her smile.

Elena covered her mouth with both hands, her eyes huge. Then she reached for Jane's hand. "My goodness. Look at that ring. It's gorgeous."

"Isn't it? Banan did such a good job designing it."

A wistful look overtook Elena for a moment before it vanished. "Yes, Banan did good. When is the binding?"

"At midnight."

"Tonight?" Elena squawked.

Jane frowned, unsure of why Elena found that alarming. "Yes. Why?"

"What are you going to wear?" Elena asked as she threw open the closet door. "Did you already buy a dress?"

"Well . . . no." That's when it hit her. "What am I going to wear?"

"First, we need to call Cassie and Hal so they can be back. No, I'm sure Con or Banan will take care of that." Elena paced back and forth in front of the bed, one hand on her hip and the other held in front of her face as her finger tapped her chin. "There might be enough time to drive into Inverness and find something."

"At almost six in the evening?" Jane shook her head and walked to her closet. "No. I'm going to have to make do with what I have."

She began to pull out the five or so dresses that she had bought to wear to the parties, balls, and charity events those from Dreagan had to attend throughout the year. Since Banan, Hal, and Guy were the ones with women, it was usually at least one of the three couples going.

That was the only reason Jane had anything even remotely acceptable to wear to her own binding ceremony.

"Do you have a blue one?" Elena asked.

Jane looked up and grinned. "Because Banan is King of the Blues."

"I think it's fitting."

"I agree."

Jane unzipped one of the protective garment bags and pulled out the blue dress. It was the loveliest shade of sapphire. The chiffon gown had a strapless sweetheart neckline bordered with clear Swarovski crystals that continued to the plunging V-neck. The same Swarovski crystals made up the two-inch-wide belt, adding to the beauty of the gown.

"I remember that gown. Banan couldn't take his eyes off you," Elena said as she fingered the chiffon skirt.

Jane held the dress in front of her. "It was our first party we attended together. I felt like a princess. No matter how many times I tripped or spilled my drink, he was always there."

There was a quick rap and the bedroom door flew open. Cassie poked her dark head in and hurried inside once she saw them. "We rushed back as soon as Hal heard Banan's news through their link," Cassie said as she hugged Jane.

"So glad you arrived," Elena said as she pulled back her dark blond hair into a ponytail. "Jane found a dress to wear, but the binding is at midnight."

"Midnight?" Cassie asked, surprised. "What a neat idea."

"But leaves very little time to get ready."

Jane hung the dress over the door and smiled at her two friends. "Stop, both of you. There is no need for any of this."

"It is. This is your wedding," Elena said. "The Kings may call it a binding, but it's a wedding either way you look at it."

Cassie nodded as she sat on the bed. “Will you be having an actual wedding as well?”

“No,” Jane said as she returned the other gowns to her closet. “The binding is enough for me.”

Elena raised both brows. “So you’ll get ready for your binding like any other day? You won’t take that extra time or get your hair done as you do when we go to the parties or charity events?”

That made Jane stop and think. It was her wedding. How often had she dreamed of her wedding as a little girl? If she didn’t do everything she wanted she would regret it later.

She faced Cassie and Elena. “All right. What do we have time for?”

Cassie jumped up from the bed as she and Elena began talking at once. Elena pushed Jane into the bathroom, urging her to take a nice long soak.

The next thing she knew, Jane was alone. She drew her bath and filled it full with bubbles. When the water was deep enough, she climbed in just in time for Cassie to be heard outside the bathroom telling her she’d found someone to come do her hair.

A few minutes later and Elena was asking her about makeup, then didn’t wait for Jane to answer before she left again.

Jane smiled as she leaned her head back against the tub. She was getting bound to a Dragon King, a man who filled her nights with passion and her days with laughter.

How had she gotten so impossibly lucky?

CHAPTER FOUR

Banan stood at the back of the manor on the paved patio and gazed at the moon. He moved through thousands of years of memories to his earliest ones, before he had been able to shift into human form.

There were times the moon had hung low and large in the sky. During those times, Banan had thought he could touch the moon. And there had been times it almost seemed as if he did.

Throughout those early years it had all been about being a good King to his dragons. How he missed his dragons. There was an emptiness in his chest that would never be filled until he was with them once more.

But Jane had helped fill most of that hole. She had given him everything he hadn't even known he needed. What a fool he had been to think he was content. He hadn't been remotely happy, but it hadn't been clear until the first time he held Jane in his arms.

At the time he had hoped it was merely lust. Though he hated to admit it, it was because he had been afraid of what might grow between them.

Then he had tasted her kisses and learned her body. There had been no holding back then. He wanted all of her, and in return, she had silently and gently demanded all of him. It never entered Banan's mind to deny her.

Rhys kept his distance from any woman who might want more than an hour in his bed, and the other Kings were just as bad. They might accept Cassie, Elena, and Jane, but they had no interest in their emotions being tied to humans.

Banan couldn't wait until each was brought low by a woman, because he had no doubt it would happen.

"Why are you smiling?" Guy asked as he walked up.

Banan glanced at his friend. "Because I know some of the other Kings think I've lost my mind."

"They doona realize what they're missing," Hal said as he walked up holding three glasses of whisky. "We do."

Banan took two of the glasses and handed one to Guy. "I'll drink to that."

The three held up their glasses and clinked them together. "To our women," Guy said.

"To our women," Hal and Banan repeated in unison.

They drained their glasses, and Guy was quick to refill them. "I expected this from you and Jane months ago."

Banan swirled the whisky in his glass. "I desired it the moment we returned from London, but I wanted to give her time. I guess I took too long because she thought I'd changed my mind."

"Women," Hal said with a smile. "It certainly is difficult to keep up with how their minds work."

Guy snorted. "I doona even try anymore. I just nod my head anytime Elena says something."

"Smart man," Banan said as he raised his glass in salute.

Hal's brow furrowed. "Keep that to yourself, mate. I doona want Cassie getting any ideas."

Banan and Guy burst out laughing.

Hal was affronted. "What?"

"As if Cassie didna already have you wrapped around her finger," Guy said.

Hal just grinned in response.

Banan took a sip of the fifty-year-old scotch and studied Guy. "When will you and Elena bind yourselves?"

The smile slipped from Guy's face. For several tense seconds he stared at the ground before he shrugged. "I doona believe she wishes to bind herself to me."

"Bollocks," Hal said. "She loves you."

Guy's smile was suddenly back in place as he reached for the bottle and refilled their glasses once more. "What did Jane think of the sailboat?"

Banan knew Guy was changing the subject for a reason, and Banan would let it go. For now. Tonight was meant to be Jane's. Tomorrow, however, Banan intended to get to the bottom of what was going on with Guy and Elena.

"She loved it," Banan said. "I had to point out the name of the boat before she realized it was hers though."

Hal sat on one of the teak chairs and drolly lifted an eyebrow. "You do know you keep doing things like that and we have to try to either catch up or outdo you?"

Banan lifted his glass to his lips, and right before he took a drink asked, "Afraid I'll win?"

"As if," Hal said with a roll of his eyes.

"I think we should take bets on who will be the next King to fall for a woman," Guy said.

Banan shrugged. "I'll take that bet. My money is on Rhys. He's trying too hard no' to be snared."

"My bet is on Ryder. He just awoke from how long?" Hal asked. "Ryder is looking at every woman as if she's his last meal. He'll be felled quick enough."

Guy merely shook his head. "You both have it all wrong. It's going to be Con."

"Con?" Banan repeated in dismay. Then he realized Guy might have a point.

"He's gone more often than no' of late," Guy pointed out. "Where is he going to? I sure doona know."

Hal said, "He goes to check on Ulrik."

"Every time?" Banan asked.

Hal didn't have an answer, but with their bets in place, Banan was sure he would win.

The patio door opened and Elena looked out. "I wondered where you three had gone off to. Is everything ready?"

"There isna much on our part to be ready for," Hal said. "How is Jane?"

"Calm," Elena said with a chuckle. "I think I'm more nervous than she is."

She gave a wave to Guy, then ducked back inside.

Banan saw Guy's guarded expression. "You have no' told her she can no' watch the binding, have you?"

"Nay," Guy said. "She's so excited I couldna tell her."

Hal set his empty glass down on the table next to him. "Cassie said she would stay behind so Elena wouldna be alone."

"I doona want to leave her behind," Guy said angrily. "Elena is part of me. She should get to come."

"Aye, but you two are no' bound. Until that happens, you know the rules," Hal reminded him.

Banan had been concerned about Jane not wanting a traditional wedding. He understood her reasoning, but she did have family she should get to celebrate with. And then a thought took root.

"How long do you think it would take for us to put together a party?" he asked his friends. "Nothing big, just us and Jane's parents and half-sister."

"Um . . . no' to get in the middle of things," Hal said, "but has Jane even told her parents about Sammi?"

Banan groaned. "No' yet. I just wanted Jane to celebrate with her family."

"I've no doubt you'll meet them soon enough," Guy said.

Banan ran a hand through his short hair. "Then a party with all of us, and we invite Sammi."

"That could be arranged by tomorrow evening," Hal said.

Guy finished off his drink. "I'll get on it right now. Maybe it'll be enough to soothe Elena."

Jane glanced at the clock. Ten minutes until midnight. Her stomach was such a ball of nerves that she hadn't been able to eat the delicious sandwiches Cassie had made. Jane had, however, drank several glasses of wine.

No matter how many times she asked, Cassie wouldn't tell her what to expect. Cassie kept saying that was part of the surprise of it all.

It had only been an hour before when they'd learned Elena wouldn't be allowed into the mountain to witness the binding. Only Dragon Kings and their mates could be there.

Elena had laughed it off, but Jane had seen the hurt in her eyes. The three of them had been close since living at Dreagan, and Jane didn't like Elena being left out for any reason.

There was a rap at her door, and she turned, knowing it was Con come to take her to the mountain.

Constantine walked in wearing black slacks and a pale silver dress shirt with silver dragon-head cuff links. "You look beautiful, Jane."

"Thank you," she said and licked her lips. "Con, I know I may be out of line, but is there any way the rules can be bent for Elena? I don't like leaving her out of the ceremony."

He gave a single shake of his blond head. "I'm sorry, nay."

"Then can we have the ceremony outside? If she can't

be allowed in the cave, she could come to the ceremony if it was held elsewhere."

"I know you doona want Elena to stay behind, but we have our traditions, Jane. All binding ceremonies for every Dragon King take place in the mountain. Once you're there, you'll understand why we continue to adhere to tradition."

She felt defeated. It was the day of her binding, and she wanted Elena with her, just as Cassie would be. It just didn't seem fair.

"It is the duty of the King of Kings to present a King's bride with a gift," Con said as he pulled a black box from his pocket and stepped toward her. "Thank you for loving Banan as he deserves."

Jane took the box with both hands and opened the lid. Her brows raised as she stared, dumbfounded, at the silver cuff bracelet that was at least three inches wide. Upon it was a dragon, wings spread, covered with sapphires that went the width of the bracelet.

"It's stunning, Con. Thank you," she said as she put it on her wrist, admiring her reflection in the mirror.

"Your Dragon King awaits you. Shall we go?"

Jane looked into Con's black eyes and accepted his arm. She wondered how different she would feel the next time she and Banan stepped into their rooms. Did one feel different once they became immortal?

She forgot all about being immortal as Con led her into the library and through a hidden door. As soon as she stepped over the threshold, Jane realized she was inside the cave.

"This section is kept sealed except for binding ceremonies," Con whispered as she looked around the corridor she had to walk down.

It was wide enough for two people to walk through side by side. The ceiling was arched and covered with drawings she couldn't quite make out in the dim light of the torches that lined the hallway.

The narrow corridor quickly opened up and that's where the Kings were lined up on either side of the passage. She spotted Hal, Tristan, Rhys, Laith, Ryder, Kiril, and Darius, but there were dozens more she hadn't met or even seen.

Their eyes watched her intently, but Jane forgot all about them as she spotted Banan standing at the end of the passageway with Guy standing beside him.

"Nervous?" Con asked in a whisper.

Jane smiled as Banan winked at her. "He's the only thing in this world that doesn't make me nervous."

When they finally stopped next to Banan, Con handed her into his care, and Jane felt as if everything had finally come together in her world.

Banan gave her an appreciative once-over before he leaned close and whispered, "Lovely gown. It'll look even better puddled next to the bed."

He always had a way of making her heart race, and now was no exception. The desire she saw in his gray eyes made her blood heat.

Banan looked at the bracelet and then up at Con. The two shared a smile before Banan tucked her hand into the crook of his arm.

"Last chance you'll get to back out," he told her.

"Just try and make me," she responded.

Behind them, Guy chuckled.

The teasing ended as soon as Banan walked her into the cavern. She looked around in awe at the time it must have taken them to carve the stone and granite into such intricate detail. Dragons were depicted in various ways—some flying, some sleeping, some rearing on hind legs, and some breathing fire.

But all of them were larger than life. She could see each and every scale carved into the stones. The craftsmanship boggled her mind, and she wanted a closer look.

While she had been ogling the cavern, the Dragon Kings had filed in behind her and Con and took their places around them.

Banan brought her to a halt before Con who now faced them. Con looked at each of them, before he took a deep breath and said, "Few have been worthy enough to bind themselves to one of us. Jane Holden is one of those. She has lived among us for months, but now we will officially welcome her as mate to Banan."

Jane found herself facing Banan as he held both of her hands. His eyes crinkled in the corners as he smiled at her.

"Banan, do you bind yourself to the human, Jane Holden? Do you vow to love her, protect her, and cherish her above all others?"

Banan's eyes were intense as he stared at her. "Aye."

Jane blinked back a rush of tears. The truth shone in Banan's eyes, and she wondered how she could have ever doubted his love for her. It had been foolish and stupid, but she would never doubt him again.

"Jane," Con said. "Do you bind yourself to the Dragon King Banan, lord of the Blues? Do you swear to love him, care for him, and cherish him above all others?"

"A thousand times yes," she said.

Jane knew what was coming next, but she didn't expect the pain on her arm to nearly double her over. She gripped Banan's hands as he calmly waited until she could open her eyes.

"The proof of your vows and your love," Con told them. He then raised his voice to the others. "Jane is officially marked as Banan's!"

The cavern erupted in cheers as Jane looked upon her left upper arm to see the tattoo done in the same black and red ink as the dragon tats on each of the Kings.

Jane had seen Cassie's mark often enough, but now she had her own. It was the size of her fist and so lovely she could scarcely believe it was now a part of her.

Banan traced the dragon's eye and the flames surrounding it on her arm. "Do you know why the mates were chosen to wear a dragon's eye?"

"No. Why?"

"Because a dragon recognizes one of its own. You may no' be able to shift into a dragon, but you hold my heart."

"As you hold mine," she said before she leaned up to kiss him.

They weren't left alone long. The other Dragon Kings wanted to personally welcome her. It was Banan who finally called a halt to things by lifting Jane into his arms and striding from the cavern.

He took her out of the mountain and back into the house, but he didn't stop there. Outside, the massive patio was ablaze with candles.

As soon as Jane saw Elena and Cassie they ran to her, looking at her tattoo. The party was just getting started, and Banan wouldn't be denied.

He danced song after song with Jane until dawn streaked the sky. Only then did they stop to watch the sunrise. Once the sun was up, Banan had Jane in his arms once more.

She waved to everyone as he quickly tugged her inside the house and up to their rooms where he hastily had her gown puddled on the floor next to the bed.

Part 2

CHAPTER ONE

Dreagan Manor
December 29

Elena got out another package of ground meat and began mixing in the ingredients for her special hamburgers. No matter how many she made, there never seemed to be enough to go around.

The large kitchen at Dreagan Manor was empty except for her, and she liked it that way. It was becoming harder to keep the smile on her face and act as if nothing was wrong.

Something was very wrong.

Her life had been, if not perfect—close. She had left her career at PureGems because of her love for Guy, and though there was plenty for her to do at Dreagan, it just wasn't enough anymore.

She dug her hands into the raw meat as she mixed in all the ingredients. Her world had begun to fall apart the night Jane and Banan were bonded.

As difficult as it was, she had put aside her frustration in not being able to see the ceremony. Cassie had made it easier by staying behind with her, but the sting of it hit home to what had been bothering her.

She might be Guy's lover, but that's all she was. Until she was bonded to him that is all anyone at Dreagan would see her as—his lover.

Elena formed another patty and set it on the foil-wrapped tray. All the while she made the hamburgers she was thinking about Guy. He had shown her an incredible world, a world she had come to love. And need.

Why then had he left? She glanced at her cell phone that sat on the counter and debated whether to call him again. She had called three times and left messages each time, but he hadn't returned any of the calls. No texts, nothing.

It was so unlike Guy that Elena was unsure of what to do. The other Kings assured her he had been sent on a mission by Con, but somehow she didn't believe them. Maybe it was the way none of them could look her in the eye as they said it that confirmed her suspicions.

"Hey," Cassie said as she walked into the kitchen. "How many more are you going to make?"

Elena set down the finished patty and rested her hands on the large stainless steel bowl. "Are you my friend, Cassie?"

The brunette raised a brow, her dark eyes suddenly serious. "You know I am."

"Are you my friend because of the Kings, or would you have been my friend without our connection to this place?"

"Elena, what—"

"Please," she interrupted Cassie. "Just answer me. Honestly."

Cassie sighed and leaned her hip against the counter as she faced Elena. "I'd have been your friend with or without the Kings or this place. I thought you knew that."

"I'm not sure of anything anymore."

"Is this because Guy left on that mission?"

Elena snorted. "Did he? Did he really leave on a mission? How many times has Con sent Hal, Guy, or Banan on a mission since we came here? Not when he has many other Kings to choose from."

"I hadn't thought of that," Cassie said as her forehead furrowed. "Where do you think Guy is?"

"Hiding from me."

Elena washed her hands to give Cassie time to close her gaping mouth after dropping such a bombshell. It had been in the back of Elena's mind for days, but now she knew it with a certainty she couldn't shake.

"He loves you," Cassie argued.

Elena wiped her now-clean hands and set aside the dish towel. "I know he did. Not all relationships last. I knew something wasn't right after Jane and Banan's binding when Guy refused to acknowledge anything I said about our future."

"It's just miscommunication like Banan and Jane had."

Elena tried to smile, but she couldn't quite pull it off. "I've been telling myself that for weeks. It's time I stopped lying to myself and gave Guy the freedom he doesn't have the courage to ask for himself."

Jane opened the door from outside and tripped as she stepped over the threshold, banging her shoulder into the doorway. "Ugh," she said as she righted herself and closed the door. "Banan says he's ready for the hamburgers."

Elena kept her face turned away from Jane. She was barely keeping her tears at bay, and if Jane began to ask questions, Elena knew she would break down.

"What's going on?" Jane asked softly into the silence.

Out of the corner of her eye Elena saw Cassie give a shake of her head.

"Damn Guy," Jane stated angrily. "Let me call him, Elena. Let me talk to him and see what can be done."

Elena furiously shook her head. "No. If you two don't know anything it's because Hal and Banan don't know either or they've been forbidden to talk to you about it."

"Hal better not be keeping anything from me," Cassie said as she crossed her arms over her chest.

Jane came to stand beside Elena and put a comforting arm around her. "You know we'd tell you if we knew anything."

"I know."

"What are you going to do?" Cassie asked.

Elena glanced out the kitchen window to see the vast garden and the hills beyond dotted with sheep. "My being here has forced Guy to leave his home. It's not right."

"You can't leave," Jane said.

Cassie dropped her arms, her eyes wide. "Jane's right. You can't leave. You're as much a part of Dreagan as any of us."

"I know Guy better than either of you. He doesn't look at me with the same desire, and he rarely kisses me anymore. His gift to me at Christmas was a ticket back to Atlanta to see my family. It was one ticket. He had no intention of coming with me. All the signs are there."

"It's bullshit," Jane said.

Elena shrugged. "I could force a confrontation, but then words will be spoken to hurt both of us. It's better if I leave now."

"Today?" Cassie asked, anxiety shading her voice.

"Today." Elena pushed past her friends and hurried from the kitchen as the tears started. She couldn't hold them back anymore, but she wanted to mourn alone.

"You bastard," Hal said as he stalked into the mountain.

Guy didn't bother to move as he sat, his chin touching his chest. Both of his hands were plunged in his hair as his mind thought of Elena.

"What the hell are you doing?" Hal demanded. "Explain it to me, because obviously I'm too dim to comprehend what the fuck is going through your small mind."

Hal's anger didn't bother him. Nothing could touch

Guy now, not after his heart was being ripped from his chest minute by agonizing minute.

"Guy."

He closed his eyes, but all he could see was Elena's beautiful face. All he could hear was her throaty laughter, her sighs of pleasure.

"Do you no' love her anymore?" Hal asked.

Guy shook his head and he laughed wryly. "I love her more than life itself."

"Then I doona understand," Hal said as he sat beside him. "The other Kings are beginning to wonder at your sanity. They're doing their best to cover for you with Elena, but none of us like it. It willna be long before Cassie and Jane confront Banan and me. Tell me why I risk the ire of my bride for a friend?"

Guy slowly sat up and looked around one of the many caves in the mountains surrounding Dreagan. This had been one he had withdrawn to many times over the millenniums. When he came here, it was known that he was to be left alone, yet somehow he wasn't surprised that Hal had invaded his space.

"Do you know what she walked away from to come here with me?" he asked. "She had an amazing career and opportunities ahead of her. She gave that up. For me."

"Because she loves you."

"And that's the rub of it, old friend. I know she loves me, but you have no' seen her face when she gets offers from other companies to come work for them. She's tried to hide her longing for that life from me, but I see it anyway. I tried to ignore it because I didna want to let her go."

Hal leaned his hands on his knees. "And now?"

"It's no' fair to her. As hard as it is, I have to let her go."

"Is she your bride? Is she the one mate who is the perfect match for you?"

The words wouldn't come, so Guy nodded his head.

"And you'll just let her go?" Hal ran a hand down his face, perplexed. "You're a bigger man than me, because there is nothing I wouldna do to hold onto Cassie."

"I've been holding onto Elena for months," Guy said. "I'm crushing the life from her. And it's killing me."

They sat in silence for several minutes before Hal asked, "When will you tell her?"

"I'm no' sure I can. You've no idea how hard it was to walk away from her, and it's even more difficult to remain apart from her. If I hear her voice, if I see her, I may no' be able to carry through with it."

Hal stood with a loud exhale. "How do you know Elena doesna want to be with you?"

"She had to choose between this life and the other. She chose this one, but that was before she really knew what she was getting into. I gave her the time to get adjusted, just as Banan did with Jane. The difference was that I saw how much Elena missed her career."

"So you're willing to let her go to see if she comes back to you?"

Guy shrugged. "Something like that."

"And what if she's too hurt to ever come back even if it's what she wants to do?"

Guy had already thought of that. It was a chance he was taking, a big chance. He had never loved anyone as deeply as he did Elena. He would pluck the stars from the sky if she but asked it of him.

No matter how much he loved her, no matter how much he needed her by his side, it wasn't worth her happiness. What he hadn't told Hal is that he fully expected to lose Elena.

And if that is what it took to bring back her smile, Guy would happily give up his heart to see it happen.

"That's why you bought her the ticket for Christmas," Hal said as he pieced everything together. "Doona leave her as she is. At least give her the answers she's trying to find."

Guy waited until Hal walked away before he pulled out his mobile. He had listened to her messages a thousand times already, and he knew in the endless centuries before him that he would play them every day.

He understood what it was to love.

He realized what it meant to be loved.

And he would never be the same because of it.

Whether Elena knew it or not, she had given him the world. For a few exquisite months Guy really had had it all. Once she was gone from Dreagan, Guy would sleep. It was the only way to ensure that he let Elena go as she deserved.

He played her most recent message, the uncertainty in her voice breaking his heart all over again. Hal was right. He had to call her.

Guy dialed her number before he could second-guess himself. She answered after the first ring with a breathless, "Hello."

"Elena," he said as he closed his eyes, savoring the sound of her voice.

"Are you all right?" she asked.

Guy swallowed and knew the time for lies had stopped. "Nay, lass, I'm no'."

The silence on the other end of the line was like a knife in his gut. "Is it me?"

"Nay," he hurried to tell her, struggling to contain the emotions choking him.

"Is there anything I can do?"

He could hear the tears in her voice and it was everything he could do to remember why he was letting her go. "Aye. You can live, be happy, Elena, as you deserve to be."

"You want me to leave?"

The fact there was no surprise in her voice meant she

had come to that conclusion already and just needed his confirmation. This was it. This was when he could let her go, or he could keep her by his side.

How could he go on without her? Yet, how could he continue to watch her wonder what her life would have been like had she remained in London with her career?

Even though he knew he should tell her yes, he couldn't manage it. Instead, he said, "I want you to be happy."

If she stayed, he would know she would be happy with him.

If she left . . . he had all the answers he needed.

"Good-bye, Guy."

The click of the phone was like a nail in his coffin.

CHAPTER TWO

Elena hung up the phone and sank onto the bed she and Guy had shared. He hadn't come right out and asked her to leave, but he hadn't told her he wanted her to stay either.

She fell back on the bed and stared at the ceiling. How many nights had she lain in Guy's arms looking at the ceiling as they spoke of their wishes and desires for the future?

Stupidly, she had thought she'd found her happily ever after. It existed. All she had to do was look at Cassie and Jane to see that. But for some reason, it wasn't meant to be hers.

What had she done wrong? How had she lost him? Guy wasn't the type to lead a woman on. He had wanted her at Dreagan at one time, but something had changed.

They used to communicate so well, but somewhere, somehow everything had changed.

She wanted to cry the tears building up inside her, but she feared if she let them out she might never stop. And there was no way she wanted to leave Dreagan sobbing uncontrollably.

But deep inside, in the furthest reaches of her soul, she was shattered, devastated.

Destroyed.

An emptiness, colossal and vast, filled her chest where her heart used to be. She might be leaving Dreagan, but her heart would remain behind. Forever.

It was Guy's. Her heart had been Guy's from the first moment he had come upon her in the caves when she thought she would die. He had lifted her into his arms, his hard body and warmth tying her to a world she had been drifting from.

And then he had touched her.

Elena sat up and rubbed her hands up and down her arms as she thought of the first time they had made love. Each time after had been as glorious and exciting as that first time.

That was Guy. He had a way of touching her as no one else could, as no one else would dare. He had seen her, the girl she had only dreamed she could be. Then he had given her the courage to reach for any dream, any possibility.

Which had been him.

Elena had given all of herself to Guy. She'd held nothing back, had never thought to. He had a way of pulling everything from her without even trying, and she was powerless to resist.

He was a Dragon King after all.

Elena stood and pulled out her suitcase. Not everything would fit, but she could have the rest sent to her once she got settled.

Her gaze went to her purse where the airline ticket Guy had given her waited. Now she knew the reason for his gift. She doubled over from the pain, her mouth opened on a silent scream.

How long had he been trying to get rid of her?

Elena covered her face with her hands and squeezed her eyes closed. Just before he left, they had made such sweet love. His kisses had been long and lingering, his gaze filled with some unnameable emotion.

He had been saying good-bye.

The realization hit her hard enough to take her breath. Elena had to brace her hands on her luggage just to stay upright. She gave herself a few minutes to collect her emotions before she began to pack.

Part of her wanted to wait until Guy returned and demand a confrontation. But what would she say? She couldn't make him love her again. Nor could she turn back the clock and try to discover what had gone wrong. No, she would give him what he wanted and leave.

An hour later, Elena came down the stairs, but she couldn't meet Banan's or Jane's eyes. When she reached the bottom, Banan silently took her suitcase and walked out the front door.

"This is complete shit," Jane said, her voice heavy with anger.

Elena took a deep breath and forced a smile. "My time here is done. I'll never forget any of you."

"I'll stay in touch."

"No," Elena said, more harshly than she intended. She swallowed and took Jane's hands. "It would be too much for me. I have to make a clean break or I might never leave."

"Guy loves you. I don't understand."

She squeezed Jane's hands. "Give Cassie my love."

And then, before she broke down in tears, Elena turned on her heel and walked from the manor. She found Banan standing beside Guy's bronze Aston Martin DB9 with the door open.

"I called a cab," she told Banan.

He shrugged. "And I sent it away. Take the car, Elena. Just let us know where to pick it up. You willna leave here in a cab."

A few tears escaped when Banan enfolded her in a hug. She returned his hug and whispered, "I wish you and Jane all the best."

Elena pulled out of his arms and got into the car blinking back her tears all the while. She started Guy's car and backed out. As she put the car in drive, Elena took a second to gaze at the manor and lands she had come to think of as home.

Then she drove away.

Banan curled his hands into fists as he watched Elena. Once she was out of sight, he strode away from the manor and Jane's questions he wouldn't be able to answer.

He knew exactly where Guy was. Banan didn't stop until he stepped into the mountain to find Hal and Rhys already there. Their gloomy looks said it all.

Banan walked into the narrow opening to find the cavern dark except for a single candle set off to the right. There he spotted Guy with his head in his hands.

"I've never known a bigger piece of shite than what I'm looking at now," Banan said.

Guy didn't even twitch at his words. "I'm trying to make her happy."

"Happy?" Banan snorted his derision. "If you had seen her before she drove off, you'd know she was anything but happy."

The silence was almost eerie as Guy slowly lifted his head, his pale brown eyes haunted and hollow. "She's . . . gone?"

Banan frowned, seeing for the first time just how hard Guy was taking it. His friend was barely holding it together. And with Elena gone? What would happen to Guy now?

"Aye," Banan finally answered.

Guy threw back his head and bellowed, the sound forlorn and enraged. In the next instant Guy shifted into dragon form. Guy let out a loud roar as Rhys and Hal came running into the cavern.

But it was too late. The Dragon King they knew was gone. Banan held the others back when they attempted to stop Guy from crashing through the back entrance and taking flight.

"Con is going to be pissed," Hal said.

Banan ground his teeth together. "Con can go sod himself. He didna just see what I did."

"I agree with Banan," Rhys said. "And you all wonder why I have a different woman every night. I doona want to feel that kind of pain."

Hal narrowed his gaze on Rhys. "And the happiness of finding your mate? You doona want that?"

"Happiness?" Rhys pointed to where Guy had left. "Does that look like happiness to you, because it sure didna to me."

Banan raked a hand through his short hair. "We need to do something. We'll lose Guy if Elena doesna return."

"And how do you suppose to get her back?" Con asked.

Banan stilled, hating when Con snuck up on them as he loved to do. Banan turned to face his King. "How much did you see?"

"Enough," Constantine said, his voice holding a note of sadness Banan hadn't expected.

Rhys crossed his arms over his chest. "One of these days we're going to sneak up on you. I thought you were out of the country."

"I was. I sensed something wrong, so I returned." Con looked at each of them before he said, "Guy did what he had to do for Elena. It's now up to her."

Hal spread his arms wide. "Really? You want to leave it up to Elena? She's gone, Con. Gone."

"How could Elena think Guy wanted her to stay anyway?" Rhys asked. "He's made her think he was gone while he's been hiding here."

Banan knew he couldn't just sit back and watch Elena and Guy be destroyed by their love for each other. "Those two are meant for each other. We all knew it the instant they met. I'll go talk to Elena."

"Nay." Con's voice was hard, the edge giving the word a finality to it. "No one will speak to Elena. She must come back on her own."

"Then Guy is fucked," Rhys said and walked away.

Hal sighed loudly. "I agree with Rhys. Neither Guy nor Elena will be happy now."

When Hal departed, it left only Banan and Con. Banan wanted to argue the point with Con, and he opened his mouth to do just that when Con held up a hand.

"I know you think I'm cold, and in this I am being a cold bastard. But think about it. If Elena doesna return on her own, Guy will forever doubt if she returned because she truly loves him. Then we will be back to repeating this same scenario."

"You really doona want us to find our mates, do you?" Banan gave a sad shake of his head. "I stood up for you, but I think the others are right. You would rather us be alone."

Con raised a blond brow. "Would I rather none of you experience pain or betrayal if it meant you never found your brides? You're bloody damn right," Con said, his voice rising an octave. "I've seen too much. Need I remind you about Ulrik?"

"That was one fekking woman millions and millions of years ago! Let it go, Con."

"I'll gladly be the bad guy in this. None of you were there when I talked to Ulrik. You didna see what I saw, didna hear what I heard. And I never want to see or hear that again. If it means we spend eternity alone, then so be it."

Banan could only stare at Con. It was the first time he had ever hinted that he had gone to Ulrik after they had killed his woman. Why tell him now? What point was Con trying to make? But it didn't matter.

"You're one cold bastard," Banan said and stormed past him before he let his temper loose.

Con casually put his hands in his slacks and stared at the rocks now crumbled at the back entrance to Guy's cave. There was more than enough room for Guy to leave in his dragon form. The fact he had nearly taken out half his cave in his bid to get free said more than any words.

Con turned on his heel and walked away. There was business he needed to see to.

CHAPTER THREE

It was the roar that had Elena jerking the car to the side of the road. She threw it in park and opened the door to step out just in time to see the deep red scales of the dragon disappear into the clouds.

"Guy," she whispered.

He had been at Dreagan the entire time. There had been no mission. He had simply wanted to be away from her. Anger sizzled through her.

Elena got back in the car, her hands on the wheel as her sadness turned to rage. She threw the car in drive and smoked the tires on the road before she sped off. Her destination was Edinburgh where she could get a flight back to the States.

Except the hours it took to reach Edinburgh were plagued with the memories of her time with Guy. His smile, the desire in his eyes, the way his hands knew how to touch her to bring about the most exquisite pleasure. Elena forced herself to stop thinking of all the wonderful ways Guy had enriched her life. Despite how angry she was, she couldn't turn it on him.

Her ire was aimed more at the world. She had done everything right, had given all of herself to Guy.

Or had she?

At the back of her mind, something twinged, a memory she didn't recognize that suddenly sprang up reminding her of how she had struggled and worked to climb the corporate ladder at PureGems.

That part of her life was over. Or at least it had been. Elena didn't want to think of the future yet. Her pain was still too raw, too visceral to manage.

Instead of breaking down into a pile of sobs, she focused on the road. She turned on the stereo, glad to hear an AC/DC CD. While the strings of "Back in Black" roared through the speakers, she sang at the top of her lungs.

With AC/DC she didn't have to worry about hearing a sad love song. They would maintain her resolve to hold things together. For how long she couldn't be sure, but at least long enough to reach Edinburgh.

And two hours later, the CD had done the trick. She turned off the stereo as the road took her through the city to the airport.

Elena circled the airport twice before deciding to spend the night at a hotel. Yet, as she drove to the hotel, she didn't think she could stay another minute in Scotland. Guy was too close, and her willpower too low.

Sitting in his car, it was all she could do not to call him and try to talk. Then she remembered seeing him fly away after she had left.

Elena turned the car around and headed back to the airport. She parked the car and pulled out her luggage before she tossed the keys into the trunk. She sent a quick text to Banan telling him where the car was just as she'd promised.

With her shoulders back and her head held high, Elena walked into Edinburgh Airport to the United terminal and redeemed her ticket to Atlanta. It wasn't until Elena was sitting at her gate that she wondered why she was going home.

Elena leaned back in the chair and stared out the window at the planes. Her flight didn't leave for another six hours. How she was going to make it through until then she didn't know.

To keep her mind off Guy she played games on her phone, watched a movie on her iPad, wandered the airport visiting the gift shops and eating, and then she tried reading.

It worked. Until she fell asleep. Then she dreamed of bloodred scales and white eyes, of Guy's tattoo and the first time she saw it move. She dreamed of his tantalizing kisses and his deep voice.

Her eyes flew open as her body trembled with need. Is this what her future held? Would her body, her heart even allow her to forget Guy and the love they had shared? Would time dim her feelings?

"Oh, God," she moaned as the truth slammed into her.

There would never be another for her. What she and Guy shared was special, too special to ever attempt to repeat. There was no man on earth who could compare. She would spend the rest of her life alone with only her memories of Guy and Dreagan to see her through the long, lonely years of her life.

As thunder boomed around her, the rain fell in thick sheets. Elena rose and walked to the large windows. Up in the clouds she knew Guy and the other Dragon Kings were flying. He never passed up an opportunity to take to the skies.

Guy would often tell her stories of his time before there were humans and how the dragons had ruled the earth. His pale brown eyes would grow distant as he talked of how it felt to feel the wind beneath his wings, of how he soared through the air, his Reds behind him.

She knew how terribly he missed his Reds, and how fiercely he fought for both the dragons and humans in that awful war that had divided the two races.

* * *

Guy tucked his wings and dove from the clouds while the lightning forked around him. The air crackled with electrical currents, but he didn't care. He flew higher, farther than he had in ages, but no matter how fast he went—or how far—he couldn't outrun the pain that was threatening to swallow him.

The air whooshed around him a second before lightning struck him through his left wing. Guy rolled and then spread his wings again, daring the lightning to take him down.

His heart was heavy with anguish, leaden with grief. The sadness, the regret bombarded him as steadily as the rain, and all the while he wished he could have been the man Elena needed to fill the void her job had left.

He thought of her hands gliding over his back as he made love to her, he recalled how her sighs turned to soft cries as her passion grew. And he remembered how she clung to him as their bodies peaked and they shared their souls.

Guy let out a roar and turned back to Dreagan. He would seek out his cave and sleep. In his dreams he would relive every second he'd had with Elena, and hopefully, thousands of years from now when he woke, he would be able to walk into Dreagan Manor without thinking of the woman who had stolen his heart.

By the time Guy reached Dreagan land the sky was full of Dragon Kings. He made sure to fly higher than any of them. He wanted no words of comfort, no talk of finding his true mate later, because he knew Elena was his bride.

Guy spotted an amber dragon below him who casually turned another away who had been on his way to Guy. It didn't take long for Guy to spot Rhys and Hal doing the same as Tristan.

When Hal tried to open their mental link, Guy hastily

shut him off. He then used the time to dive to earth, spreading his wings to slow just before he reached the back entrance to his cave.

Guy landed and tucked his wings. He turned his great head to the manor wishing Elena was waiting for him. With one last look at the window of their rooms, Guy walked into the mountain.

Darkness met him, but with his dragon eyes the night didn't bother him. He curled up in a back corner hidden by boulders and rested his head upon his arm.

After a long sigh, he closed his eyes even as he picked up the sounds of approaching footsteps. Guy didn't need to open his eyes to know it was Con coming to pay him a visit. It had only been a matter of time before Con came to him. Before every King took to their sleep, Con would spend time with them. Guy would be no different.

Con's steps slowed before he entered the cave. Guy shifted into human form and waited for Con to speak. For several minutes Con's eyes searched the darkness for Guy before he leaned back against the rock and crossed one ankle over the other.

"How long will you sleep?" Con asked.

Guy was surprised Con hadn't wanted to know what went wrong with Elena, but no matter. Guy was grateful not to be talking about her. "I doona know. A couple of millennia at least."

"Will that be enough?"

Guy understood Con was asking if it would be enough time to ease his shattered heart. "Nay."

"Is there anything I can do?"

"Keep the others away. I know they mean well, but I doona want to talk of her."

Con rubbed his jaw as he looked at the ground. "Sleeping will no' erase her from your memories."

"I know, but if I doona sleep, I'll go to her."

"Would that be so bad?"

Guy fisted his hands, hands that had held Elena just a few nights earlier. "She has a career, Con. I need to let her go and no' tie her here."

"Have you thought you might be making a mistake?"

Guy frowned. Mistake? He knew what he had seen, and it hadn't been easy to come to his decision. It had nigh killed him to leave her the way he had. "Nay."

Con shrugged and straightened from the wall. "I'm sure it's all for the best. We're better off without the pain the humans bring us."

Guy waited until Con's footsteps faded before he shifted back into a dragon and resumed his position. Only then did he force his eyes closed.

And an image of Elena filled his mind.

CHAPTER FOUR

"Last call for boarding flight 1683 to Newark," came the nasally female voice over the intercom of the airport.

Yet Elena remained in her seat. If she got on the plane and returned to the States, she would never come back to Scotland. Ever. It would be too hard.

But to stay . . . that was just as difficult.

If she remained, there was a chance she would run into Guy. What if he was with another woman? How could she survive that? Then again, how could she leave Scotland and never see him again?

Elena bent over at the waist and squeezed her head with her hands. She didn't know what to do or where to go. Her mind was full of Guy and decisions were impossible to make.

She grabbed her purse and found the customer-service desk for United. There she cancelled her ticket and gave the address to her hotel for her luggage to be returned to her.

Elena walked out of the airport and waited for a taxi. She didn't know how long she stood there before she noticed someone was beside her.

She slowly turned her head to find Constantine. Elena hastily looked away. He was a reminder of the life she had left, of the man who had loved her—if only for a brief time.

"I've been watching you," Con said.

Elena shrugged, still refusing to look at him. "That's nice."

"You look like shite, Elena."

"Bugger off, Con."

He sighed loudly. "You didna use your ticket."

"How very observant of you." She was tired of being polite, tired of holding the rage and pain back. Con was the perfect person for her to take everything out on. And she intended to do just that.

"Why did you stay?"

"None of your business. You may rule the Kings, but you don't command me anymore."

He made a sound at the back of his throat. "You're a fool if you thought I ever commanded you or any of the women, Elena."

"What do you want, Con?"

"I want to know why you didna get on the plane."

Elena swallowed and looked out over all the parked cars, not seeing the people milling about. "I knew if I left Scotland that I'd never return."

"Nothing would prevent you from returning."

"Memories. If I put that kind of distance between what once was and a new life, I'd never be strong enough to return."

Con turned so that he leaned against a column to face her. "So you stay?"

"I couldn't get on the plane today, but I'm tired of sitting at the airport. I want a bath and a bed." So she could cry the tears she had been holding back all day. "I'll face tomorrow and any decisions when it arrives."

"So you doona have a job waiting for you?"

Elena's head jerked to Con to find his black eyes watching her with amusement. "Job? No."

"You doona have offers?"

"I've had a couple. What difference does that make?" She hated when Con didn't come right to the point. He loved to take the long way around things as if he had all the time in the world—which he did. And it infuriated her.

Con shrugged one shoulder. "Have you accepted an offer?"

"No," she said angrily, and she didn't try to hide it from him. "Why? Why would you care if I had a job or not?"

"No job and you are no' returning to Atlanta. What are you going to do?"

Elena turned and walked away. She had taken only three steps when she whirled back around and stalked to Con. "Ask what you really want to know."

"Why did you leave Guy?" Gone was the delight she had seen in his black eyes earlier. Now they stared at her with a singular intensity that left her shaken.

Emotions too tightly bundled and shoved aside suddenly enveloped her. She hastily blinked away the tears, not wanting Con to see how devastated she was. No matter how hard she tried, she couldn't keep everything at bay.

With her heart ripping in half, the flood of tears broke. She ducked her head and turned away. The pain was too raw, too fresh for her to share it with anyone else.

To her surprise, Con wrapped an arm around her and started walking, leading her she knew not where. When he finally stopped, she looked up through her tears to see his car, a bright blue Maserati.

He opened her door and waited for her to climb inside before he shut it and walked to the driver's side. Once he was behind the wheel, he looked at her and asked, "Where do you want to go?"

She couldn't tell him Dreagan, so she told him of the hotel she had given the airport.

The car roared to life and they drove away, the silence growing with each turn of the wheels. Con hadn't pressed her to answer his question, but he waited patiently for the answer.

"I left because he doesn't want me anymore. He deserves happiness, and I don't want to be in his way."

Con didn't respond as he continued to weave through the dense traffic of Edinburgh.

Elena shifted in the seat. The longer there was no response, the more antsy she became. She grew confused when he passed the hotel where she had planned to stay. By the time he pulled up to the curb of another hotel, Elena couldn't wait to get out of the car.

With her hand on the handle ready to open the door, Con said, "Tell me, Elena. Would Guy ask you to stay at Dreagan if he didna love you?"

"No. I know he loved me. I guess something went wrong. These things happen. I didn't expect it to happen to us."

"And you willna fight for him?"

She looked at Con with narrowed eyes. "Is that what this is? A test?"

"Nay, lass," he said casually. "It is merely a question I pose to you. You claim to love him."

"I do. More than I could possibly explain."

"But you'll just walk away from him?"

Elena briefly closed her eyes. "It's what he wants, Con. Whatever we had is over."

"I didna expect this from a woman who went back into the caves after she nearly died there. I thought you were stronger than that."

Elena glared at him, hating Con more than she thought possible. "You like hurting me, don't you?"

"Nay. I also doona like to see my men hurting."

"Con," she said with as much patience as she could muster. "You're making my head hurt. What do you want from me?"

"I wanted to see if you were worthy of Guy." He turned his head to stare out the windshield. "I was wrong."

Her door was suddenly opened by a bellman. Elena got out of the car. The door had barely closed when Con drove off. She tried to walk away, but the bellman knew her name and urged her inside. She woodenly walked into the hotel only to learn Con had paid for her room in advance for as long as she wanted to stay.

In the room, Elena did exactly what she'd told Con she wanted to do. After she ordered room service, she took a long, hot shower as sobs wracked her body.

If Elena thought she would sleep that night, she was dead wrong. In between bouts of crying, she would alternately curse Guy and wish he was with her.

But what she kept coming back to was Con's question.

And you willna fight for him?

She hadn't fought for him. He had pulled away, and she had let him. She hadn't made him sit down and talk to her about what was wrong. No, she had simply left.

What a damn coward she was. She had railed against Guy all night, but the one she should be angry at was herself. Elena threw off the covers and rose from the bed. She walked into the bathroom and looked at the clothes she had worn the day before.

With her suitcase God only knew where, she had no makeup, no clothes . . . nothing. As angry as she was at Con, he hadn't left her. He had paid for the room for as long as she wanted to stay.

Elena picked up the phone and called the front desk. "Yes, hi. Can I get a toothbrush and toothpaste, please?"

"Of course, Miss Griffin," the man on the other end of the line said. "Is there anything else I can get you?"

"Actually, there is. My luggage is on a plane. I don't have anything."

"No' a problem. Let me send Janet up to you so she

can get your measurements and a list of anything you need. Are you in a rush?"

"Um . . . a bit, yes."

"Expect Janet in a matter of minutes, Miss Griffin. And if there is anything else I can get you, please doona hesitate to let me know."

Elena hung up the phone and gave a bark of laughter. So, that's what money could do. She had expected to be told there was a gift shop or something since she hadn't paid much attention the previous night.

No sooner had she ordered breakfast than there was a soft knock on the door. Elena opened it to let in an older woman with graying dark blond hair and kind blue eyes. In less than ten minutes she had given a list of items to Janet as well as her measurements with Janet promising to return within two hours.

Elena wasn't going to waste that time. When breakfast arrived, she ate, making up for the lackluster food she had managed to get down the day before.

Then she showered and let her hair dry naturally as Guy liked. While she tried to plan out what she would say to Guy, Janet returned with everything she'd asked for.

Elena gave Janet a nice tip and a wide smile she didn't quite feel. If anyone thought she was armoring up, that's exactly what she was doing.

Because if she was going to return to Dreagan, she was going to fight for her Dragon King as she'd never fought for anything in her life.

Elena stepped out of the hotel, about to ask the bellman for a taxi to take her to rent a car when she saw the bronze Aston Martin parked along the street.

"These belong to you, ma'am," the bellhop said as he gave her the same keys she had tossed in the trunk when she'd parked the car at the airport.

Elena stared at the car, then said a belated thank you to

the bellman before she walked to the DB9 and slid into the driver's seat.

There was a piece of paper laying on the passenger seat with one word: Hurry.

Elena started the car and pulled into traffic. In seconds she was headed back to Dreagan, and this time she pushed the sports car to its limit.

CHAPTER FIVE

Guy knew he was sinking further into his memories than was safe. Most Dragon Kings would sleep just deeply enough not to realize the passing of time, but sufficiently alert for when Con would come to them every decade or so and fill them in on what was happening around the globe.

It's what Guy intended, but as memories of Elena poured through his mind, as well as the realization that he would never hold her again, it became too much.

He knew he was treading dangerous ground even as he slipped further into sleep. If he went too far, he would never be woken again.

It was preferable to living in a world without Elena.

Elena put the car in park in front of Dreagan Manor and shut off the engine. She'd made it in record time, and though she knew exactly what she was going to say to Guy, a thread of uncertainty ran through her.

After all of this, he might not want her. It would kill her, but at least she would know for sure. At least she could say she'd fought for him, for their love.

Elena took a deep breath and stepped out of the car. She looked up at the imposing structure of the house. She didn't relish trying to talk to Guy in front of everyone, but at this point, she was willing to do whatever it took.

"Elena."

She turned to find Rhys walking to her. His surprised expression meant that not everyone had known she would come back. "Hi."

"Hi, yourself. Did you come back for your things?"

Elena licked her lips and shut the car door. "I need to see Guy."

Rhys shifted from foot to foot, his unease apparent. "Elena . . . ah . . ."

"Just spit it out, Rhys. Is he with someone?"

"No," Rhys said hurriedly, his brow furrowed deeply. "He's sleeping."

Elena hadn't expected that. Why would he sleep now? "I have to see him."

"I'm no' even sure he'll hear you."

"I have to try."

Rhys motioned for her to follow him. Elena had never asked where it was that Guy slept. She knew it was in one of the many mountains on Dreagan, but she hadn't expected it to be so far from the house. She huddled into her coat and tried to keep up with Rhys.

It took nearly an hour to walk to the mountain. When Rhys stopped near an entrance Elena could tell he was struggling with something.

"Guy chose his cave carefully," Rhys said as he walked into the opening. "When Guy sleeps he likes to be isolated. The only one who ever visits after he sleeps is Con."

Elena looked around the passage they were walking through, thankful Rhys held a flashlight so she could see where she was going. "In other words, you aren't sure how Guy will react to me being here."

"Nay, I doona. I've seen him get ready for his sleeps many times over our lives, but this time was different. He was different." Rhys paused and turned to her. "I worry about taking you to him, but I think you may be the only one who can talk to him."

Elena put her hand on Rhys's arm when he started to turn away. "Am I wrong to be here? I want to fight for Guy, for the love I have for him."

"Go to him," Rhys said and handed her the flashlight.

When Elena paused, he gave her a little push, and that's when she saw the opening on the left. She glanced over her shoulder, but Rhys was already gone.

Elena drew her courage around her and walked into the cave. She shone her light around her, noting how large it was. The shadows gave the cavern an eerie feeling, or maybe that was just the coldness around her heart at the thought of losing Guy.

The light moved from one end of the cavern to the other, but she saw no sign of Guy. And then a beam of light caught red. Elena jerked the flashlight back to where she saw the color and glimpsed a red scale between two huge boulders.

Of course Guy would settle into a spot that would hide him from anyone searching the caves, even if those caves were on Dreagan. There was a very private side of Guy that he rarely showed anyone.

But he had shared it with her.

Elena kept the flashlight focused on the boulders as she picked her way through the cave, stumbling over rocks as she did. It brought back the memory of being lost when she went caving and her boss had died.

She shuddered, recalling how disoriented and alone she had felt. Until Guy appeared. He had been so calm. Now she knew why, but at the time it was all that kept her from falling apart.

Elena came around the boulders to find Guy laying with his massive dragon head resting on one paw. His breathing was deep and even, and the light from her flashlight didn't seem to penetrate his sleep.

"Oh, Guy," she whispered and leaned back against another boulder. "What happened to us? Did you stop loving me?"

He didn't answer. Not that she expected him to since he was sleeping. And how did one go about waking a sleeping dragon? That was something she hadn't bothered to ask Rhys.

"Smooth, Elena. Real smooth," she murmured to herself.

She had been so hell bent on confronting Guy and looking her best when she did that she hadn't thought of the details—details, which were obviously important.

Elena walked to Guy and ran her hands over the scales on the side of his head. She was always amazed at how smooth they were. "Wake up, Guy. I need to talk to you."

When he didn't stir, she bit her lip and looked around. That's when she decided to get comfortable. Elena settled herself in the crook of Guy's bent arm. She leaned her head back against his warm scales so she could see his face.

"I don't know how to wake you," she said. "I know Con doesn't wake any of the dragons when he visits those still sleeping to update them on the world. Will just talking to you work? Or is there magic involved?"

She gave a snort. "I'm royally screwed if there is magic needed. You know there isn't an ounce of magic in me anywhere. Too bad I'm not a Druid, huh? No, I'm just a human. As regular as they come. Except for one thing. I fell in love with a Dragon King. That I never saw coming.

"I did see my rise in PureGems. I had my eyes set on running the company worldwide. I was never concerned with marriage and children. If they happened, they happened."

She settled more comfortably as fatigue set in and propped her feet up near Guy's mouth. "Instead, I go caving, watch my boss fall to her death, sprain my ankle, and get lost in the mountain. I thought I would die. Then you were there with those pale brown eyes of yours, watching me. I'd love to know what you thought of me when you first saw me . . ."

"I thought you were the most beautiful thing I'd ever seen."

Guy had never talked to his memories before, but then again, he had never known anyone like Elena before. He wished he could hold her one last time. The need was so great that Guy could almost feel her lounging against him, her sweet scent filling his nostrils.

He could feel her sage green eyes on him, her blond hair tickling his scales. She had embraced him as a Dragon King. He could still recall when he'd watched her eyes blaze with pride and excitement as he took to the skies.

To never see that again, to never know that again. He was defeated, wrecked.

Obliterated.

His emotions were jumbled, muddled. His mind was in complete disarray except for one fixed point—Elena. Even as crushed as he was, she was his link to the last shreds of sanity.

Like a beacon she beckoned, compelled. Urged.

And he was powerless to deny even her memories. She was an enchantress, her call as seductive and erotic as her kiss. With her amazing eyes she bewitched, captivated.

Enticed.

Through all of eternity Guy knew he would forever crave her touch. She was the only one who had reached the part of him he had kept hidden away.

Elena idly ran her fingers along Guy's scales as her eyes drifted shut. "I couldn't sleep last night. While you've been off in la-la land, I've been wracked with memories of you. It's pretty shitty of you to leave me here talking to myself. What if I say something important? You'll miss it. Open your eyes, dammit."

Elena cracked open one of her eyes to see if he had done as she asked. Once more, no response. She closed her eye and went back to talking.

"Do you remember when you carried me out of that mountain? I was so scared. But as frightened as I was then, it doesn't compare to what I feel now at the thought of losing you. I'm terrified, Guy. Absolutely petrified at the idea of you out of my life."

She yawned loudly. "I wish you would talk to me. If you want me gone, I'll go. Just tell me. That's all I'm asking. Well, that and why. I want to know what happened, what I did wrong. And if I can fix it.

"I love you, Guy. I love you more than I thought a person could love. It doesn't seem fair to love like this and lose it. Frankly, I think it's bullshit. You loved me once. I know you did."

"Aye, I loved you. I love you still. I'll always love you."

His memories were taking Guy into an almost waking state. He fought against it, wanting—nay, *needing*—to return to the Elena who still loved him. It didn't matter if the world was falling down around him, he never wanted to leave Elena.

Her voice sounded so close, as if his memories were in stereo.

Despite his attempts to fall back into that deep sleep that would hold him forever, time and again he was dragged back. Guy dug his claws into the rocks and tried again, but once more he failed.

"I need you, Guy."

He stilled. His breath locked within him. That voice hadn't been in his memories. That voice, that beautiful, seductive voice was beside him.

Elena.

That's when he felt something against him, a warm presence that was all too familiar. Had he lost his mind? Had he tumbled into the void of his memories and just not known it?

Guy drew in a deep breath and opened his eyes. The first thing he saw was the beam of light shining against the wall opposite him. When he followed the light, he found the source nestled against him.

He raised his head and looked down at the only woman who could ever hold claim to him—Elena. She was on her back resting against his arm.

How long had she been there? More importantly, why was she there?

Guy took in her beauty from her long, dark blond hair that fell around her shoulders. She wore a chocolate-colored sweater that hugged her mouthwatering curves. Her lean legs were encased in dark denim tucked into brown boots that laced all the way up to her knee and had at least a four-inch heel.

She looked amazing, but then she always did. Elena had a way of looking sexy without even trying.

"I shouldn't have left," she said with her eyes closed, and by the tone of her voice, she was half asleep. "I should have confronted you. But I was a coward. You're the one thing I never factored into my life, and I didn't know what to do to save us. So I left."

Guy shifted into human form, careful to keep hold of Elena so she didn't hit her head on the rocks. He rubbed a strand of her hair between his fingers as he stared at her face, wishing she would open her eyes.

And hoping she didn't.

"As I drove off I saw you fly away. That's when I knew you had been at Dreagan the whole time. I was so angry."

CHAPTER SIX

"What did you do then?"

Elena realized two things in that instant: she was no longer leaning against a dragon but being held by arms she knew intimately, and it was a voice she had been hoping to hear since she walked into the cave.

She slowly opened her eyes to find Guy. His face looked haggard, gaunt, but in his eyes she saw . . . hope. Elena remained still, hoping he wouldn't release her.

"I drove to the airport and used the ticket you gave me," she said in answer to his question. "I sat there for hours waiting for the flight, but when it came . . . I couldn't get on the plane."

"Why?"

She frowned. "Why? Don't you know? You're my world, Guy. I love you brighter than the sun, deeper than the oceans, wider than the sky."

"And your career?"

It hit her like a bulldozer then. The e-mails she had been getting trying to recruit her back into the jewelry business had set all of this off. She had enjoyed the e-mails because they proved to her how good she had been, but Guy must have taken them a different way.

Elena pushed him away and got to her feet. Then she whirled to face him as she stood. She ignored his perfectly formed nude body and kept her gaze on his face—as difficult as it was.

"You thought I wanted my career more than I wanted you." She let the statement hang in the air, silently demanding he answer it truthfully.

Guy looked at the ground and nervously ran a hand through his hair. When he looked at her again, his gaze was hooded, as if he didn't want her to see what he was feeling. "Aye."

"Because I got some e-mails?"

"Because you looked as if you miss it."

She shrugged. "I do sometimes, but then I look at you and the life we have. I would never have left my career if I didn't know exactly what I wanted. Which is you, by the way."

"I doona want you to stay because you feel you have to."

Of all the ways she thought she could have ruined their relationship, of all the things that she might have said wrong, not once had it even remotely occurred to her that Guy thought she wanted her career back.

The more she thought about it, the angrier she got. "You were going to let me leave? You were going to throw everything we have away because of something you *thought*? Did it ever cross your mind to *ask* me?"

"I didna need to ask. I saw how you looked after those e-mails. You longed for it." A muscle ticked in his jaw. "Admit it. You yearn for all of it again."

Elena shook her head and looked away, too upset to even form any words immediately. "I thought you knew me. I thought you understood that I left all of that behind for you, and that if I had ever changed my mind I would talk to you about it."

When he didn't respond, Elena started to walk out of

the cave. She had no choice but to pass by Guy in order to get around the boulders and then out.

As soon as she drew even with him, he reached out and grasped her arm. In a blur he had her pressed against the boulder, his hot, hard body against hers. Elena tried to calm her racing heart, but she would never be immune to Guy's enthralling charms.

He kissed her and she melted. He beckoned and she went. He touched . . . and she was his.

"Where are you going?" he asked in a low, husky voice.

"For a walk."

His hand slid around her neck, sending chills racing over her skin. "You brought me out of my sleep."

"I wanted to talk to you."

He gave one shake of his head, his long honey-brown hair moving with him. "You doona understand. I wasna just sleeping, Elena, I was going to the Void—and happily."

"The Void?" she repeated.

"I let my memories consume me. I was sinking into an abyss which I wouldna have been able to come back from."

Guy watched the play of emotions over her lovely face. First there was confusion, then understanding. And then anger. She slapped his shoulder and gave him a meaningful glare.

"That was just stupid," she said. "Not only did you let me leave, you weren't going to try and win me back."

"I wanted what was best for you."

"What you *thought* was best for me."

Guy shrugged, not wanting to debate the issue. He would do it all again if it was what he felt in his heart that Elena wanted or needed. All that mattered to him was her.

"I was willing to let you go because I love you so much," he said as he leaned close to her. "But you, you amazing, beautiful, stubborn woman, were ready to fight for us."

Her sage green eyes met his. "Yes. Always."

"I love you. I will always love you. I'll love you when the earth fades into nothing and all that is left are the stars. I asked you once, but I'll ask again. Would you stay here with me, Elena Griffin? Will you bind yourself to me, becoming my bride and remaining by my side until I breathe my last?"

Her lip trembled. "I said yes then. I say yes now. I belong with you, and you belong with me."

Guy's heart felt as if it were going to burst he was so happy. "No waiting this time. I want the binding done immediately."

Elena's smile was coy as her hands reached down to stroke his cock, which had been hard since he'd shifted into human form. "It can wait a little while."

"A verra wee bit," he said as he unbuttoned her jeans and shoved them down her hips.

Elena tried to unzip her boots at the same time and they fell over laughing. The laughter died when her clothes were finally removed and he crawled over her.

She reached for him, urging him closer with her hands and wrapping her legs around him. He closed his eyes on a groan as he slid inside her tight wetness.

He would never let her go again. He would fight for her.

Always.

Five hours later . . .

Guy couldn't take his eyes off his bride. Elena, in a seductive, body-skimming red gown, was with Cassie and Jane looking over the tattoo that now graced her left upper arm, a tat that signaled her as his.

"I'm glad she came back," Banan said as he handed Guy a glass of whisky.

Hal moved to Guy's other side. "We wanted to go after her and bring her back, but Con wouldna let us."

Guy frowned as his gaze sought out Constantine. The King of Kings stood off by himself, an island among people. He merely watched and observed as others interacted. "Con is the one who went to Elena at the airport. He drove her to the hotel and made sure my car was there for her to return."

"I'll never figure him out," Banan said with a shake of his head.

Hal swirled his whisky. "If you asked me, I would've told you he was happy Elena was gone. He fought hard to have Cassie sent away."

"I'll fight Con to the death for Elena," Guy vowed.

As if she knew he was speaking of her, she turned to him, her eyes smiling. Guy handed Banan his whisky as he walked to his new bride.

Guy took her in his arms as a slow melody played through the speakers. The cold wind of the last day of December blew across the land and more snow was on the way, but in his arms was a fire that matched his own in every way.

"Wife."

"Husband," she whispered as they twirled around the floor.

He rubbed his thumb over the teardrop ruby nestled atop a platinum band on her finger. "There willna be any leaving me now."

"I never wanted to leave, you silly man."

Guy chuckled. "No one has ever called me silly."

"Someone has to keep you from thinking you're all that."

"But I am all that," he said with a frown. "I'm a Dragon King."

She lifted a brow. "You're my Dragon King."

"Oh, aye," he murmured.

"Tell me this isn't a dream. Tell me I'll wake in your arms in the morning."

Guy stopped them and shifted to the right, bending her over his arm as he leaned in for a kiss. "You'll wake in my arms every morning from now until eternity."

"Have we stayed long enough?" she asked between kisses.

He smiled as he took her hand in his. "Definitely."

Elena twined her fingers with Guy's as he straightened them. She caught sight of Jane and Cassie watching her. Several people tried to stop them, but Guy refused to halt.

They were laughing as they ran into the house while the others jokingly shouted for them to remain. Guy didn't stop, and Elena wouldn't have let him.

Once in their room, Guy shut the door and pressed her against it. "I'll never let you go again. I'll fight for you, Elena. Always."

"And I will always fight for you," she said as he unzipped her gown and watched it fall to the ground.

"You're no' wearing . . . anything," he said in a strained voice.

Elena smiled. "Just as you like it, my Dragon King."

Read on for an excerpt from ***DARKEST FLAME***,
the next epic romance from Donna Grant.
Coming Soon from St. Martin's Paperbacks

Denae gripped the sink in an effort to combat the pain from getting out of the bed and making her way to the bathroom. When it was under control, she lifted the pale yellow tee to see her wound.

A large strip of gauze covered it. She peeled back the gauze and stared dumbfounded at the wound through the mirror.

"Is something wrong?"

At the sound of the deep, sensual voice Denae spun around, forgetting her wound in her surprise. The pain struck instantly and caused her to gasp and try to grab for anything to stay upright.

She found herself in Kellan's arms as he held her gently but securely. Denae gripped his strong arms while she absorbed the heat radiating off him. She looked up and was snagged in his gaze and lashes so thick and black they would have looked feminine on anyone else.

Her body responded instantly to his touch. Her blood pounded through her while a slow, steady heat settled between her legs. Denae couldn't explain the irresistible and seductive attraction she felt for Kellan. It was there, as if it always had been and was just waiting for her to meet him.

As beautiful as his eyes were, there were no emotions there. It was like a bucket of ice water thrown on her. Denae pushed away from him, trying to ignore the rigid muscles of his chest beneath her palms as she did.

"You can leave now," she said as she faced the mirror once more.

"You're pale."

Denae gripped the sink once more. "Yep. That tends to happen when a person is wounded and loses a lot of blood."

"You should be feeling better."

She lifted her gaze to look at him through the mirror. His words, combined with the way her wound looked as if it was a week old instead of just a few hours, made her scowl at him. "What did y'all do to me?"

Denae cringed as she finished. It had taken meticulous work on her part to eradicate all Texas twang from her speech, especially the y'alls.

"We tended to you."

She turned to face him making sure to move slowly so as not to pull her side. "What else did you do? I know how deep that wound was. I know I was bleeding badly."

"The cave was dark," he said and leaned a shoulder against the doorframe before he crossed his arms over his chest.

It caused his shirt to stretch even tighter over the thick sinew. Denae had to look away. "You just happened to be in the cave?"

"It is my cave."

Her eyes snapped to him as she frowned. "*Your* cave? What does that mean exactly?"

"If I hadna been there, you'd be dead."

"I think it would've been better for everyone if that were the case." Denae faced the sink again and turned on the faucets. She splashed water on her face, suddenly exhausted to the marrow of her bones.

She dried her face and spotted a brush. Without thinking, she unpinned her hair and let it fall around her. It was still damp in places as she ran the brush through it.

Denae caught Kellan watching her hand as she ran the brush through her thick hair. Something flickered in his eyes, some nameless emotion that caused her to pause.

When she did, his eyes jerked to hers and the coldness returned. For several tense seconds, they simply stared at each other. He made her edgy, as if there was an undercurrent of something primal and sexual she couldn't grasp.

Denae wished she knew how to use her body as some agents did. Seduction wasn't one of her skill sets, and it hadn't been cultivated at MI5. If only she had paid closer attention to the agents who went undercover using their bodies she might know what was happening to her now.

She returned the brush to its place and fidgeted, suddenly unsure of herself. The only time she felt such . . . restlessness was in Kellan's presence.

Was he doing this to her on purpose? If so, it was a great tactic because it was working perfectly.

"Do I make you uncomfortable?" he asked.

She refused to make eye contact with him again, even through the mirror. "Isn't that what you want?"

"Why would you think that?"

"Why are you in my room?"

"Is that no' obvious?"

Denae shook her and gave a rueful laugh. "I've already said I would tell you all I know of MI5's plans regarding Dreagan. I don't need someone watching over me. I doubt I could escape even if I was up for it."

"You got onto our land and into my cave without us knowing."

"I think we got lucky," she said and started for the doorway making sure to look anywhere but at him.

Just when she thought he might step out of her way, he blocked it, forcing her to look at him. "What were you searching for?"

"Anything. Everything. As far as I know there is nothing specific. When I asked why Dreagan was targeted, I was told there was suspicion. Matt knew more."

"And you killed him."

"It was kill or be killed," she said through clenched teeth.

Her strength was waning fast. As if sensing it, Kellan moved out of the way and she walked the few steps to the bed and gingerly sat down.

"Cassie brought you pain medication," Kellan said as he sat in the chair Con vacated earlier.

Denae bit back a wince as she twisted to get both legs into bed. "I have a high tolerance for pain."

"You mean you doona trust what's in the medicine."

"Something like that. I'm sure you understand."

To her surprise, there was a softening of his lips as if he had almost smiled. "Aye. It could be you're just obstinate."

"I don't enjoy pain," she said and pulled the covers over her bare legs. The shorts she wore had ridden up, exposing almost everything.

She might have left off the covers had she thought Kellan was interested, but his aloofness said it all. If only she could convince her own body that he wasn't worth the time she might feel more in control of things.

"If you doona enjoy pain then take the medicine."

"Fine. I'll take the damn meds."

One caramel brow lifted. "Your easily riled. No' something I expected from an MI5 agent."

"Yeah, well, you seem to bring it out of me."